SEEING GLORY

"A thrilling and dynamic adventure across four diverse characters during a fascinating period of American history, littered with engaging moments of drama and excellent character development. *Seeing Glory* is an essential read for people with an interest in the Civil War and its cultural context."

— *USA Today* Bestselling Author K. C. Finn,
Readers' Favorite Reviewer, Author of *The Mind's Eye*

"A page-turner in every sense. As a student of the Civil War myself, I can attest that the historical background of Bruce Gardner's novel is spot-on and incredibly well researched. As it covers the issues of slavery, abolition, and a deep undercurrent of racism, *Seeing Glory* is also quite thought-provoking and relevant to today's America . . . everything I want in historical fiction."

—Stacie Haas, Readers' Favorite Reviewer,
Author of *Freedom for Me: A Chinese Yankee*

"An extremely powerful and emotional read. Bruce Gardner has crafted a wonderful story of the conflicting emotions and motivations around the time, seamlessly melded into real events, historical Civil War battles, and names that even today resonate through history, such as Lincoln, Harriet Tubman, Frederick Douglass, and Stonewall Jackson . . . This is one of the best Civil War novels I have read."

—Grant Leishman, Readers' Favorite Reviewer,
Author of *Just a Drop in the Ocean*

Bruce Gardner

Seeing Glory

A Novel of Family Strife, Faith & the American Civil War

*This work of fiction is dedicated to
the memory of the radical northern social reformers and
the rare though inspiring examples of
anti-slavery southerners who joined with them
in advancing the "Great Cause" of abolition.*

John Brown, Frederick Douglass, William Lloyd Garrison,
Harriet Beecher-Stowe, Sojourner Truth,
Thaddeus Stevens, Charles Sumner, Charles Finney,
Harriet Tubman, Angelina and Sarah Grimké,
David Walker, Mattie Griffith-Browne, Levi Coffin,
Elizabeth Van Lew, Moncure Conway, Thomas Garrett,
and others

CAST OF FICTIONAL CHARACTERS

(In Order of First Mention or Appearance in Initial Role)

Abel Bowman
- Only son of Kansas farmer

Emma "Em" Hodge
- Younger daughter of Lawrence Hodge (southern Virginia plantation owner)

Catherine "Cat" Hodge
- Elder daughter of Lawrence Hodge

David Hodge
- Only son and eldest child of Lawrence Hodge

Horace Jones
- Local country Baptist preacher

Sallie Cobb
- Domestic servant for Hodge Family Plantation; Emma's personal maid

Charles Cobb
- Fieldworker; Sallie's elder stepbrother

Lew Cobb
- Fieldworker; Sallie's younger stepbrother

Sam Taylor
- Field supervisor; son of the Hodge Family Plantation overseer (Philip Taylor)

Lieutenant Joseph Hartwell
- Virginia Military Institute cadet corps officer

Daniel Samson
- Supplies procurer for Eppes Plantation; cousin of Sallie Cobb's stepfather

Sarah Krause
- Young widow from Frederick City, Maryland; mother of Jenny

Lieutenant Colonel Jonathan "Jack" Hurley
- Assistant Inspector General, XII Corps, Union Army of the Potomac

William Johnson
- Assistant supervisor, American Missionary Association (Washington Office)

George Skipwith
- Field foreman, Magnolia Plantation (Sea Islands, South Carolina)

REAL HISTORICAL FIGURES

(In Order of First Mention or Appearance)

John Brown
- New England abolitionist

Owen Brown
- John's third son

James Doyle
- Kansas farmer with connections to local proslavery violence

Charles Faulkner
- US Ambassador to France (pending appointment)

Edwin Cowles
- Head Editor of the *Cleveland Leader* newspaper

Charles Finney
- Famous evangelist and president of Oberlin College (Ohio)

Frederick Douglass
- Nationally known abolitionist (former Maryland slave)

Lieutenant Colonel William Creighton
- Commander, 7th Ohio Volunteer Infantry Regiment

Angelina Grimké-Weld
- Nationally known abolitionist (former plantation daughter from South Carolina)

John Rodgers
- Commander, *USS Galena* (Union navy ironclad gunboat)

Abraham Lincoln
- President of the United States, 1860–1865

General Rufus Saxton
- Union military governor for Sea Islands District (South Carolina)

CONTENTS

Historical Preface xv

Prologue   Judgment Night (1856) 1

Part I   Hearts Divided (1859) 17

Part II   Flight and Fury (1861–1862) 109

Part III   New Vision (1862–1863) 217

Part IV   Glory (1864–1865) 335

Epilogue   Restoration (1865) 455

Author's Note 465

Select Bibliography 473

Acknowledgments 475

About the Author 477

Then Moses said,
"Please, let me see Your glory."

Exodus 33:18

HISTORICAL PREFACE

John Brown had long believed the explosion would come, and that God had appointed *him* to be its spark. For the fifty-five-year-old New England tanner, wool trader, and committed abolitionist inspired by his strong Calvinist religious beliefs, it was only a question of when and where.

By 1855, his answer was coming into clearer focus as national tensions spiraled toward the boiling point over the status of nearly four million enslaved people and the relentless, westward spread of the system oppressing them. With the passage of the Fugitive Slave Act of 1850 and the Kansas–Nebraska Act four years later, it appeared that the proslavery forces dominating the southern states were well on their way to successfully imposing their desires on the rest of the rapidly expanding country.

Brown—a part-time Underground Railroad conductor who, nineteen years earlier, had sworn "before God, from this time, to consecrate my life to the destruction of slavery"—saw that the situation had become intolerable. He was especially concerned about the need to protect his five adult sons and their families who had previously migrated to the Kansas Territory from the threats and advances of proslavery forces in the area. In late 1855, Brown left the utopian, biracial community he'd personally established in the mountains near Lake Placid, New York, and moved west to join them.

Over the next several months, violent episodes increased in frequency across Kansas and the nation. Then, on the afternoon of May 22, 1856, something unthinkable happened. Preston Brooks—the proslavery representative from South Carolina—employed his gold-headed walking cane to mercilessly beat Senator Charles Sumner, the famous abolitionist from Massachusetts, to the point of near death on the floor of the US Senate chamber. Some southern lawmakers afterward made rings out of the broken cane pieces and wore them on necklaces to proclaim their solidarity with Brooks, who boasted the pieces were "begged for as sacred relics."

It was the last straw for John Brown. Something had to be done . . .

PROLOGUE

JUDGMENT NIGHT

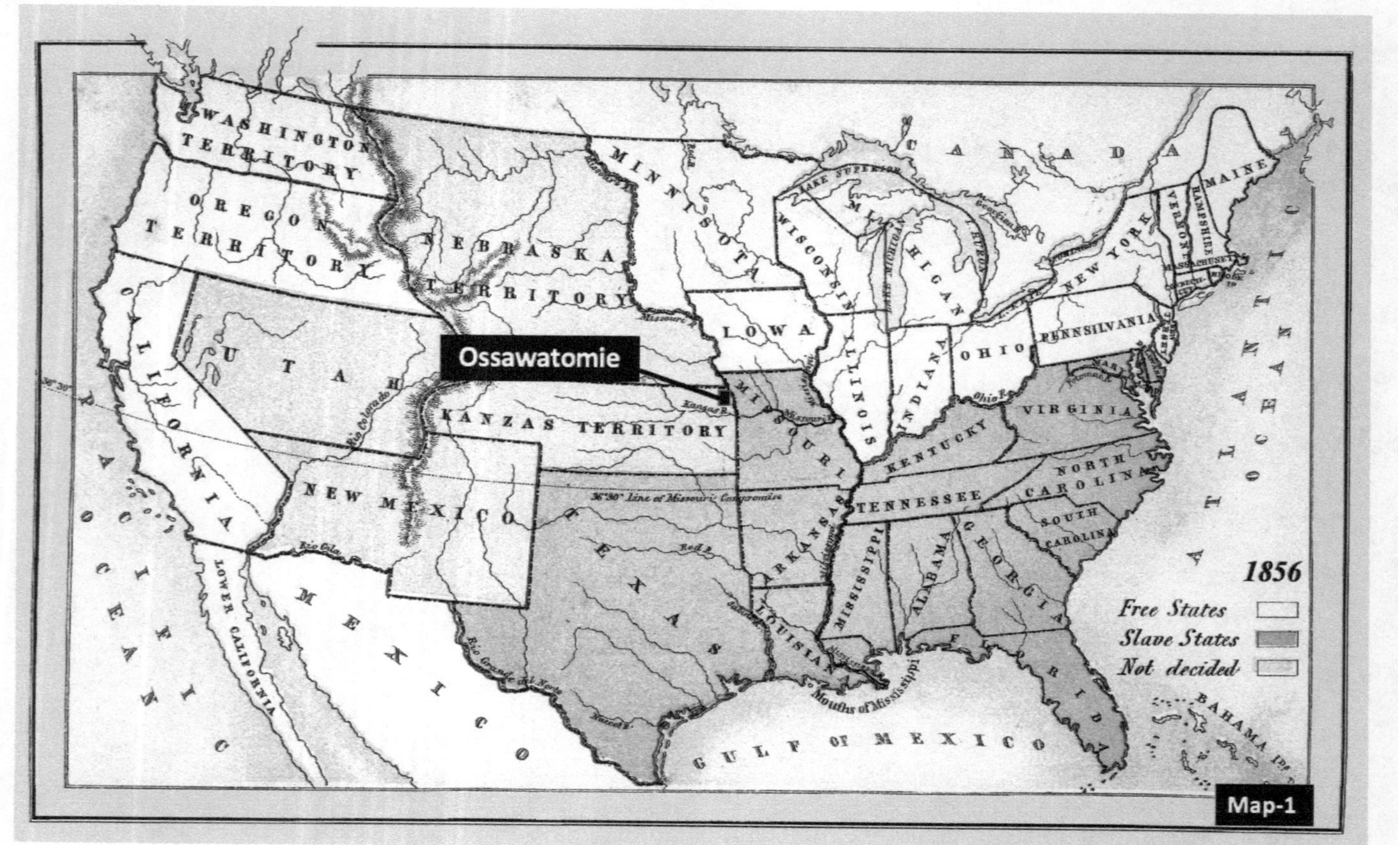
Map-1
1856
Free States
Slave States
Not decided
Ossawatomie
WASHINGTON TERRITORY
OREGON TERRITORY
CALIFORNIA
UTAH
NEW MEXICO
NEBRASKA TERRITORY
KANZAS TERRITORY
TEXAS
MINNESOTA
IOWA
MISSOURI
ARKANSAS
LOUISIANA
WISCONSIN
ILLINOIS
MICHIGAN
INDIANA
OHIO
KENTUCKY
TENNESSEE
MISSISSIPPI
ALABAMA
GEORGIA
FLORIDA
NORTH CAROLINA
SOUTH CAROLINA
VIRGINIA
PENNSILVANIA
NEW YORK
VERMONT
HAMPSHIRE
MAINE
MASSACHUSETTS
CANADA
MEXICO
LOWER CALIFORNIA
GULF OF MEXICO
PACIFIC OCEAN
ATLANTIC OCEAN
BAHAMA IS.
LAKE SUPERIOR
L. HURON
Kanzas R.
Missouri R.
Ohio R.
Red R.
Rio Colorado
Rio Gila
Rio Grande del Norte
Nueces R.
Mouths of Mississippi
36°30' Line of Missouri Compromise

CHAPTER 1

Ossawatomie, Kansas Territory
May 24, 1856

Abel Bowman barely noticed the low, angry rumble of distant thunder. Picking idly with his fork at the meal of corn mush, mashed plums, and strips of buffalo jerky that his mother had managed to scrape together, he made his decision.

"Ma, I can do it, and I'm going to do it. Will you just stop fretting?"

Abel was sick of being coddled like a five-year-old. *Enough* of being cooped up in his family's one-room log cabin on the windswept, northeastern Kansas prairie outside town. The time had come for a change in his life—a big one.

Eyes flashing, Ma glared at him from across the table. "I'm telling you, I just don't like the sound of it. Dan, you really gonna let your son go along with those men?"

Abel's father put his spoon down slowly. Surprisingly, instead of launching into his usual fit of temper, he reached over and placed his hand on his wife's forearm.

"It's all right, Kate. The boy's sixteen, built like he's twenty. High time we let 'im do a man's duty."

Ma jerked her arm away. "Don't see how a 'man's duty' calls for participating in this kind of nonsense. Honestly, Dan, I can't help thinking this Mr. Brown fellow's up to no good, regardless of all his highfalutin words and ideas. You *really* want Abel to help him and his sons out tonight?"

Abel rolled his eyes and gawked at his father in exasperation. Ma just never knew when to stop. But tonight, for once, it was clear Pa had no intention of allowing himself to be rattled by her constant second-guessing.

"I've told you before, Kate," he said softly, "and I'll tell you again. There's not one boy wanting to become a man in this Kansas Territory who can sit at home, doing nothing in the face of all we seen happen around here lately. And no boy who'll know what to do without someone like Mr. Brown teaching him."

Pa couldn't have put it better, Abel thought. His family—like many others in Kansas who opposed slavery and wanted to see the Territory admitted to the Union as a free state—was living constantly on the edge of fear. It had been that way ever since the proslavery Border Ruffians from neighboring Missouri had begun infiltrating the Territory a couple of years ago. The Ruffians were happy to put their vicious methods on display for all to see. And according to Pa, there was only one man in the local area showing any real willingness to stand tall for the Free-Staters in opposing their intimidation: Mr. John Brown, the strange, new neighbor who'd recently arrived from New England to support his five sons who had settled earlier in the area.

"Well, that may be," Ma retorted, "but you know those Ruffians aren't likely to take kindly to Free-Stater boys trying to become men with Mr. Brown's help."

Abel slammed his hand down on the table. "Ma, you can't keep on protecting me forever! I can fend for myself now." He uttered a foul word—under his breath, or so he thought.

"You watch your language, young man!" Ma hollered. "And don't act so cocksure of yourself. You want to end up like those poor boys from Lawrence?"

Abel sat back in his chair, folded his arms, and sighed. On that point, he knew his mother had some good reason for concern. The Bowmans and other local families had been shocked at the reports received two days ago from the nearby city. Not only had a Ruffian-led gang burned down two abolitionist newspaper offices and the house of the city's Free-Stater militia leader, but there were rumors that they'd also seized and cruelly bullwhipped two local teenage boys they claimed were somehow trying to interfere. Shouting racial slurs and other obscenities, they'd then rampaged through the town, threatening even worse consequences to come for antislavery proponents. No question, the Ruffians were not the ordinary breed of local troublemakers.

Pa took up the defense. "That's exactly the problem, Kate. Unless *somebody* faces up to them, Abel and other Free-Stater boys like him'll always be trembling in their boots every time a Ruffian happens to cross their path. And up to now, we all know Mr. Brown's the only one around here who's seemed willing and able to confront those thugs, talk sense, and put the fear of God in 'em. We all heard him speak at the rally last Saturday, dressing down that proslavery idiot. There isn't *anybody* who can talk to people of that ilk like John Brown can, I guarantee it."

"Well then," Ma shot back, "why can't we just let Mr. Brown and his people take care of the Ruffians themselves, without our Abel's help?"

"Because, Kate, there comes a time when Free-Stater families can't just sit back and let others do our unpleasant work for us. It just ain't right."

Pa pushed his chair back and rose slowly and painfully from the table. Favoring the badly healed leg wound he'd received in the Mexican–American War, he hobbled over to the hearth. He refilled his mug with hot coffee from the smaller kettle, then sat down again in his high-backed rocking chair by the cabin's single window.

Abel watched his father closely while his mother, clearly unhappy with her husband's view of the situation, clanked the dishes together and carried them to the washtub.

To an extent, he could understand her reaction. It wasn't like Pa to express such confidence in the capabilities of a man he'd met only once—at last month's outdoor supper hosted by the local Baptist church where, years before, in response to the fire and brimstone warnings of the visiting preacher and a strong sense of God's call on his heart, young Abel had come to believe and trust in Christ as his Lord and Savior. Yet here Pa was now, staring serenely out the window at the gathering evening storm, expecting the imminent arrival of that same man to shepherd Abel—his only child—on a potentially dangerous mission involving some kind of "discussions" with a couple of local proslavery families.

On the other hand, who could deny that Pa had plenty of army experience in judging the characters and abilities of his superior officers? There was no doubt he'd carefully considered Brown's qualifications in that light and had judged him positively. Otherwise, he would never have agreed to Abel's involvement.

Besides, hadn't Mr. Brown assured Pa yesterday that tending some horses during the discussions would be Abel's only required support task? Abel would be back by tomorrow night, safe and sound. His parents could then rest proudly, knowing they'd contributed their son's services to a worthy cause, a "God-ordained purpose," according to Mr. Brown. Abel could also rest knowing he'd taken a big step toward becoming the kind of man he'd always wanted to be: a man of courage and conviction, just like Pa. Yes, the rewards were clear . . . and he could hardly wait for this exciting mission to begin.

Lightning, followed by a loud clap of thunder, signaled the evening storm had arrived. Seconds later, Abel nearly jumped out of his chair at the sound of the loud pounding at the cabin's front door.

"He's here," Pa muttered as Ma folded her arms and stared at him coldly. "Go greet him, boy."

Abel crossed the room. He lifted the latch and opened the door, recoiling at the sight of the tall, slightly stooped, narrow-shouldered man now standing in front of him with hat held politely in both hands. It wasn't the man's wiry, gaunt physique that sparked Abel's reaction so much as his dark, severely chiseled face featuring a firmly set wide mouth and square jaw. Most unnerving of all were his piercing, steely blue-gray eyes that seemed to bore in on Abel with unwavering intensity.

Abel averted his own gaze, cowed to feel the very core of his soul probed by a man with such a stern, eagle-like countenance.

"Good evening, son." John Brown's deep, metallic voice sent a shiver down Abel's spine. "Looks like we got us a storm brewing tonight. You ready to help us do the Lord's appointed work?"

Abel stood at the edge of the clearing, twenty yards back from the cabin belonging to the first of the families on John Brown's list to be visited tonight. A strong breeze off the Pottawatomie Creek blew suddenly through the surrounding woods, sparking a spasmodic trembling that coursed through his entire body. Strangely, the confidence and bravado he'd felt earlier this evening seemed to be fading quickly. *Please, Mr. Brown, just hurry up and get this thing over with, before I turn chicken and bolt.*

Brown knocked loudly on the cabin's front door as the seven other men supporting tonight's mission, including four of Brown's adult sons, gathered close behind him, lanterns or pistols in hand. "Come on out now, Mr. Doyle. You and your boys." His voice left no room for compromise.

Abel gripped the reins of the men's horses and held his breath, praying for a quick and appropriate response from someone inside. It was nearly 11:00 P.M. God alone knew who or what the Doyles imagined was descending upon them at this odd hour.

Brown pounded once again.

No response. Things seemed too quiet, the silence broken only by residual drippings from the early evening storm and the haunting song of a distant whip-poor-will.

Finally: the sound of a bolt being lifted. The door cracked open.

"Who the hell are you to be botherin' my family this time o' night?" a grumpy voice snarled from behind the door.

"John Brown, Captain of the Northern Army. It's the night of reckoning, Mr. Doyle, and we need to talk."

"John . . . who? Oh, yeah, I heard 'bout you. You're one o' them New England abolitionists, ain't ya? I can smell your type a mile off. I'm tellin' ya now, mister, get off my property . . . 'fore I blow your rotten head off!"

"I wouldn't be so quick to try that, Mr. Doyle," Brown replied calmly. "We don't want any trouble, but as you can see, we're well prepared to defend ourselves."

The door cracked open a bit wider for a moment, then it shut. A long pause ensued. Abel could hear what sounded like frantic voices arguing with each other inside the cabin. The door at last opened wide. Mr. Brown and three others barged their way inside. Less than a minute later, at gunpoint, James Doyle and three of his sons emerged one by one into the light of the lantern held by John Brown's third-born son, Owen. As the Doyles stood together in front of the doorway, it occurred to Abel that he'd never seen such a drab, slovenly looking bunch.

"All right, now we're all outside. So what exactly are you here for, Mr. Brown?" James asked, sounding far less cocky than before.

"Mr. Doyle," Mr. Brown responded firmly, "you know good and well your irresponsible speech and actions have helped to heat up every proslavery settler and Border Ruffian in this area. Your sons have threatened Free-Staters with guns to keep them away from the polls. Because of people like you, God-fearing antislavery Kansas men are being murdered, their properties destroyed, and their wives and children threatened. All so you can ensure Kansas will become a state that keeps the colored man in chains and misery forever. For too long, Free-Staters have shied away from resisting. But that all ends tonight, Mr. Doyle. The Northern Army is here to take you prisoner."

Doyle's body stiffened. "Mister," he spouted indignantly, "you got it all wrong. Me and my boys, we never threatened nobody. You talk like we're some kind o' rich plantation owners, runnin' our slaves into the ground! Why, we're just poor folk from Tennessee. Ain't rich enough to own no slaves. And we sure don't got time or interest to be baitin' the antislavery crowd like you're accusing us of. Right, boys?"

All three of Doyle's sons nodded vigorously in wide-eyed unison.

Brown's voice took on a harder edge. "You're lying, sir, and you know it. It's on record at the Lawrence courthouse that you and your sons are all members of the proslavery Law and Order Party and have participated in those recent voter intimidation actions by the Ruffians. Now accept your lot as our prisoners—come along without resisting, and you have my promise you won't be hurt."

Doyle cocked his head back as if momentarily confused, then looked at his sons and smiled resignedly. "Well, boys, Captain Brown here's convinced he has something on us. Guess there's no use for us trying to deny it." Turning back toward Brown, Doyle bowed slightly with open arms. "All right, sir, fair 'nough. We surrender. Go ahead—*take* us prisoner, whatever the hell that means. But I guarantee, you'll never get away with this. Every single Ruffian in this state'll be hot on your tail within five seconds once word gets out we're missing."

Mr. Brown smiled pleasantly. "Why, thank you, Mr. Doyle. I was hoping you'd see it our way. And I'm so glad you admitted to your admiration for the Ruffians. That serves to confirm my accusations against you, doesn't it? But don't worry, we'll take good care of you and see that you get a fair trial real soon. If the Ruffians find us, before that, so be it. We'll deal with them as we need to. Now, gentlemen, it's high time we all get going. Where are your horses, Mr. Doyle?"

"Left 'em grazin' out on the prairie—back down the road a little ways, near the woods."

"Let's go find them, then. You're going to need 'em."

The men fell in line and began to walk past Abel, Mr. Brown in the lead followed by the Doyles, with the pistol-wielding Owen along with his three brothers and the rest of Brown's men bringing up the rear.

"Just wait here with our own horses, son," Mr. Brown said as he passed by with an oddly serene smile on his face. "We'll be back before you know it."

Abel nodded, breathing a sigh of relief that things were wrapping up so peacefully. A loud shriek caused him to jump and the other men to stop dead in their tracks.

"James Doyle, didn't I tell you nothin' good would come from the course you been takin'?" Doyle's wife ran up to her husband and threw herself in his arms, pulling him aside and crying hysterically.

"Hush now, Mother, hush," said Doyle softly. "Everything'll be all right." Cradling his wife, Doyle called out toward the front of the group, "Hey, Mr. Brown, got a question for you."

Brown peered at him intently. "What's that, sir?"

"What makes you New England do-gooders think you're so much better than the rest of us?"

Abel's jaw dropped. Was Doyle *crazy*, asking such a question in his position? He must be counting on Mr. Brown's promise of good treatment.

Even in the dim moonlight, Abel could see Brown's face contort. "Now what would make you ask such a thing, Mr. Doyle?"

Doyle kept gently stroking his wife's back. "Guess it's just that, try as I might, I can't figure why you abolitionist people get so riled up over the s'posed bad treatment of slaves in the South, especially when I hear most northerners—even most Kansas Free-Staters—agree they're an inferior breed. Only difference between North and South, far as I can tell, is the South offers steady, honest, hard work for 'em—work they're good at when they're not loafing or running off."

"You're wrong, Mr. Doyle. As God created all men equal in his sight, the negro is *not* inferior. And regardless, the man who owns slaves certainly has no justification before God to mistreat them in the manner that the South has long been doing."

"Well then," Doyle retorted in a slightly mocking tone, "seein' as we're your prisoners, I sure am glad to confirm that *we* don't own no slaves, so obviously we ain't mistreating any. But if I did own some, I can assure you I wouldn't hesitate to whip any lazy good-for-nothings every day if that's what it took to make 'em do the work I was feeding and sheltering 'em to do. It's only fair justice. That's all I got to say, and I guarantee I ain't afraid to tell it to whatever judge you're takin' us to."

Abel felt the blood surge to his face. *Come on, Mr. Brown, smash his face with your pistol butt!*

Brown stared hard at Doyle, saying nothing for several seconds. "If that's what you believe, Mr. Doyle, then let it be so," he said finally. "Let's go."

Abel's jaw dropped. *That's it? Mr. Brown's gonna let that no-good yokel get away with talking like that?*

Doyle's wife, her face stricken with terror, pulled on her husband's arm and whispered something in his ear. Whatever she'd said, he stared at her intently, then nodded and patted her hand.

"All right, Mr. Brown, all right. We'll go with you. Just one last question."

"One last question? Then ask it, sir."

For the first time, Doyle's voice seemed to tremble slightly. "You believe in the Lord Jesus our Savior?"

Brown hesitated. "Yes, Mr. Doyle . . . I certainly do. Why do you ask?"

Doyle pulled his wife closer. "Well, if that's the case, whatever sins you think me and my boys might be guilty of, I just hope you'll remember Christ alone is our only righteous judge."

Abel recoiled. *A professing Christian? Seriously?* He felt a momentary stab of guilt for wishing Doyle physical harm, even if the man's views on slavery were obviously misguided and despicable. But why would Doyle be making such a point about Christ? Was it a manipulative appeal for understanding and leniency?

Mr. Brown gazed up at the sky and closed his eyes. He took a deep breath, then returned his attention to Doyle. "I have just prayed that the Lord will soon make his righteous judgment in this matter known to all of us, Mr. Doyle."

Mrs. Doyle grabbed the arm of her youngest son. "Please, Mr. Brown, sir, let my boy John stay back here with me and my daughter. He's only sixteen."

Brown looked at the boy and smiled sympathetically. "Of course, ma'am. No need for every man from this house to lose more sleep than necessary tonight. Go with your mother, son."

It was a kind gesture, Abel thought, as he watched Mrs. Doyle and her youngest son return to the house while the men resumed their walk off into the dark. Mr. Brown certainly seemed to have an admirable inclination for mercy.

Ten minutes passed. Abel continued to wait by the house as Mr. Brown had requested, holding the reins of the horses and wondering how much longer it would take the others to return with the Doyles' steeds so they could all move on together. He glanced up through the branches at the half-moon that had suddenly emerged from behind some clouds. Bitter anger and frustration began to overwhelm him. Mercy had its limits. The Doyle men—especially the father, given his unrepentant, arrogant attitude—shouldn't be getting off as easily as Mr. Brown was apparently planning.

Abel peered down the dark path. He noticed someone returning but couldn't tell who. He blinked hard and squinted, but even that didn't help. Whoever it was, they were running quickly and deliberately toward him.

Owen Brown's excited voice crackled through the dark stillness. "Kid, tie the horses to the tree, quick—we need your help!"

"W-What? What's goin' on, Owen?"

Owen didn't reply. He walked over to one of the horses that had a large burlap satchel attached to its saddle, reached in, and pulled something out. Abel gasped at his first sight of the two-foot-long, brass-hilted broadsword that gleamed in the moonlight. Owen held it up and ran his finger along one side of the double-edged blade.

"Having more trouble than we figured with the Doyles, Abel. Father says the Lord's told him that the time has come—the inevitable war needs to begin. He said to ask if you'd be willing to help us teach the proslavery crowd a lesson. How about it, kid? Want to partake in the Northern Army's first strike against the abomination of slavery?"

Abel gulped, his mind torn and his body trembling with a strange mixture of elation and dread over Owen's proposal and his apparent means for carrying it out. He opened his mouth to reply but was unable to speak.

Owen seemed to recognize his dilemma. "There are times in history, kid," he said softly, "when the evil in the land rises to such a level that God requires his true followers to confront it—without timidity and with no reservations. We've reached such a point."

Abel looked down at the ground, scuffing it with his foot as he wrestled with Owen's provocative words in light of what Abel knew from the Bible about the nature of God and Jesus. He recalled God describing himself as slow to anger, merciful, and abounding in love. And yet . . . had not even the loving Christ, in his righteous anger, violently overthrown the tables of the corrupt temple moneychangers and said to his followers that he had come not to bring peace, but a sword?

Owen shrugged impatiently. "What's it going to be, Abel? I gotta get back now."

Abel let out his pent-up breath. The time to prove himself, to stand tall and firm against the doers of evil, had come. He grinned weakly back at Owen. "I'll help you, sir. What do I need to do?"

Owen reached into the satchel and pulled out two more broadswords, handing them to Abel. "Bring these along, just in case we need 'em to calm the Doyles down. The Lord's Glory will be praised tonight, Abel!"

Abel gripped the two swords in his hands. Each felt like it weighed at least ten pounds. He swallowed hard, then started to follow Owen down the path. No more hanging back. He would aid the fight for a noble cause—as any real man should.

Yes, Abel thought, *Owen's right . . . the Lord's Glory will be praised tonight, indeed!*

Pa would be proud of him.

Three days later, after a long day planting corn and cotton in the field while his father went to town for supplies, Abel sat exhausted on the ground with his back propped against the outside wall of the cabin just beside the front door. He dreaded Pa's return, knowing he'd probably be upset to have heard in town the first official accounts of what had happened last Saturday night.

Before long, Pa rode up, dismounted, and tied his horse to the rail. Sure enough, he had a newssheet with him, folded and tucked under his arm. Pa walked up and threw the paper into Abel's lap. "Read that," he said sternly.

It was one of the local proslavery publications. Abel unfolded the paper and read the short article just under the headline on the first page:

POTTAWATOMIE MASSACRE

Near midnight on May 24, the homes of three innocent Kansas families were invaded by an abolitionist gang bent on spreading their prejudiced message concerning the supposed evils of slavery in the most venomous fashion imaginable. The Doyle family men were the first victims to be murdered in cold blood, each suffering horrible wounds inflicted by heavy swords. James Doyle, the father, was found in the creek, stabbed through the chest and shot in the head. One of his sons had his fingers and arms severed and his skull split, apparently from trying to fend off blows. Another son had been stabbed through the head, jaw, and side. The other two families encountered similar fates. A total of five brave settlers lost their lives to the senseless violence of the abolitionist gang led by a man referred to as "Captain John Brown," and which is still on the loose. More details will follow in the next edition.

Abel gulped and peeked up hesitantly at his father, fearing his reaction.

Pa's face was like granite. "Like you said—you were just tending the horses, that's all . . . right, son?"

Abel averted his eyes. The blood drained from his face as he tried to subdue the bile that begged to erupt from this throat. "Pa . . . I . . ."

"*Right*, son?"

"Of course, Pa. Did just what I was told."

Pa nodded and smiled. "If that's the case, then I'm proud of you, boy." He brushed past Abel and went inside.

Abel closed his eyes and breathed a sigh of relief. Finally forcing himself to rise, he walked to the small storage shed adjoining the barn and went inside. The light was dim, and he could barely see. He stood on his toes, reached up, and moved his hand along the top shelf at the rear of the shed, wondering whether Pa might have already discovered and—for Abel's own good—removed what he was now searching for.

His hand found it . . . in exactly the same spot he'd laid it two nights ago after returning from the mission. He grasped the handle of the heavy, cold object and pulled it down from the shelf. Dried blood covered three-quarters of the blade; he'd never given a thought to washing it off before hiding it away. He moved his fingers along the blade's edge, marveling at its sharpness.

Something about the feel of the handle caught his attention. He turned it over and noticed what appeared to be an engraving of some type that was difficult to make out in the darkness. Holding the heavy weapon's blade with his left hand and the butt of the handle with his right, he raised it to the level of the room's small, dirt-smeared window through which some late afternoon light barely managed to filter. The handle's finely etched engraving suddenly came into clear focus:

The word stared back at him like some divinely inspired inscription on the head of a tombstone. The third "letter," artistically carved to appear as some sort of radiance-projecting human or divine eye, seemed to bore straight into his own with a message that made Abel's throat constrict and his chest heave with sobs.

There was no denying it: in last Saturday night's personal test of manhood and courage, he had failed miserably. After it was all over, when John Brown had handed him the sword still dripping with blood,

Abel had fallen to his knees with tears of shame. And yet, Brown had not condemned him. Instead, he had offered him hope—hope for another chance, if he was willing.

With both hands, Abel drew the sword reverently to his lips and kissed the blood-crusted blade. He knew now without a doubt that God and John Brown had called him to a grand new purpose in life. And from this day forward, he swore to himself, he would never again try to avoid it.

PART I

HEARTS DIVIDED

(1859)

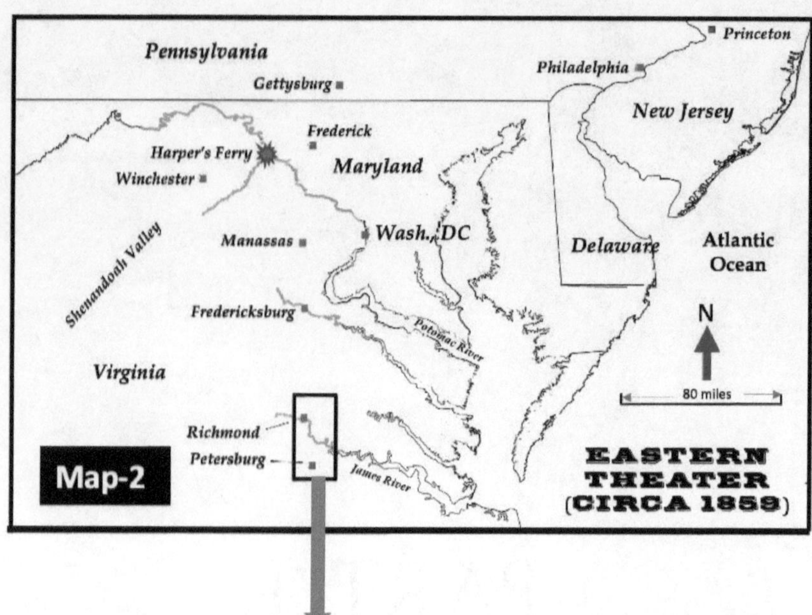

Pennsylvania
Gettysburg
Harper's Ferry
Frederick
Winchester
Maryland
Manassas
Wash. DC
Shenandoah Valley
Fredericksburg
Potomac River
Virginia
Richmond
Petersburg
James River
Map-2
Princeton
Philadelphia
New Jersey
Delaware
Atlantic Ocean
N
80 miles
EASTERN THEATER (CIRCA 1859)

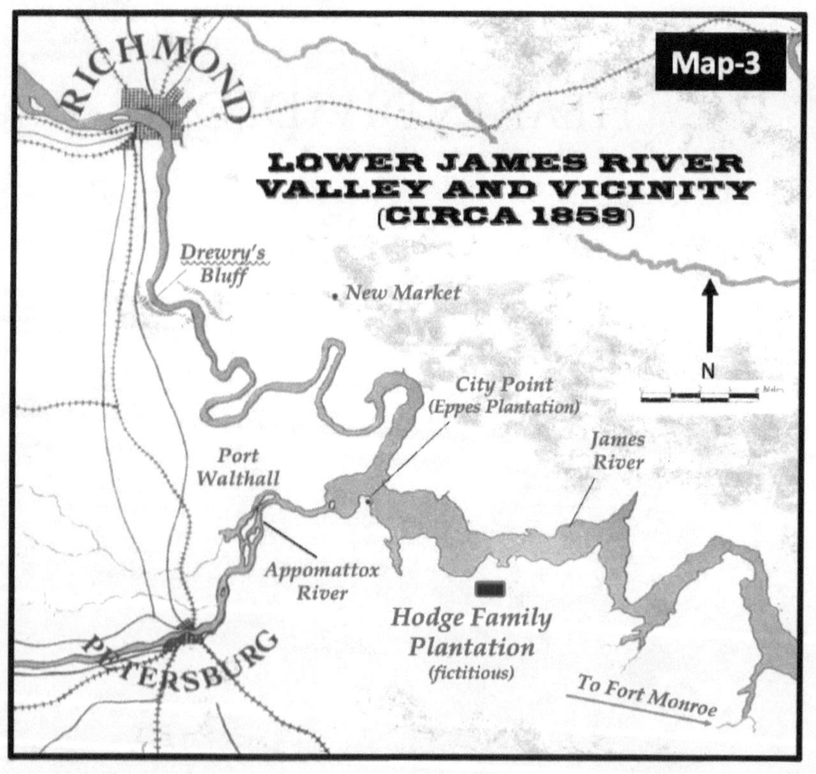

RICHMOND
Map-3
LOWER JAMES RIVER VALLEY AND VICINITY (CIRCA 1859)
Drewry's Bluff
New Market
City Point
(Eppes Plantation)
James River
Port Walthall
Appomattox River
Hodge Family Plantation
(fictitious)
To Fort Monroe
PETERSBURG
N

Chapter 2

Hodge Family Plantation, Northeast of Petersburg, Virginia
November 17, 1859
(Three and a half years later)

Awaking suddenly from her short afternoon nap, Emma Hodge struggled to focus. She sat up straight and rubbed her eyes, then folded her hands in her lap and glanced casually over the side of the damask-upholstered parlor room sofa. Her eyes came to rest on the local city newspaper that her father had left on the adjoining end table earlier this morning.

The extra-large boldface letters of the headline screamed out the message that most, if not all, loyal Virginians had been longing to hear for over a month now:

JOHN BROWN EXECUTION SET FOR DECEMBER 2nd
Five Other Members of Gang Also Sentenced for Roles
in Harpers Ferry Attack

Emma leaned back, closed her eyes, took a deep breath, and let it out slowly. The *last* thing the seventeen-year-old daughter of a wealthy Virginia planter felt like thinking about this late in the afternoon was the fates of some fanatical abolitionist and his wild-eyed cronies.

It had been a long and tedious day so far: piano scales practice first thing in the morning followed by another dull sewing lesson with her private tutor; a chilly, rain-interrupted picnic dinner by the pond with her sister; an exhausting review of the main house's kitchen supply needs—revealing that one of the house servants must be pilfering sugar. Even the midafternoon tea and pastries with the visiting ladies from the Petersburg Charity Society had turned out to be a dreary, taxing affair. In all her years of living on her family's seven-hundred-acre tobacco plantation serviced by over eighty slaves, Emma had rarely felt so spiritless.

And now, there was another unpleasant little task that her father had requested of her: to inform her sister Catherine of their elder brother David's imminent arrival home on break from college. Given the strained relationship between her two siblings, it was news that Emma feared could easily provoke Catherine's ire, and dealing with one of her sister's petulant fits was never a pleasant prospect.

Emma forced herself up from the comfortable sofa and trudged up the carved walnut spiral staircase, favoring the nagging limp that had plagued her ever since the terrible accident seven years ago. Arriving at her sister's bedroom at the end of the hall, she paused in front of the closed door. She raised her hand to knock but then suddenly lowered it and bit her lower lip, uncertain how or even whether to proceed.

Just get it over with, she told herself, nervously brushing a stray lock of hair behind her ear. *Deliver the news, don't get into an argument, and everything will be fine.* Catherine might fly off the handle, but she would eventually calm down.

Emma steeled herself, raised her arm once again, and knocked lightly.

There was a long pause before a grumpy-sounding female voice finally responded. "Sister, the least you can do is try opening the door."

Emma gritted her teeth. *Lord, grant me your patience.* She turned the knob and opened the door partway.

It was a familiar sight. Catherine sat on the edge of her velvet-tufted vanity bench, leaning forward to examine some imagined tiny flaw in the dressing mirror's reflection of her face.

"Hey, Cat . . . getting ready for supper?" Emma asked as sweetly as she could.

Catherine slightly turned her head to study her long blond hair pinned up in back, the lengths forced into tight curls draping her shoulders.

"Of course I'm getting ready for supper, Em," she replied irritably. "And why is it you always seem to show up when I'm right in the middle of making myself presentable?" With a resigned sigh, she returned to the careful study of her appearance, obviously pretending not to see the mirror's reflection of Emma approaching from behind.

Emma leaned over and threw her arms around Catherine's shoulders. She nestled her own cheek against Catherine's and gazed at the mirror with her.

"O classic, elegant face," Emma teased, cupping her nineteen-year-old sister's chin with her small, delicate fingers. "What more can I do to improve upon you? Those lovely big brown eyes, these high cheekbones, this perfectly sculpted chin and jawline, those enticing lips that men would—"

"Em, enough!" Catherine protested, wrestling to extricate herself. "Will you . . . just . . . *let me be*?"

Finally, she allowed herself a small laugh over her sister's playful prodding. "Now get away from my face and sit like a proper lady while I finish up here."

Emma sat on the end of the bench and began brushing her own light-auburn, naturally wavy, shoulder-length hair using one of the seven different styling brushes that Catherine kept handy on the dressing table. Glancing discretely at her sister's reflection beside her own, she marveled as usual at the degree to which Catherine had been graced with their mother's sharp, angular facial features, while she herself—with her hazel eyes and heart-shaped face—bore an uncanny resemblance to their father's sister.

"So," Catherine ventured as she reached for her makeup box, "what are *you* wearing to our 'famous' Hodge Family Plantation's annual harvest party tomorrow night? Not that awful yellow gown with the fancy embroidery, I hope."

"Oh, Cat," Emma groaned, "you think every dress I own makes me look like some gaudy flower—or an overripe piece of tropical fruit."

"Or sometimes both. Why don't you wear that lavender dress that Aunt Lyla bought for you when we all visited Washington last year? It shows that shapely figure of yours nicely, and it doesn't make you look like the perfect little prude that Mother constantly tried to turn us both into."

Emma laughed. "You better hope Mother isn't listening in from heaven on this conversation!" Martha Hodge, a beautiful lady in her own right prior to the ravages of her illness and eventual death from cancer three years ago, had never seemed comfortable with either of her daughters' attempts to display—even modestly—any of their own blossoming physical assets. "Young ladies should never dress in a way that will tempt gentlemen to entertain ungodly thoughts," their mother had admonished them separately on more than one occasion.

Catherine grimaced and shook her head. For her sister, Emma knew, even the lighter memories of their mother's pristine ways seemed to produce mixed emotions. As if she were still torn between her intense disdain for Mother's overly restrictive dictates and her appreciation for the loving intent behind them.

The ice now melted, Emma broke the news. "Cat, just before my nap, Papa got back from the city and told me that David arrived this morning. He wanted me to let you know."

Catherine froze in the middle of applying a touch of rouge to her cheek. Slowly, she turned her face toward Emma.

"He's a week early, isn't he?"

"Papa said he convinced his professors to let him take his fall exams a little early so he could be here in time for the party. You know it's always been his favorite social event of the year."

Catherine stared at her coldly, then turned back to the mirror. "So, I suppose he'll be joining us for supper tonight?" she asked finally.

"I think so. He was up at the Wheelers' farm this afternoon, helping that country preacher—Pastor Jones—get ready for his special revival service on Saturday evening. But he should be back soon."

Catherine smacked her small rouge jar down on the vanity. "There he goes again! Mr. Holier-Than-Thou trying to show everyone in this family—if not everyone in the whole county—what it takes to be a *true* Christian according to his own personal standards."

Though she'd half anticipated the reaction, Emma drew back, her eyes ablaze. "*Cat!* How could you say that?"

"Em, you know as well as I do that all David can talk about these days is '*prove* your faith is real and *live* like Christ.' Next thing you know he'll be asking Pastor Jones if he can preach his sermons for him."

Emma sighed. "Well, David does seem sincere about it all. Do the rest of us need to pile on, just because he tries to set a good example of Christian living for us? Shouldn't we all be striving to live more as the Bible teaches us? What's wrong with having someone in our family willing to challenge us on that?"

"There you go, protecting him again," Catherine groaned. "Why, Em? After all David's said and done to embarrass Papa these past few months? All his crazy talk about how we should all be so *ashamed* of ourselves as Christians for supposedly 'treating our negroes like cattle' or 'speaking with such hatred' toward the northerners?"

Not receiving any response, she shook her head in disgust. "David acts like he's found the secret for living a perfect, sinless life. He frowns down his nose on us 'pretend Christians,' even though we've clearly professed our faith in the Savior and strive our best to live as he commands. Whatever good we try to do, it never seems good enough for our dear brother, and the more time he spends helping that Pastor Jones fellow, the more pushy and annoying he seems to get."

Emma pressed her lips together, struggling mightily to contain her indignation. She'd always had a tender spot for her twenty-three-year-old brother and his obvious enthusiasm for matters of the Spirit. It was David who, four years ago, had escorted her on that long walk in the countryside, patiently answering her questions about what she was hearing in church concerning the salvation offered by Christ. Shortly after that, he'd been witness to her heartfelt prayer expressing sorrow for her sins and committing her life in submission to the Lord's leading.

"Cat," she said softly, "you know how much David loves our family. He's just encouraging us to—"

Catherine slapped the vanity top with her palm and twisted on the bench to face her. "Em, can't you see? It's not just about religion. David's in love with *all* his grand, new ideas. Especially when it comes to the supposed evils of slavery and secession. It's so ridiculous. Now he's even presuming to defend the actions of that murdering abolitionist John Brown and his band of slave lovers . . . even after they attempted to start a national slave rebellion with that raid on the Harpers Ferry arsenal last month."

"*What*?" Emma frowned, stopping her hair brushing mid-stroke. "How do you know that?"

"Papa told me he received a letter from David last week. He said how much he was looking forward to his semester break and being home again. He also proudly wrote that he'd just turned in his term paper reflecting on the crimes of Brown and his thugs, including those horrible Pottawatomie killings in Kansas three years ago. He said while he didn't agree with Brown's methods, he did have some sympathy for his motives and that he'd carefully explained why in his paper." Catherine shook her head. "I can't believe anyone from this household would ever come to think that way. Sympathy for a murdering insurrectionist? Really?"

"Well," Emma said cautiously, "doesn't he have a right to his opinions?"

Catherine glared at her sister's reflection in the mirror as she reached behind her head to fasten the clasp of her favorite gold locket evening necklace. "Seems to me that if David really cared about the rest of us, he'd show more respect for Papa's views and, heaven forbid, even a little respect for *my* views on such things once in a while. Honestly, every time he comes back on break from that college in Yankee Land, David acts like I have only half a brain. Like a planter's daughter might be able to learn French, but she couldn't possibly have anything intelligent to say about important 'manly' things like politics or national affairs."

"Cat, you know that's not true. You know David just likes to joust with all of us on those subjects. And just because he disagrees with Papa or you doesn't mean he disrespects your views or your intelligence."

"If you say so." Catherine huffed. "And it's true he *does* seem to respect whatever *you* have to say on such things. No doubt he's impressed with all those high-minded books you love to read." She waved her hand wearily. "Or maybe it's because you're so sweet and compassionate and never give him as hard a time as I do."

Emma could tell the conversation had taken the expected counter-productive turn. It was clear that the extra family duties her elder sister had felt obligated to assume following Mother's death were exacting a huge toll on her disposition toward just about everyone lately. Standing up, she gently squeezed Catherine's shoulder, then turned away and limped toward the door.

Catherine picked up an emery stick and began filing her nails. "By the way, Em . . . while we're on the subject of respect . . . I hope *you'll* be careful not to disrespect Papa by pursuing your little romance with that slave boy."

Emma's face turned ashen. She spun around, hands on hips. "What are you talking about, Cat?"

"Oh, it's hard to miss. All I had to do was watch Charles's face and yours light up like the sun itself when we passed him on our walk yesterday afternoon. And trust me, it's not the first time I've noticed you two slyly eyeing and smiling at each other—even in front of some of the other slaves."

Emma stood frozen with mouth agape as she tried to process things. She had thought she was being discrete with her innocent exchanges but had forgotten that Catherine always seemed to have extra sets of eyes in the back and sides of her head. And now that Catherine had peeked through the curtain, who knew what else she might now be thinking?

She tried to control the quavering in her voice. "*Cat*, it's not like Charles and I are . . ."

"Oh, I never said you were," Catherine said as she continued to file her nails. "I'm just saying, be careful. I know Charles saved your life once, and I can understand why you'd still feel some gratitude toward him. But you know what Papa would do to that boy, not to mention you, if he ever got the slightest wind of anything even hinting at, well, you know . . ."

"Cat, how could you even *think* something like that?" Emma said, her voice breaking. "I promise, you don't have to worry—there's nothing between Charles and me beyond a shared memory."

"Well, *that's* certainly a relief to hear. The last thing this family needs is an illegitimate, mixed-raced child of a slave whom we always have to keep out of sight."

"I'll see you at supper, Cat." Emma slammed the door behind her and stood in the hallway. Her whole body trembled with a confused mixture of indignation and dismay over the possibility that her own sister might consider her capable of committing the sin most despised among southern gentry: sexual relations between a White woman and a Black slave.

Alone in her room, Catherine glared at the tear-stained face staring back at her in the mirror. *You heartless witch! How could you have said something so cruel to your own sister? Hasn't Papa admonished you constantly to be kind and understanding toward her like Mother was . . . but you're doing exactly the opposite! Yet another reason for Papa and God to be disappointed in you. You just never seem to stop giving them reasons, do you?*

Then again, she thought, Papa never seemed to need much of a reason for his frequent verbal criticisms and other subtle expressions of disapproval of Catherine's efforts to fill the role that Mother had performed so admirably as plantation mistress. It all felt like a natural extension of her earlier years—between ten and fourteen—when her father, stressed by the plantation's business situation and seeking solace in his bourbon, would often lash out physically over some perceived small violation of proper behavior on Catherine's part. Angry dressing-downs and slaps to the face for her "bratty, tomboyish antics" or "petulant, disrespectful looks" had been commonplace, and the occasional use of his leather belt to whip her bare legs had more than once drawn some blood and left painful welts. When she'd once screamed out in distress and asked him why neither David nor Emma ever received such correction, he'd simply answered that "they don't act silly or talk back like you."

Thankfully, Mother's cries for mercy had spared Catherine from even worse treatment then, and it was true that over time Papa's physical punishments had gradually transitioned to less overtly abusive forms. Still, the fact that—unlike David and Emma—she never seemed able to genuinely please him led her to one inescapable conclusion: somehow, she was failing to perform as Papa expected of her as his eldest daughter. *And if I'm failing in Papa's eyes, then I must be failing in God's eyes as well.*

As the painful memories and confused thoughts of anger and self-condemnation took hold, the familiar pang in the pit of her stomach began to spread. Opening the vanity drawer, she pulled out the small instrument that she'd discovered as the only reliable antidote for the head-spinning, stomach-cramping episodes of depression that were plaguing her more and more these past two years since Mother's death. Nothing the family doctor had prescribed had helped in the slightest. One dark night several months ago, overwhelmed with her dark ideas and physical distress, the bizarre idea had first occurred to her. Amazingly, it had helped then, and—like a magic ritual—she'd employed it ever since.

Taking the penknife in her right hand, she placed her left palm upward on the vanity surface. She gritted her teeth, then made a small cut at the base of her thumb—enough to draw blood. It was the tenth incision she'd inflicted since that first episode in various places on her body. The previous ones had been completely hidden from view. Not this one.

She allowed the blood to drip into a small bowl for almost a minute, then applied a dab of cotton to the cut to stem the flow. After cleaning the bowl, she wiped off the knife and returned it to the drawer. With the entire ritual now finally over, she gazed at her reflection in the mirror. As if on cue, the tears had dried and the gnawing pain in her abdomen had begun to subside. She rose from the vanity, a small smile of relief on her lips. Once again, the ritual had worked to perfection.

I can handle this . . . and I will never, ever let anyone know. Yes, as difficult as it was, she would do everything in her power to honor her mother's memory and make her father proud. And then maybe one day, she hoped desperately, Papa would grant at least a fraction of the tender love and affection that she still remembered receiving from him as a small child.

CHAPTER 3

Hodge Family Plantation
November 17, 1859

Emma stared out her bedroom window at the late fall sunset, clutching the small, cloth-wrapped package close to her chest. The sting of Catherine's rebuke was still fresh, but she was determined not to let it spoil the eighteenth birthday surprise she'd been eagerly planning since late last week for Sallie Cobb, her personal maid.

Sallie, what on earth is taking you so long? Supper was now only a half hour away, and there was little time to spare. Moving as close to the glass as the billowing swell of her white silk hoopskirt would allow, she peered down and off to the side toward the loom house. Hopefully, Sallie, having completed her late-afternoon assignment helping the domestic production workers with their annual weaving project, would appear soon at the exit and start making her way toward Emma's room on the second floor of the main house.

Her gaze drifted to the backyard vegetable garden where she spotted the familiar wooden child's chair underneath the sweet gum tree at the garden's far edge. The sight caused the frightening event of seven years ago to unfold in her mind, as if it had occurred only yesterday . . .

After dinner on a hot July afternoon, ten-year-old Emma had been sitting in her favorite backyard chair, engaged in her favorite activity. Having already read three illustrated storybooks over the past two weeks, she was halfway through devouring a fourth. Her parents, discovering that Emma possessed special talents for reading and writing, had kept her well supplied with books like these along with a variety of other reading materials considered to be quite advanced for her age.

Tired from her concentrated effort—and noticing Catherine napping on the rear veranda's settee while the girls' nanny, Priscilla, dozed in one of the chairs—Emma had brashly ventured out on an exploratory walk along the path through the nearby woods leading to the slave quarters. It was her first time traversing the narrow trail alone, and she'd been mesmerized by the intoxicating aroma of pine needles and cedarwood, as well as the spectacle of squirrels and other small creatures scurrying along the ground.

A few hundred yards from the main house, the seemingly idyllic path had meandered perilously close to an eroded, rain-slickened creek embankment. Without warning, the muddy dirt had crumbled under Emma's feet. Despite her frantic attempts to grasp hold of several exposed tree roots, she'd slipped down the bank and gashed her shin on a sharp rock protruding from the swirling water that was now running deep and fast due to recent storms. Pulled into the current and unable to swim, she'd struggled mightily to keep her head afloat as each attempt to scream drew a batch of water into her mouth and down her throat. She'd tired quickly and was on the verge of blacking out.

Thank the Lord that twelve-year-old Charles Cobb, Sallie's stepbrother, was picking wild berries near the opposite bank and had heard her muffled cries for help. Jumping in downstream and fighting the current, Charles—a head taller and stronger than most boys his age—had somehow managed to swim the twenty feet across the water to reach her. Fighting against the little girl's panicked flailings, he'd secured her safely under his arm and traversed the remaining distance to the bank. With Emma clinging to his back, he'd then worked his way hand over hand up a low overhanging branch, out of the water and up the embankment to safety.

The ordeal hadn't ended there. Emma, her left shin throbbing and bleeding badly from her fall into the creek, was unable to stand. Charles had wrapped his wet shirt around the wound and carried her home. Mother, first to respond to the butler's distraught cry from the side yard, had nearly fainted at the sight of her youngest daughter in the arms of a shirtless negro boy. Papa, equally aghast, had yanked Emma from Charles's arms but—after hearing the story—had thanked and politely dismissed him with an offer of dry clothes and some left-overs from dinner in the back of the house. He'd then ordered a sound whipping and six-month consignment to fieldwork for Priscilla, whose dozing had allowed Emma to wander off. Were it not for Catherine and Emma's pleas and Priscilla's excellent service up to that point, Papa said he would have permanently banned her from household support work.

Within two days, more trouble had arrived for Emma in the form of a seething infection to the gash she'd incurred. It had required Dr. Haynes to cut deeply into the flesh just below the knee. The wound had healed badly, resulting in an ugly scar and a noticeable limp that had plagued her ever since.

The whole experience was one she would have longed to forget were it not for the tender recollection of Charles Cobb and his heroic action on her behalf that day.

"I'm so happy you still 'live, Miss Emma," was the last thing Charles had said when Papa had lifted her away from his arms . . .

"Sallie?"

"Yes, it's me."

Emma opened her bedroom door and smiled at the welcome sight of the petite young woman with the mahogany complexion and attractive, oval-shaped face. "One of the prettiest, most intelligent slave girls in the county," Papa had boasted to visiting socialites from the city more than once. Garbed in the loose-fitting bright-white dress with starched apron and headwrap that Mother had made as part of a previous year's clothing allotment for the female domestic servants, Sallie reminded Emma of the beautiful, dark-skinned angel she'd once seen in a storybook illustration.

"Finally! I thought you'd never get here! Now come over here and sit beside me so I can give you your birthday present."

Sallie stared at her suspiciously. "*Present*? You got *me* a present?"

Emma laughed. "What, are you suddenly doubting your mistress's kindness and good intentions?" She grabbed Sallie's hand and led her to the sofa. Once the girls were settled on it, she laid the package between them. "Now, you know I never break my promises to you, right?"

"Well, yes, but . . . what's this?"

"Just open it and see."

Sallie's hands shook as she unwrapped the cloth and read the title of the leather-bound book: "*The Wide, Wide World* by Elizabeth Wetherell."

"Oh, Miss Em! Oh, I . . . I can't believe you got this for us!"

"Told you I would, didn't I? Do you think I'd spend all those Sunday afternoons locked up in here, teaching you to read, if I wasn't eventually going to get us something a little more challenging to practice on?"

The girls hugged, their delighted laughs mixed with tears.

Sallie opened the book to the first page. "Oh my," she said, frowning. "I never seen hardly none o' the words on this page before. How long you think it gonna take me to learn how to read *this*?"

"Well, it's definitely more advanced than anything you've tried so far. But as smart as you are, and with the amazing rate you're progressing with my teaching you? I'm sure we'll be able to do a chapter each month. It's about a young girl who gets separated from her mother who'd meant everything to her, how she struggles to be a good Christian, and how she deals with people who don't care about her."

Sallie closed her eyes and bit her lip as she stared down at her lap. Emma wasn't surprised by the reaction. Who would know better than Sallie Cobb what the word *separation* meant?

As she'd related her fuzzily recalled childhood story to Emma, Sallie had been born to poor but free Black parents in a tiny shack outside Baltimore, Maryland. When she was eight, kidnappers bent on supplying slave traders with some "fresh young meat" for the southern market had barged into the shack, ripping Sallie away from her recently widowed mother's arms. The weeklong journey southward—hidden in the back of a rickety covered wagon under the watchful eye of an unsympathetic older slave woman—had been arduous. It had finally ended in Richmond, Virginia. Emma's father, seeing young Sallie for sale at a city slave auction, had purchased her with the idea of having her trained to become a domestic servant for the household.

Upon bringing her home, Papa had introduced Sallie to Tom and Mary Cobb, a thirtyish slave couple with a reputation for being honest and hardworking fieldworkers. The Cobbs had agreed to take Sallie in and raise her as their own along with their own nine-year-old son Charles and baby Lew—with the understanding that the girl's day job would be learning to work in the main house as a personal attendant for her young mistress Emma under the watchful eye of Priscilla.

When Sallie had completed her training and first entered service at the age of eleven as young Emma's official personal maid, their bonding had been immediate. Emma had embraced her like a newfound sister—never hesitating when the two were alone to joke, complain, gossip, express affection, or confide. It was all quite unlike the cold, austere treatment the girl would usually receive from Emma's sister and parents. Within a year, Sallie had privately become Emma's closest companion and primary focus of the growing empathy Emma had been experiencing—ever since the day of her accident and rescue by Sallie's stepbrother Charles—for the Hodge family slaves and the hard lives she knew they were destined from birth to endure.

"Miss Em," Sallie said finally after wiping her eyes, "you think maybe you doin' too much for me? Don't wanna get you in trouble with Master."

Emma winced. That *was* a possibility, she knew, even though she believed in her heart that her actions had the purest possible motivation. After all, didn't they reflect her church pastor's constant reminders of Christ's call to show benevolence and kindness toward the "least of these"? And weren't they a natural extension of the charitable work she'd begun at age eleven—assisting Mother in ministering to ill slaves in their quarters and conducting Sunday evening prayer sessions on the main house's rear veranda for the domestic servants and a few interested field slaves?

As time had gone on, she'd wanted to do something more. Something compatible with her growing desire to share her passion and gift for reading. And so, starting a little over two years ago, she had initiated a far more controversial activity: secretly teaching Sallie the ABCs and to read selected, simple verses from the Bible.

It was an undertaking which Emma was convinced that Papa— should he ever find out—would easily forgive despite Virginia's strict anti-literacy laws forbidding such activity with slaves. Her confidence was based on her father's often-stated personal conviction that "slaves deserve to hear and know the Word of God, especially as it instructs them in the rewards of obedience to their masters." Though she'd long recognized and been troubled by his seemingly self-serving motivation, she took solace in knowing that at least Papa appreciated the inherent value of the Good Book for the slaves' spiritual welfare.

Still, to avoid the possibility of her father discovering and being forced to confront the illegality of her actions, Emma had held her two-hour, early Sunday afternoon tutoring sessions with Sallie in the privacy and security of her own bedroom. The scheme had worked perfectly, and, enticed by Sallie's rapid development and Emma's own enjoyment of her teaching role, she had gradually abandoned any effort to limit the reading materials to Bible verses alone. Her childhood reading primers and simple storybooks had been introduced into the "curriculum," and Sallie was now ready for her next big step. The potential rewards of taking it definitely seemed worth the risk.

"Leave Papa to me," Emma said, patting Sallie's hand as she rose from the sofa. "You just worry about making me proud of your progress."

"So . . . how you gonna teach me this book?" Sallie asked.

"Just like with the last one—a chapter at a time. I'll read it to you first, then we'll have you take your turn, sentence by sentence. Of course, this one's *much* harder with a lot of new words, so we'll spend more meetings on each chapter."

Sallie stood up and hugged her mistress closely.

"Love you, Miss Em! Thank you, thank you."

Suddenly, looking into Sallie's grateful eyes, Emma remembered her sister's words. She pulled Sallie's hands away, then ambled over to the window.

"What's wrong, Emmy?"

Emma turned to face her. Her lips trembled as she spoke. "Cat suspects me and Charles."

Sallie tilted her head. "What she suspect? You and Charles never . . ."

"No, of course not. But Cat knows me all too well. I know she loves me and she's always tried to protect me, especially now with Mother gone. But *nothing* I do these days seems to escape her eye—especially when it comes to any supposed 'flirtations' with men. When we passed by Charles yesterday, she saw us smile at each other, and she accused me of having a 'little romance' going on with him."

"Well, how would *you* describe it?"

Emma blushed. "Oh, he's a really nice boy . . . and I *love* the way he so faithfully participates in our Sunday evening prayer sessions, even though he could have chosen to take a nap or go fishing. I-I try to be friendly to him, that's all—especially since he's your stepbrother."

"And the fact that a really nice, good-lookin' boy saved your life don't have nothin' to do with it, right?" Sallie chided gently, eyebrow arched.

Emma flashed an annoyed look. Sallie always knew how to bring out the true motives behind her feelings.

Letting out a long sigh, she admitted the obvious. "I'd be lying if I said that sweet memory doesn't register strongly in my mind every time I see him."

"So you like him then?" Sallie asked with a coy smile. "Lord, I know he sure likes you. Every day, he carries in his pocket that handkerchief you made special for him last Christmas."

"*Really?*" Emma gasped, her heart leaping. "Oh, that makes me so happy to hear. And . . . yes, of course I like Charles. Very much. But just because I *like* him doesn't mean I have a 'little romance' going on with him."

"*I* know, Miss Em, but still . . . maybe you takin' too many chances, like stoppin' to smile and wave and say somethin' nice to him when he passed us on his way back from the fields last Friday. There're too many gossips around here, Emmy—a lotta colored girls wishin' a handsome young man like Charles would pay more attention to 'em. And they just lookin' for a chance to stir up nasty rumors."

Emma nodded. "You're right. I had no idea I was being so obvious. I definitely need to take more care. And I suppose I should *thank* Cat for telling me the truth—even if she did make me feel like a naughty two-year-old. Seems I deserved it."

Sallie's eyes narrowed. "You don't think Miss Cat will blab on you and Charles to your father, do you?" she asked, her voice trembling slightly.

"Oh, definitely not." She waved the notion away. "We've *always* trusted each other completely with our little secrets."

"And you haven't told her about our readin' sessions, have you?"

Emma hesitated. "Well . . . no, but—"

Both girls flinched at the sound of the supper bell clanging.

"Miss Em, I need to get back to my shack. Daddy'll skin my hide if I don't at least have supper started 'fore they all get back from the fields."

"All right, but before you go, I've got one more present for you."

Emma limped to her writing desk and picked up a small, framed print. Returning, she presented it reverently with both hands to Sallie.

"What's this?"

"Keep this close to you always. Hide it under your mattress if you have to. You know what these verses say because you can read them now. Let them be an encouragement to you whenever you're feeling low. And remember, Jesus is always there with us in those times. We're never alone."

Sallie's eyes glistened as she peered at the three simple Bible verses that Emma had hand-written on colored cardboard and framed herself.

"I promise, Miss Em, I'll learn these by heart."

Emma smiled. "I know you will. Now, shoo! You've got to get going, and I need to get to supper." Her throat constricted as she watched Sallie wave goodbye from the doorway before hurrying off down the hallway.

Along the beaten path through the woods to the slave quarters, a twig snapped and jolted Sallie out of her reverie. Glancing up from the framed Bible verses she'd been staring at while walking along, she peered through the branches, searching for the disruption. There was nothing.

"Who's there?" she said softly. No answer.

Another soft crunching noise, this time closer and a little off to the side.

"Hello, someone there?"

Again, no response. Probably just a skunk or raccoon—Daddy said they'd been overrunning the woods lately. She began walking swiftly again toward the quarter. If she wasted no more time, she would make it back to the shack before her family arrived and chop up and boil the collards, kale, and turnips that Momma had harvested last night from the family's tiny garden plot. Daddy, of course, would expect her to mix in some pieces of raw beef from their weekly ration and spice up the whole mixture with red pepper. Hopefully, there'd be enough for seconds for Charles, who never failed to plead for them on the laughable excuse that he was "still a growing boy."

A movement just ahead caused her to stop. She barely stifled a scream at the unwelcome sight of Sam Taylor—the twenty-six-year-old fieldwork supervisor and son of the plantation overseer—blocking the path ahead. The tall, muscular man held a shotgun casually in his hand, its barrel resting against his shoulder.

She made an awkward attempt to hide the frame-print under her shawl.

"Well now, Sallie, what you doin' out here?" Sam grinned, tipping back his light-gray, wide-brimmed bowler hat to reveal a short fringe of oily black bangs and a horizontal, purplish scar on the right side of his forehead.

Something about his narrowed eyes and mocking tone of voice suggested this was not a chance encounter. Nor was it the first time he'd ogled her with that merchandise-appraising stare. In fact, one of the fieldworkers recently said he'd overheard Sam tell his assistant that he'd long "admired" Sallie's looks, and that he'd love to "get to know her a little better" someday. *That*, of course, could mean only one thing.

Sallie pulled the shawl closer around her shoulder, praying Sam hadn't noticed the frame. "Hello, Mr. Taylor. I-I's just walkin' back to my shack to get supper started for my family, just like I do every day."

"That so?" Sam sounded genuinely surprised. "Can't say I've ever known you to take this ole broke-down path to your shack the entire ten years I been workin' here, Sallie. Why aren't you just walkin' down the main lane in plain sight, like usual?"

Sallie shrugged. "Just thought I'd try a different way this time, that's all. Mr. Taylor, sir, it be all right if I get on to my shack now? Gotta get supper ready for my family."

"Oh, sure, sure, Sallie," he said, stepping aside ever so slowly. "Didn't mean to hold you up. In fact, I was out here just takin' a little walk myself . . . checking for a sign of that no-good stepbrother of yours I sent to fetch me a couple o' grub hoes from the Wheelers' barn. Been over two hours since I sent him, and the workday's over. Wonder what that boy's up to. No sign of him in the quarter. Don't suppose you happened to see any sign of Charles while you were walkin' through these woods, did you, Sallie?"

She froze in her tracks, her heart beating wildly.

"N-No, Mr. Taylor. I ain't seen Charles since the crack o' dawn. But if he shows up after I get to the shack, I'll let him know you're lookin' for 'im."

Sam looked at her suspiciously. "That's real good, Sallie, because that boy's got a hell of a whippin' coming once I find him. Might even need a little somethin' extra to help him learn . . . I'll have to think what that might be. Anyways, enjoy your family time and supper tonight. And please give Miss Emma my regards tomorrow!"

Sallie tried her best to resume her walk as calmly as possible.

"Oh, Sallie!"

"Y-Yes, sir?"

"Just curious . . . what you think you're tryin' to hide under that shawl of yours?"

Sallie reluctantly opened her shawl to reveal the frame. "I-It's a birthday present from Miss Emma."

"A present from Miss Emma? How about I just take a peek at that."

Sallie's hand shook as she handed the frame over. After studying it for a few moments, Sam glanced up at her, his eyebrow cocked suspiciously. "You lyin' to me, Sallie?"

Her heart in her throat, Sallie's voice quavered as she spoke. "No, sir. I-I promise I'm not lyin'."

"Well, what I want to know is . . . why would Miss Emma give you a real nice present like this if she knows you can't even read? I know you've somehow learned to speak the King's English better 'n' all the other slaves around here—and I don't doubt you hangin' around Miss Emma so much helped you with that. But are you gonna tell me she's taught you how to *read* even though it's against the law? You didn't steal this from Miss Emma's room, now did you, Sallie?"

"No, sir. Miss Em just read those verses to me, and I liked 'em, so she framed 'em and said I could keep it for my birthday present."

Sam rubbed his chin. "Tell you what, Sallie. I'm a fair man. How about I keep this with me and check with Miss Emma next time I see her. If your story's true, I'll bring this right back to your shack and hand it to you myself with a big ole apology. That sound like a fair deal?"

Just tell him what he wants to hear. "Oh, yes, sir . . . it sound real fair to me."

"Well, you better get on home now, right?"

Trying desperately to maintain her calm, she began walking once again down the path. It was a losing cause—after three steps, she broke into a frantic run toward her shack.

CHAPTER 4

Hodge Family Plantation
November 17, 1859

At precisely 7:30 P.M., Ben Edgefield, the Hodge family butler, opened the dining room doors with his usual flourish. "Master Hodge, supper's ready to serve whenever you're ready, sir."

Setting his empty bourbon glass down on the rosewood sidetable next to his favorite parlor armchair, Lawrence Hodge smiled across the room at his two daughters.

"Fine, Ben, thank you," Lawrence said. "We'll be there as soon as David and his guest arrive. They should be here any minute now. And Ben, tell Dorothy we'll need two portions each of that delicious broiled quail for my boy David and his friend."

"Two, sir?"

"That's right. We have to welcome our prodigal son home—and no doubt he and his friend will be expecting at least *some* earthly reward for all their work preparing for that revival service on Saturday night."

Seated near Emma on the sofa next to the hearth, Catherine looked up from her French lesson book.

"Papa, who is David's guest?"

"Pastor Jones. Your brother asked if he could invite him, since it would give us all a chance to meet and get to know him. They should be getting here any minute now."

Struggling to keep her tongue in check, Catherine stared across the parlor at her father in wide-eyed amazement. She knew that Papa—a successful planter, businessman, lawyer, and ruling elder for the Second Presbyterian Church of Petersburg—was already disturbed by David's increasingly radical views on the slavery issue. So why was he now so ready to offer the family's hospitality to that country *Baptist* preacher, who Papa said had recently expressed some strange opinions on slavery that ran counter to the prevailing sentiment of other city clergymen and local slaveowners?

Catherine shot a quick glance at her sister. Emma had been strangely quiet since arriving in the parlor, seemingly lost in her own thoughts. *She's probably still angry about my warning this afternoon,* Catherine thought with a flash of lingering remorse over the harsh way she'd delivered it.

"Oh," Papa said, "did I mention that Mr. and Mrs. Faulkner will be attending our party tomorrow night?"

Catherine groaned silently, knowing exactly the implications. Charles Faulkner, an old acquaintance of Papa's, was rumored to be President Buchanan's preferred choice for succeeding the recently deceased US ambassador to France. He was visiting relatives in Petersburg, and Papa would certainly not want to miss the perfect opportunity to impress him and his wife with Hodge family assets and talents. Papa had invested far more than the average planter in his children's education beyond the typical vocational or domestic subjects, and he expected to see some reward for it all. Catherine and Emma would be expected to play their part.

Papa tapped his hand on the top of the chair arm. "I suppose we'll have to brag a little about Emma's writing award, and I know you'll be putting your best French on display for the Faulkners, won't you, Catherine?"

"Yes, Papa, have I ever let you down on that score?" she replied with the sweetest smile she could muster.

"That's good. Never hurts to let people in high places know what this family is made of. Especially important people like Charles Faulkner who help keep this country in good standing around the world."

Before Catherine could roll her eyes, a familiar figure appeared in the side doorway.

"Papa . . . did I just hear someone mention 'important people'?" quipped David Hodge with a wide grin. Catherine tried her best to appear as delighted as her father and sister at her brother's arrival.

"Well, better late than never!" Papa declared, rising from his chair. "Where's your guest?"

"Right here," David said, stepping aside to reveal the presence of a short, thin, fiftyish-looking gentleman with curly, grayish white hair, balding temples, wire-framed glasses, and the plain, dark attire and white cravat typical of an itinerant country preacher. The man's vanilla-brown skin tone led Catherine to wonder if he might be of mixed-race descent.

"Pastor Horace Jones," David intoned, "allow me to introduce my father—Lawrence Hodge—and my two sisters, Catherine and Emma."

"It's an honor and pleasure, my ladies and sir." Pastor Jones stepped into the room and bowed modestly in a way that seemed quite sincere. "It was so kind of you to invite me."

Papa walked over to shake his hand. "Welcome to our home, Pastor. Please, come join us at our table. Are we all ready, ladies?"

Catherine stood and walked over to grasp her father's hand. "Of course we're ready, Papa." With Mother's passing, she'd become an expert at performing the little rituals she knew he'd always expected.

In the dining room, Ben seated the women along one side of the rectangular table across from David and Pastor Jones while Papa took his seat at the head. As he did so, Catherine noticed him gazing sadly at the jewel-adorned glass candelabra gracing the table's center. It was the piece that he'd had specially made for Mother as an anniversary gift, and one which she'd always treasured dearly.

After catching his eye, Catherine leaned over and placed her hand on his forearm. "I know she's with us even now, Papa," she said softly. Papa stared at her vacantly for a couple of seconds, then lowered his head and patted her hand lightly.

Breaking the brief awkward silence, Dorothy, the family cook, entered the room and started to ladle out the supper's first course: oyster stew. Papa invited Pastor Jones to say grace, after which he took over the conversation in his usual gregarious fashion.

"So, Pastor, we've heard some interesting reports about your Saturday night revival meetings at the Wheelers' farm. Seems you're stirring up quite a frenzied following for the Lord among our rural folk!"

Pastor Jones chuckled. "I certainly try to do my best. Though I must admit it's been quite a challenge locating enough *snake oil* around these parts to anoint the heads of all our prospective converts! I just hope I haven't been too much trouble for the Wheelers. They've been so kind to provide lodging for my wife and me, as well as a place to preach outside the city."

His self-deprecating comments drew appreciative laughs from everyone, especially Papa, who Catherine knew was well aware of all the recent talk in their own church concerning "arrogant, out-of-control" local country preachers bent on bringing their own version of the gospel message to poor Whites and ignorant slaves.

Papa went on to observe how challenging he imagined the life of a country clergyman must be. How he'd once gone to a barn revival meeting himself as a youth but hadn't quite resonated with the preacher's frantic urging to "make a voluntary decision *now*" to approach the makeshift altar, fall on his knees, and pray for his own sudden, emotion-filled, born-again conversion experience right then and there. While such an orchestrated, public solicitation certainly might be God's means of conversion for *some* people, Papa conceded, his own had been brought about by consistently hearing the Bible preached in church—resulting gradually over time in a sincere inner conviction of his "incurable, hell-deserving sin" that had led him to privately repent, believe, and call on the Lord for salvation.

Pastor Jones seemed to take it all in stride with gentle nods and a peaceful smile. His only response was to quietly point out that God's ways are often mysterious, especially when it came to the process and timing of conversion.

He seems to be a humble man with nice manners and a great sense of humor, Catherine had to admit. *Not at all the thundering, hell-fire-spewing prophet I'd half expected.*

The conversation switched to talk of the weather, the challenges with this year's tobacco harvest, and the latest theories on crop rotation. Emma said nothing, apparently still preoccupied with her own troubled thoughts. Catherine, bored nearly to tears, took the opportunity to gaze discreetly at her brother and wonder what provocations he'd eventually bring to the table tonight. It wasn't like David to allow a family meal to proceed in total serenity from beginning to end.

It hadn't always been that way, Catherine thought. David used to be the model of quiet decorum. Never questioning anything Papa said. The perfect choirboy at church; the fawned-over, favorite child at home. Even Emma—with all her lovable, compassionate qualities—hadn't received half the adulation and affection that Lawrence and Martha Hodge had showered on their only son, the firstborn of their three children.

True, Catherine had to admit, any parent—or sister, for that matter—would be hard-pressed *not* to adore David. Especially in recent years as his face had matured, reflecting Papa's strong, square jawline combined with Mother's high cheekbones, large brown eyes, and sleek, narrow nose. But it wasn't just his attractive physical features that had captured their hearts. David had always displayed an unusual sensitivity, an earnest concern for the feelings of others. Like all those times as children that he'd make a disastrous late move resulting in Catherine's winning at checkers, even though David was by far the better player. Catherine just *knew* that David had recognized her desperate desire to win, and she loved him for unselfishly allowing her to do so.

So much had changed over the past four years. David had graduated first in his class at L. S. Squire's prep school for boys, one of Richmond's finest. After admission to the College of New Jersey at Princeton, his confidence in his own intellectual capabilities had soared, as had his interest in the wider world and its challenges. Now in his senior year, it was not enough simply to gain his BA degree in preparation for an anticipated career in journalism. Reading abolitionist-leaning newspapers, attending radical political speeches, and devouring books on history and religion had become his favorite extracurricular pastimes. And along with these had come an insatiable tendency to test his new-found knowledge and ideas against the codified beliefs and thinking of his own family.

Lifting her eyes, Catherine was taken aback to find Pastor Jones looking at her. It didn't seem at all to be a look of ill intent, but rather one of almost tender concern, even empathy. Had he read her thoughts? She quickly averted her eyes back to Papa, who thankfully seemed to be wrapping up his long discourse on one of his favorite topics: the price of cotton in English markets.

A blessed, temporary pause in the conversation allowed Dorothy to distribute the supper's main course of broiled, spiced quail accompanied by sweet potatoes and corn.

Papa cooed with pleasure as Ben lifted the cover and released the steam from the platter of quail. "Sweet heavens, thank you, Dorothy . . . I can already tell from the delightful aroma that you've captured exactly my dear wife's recipe for this."

Dorothy beamed. "You're welcome, sir. Dear Missus sho' was a good cookin' teacher."

As the eating commenced, Catherine's attention once again began to wander. Her gaze fell on the large reproduction of Da Vinci's "The Last Supper" on the wall directly behind and above Pastor Jones and David. She wondered wryly if it held any special, divine portent for tonight's meal and its aftermath.

"Pastor Jones," David said, lifting his water glass in an informal toast, "I should mention how proud I am of my two beautiful sisters here. Why, it was just last month that Emma beat out twenty other contestants to win the Piedmont County writing contest for girls under eighteen."

"My, that's wonderful, Miss Emma! May I ask . . . what topic did you write on?"

Emma blushed. "Oh, it was nothing much, sir. We were given two hours to write an essay on a memorable life experience that involved helping others in some way."

"I'm sure you've had many. Was it hard picking just one out?"

"Oh, no, sir—that was the easy part. I wrote about the time I was taking one of my occasional nature walks around the plantation and one of our fieldworkers came running up to me. She was crying hysterically and holding her baby, who was spitting up and clearly in distress. The woman said she was taking him back home but was so afraid because she hadn't yet finished hoeing and seeding her quota of tobacco for the day. She said the field supervisor had told her she better get back soon and finish up, or he'd give her a good whipping, but she knew she'd never make it back before the day ended. I told her to go on home and that I'd go and speak with her supervisor, which I did after praying for help to know what to say . . ."

Emma paused and peeked hesitantly at her father.

"It's fine, dear, tell the rest of the story." He glanced with raised eyebrow at Pastor Jones. "Assuming, of course, that our guest is willing to hear it."

Jones grinned. "You have me on the edge of my seat, Emma. By all means, please do continue."

"Well," she said, "I went to the supervisor and said I didn't think any nursing mother deserved to be threatened with a whipping. He told me he was sorry, but he was under strict orders from Papa to make sure each of our slaves filled their quota every single day. I told him if that was the case, then *I* would take the woman's place. He didn't believe me, so I walked right over to her plot, picked up her hoe, and started chopping away. After just fifteen minutes, I was so tired I thought I'd die, but fortunately the supervisor came over and asked me to please stop and go on home, that he'd 'somehow' figure out another way to get the work done."

Emma cast a sly glance her father's way. "I think he finally realized he would get in far more trouble with Papa by forcing his daughter to work the fields than by falling a bit short on the day's quota."

Papa sighed. "True, true . . . Sam Taylor's a good, faithful supervisor, but he can get a little overzealous at times. He made the right decision in this case."

"Afterward," Emma continued, "I went to the woman's cabin to check on her and her baby, who was doing much better. She was so appreciative, and we talked for over two hours about her life and how she so missed her husband, who'd recently died. I asked her if she'd like to start coming to our Sunday evening prayer services, and she's been a regular there ever since."

Pastor Jones nodded approvingly. "So, what would you say was the most important thing that you learned from all this, Emma?"

She thought for a moment. "That when I make an effort to help others, I learn about the real struggles they face . . . and that helps *me* to stop feeling so much self-pity over my own comparatively trivial problems."

"It certainly sounds like you've put into practice what you've learned from the Scriptures about 'loving thy neighbor' in a meaningful way. God knows there are a lot of people in my own congregation who should hear your story."

Oh, for a wonderful, compassionate Christian heart like my sister's! Catherine thought irritably. She'd heard Emma tell her story to adoring family visitors one too many times and was sick and tired of the predictable, fawning reactions.

"Emma's always been one who tries to put into practice what she reads in the Bible," David chimed in proudly. "I daresay it's not just your congregation, Pastor Jones, but all of us who can benefit from her testimony about living as Christ commands."

Catherine gritted her teeth. *Look out, here it comes.*

"Oh, and Pastor," David said with an impish smile, "did you know my other beautiful sister Catherine here can speak fluent French?"

Catherine stared at her brother. One of his typical patronizing compliments, she thought, intended mainly to point out the relatively narrow extent of Catherine's intellectual pursuits compared to his own. Well, this time she wouldn't play his game.

"Oh, David, we needn't trouble Pastor Jones with references to my silly little talents. I think we'd all be far more interested in hearing from *him* about his views on all this John Brown business. Especially since, as I've heard, he owns no slaves himself."

Papa shifted uncomfortably in his chair as a dead silence fell around the table.

"Uh . . . Cat," David said softly, "are you sure you want to be getting into that now? It's a very complex subject that really requires a lot of clear thinking, and . . . well . . ."

"And well *what*, David?" Catherine asked with barely disguised indignation. "I know you wrote a term paper on the subject and have thought a lot about it, but why shouldn't the rest of us be allowed to hear a variety of opinions? After all, it *is* an important national issue that could affect our entire future, so I'd like to learn as much as I can about it." She blinked at him defiantly, then turned to face Pastor Jones. "I'm especially curious to know what the pastor thinks about all those other Baptist and Presbyterian preachers around here who do own slaves. Most of them are saying that raid by Brown's gang on the federal arsenal at Harpers Ferry in order to 'free and arm the slaves' was not only treasonous, but an affront to God's natural order. Are they wrong? Or—"

Papa, his face the color of the rose tablecloth, slapped his hand down emphatically on the arm of his chair. "*Catherine . . . that's enough!* We did not invite Pastor Jones here to berate him with controversial, pointless questions like this."

Mortified to see her father's displeasure over her impolitic outburst, Catherine reached for his hand. "Papa, I am so sorry. I didn't mean to embarrass or make our guest uncomfortable. I . . ."

Pastor Jones raised his hand just above the table with open palm, as if calling for the peace of God to calm the turbulent waters. He cleared his throat, bowed his head for a brief moment with eyes closed, then looked up again—this time straight into Catherine's eyes. He didn't seem at all angry.

"Miss Catherine, you've asked an important question. And with your father's permission, I'd be honored to try to answer it to the best of my ability."

Papa looked toward the dining room door beside which Ben stood quietly with hands clasped behind his back, awaiting further service orders. "Ben, please allow us some privacy for a bit," Papa said. Once the door was closed, he sighed, leaned back in his chair, and—after casting one more scowling glance at Catherine—nodded his approval to Pastor Jones.

Jones continued softly, his voice calm. "You asked for my personal position on the John Brown matter, so I'll give it to you straight from my heart. I agree with Brown on one thing: slavery is not the intended plan of God, and I fervently wish it had never been introduced any-where in this great land of ours. I know this view puts me at odds with almost all of my fellow Southern Baptist preachers and civic leaders. But I can't go against what my conscience dictates, and by the grace of God, I never shall."

Catherine's gasp was almost as noticeable as her father's. Never before had such a position been so directly and clearly voiced in the Hodge family presence. Even David's recent controversial assertions hadn't gone so far as to unambiguously condemn the entire institution of slavery. Pastor Jones had just fired a moral artillery shell through the very fabric that held the entire southern economy and way of life together.

At least now Papa can see that my question for the pastor wasn't so pointless after all, Catherine thought with immense relief. *He volun-teered an answer, and now we've exposed him.*

Lawrence folded his arms and sat up straight in his chair. His voice had a hard edge. "So, Pastor . . . how is it that this plantation-owning family you're dining with tonight—whose slaves are literally serving this table—is supposed to believe that you're not out there in between your revival meetings secretly exhorting other slaves to rise up against us? Sir, you know we've experienced quite enough of that dastardly practice in our beloved southern states over the years. And I, for one, cannot stomach the thought of White people being murdered in their beds at night by another Nat Turner–type slave rebellion. Especially one that starts right under my nose in what is practically my own backyard!"

Pastor Jones made no immediate response other than to close his eyes and nod slightly.

He's trapped, Catherine thought.

"Mr. Hodge," Jones said finally, "you shouldn't assume that my loathing of slavery leads me to follow the practices, or even the vision, of the most radical of the northern abolitionists. I don't support violent actions or conspiracies that would attempt to immediately break the existing relations between slaves and masters. Only God can rightly change those relations. And he'll do so by eventually softening the hearts of the men who make the laws of this nation to improve them in a gradual and orderly manner. But I believe strongly that God will do that in *his* own time, *not* at the beck and whim of wild men like John Brown who are determined to take the law into their own hands."

Catherine cringed at David's delighted grin, Emma's relieved smile, and—worst of all—Papa's pursed lips and seemingly understanding, respectful nod. *How can Papa allow himself to be mollified so easily*? It was one thing to receive assurance that at least Pastor Jones didn't support slave rebellions—only "gradual and orderly" emancipation. But had Papa forgotten his own firm opposition to emancipation—*ever*, under any circumstances? Had he forgotten what their entire family had heard preached on numerous occasions in their own church? She could not let this slide. She would make Papa proud that she, at least, had been paying attention to what they were all being taught on Sundays.

"Pastor, isn't there something else that should be considered?"

"And what might that be, Miss Catherine?"

Ignoring David's exaggerated eyeroll and Emma's hand on her forearm under the table, she pressed ahead.

"What about the points we've heard repeatedly from our own church's pastor: that slavery is never actually condemned in the Bible; that instead it was regarded as a fact of life; and that even the Apostle Paul said in the book of Ephesians that slaves should obey and honor their masters? And besides that, doesn't slavery serve a doubly useful purpose for society—because it supports not only our southern economy but also the continuing civilization and Christian enlightenment of the slaves themselves? So . . . for all those reasons, Pastor, I'm trying to understand . . . why shouldn't the institution of slavery be permanently endorsed and protected?"

Pastor Jones's body tensed, and his face darkened. Still, he spoke in a soft, measured tone. "Miss Catherine, my paternal grandmother was an African slave. She was nearly starved to death and violated repeatedly by the White captain of a transatlantic ship that packed her along with two hundred other unfortunate negroes into its steaming, filthy cargo hold for nearly a month. All to transport the poor, miserable souls to a 'better life' in the New England colonies, or so they were told.

"At the age of ten, my grandmother's illicit mulatto son—my own father—witnessed the day when my grandmother was falsely accused of stealing jewelry from her White master's wife. The master, in a drunken rage, barged into her cabin, yanked my grandmother out of bed, took her outside, and tied her outstretched arms to two stout trees. My terrified father—who the master had locked inside the cabin—watched from the window as the master gathered some wood and lit a fire at my grandmother's feet. It took over ten minutes for the flames to consume her and finally stop the horrible . . ."

Unable or unwilling to continue, Pastor Jones lowered his head and shook it slowly from side to side.

"Oh, dear God." Catherine's hand flew to her mouth.

After composing himself, Jones continued where he left off: "That my father retained his sanity and determination to survive and work on the master's farm as a young slave after witnessing such an awful scene is something I'll never be able to explain.

"Ten years later, the master—probably to assuage his own burden of guilt—approached my father. Told him he regretted having to 'deliver such stern justice,' and that as recompense he had now graciously decided to grant my father his freedom. He also said he would give him a small sum of money to begin making a new life for himself in the city of New York—just like many other freed slaves who were migrating there. The master concluded the one-way conversation by 'encouraging' my father with the idea that from now on he could always know that his mother's death had not been in vain. As the master so *kindly* explained: Just like Christ's, my grandmother's painful sacrifice had, in the end, served a wonderful purpose: it had set the captive slave free!"

Pastor Jones paused briefly as Catherine's trembling hands tried to quell the bile in her throat from spewing out her mouth. Then he continued: "And in view of such real-life incidents, Miss Catherine, I implore you: *be very wary* of defending arguments that universally glorify the Christian upbringing of slaves by their supposedly well-intended White masters. And be thankful for your own father's honorable efforts in that regard. Unfortunately, I fear he's more the exception than the rule these days."

Catherine jerked her arm away from Emma's consoling hand. Choking back tears of abject humiliation, she threw her napkin on the table, rose unsteadily, and ran out of the room.

CHAPTER 5

Hodge Family Plantation
November 17, 1859

A chilly, heavy mist shrouded the night landscape as David strolled with Pastor Jones along the lantern-illuminated carriage path toward the front gate of the property.

He ran his fingers through his hair, struggling to find the right words. "Pastor, I don't know what to say. Catherine likes to speak her mind, but never like *that* in front of our guests. Usually, I'm the one who's guilty of that sort of thing. But tonight, she obviously turned the tables on me."

Pastor Jones placed his hand on David's back. Strangely, he seemed not the least bit perturbed. "Your sister only repeated what's been drilled into her and others in this region over the last two decades by practically every White southern preacher I know. I certainly forgive her, though I do pray she'll one day see the light."

David nodded. Pastor Jones had just put into words what David had long been thinking but had never expressed so directly to his family.

"I suppose I need to be patient with her as well, much as it galls me to even think about it. Catherine hasn't been the easiest person to talk to these days."

Pastor Jones chuckled. "And what do you think Catherine would say about *you*, David? Are you the easiest person to listen to these days?"

"Not by my family's standards," David replied with a sheepish laugh. "I know Papa and Catherine think I've been spouting a lot of sanctimonious nonsense lately, that I've read too many books written by 'those godless northerners.' As long as I limit my 'nonsense' to occasional comments at private family gatherings, Papa puts up with me. But I know he's not happy with a lot my ideas. He's afraid that he's wasted his investment in my college education, because he thinks I'm succumbing to the northerners' arguments that the South is evil. That our whole way of thinking and preaching about slavery is wrong."

Jones stopped suddenly and turned to face him. "Well, *are* you succumbing to them?"

"Hmmm . . . good question." David kicked at a large pebble and sent it skimming ahead down the path. "I'll always have great respect and love for the South, Pastor. Perhaps I'm being naive, but I believe there are a lot of well-meaning and kind people—in *this* state, at least—who show wonderful hospitality to their neighbors, who treat their slaves fairly and look after their well-being. And, as you said, I *know* my father is one of them. It's just that . . ."

"It's just . . . what, David?"

"It's hard to explain. There's just something inside me that fights against so many of the things I've been taught. Things that all my friends and family—except for Emma—always seem to accept without question."

"Such as?"

"Such as . . . that the South can do no wrong. That we're inherently superior to the North in terms of culture, morals, and religion. That all abolitionists are atheists and agents of the devil. And . . . what I now consider to be the worst lie of all."

"And what's that?"

"Pastor Jones, it's the very lie that you yourself pointed out to me during one of our first conversations. The one, you said, that's being spread now by so many southern evangelical preachers, including the pastor of my own family's church—the lie that the Bible itself justifies the institution of slavery."

Jones closed his eyes and nodded, a small smile on his lips. "I'm glad you see that crazy idea for what it is, David. God knows how these people have twisted those passages about the Curse of Ham in Genesis and Paul's exhortations to slaves in the New Testament into a convenient, self-serving rationale for preserving slavery forever . . . at least for people of African descent."

Gently grasping David's arm and pointing down the path, Pastor Jones signaled his readiness to resume their walk toward the gate. They'd taken only a few steps before Jones broke the silence.

"David . . . I am curious about something. Where'd you get that bold, liberal-minded spirit I sensed in you the first time we met—the one that keeps nudging you to question the traditional beliefs of your family and friends?"

David laughed. "I hope you mean that as a compliment! I guess it's something I was born with, though I really didn't know I had it until I joined my prep school headmaster's after-school debate club. My classmates' simplistic, pro-southern arguments on everything annoyed me, and I felt an irresistible urge to challenge them. At first, I think I was just trying to knock 'em off their own proud pedestals more than anything else. But as time went on, I became more and more convicted of the logic of my own positions, especially after listening to some great debates at college.

"A few months before my mother died, she told me I was becoming exactly like one of her ancestors. He was a Lutheran pastor in Germany during the Thirty Years' War in the 1600s. She'd read his life journal and said he was basically a modest and compassionate man. But he was always challenging the militant views of his city's mayor and Lutheran religious council when it came to their prideful, no-compromise stance on rebellion against Germany's Catholic governing authorities. So, who knows, maybe this 'bold, liberal spirit' runs in our family line, showing up from time to time in unsuspecting souls like me."

Pastor Jones stopped and turned to face him once again as the two men arrived at the lantern-illuminated front gate. "David, I know you're troubled by what you see and hear these days from the politicians and preachers in our beautiful state, but may I offer you one piece of advice?"

"Of course, Pastor."

"Love her."

"Pastor, I already told you . . . I haven't lost my respect or love for the state I was born and raised in, nor for the South in general."

"I'm not talking about loving Virginia, David. I'm talking about loving your sister Catherine."

"But, Pastor, I *do* love her. It's just that she keeps trying to fight me on everything I try to—"

Jones grasped his arm. "David, listen to me. Beneath her seemingly crusty exterior, there's something inside your sister that's crying out for help. I've seen enough hurting souls in my thirty years of pastoring to know one when I see it. And I certainly saw one tonight."

"That may be true, but she's never been the sort to admit to her own weaknesses, and I really don't know what else I can do to 'love' her any more than I already do. She's my sister, after all, not my wife."

"Well, my friend, seems you've already forgotten my message from last month's revival service. Here's a small hint from Saint Paul: 'Love is patient, love is kind . . .'"

David grinned and took up the slack, completing the passage from First Corinthians that his Sunday school teacher—who years ago had helped him come to truly believe in and confess the Lord—had urged him to memorize as part of his spiritual growth. "'Love does not envy, is not boastful, is not conceited, does not act improperly, is not selfish, is not provoked, and does not keep a record of wrongs.'"

Jones squeezed his arm a bit tighter. "So the next time you're tempted to become frustrated and condemn Catherine for never admitting to her own fallibilities, what are you going to remember?"

"That I need . . . instead . . . to love her."

Pastor Jones peered at him closely. "Never forget what you just said, David. Because something tells me the day's coming when Catherine—and Emma, for that matter—is going to desperately need the kind of love that only you, as her brother, can give."

David nodded but said nothing and then looked away. Loving Emma in the way Pastor Jones was suggesting was one thing, but loving Catherine on those same terms was quite another.

Jones finally released his grip and broke the awkward silence. "So, what are your plans after this weekend? Back to the academic grind at Princeton, I presume?"

"Actually, I have a little detour planned on the way back."

"Oh? Care to divulge?"

"I'm stopping off for a couple of days at Charles Town to witness the execution."

Jones's eyes widened. *"Seriously?* David, what in heaven's name is prompting *this*? Surely you're not planning a last-minute attempt to personally yank John Brown off the gallows stand! What's the point?"

David gazed at the ground. "After all that research I did on him for my term paper, I have to admit I've become a bit obsessed with his whole public persona. I want to be there to observe him, to hear his last words . . . see how he handles the whole thing."

Pastor Jones crossed his arms and sighed. "You admire him, don't you?" he asked. "Even if he *is* guilty of the Harpers Ferry raid and supposedly that horrific Pottawatomie massacre a few years back."

David smiled forlornly. "It's the strangest thing, isn't it? I should be *ecstatic* that the man's finally going to receive his just reward for all the mayhem and murder he's responsible for. But somehow, I just . . . I . . ."

"You somehow believe that the Great Cause of abolition may justify it all. Am I right?"

David nodded grimly. "I'm starting to consider that possibility. I know it's crazy. And I know if I keep challenging my father on the matter, my days at Princeton will soon be over—my diploma never received. But, Pastor, I can't keep letting my father's unquestioning adulation of the 'southern way' dominate my thinking about what's truly good and right from God's perspective."

Pastor Jones eyed him and smiled. "And do you believe that, by watching John Brown die, you'll be able to think more clearly from 'God's perspective'? That perhaps God will show you some grand, new life direction, inspired by the noble martyrdom of a true abolitionist?"

"At this point in my spoon-fed, privileged life, that's not a bad thing to hope for, is it? And, being of colored descent yourself, wouldn't *you* hope that for me as well? That I'd come away with an even stronger motivation to do my part to help break the negroes' chains?"

A slight breeze stirred the lower limbs of a nearby tree, causing a dark shadow to pass over Jones's face. "What I hope most for you, David, is that you'll remember what we talked about earlier concerning your sisters. Yes, by all means, go and learn what you can from watching the execution. If God wills it, you'll grow in your appreciation and support of the cause. But don't forget—John Brown will soon be dead and gone. Catherine and Emma, on the other hand, still live on. Don't let over-fascination with the ideals and actions of a dead martyr obscure your vision for the human need that's right in front of you."

Pastor Jones clapped David on the shoulder, turned, and walked off down the dark lane toward his residence on the Wheelers' farm.

CHAPTER 6

Hodge Family Plantation
November 18, 1859

Bright white sunrays knifed through the bare branches of elm, sweet gum, and maple trees bordering the lonely dirt trail, helping to take the edge off the midmorning chill. Still, Emma was grateful for the warmth of Catherine's hand in her own as the two strolled wordlessly toward the pond on the far side of the Wheelers' property. It was a journey that had almost never happened.

After a nearly sleepless night of tossing and turning over concern about Catherine's perception of her "over-friendliness" with Charles, Emma had awakened to Sallie's excited knock on her door. Sallie had described her run-in with Sam Taylor the previous evening, his determination to find and punish Charles, and his confiscation of the framed Bible verses.

Thankfully, Sallie had also reported some good news. Sam had finally "found" Charles—exactly where he was supposed to have been: hoeing the soil in the apple tree orchard on the far side of the tobacco fields, just as Sam had directed him earlier but had apparently forgotten. Sam had tried to soothe his own bruised ego by giving Charles a good cursing out and warning never to cross Sam like that again if he wanted to keep the flesh on his back. After Charles had returned home safely, his story had generated quite a bit of raucous laughter and mockery of Sam Taylor's mental capacity throughout the slave quarters.

Still, Sam's ongoing threat against Charles and his audacious piracy of Emma's personal gift to Sallie did not bode well. Sam had long held animosity toward Emma, stemming from her firm rejection two years ago—when she was only fifteen—of his crude attempt to express his "affectionate feelings" and desire to court her. Ever since, he'd behaved toward her in a surly, barely respectful manner. And now that he had the Bible verse frame-print in his possession—and had even questioned Sallie as to whether Emma had illegally taught her to read it—the possibility that he might now be plotting some type of mischief against her couldn't be discounted.

Upset by the news and wishing to reduce the tension between herself and Catherine, an hour ago Emma had knocked on her sister's bedroom door. She knew Catherine would gladly have remained in bed the entire day, sulking over last night's ordeal with Pastor Jones and the embarrassment it had caused her. But Emma had finally prevailed with her suggestion that a nice walk and talk in the fresh air was bound to cheer both of them up.

Squeezing her sister's hand tighter, Emma finally broke the awkward silence. "It seems things got a little out of hand last night, didn't they?"

Catherine stared at her warily. "Em, I'm telling you right now . . . there's no way I will apologize for the questions I asked. After all, Papa and Pastor Jones *did* give me permission. And it's not like David hasn't ever said something to offend our guests."

Emma started to give an impatient retort but checked herself and looked off into the distance. *Don't say anything that'll upset her even more.* Despite being the elder sister, too often these days Catherine seemed incapable or unwilling to discuss certain things in a rational light.

"Well," Catherine blurted out finally, "aren't you now going to tell me how I deserved to be put in my place last night, especially after what I'd said earlier about you and Charles?"

Emma hesitated, overwhelmed by a desire to avoid further confrontation. Out of nowhere, a pleasant memory of past times with her sister flashed through her mind. She scanned the field to the left of the lane, envisioning the old, abandoned sawmill hidden back in the woods on the far side.

She turned toward Catherine with a playful smile.

"Cat, do you remember when we were little, and Mother would have Priscilla take us on those long Sunday afternoon walks down this very lane so she and Papa could have some quiet time napping together after church?"

Catherine rolled her eyes. "Of course I remember, Em. Sallie would come with us, and we'd all go to . . . wait a minute . . ." Catherine jerked her hands away. "Em, you can't be serious! You are *not* taking me through all those bushes and brier patches to that rundown mill. Not in these clothes, anyway. I'm going back."

"Oh, Cat, *please*! Can't you just for once try to have a little fun? Don't you remember how we used to love that place, pretending it was a schoolhouse?" Emma stared excitedly at her sister as she recalled the day of their mutual childhood discovery of the decrepit mill and their creative conversion of its dusty interior remains into a rustic stage for "playing school."

Catherine's testy gaze turned into a faint smile. "And I remember *you*, little sister, pretending you were the teacher for Priscilla, Sallie, and me—trying to get all of us to pay attention to your math lessons. I don't think you liked that time Priscilla got so confused by your wonderful teaching on how to add nineteen plus twelve."

Emma threw back her head and laughed. "I remember that too. Made her go stand in the corner with her back turned, didn't I? D'you think she ever got over a nine-year-old child disciplining her like that?"

"I don't know, I . . . Em! Where are you going?"

Emma was already ten steps across the field leading to the sawmill. In her imagination, she was nine years old again, and she could trust her older sister with anything. "Beat you there, slowpoke!"

"You're crazy, you know that, Emma Hodge?" Catherine picked up her skirt and took off in pursuit.

Catherine wrinkled her nose at the musty smell of sawdust piles, woodchips, and critter droppings pervading the dank air inside the abandoned mill's cutting room.

"Em, there's nothing here. This place gives me the creeps. How long do you think it's been since anyone was here?"

Emma looked away. She had no intention of revealing to her sister that she and Sallie had on rare occasions used the site to conduct their secret reading sessions.

"I don't know," she lied. "I heard Papa say that Mr. Wheeler came and took out all the rusty equipment about five years ago. I doubt anyone's been here since. Hey, is that what I think it is?" Emma walked over to the room's sole remaining fixture—a large wooden box attached to the far wall. "It's completely empty, Cat. No more sawdust in the waste bin. What're we going to do for our 'chalkboard'?"

Catherine groaned. "What . . . did you coax me all the way out here to deliver another one of your math lessons?"

"Given that last report from your tutor, it wouldn't do you harm!"

"Oh, *no!*" Catherine covered her face with her hands.

"Oh, come on," Emma chided. "I was just teasing."

"No, not that. My dress."

Emma groaned. "What's wrong with it now?"

"Get over here and look. It's got a big rip at the bottom. The hem's about to come off. All thanks to you, sister. *You're* the one who made me follow you through all those weeds and bushes to get to this godforsaken place. And all for nothing, obviously."

"Now, now," Emma said soothingly as she examined the rip, "it's not so bad. Don't go fretting about something that's so easy to fix when we get back."

Catherine pouted. "You sound exactly like Mother."

"Well, heaven would strike me dead if I told you what *you* sound like, *big* sister!" Emma released the skirt, walked over to the other side of the room, and sat down with her back against the wall. "Don't worry about the dress. I promise I'll sew it for you tomorrow. Why don't you just come over here and sit with me? I want to forget all our problems for once and talk about our hopes and dreams for the future."

Catherine grimaced, then sat beside her sister, stretched her legs out, and leaned her head back against the wall. "All right, Em. So what shall we 'dream' about today? Your noble desire to become a school-teacher and save all the world's downtrodden from hunger and illiteracy? God knows I don't have any grand new vision to report, besides marrying a good man and becoming a successful, happy plantation mistress like Mother."

Emma closed her eyes and sighed. "Cat, don't you want anything more out of life than *that*? With all your intelligence and foreign language skill, and with some more education at one of those colleges like Oberlin or Wesleyan that now accept women, you could be far more than a schoolteacher. You could join the diplomatic service as an interpreter, you could travel to other countries, and—"

"Don't start, Emma," Catherine interrupted, scratching furiously at some imagined small stain on her dress. "Those are all very nice ideas . . . for someone like you, maybe. I know I was born to be a plantation wife and mistress, and I know I'll excel at it. You can sneer at that like all those pinch-faced Northern women writers do if you want, but I'll always believe it's a very honorable and worthy calling. And one that I'm sure God is perfectly pleased with just in case you might be doubting that for some crazy reason."

Emma looked at her sister askance, her eyes twinkling. "Really? I would never have guessed that you held it in such high esteem . . . after listening to you moan to Papa about having to tend to Mother's charity society obligations or making up the slaves' supply list yesterday."

"Well," Catherine admitted with a resigned sigh, "I suppose yesterday was not the best for me—it's not easy trying to fill Mother's shoes. Anyway, even if I wanted to pursue some kind of advanced education, Papa certainly killed that notion when he said I couldn't even go to the Richmond Female Institute. I can still hear him: 'Too far away, Catherine. And you're doing just fine with your private home tutors.' And yet he had no problem allowing David to attend prep school in Richmond and college in New Jersey, which is twenty times farther away."

"Cat, is it remotely possible that you could ever think of just *one* nice thing to say when you're mentioning David?"

Catherine puckered her lips. "Hmmm. Let me think. Well, he's extremely smart. He's good-looking. He's . . ."

"*Goodness*! Can't you try a little harder than that?"

Catherine folded her arms and gazed up at the roof. "Oh, I suppose at times David can be very kind to certain people who don't deserve it."

"Certain people like . . . who?" Emma prodded with a coy grin.

"People like . . . oh, I don't have to explain myself to you. Never mind. Just go ahead and tell me about *your* latest dreams."

"My dreams? Hmmm. Let me think." Emma rested her head back against the wall and closed her eyes. Instantly, the memory of that blistering hot Sunday afternoon a year and a half ago in late May flooded her mind like a surging tidal wave . . .

For a change of pace, Emma had suggested that she and Sallie meet at the old sawmill instead of her bedroom for their weekly reading session. She'd also asked her if Charles might like to meet them there and do some fishing in the creek running behind the mill while the girls rehearsed their lesson.

All had started out as planned, but after a half hour or so, Charles had become frustrated at the lack of fish bites and decided to join Emma and Sallie inside to "see how y'all do dis readin' thing."

Seeing an opportunity to have a little fun, the girls challenged Sallie's eighteen-year-old stepbrother to take a stab at reading a short sentence to them. It wouldn't be the first time he'd attempted this; passing on what she'd learned with Emma, Sallie had surreptitiously taught him the ABCs and to pronounce a few simple words and phrases that she would scratch out with a stick in the loose dirt behind their shack.

Trying to suppress a giggle, Emma reclined next to Sallie against the soft cushion the two girls had formed against the wall from the old, loose hay scattered about the floor.

"No, Charles. It's not *'dessing'*—it's *'dressing.'* Now try it again. One more time. Just for me."

"All right, Miss Em, if you say so." Standing and facing the girls, Charles stared intently at the sentence from Emma's reading primer— *McGuffey's Eclectic Reader*—that had so far stymied him. He drew himself up to full stature, cleared his throat, took a breath, and let loose in a stilted, professorial voice.

"'D-Dssing was sad work for little Ellen today.'"

Sallie burst out in a hysterical fit of laughter. "Oh my goodness! Charles . . . you sound like . . . you just won't . . . oh, my!"

Emma, seeing Charles's crestfallen face, frowned and smacked Sallie's arm. "Don't mock him! He's trying hard. It's not easy."

Sallie struggled to compose herself. "Maybe he just don't care as much about 'little Ellen' and her struggles as you and I do, Emmy. That right, Charles? You be more interested in reading something more manly, maybe?"

Charles's shoulders slumped, and he broke out in an embarrassed grin. "Maybe so. Guess I'm a little tired out today after fishin' earlier this mornin' with Lew. Havin' more trouble thinkin' on dis than I thought I would. Sorry, Miss Em."

Emma smiled sympathetically. "It's all right, Charles. Don't let your mean old sister discourage you—it's not like she's been perfect herself today." She patted the pile of loose hay between herself and Sallie. "Here, take a break and come sit for a bit." Charles's face lit up, as if a judge had just granted him parole from a life sentence. He closed the book and sat down, being very careful—Emma noticed with a tinge of disappointment—not to touch her as he did so.

"Don't think I'm letting you off the hook completely now, Mr. Cobb," she said sternly, her eyes narrowed and her brow creased in a mock frown.

Charles, sitting forward with arms around his knees, looked warily over his shoulder. "What you mean, Miss Em?"

Emma shook her head slowly from side to side. "Just because your sister and I allowed you to pause your recitation doesn't mean you can just sit here for the rest of our time with no responsibilities."

"Huh? What I s'posed to do?"

Trying not to laugh, Emma cast a quick peep at Sallie. "Entertain us."

"*Entertain* you?"

"That's right. Entertain us. For the next fifteen minutes, Sallie and I are going to just sit here and listen to you tell us the story."

"Th-The story? Story 'bout what, Miss Em?"

"Tell him, Sallie."

"*What*?" Charles cocked his head, pivoting it back and forth between the two girls. "What you two talkin' 'bout?"

Sallie glanced slyly at Emma. "The story about you and your friend Billy sneakin' down the Appomattox River during last Christmas's work break for that s'posed 'catfishing party' with Uncle Jasper. We wanna know what you two were *really* up to."

Charles's eyes widened. "Now how you hear 'bout *dat*?"

Sallie and Emma burst out laughing.

"You think word wouldn't get around sooner or later, with Billy and his big mouth?" Sallie chortled. "My Lord, he couldn't stop braggin' to me about your big trip. Couldn't believe you hadn't told me about it before. When I asked him how many 'catfish' you all caught, he just kinda looked at me with that opossum-eatin' grin and said I'd better ask you. So . . . how many *did* you catch, big brother?"

Charles lay back against the hay and put his hands behind his head, still careful to preserve some space between himself and Emma. "Oh, dozen or so, I reckon. Dey sho' tasted good—except for dem bones gettin' stuck in my throat."

"Mhm," Sallie said with arched eyebrow, "and how many bottles of Uncle Jasper's famous brew did it take for you to wash all those stuck fish bones down?"

Charles grimaced. "Well . . . only a couple . . ."

"*Charles Cobb!*" Emma twisted on her side and reached over to lightly slap his arm. She was glad to see that he didn't flinch even a bit at her brief touch. "How *could* you? Last time I saw him, Pastor Jones told me you'd promised Jesus to give up all liquor out of obedience and thanks for what he did for you by dying on that cross in your place. I was so proud of you!"

"D-Dat's right, Miss Em," Charles stuttered, now staring at her with wide-eyed intensity. "Dat's exactly what I did, only I made my vow at Pastor Jones's revival the month *after* I got back. So I-I didn't break my promise to Jesus, and I been perfect clean ever since. I promise, Miss Em."

Emma nearly melted inside over Charles's obvious concern for her opinion of him and his desire not to disappoint her in any way. She felt a sudden impulse to roll over, reach out, and grasp his arm reassuringly, but she checked herself. Instead, she shook her head and sighed before finally cracking a smile. "Well, I suppose I'll just have to believe you. After all, every student in Emma Ann Hodge's Schoolhouse is required to maintain strict sobriety."

"'Strict' . . . *what*?"

Sallie guffawed. "Charles, you are a hoot! Ain't you ever heard the word '*sobriety*'? Means bein' sober, not drunk, not . . ."

Charles slapped his thigh and glared at his stepsister. "Don't you go makin' fun o' me, girl," he growled.

"Oh, all right, all right . . ." Emma sat up. "Let's get back to work. We've got only about an hour before we have to leave. Charles, up you go. And this time, I want you to go a little slower and pronounce every word clearly. And remember, it's '*dressing*,' not '*dessing*'!"

"Wait, Emmy," Sallie interjected. "We gotta let Charles finish his story about that catfish party. What else went on there besides eatin' and boozin', Charles?"

Charles laughed. "You gonna drag it all out o' me?" He looked cautiously at Emma. "You really want to hear dis, Miss Em?"

"Oh, all right. Guess now I'm hooked." Emma lay on her back once again, closed her eyes, and smiled as she listened to Charles recount the hilarious antics of the three-man party that had lasted into the wee hours of the morning. The sweet sound of his voice and close presence of his body reclining no more than two feet from hers brought back the day long ago when the young Black boy with the large, kind, dark-brown eyes had held her in his arms, carrying her to safety from the raging creek. He was handsome then, and even more so now as his matured jawline, widened mouth, and recently grown mustache and light beard all combined in a way that few young women could deny was pleasing to the eye.

As Charles continued talking, he slowly moved one arm from behind his head and laid it next to Emma's, unseen by Sallie. A shiver went up her spine as he gently touched her little finger with his own. He turned his palm upward, inviting a response.

She tentatively laid her hand in his. For a few seconds, their fingers interlocked . . . until Emma abruptly withdrew her hand and forced herself to sit up yet again as she listened and laughed to the rest of his hilarious story. Somewhere in the back of her mind, she knew she'd crossed a forbidden boundary. Yet somehow, it didn't seem like such a terrible sin.

Chapter 7

Hodge Family Plantation
November 17, 1859

"Well, are you going to say something?" Catherine asked after nearly falling asleep from waiting over a minute for Emma to reveal her thoughts. "Or should we . . . *Em*! What's wrong?"

Emma cheeks flushed red. She turned her face aside as hot tears began to roll down. How stupid to bring Catherine to this ramshackle mill with the primary intent of cheering her up. But then again, she hadn't planned on her own problems and emotions betraying her like this.

"It's Charles, isn't it?" Catherine asked softly.

"I can't help it, Cat. I know it looks bad, but I like him and I truly do *care* about him."

Catherine sighed. "Em, you've always cared so much about everybody. Especially our slaves. But, sister, you can't let your compassionate feelings for—"

"*Why not, Catherine?*" Emma exploded. "Why is it that I can't even smile at Charles, much less say something nice to him once in a while without others—including you—assuming the worst?"

Catherine looked her in the eye. "Em, listen to me. Charles *does* seem like a very sweet young man, and I definitely understand why you'd have a special heart for him considering he once saved your life. But if we heard it from Mother once, we heard it a thousand times: 'The most important traits for a young southern plantation woman are purity, piety, domesticity, and submission'—with purity being first and foremost. I'm the first to admit I sometimes wish we had a different set of priorities, but I'd never want to dishonor Papa by having him even *think* that I would compromise my reputation, especially with a slave."

"Cat, I have *not* compromised my purity with Charles—I promise you that. It's something else . . . it's . . . oh, I should never have brought this up in the first place."

"So why did you bring it up?"

Emma bit the inside of her cheek, suddenly feeling as if she might choke on the stagnant, humid cutting-room air that bore the rank odor of moldy sawdust. As she considered her reply, a fluttering noise above caused her to look up in time to see a small bat crash against the rotting wood wall before it recovered and flitted out of the room as quickly as it had entered.

"Because . . . I'm afraid that someone's about to do something terrible to him."

"Emma, what are you talking about? Who's going to hurt Charles?"

"Sam Taylor. Sallie passed him on her walk home late yesterday afternoon, and he asked her where Charles was. Said he was planning to give him an extra-hard whipping for supposedly getting back late from running an errand. Sallie told me this morning that things turned out all right this time—Sam had forgotten he'd told Charles to do something else—but still . . ."

Catherine crossed her arms and shook her head. "Sam Taylor. I never could stand that conceited, ignorant whip-cracker. Acts like he's God's gift to southern womanhood. Any question on that score, just ask Liz Wheeler, who I've heard he's secretly been sleeping with. Thank heavens . . . at least *you* put him in his place two years ago.

"But Em, if Charles or any other slave is ever derelict in their duty, there's not much we can do to stop them from being disciplined. You know Papa does his best to be kind to the slaves, but he has his rules and fitting punishments for breaking them."

Emma frowned. "You might consider Papa's punishments to be 'fitting,' Cat, but I certainly don't, and I promise you I never will. Not after that terrible whipping I happened to spot Sam's father doling out to that poor field slave last year, all because he'd supposedly stolen a few extra ears of corn from the barn for his family. It just isn't right!" She picked up a small piece of splintered wood from the ground beside her and heaved it against the far wall. "And neither is slavery, for that matter."

Catherine stared at her hard. "So, are you saying our pastor is wrong about what the Bible says—or doesn't say—about slavery?"

Emma hesitated. "He quotes his selected verses accurately," she replied carefully, "but I think he twists the meaning of the them to draw his own convenient conclusions about slavery in our country today that aren't justified. I just know God does not—and I can't believe he would *ever*—approve of slavery or any form of human bondage like we've seen practiced in modern times."

Catherine looked away, saying nothing.

She's probably too worn out from last night's thrashing to continue arguing the point, Emma thought.

"But anyway," she continued, "back to Charles . . . Sam's threat is more than just 'expected discipline.' Sallie said Sam told her he was planning on doing something really bad to Charles—something far worse than just a standard whipping. Sam seems to have it in for Charles for some reason neither Sallie nor I can figure out. Oh, Cat, I'm so very worried about him."

"Em," Catherine said soothingly, "you know Sam can't do anything 'extra' to punish Charles without first getting Papa's permission, right? Papa's been very clear about that with Sam. If Sam ever violated that rule, he knows he'd get fired and banished forever from this plantation."

"Well, yes, I suppose, but . . ."

"You should trust Papa to look out for him, Em. He knows Charles has been a good worker, and he certainly remembers that he saved your life once. He won't let Sam punish him any more than's right and absolutely necessary. Em, try not to worry. Charles will be all right." Catherine's calm voice and tender, concerned expression reminded Emma of the not-so-distant past, when Catherine had been her reliable fount of family understanding and wisdom.

"Do you really think so?"

"I *know* so."

Emma leaned over and gave Catherine a prolonged hug. It had been quite a while, and it felt wonderful. A sudden impulse bubbled up to confess everything—including Sam's confiscation of the Bible verse frame-print she'd gifted to Sallie, and the secret reading sessions that had led up to that. Who knew what Sam was planning to do with the gift now in his possession? It would be good to get it all off her chest and receive some sisterly advice on how to handle things.

"Cat, I . . ." Emma hesitated. *Can I trust her not to reveal it all to Papa?*

"What is it, Em?"

Emma smiled and grasped her sister's hand. "It's nothing—other than to say thank you and I love you. Now let's get back. I've had enough of our dreary old 'schoolhouse' for at least another ten years!"

That afternoon, mounted on her favorite saddle horse atop the crest of the small hill overlooking the plantation's main tobacco field, Catherine shaded her eyes from the blazing sun and surveyed the scene below.

With the harvest completed in early October and the auction for the last big batch of dried, graded, bundled, and pressed tobacco leaves only a week away, over a dozen male and female fieldworkers were now bent to the laborious task of hoeing and clearing the stubbled field in preparation for next spring's planting season. Johnny Wheeler, Sam Taylor's short, somewhat corpulent assistant, strolled casually among them with his coiled whip hanging from his belt, barking an occasional surly command to one or another of the workers as he passed them.

How do they manage it—day after dreary, long, toilsome day? Catherine mused. Especially in the oppressive heat and humidity of late July and August, when the growing plants needed to be painstakingly hand-weeded and the flowering top buds and unproductive "sucker" stems removed from the stalks. Certainly, such an intensive daily regimen was not one she could imagine herself being able to endure.

But, she wondered, *do the workers really hate their lives as much as those preachy northern abolitionists claim, or have they learned to adapt and be more or less happy and content with the hard conditions into which they were born?*

It was a question she'd been pondering more and more lately—but never too deeply, as she feared that doing so would stir up some uncomfortable questions about slavery in general and God's attitude toward it. Questions for which she knew she had no good answer, especially after her upbraiding by Pastor Jones at last night's supper and this morning's talk with her sister. Oh, well, at least—as Pastor Jones acknowledged—the Hodge family tries hard to treat them kindly.

Leaning forward in the saddle, Catherine scratched behind her horse's ear.

"It's all right, Zino . . . we're almost there. That's a good boy."

As always, the dark bay Morgan gelding responded with a contented snort to his rider's affectionate voice and touch—even though from long habit he surely realized that a swift, hard kick in the flanks would be coming as soon as they reached the lane leading past the tobacco field toward the plantation's front entrance.

The half-mile, all-out gallop home along the lane had become the favorite part of Catherine's biweekly, two-hour recreational ride. It was her only means besides cutting herself to completely forget—for a few exhilarating moments—the strange, stomach-knotting cramps and thoughts of self-hatred that seemed to be worsening as time went on since Mother's passing. Today, her anticipation was even greater than usual, enhanced by the lightening of her soul following this morning's adventure with her sister at the sawmill. *For once,* she thought happily, *I was the big sister that I know Emma longs for.*

Upon Catherine's command, horse and rider descended the hill and stepped out onto the lane. "Now's our time, Zino. *Get up!*"

Catherine barely breathed, and her heart pounded as she leaned forward and slightly off the saddle, striving to savor every delicious moment of the hot wind stinging her face underneath her hat and pressing the folds of her matching gray riding dress against her legs.

Racing around a slight bend in the tree-lined lane, Catherine spotted the back of a tall man with a bowler hat standing by the rail fence about a hundred yards ahead. His hands were on his hips, and he appeared to be sternly lecturing a small negro boy standing in front of him. Not wishing to alarm, she brought her horse to a gradual halt and paced him ahead cautiously until finally she was able to recognize the unlikely pair: Sam Taylor and Lew Cobb, the younger brother of Charles and Sallie. She noticed that Lew was holding a bag of something in his arms.

Suddenly Sam yelled something at Lew and slapped him in the face with his right hand, causing him to reel to the side and drop the bag at his feet.

Shocked and dismayed, Catherine spurred Zino ahead.

Sam turned at the sound of her approach, the snarl on his face quickly transforming into an innocent, friendly grin.

"Why, hello, Miss Cat! It's been a while since I've seen you perched so queenlike on that beauty of a horse."

Sam's insincere, patronizing tone and manner had always infuriated her. Barely managing to stifle a sarcastic retort, she walked Zino up close to the fence and paused as she took in the scene.

"Just what do you think you're doing, Mr. Taylor? Why did you hit Lew?"

Sam glanced at the boy, who had a cowed look on his face and appeared to be trying his best not to cry. "Well, ma'am, it turns out my boy Lew here brought me the wrong bag from the barn. Seems like every time I give clear instructions these days, one of my workers manages to ignore 'em or pretend they didn't hear 'em right."

Catherine, hot fury rising in her breast, dismounted and stomped up to the fence. "Sam, Lew's only . . . what? Nine years old? He should be back in the slave quarters playing with his young friends, not forced to run errands for you."

"Wasn't my idea, Miss Cat. Lew was visitin' his parents who're workin' in the smaller field where my junior assistant Nate's in charge. Lew asked Nate if it'd be all right for Lew to take some of their leftover rations and deliver 'em to his brother Charles out there." Sam jabbed his thumb back toward the slaves working the field behind him. "Nate said sure, so long as Lew did a stopover at the barn and picked up the bag o' mulch he knew I needed over here. So here he is . . . with the wrong bag, and now I gotta wait while he goes back to get the right one. Big waste of time."

Catherine saw that Lew was now trembling as if he had palsy. "Lew, come here for minute," she said softly. Lew peeked hesitantly at Sam. "It's all right, Lew," Catherine persisted. "I just want to see something."

Lew stepped over the bag, crossed between the fence rails, and walked tentatively to Catherine as Sam stood and watched, his eyes squinted and mouth ajar.

"Lew, look at me." The boy raised his head. Examining the boy's face closely, she noticed the faint red stripes on his left cheek.

Catherine glared at Sam. "So why did a child's simple mistake warrant this kind of violence from you, Sam?"

Sam shrugged. "He was sassin' me, Miss Cat. Can't let young slaves start gettin' in a bad habit like that."

Catherine bent over and whispered quietly in Lew's ear. "Is that true? Did you sass him? Don't lie to me, Lew."

The boy lowered his eyes and shook his head no.

Catherine sighed. She knew what she was about to do would abuse plantation propriety and offend Sam, but if that was what it took to spare this young slave child from further mistreatment, so be it. She reached down and took Lew's hand in hers. "Lew, would you like to go home now?"

The boy peered up at her, seemingly confused. She smiled and patted his hand. "It's fine, Lew, you don't have to go back to the barn. Go on home and wait for your parents to return. I promise you won't get in any trouble."

Lew's round, ebony face broke into a huge smile as his eyes met hers. He squeezed her hand, turned, and fled down the lane without glancing back.

Sam leaned against the fence, resting one arm casually along the top rail. He removed his hat with his other hand and wiped the sweat off his brow with his forearm. "Well now, that sure was a nice gesture, Miss Cat. Only problem is, you know it ain't right and proper to be floutin' my authority over the fieldworkers. Authority your own father's granted me."

"He's not one of your workers, Sam!" Catherine shot back. "You know good and well my father doesn't want the children to work the fields until they're eleven. And he certainly doesn't want them being slapped around for no good reason."

Sam scuffed the loose dirt around the fence with his shoe. "I'm not disputin' the age thing as far as workin' the fields, Miss Cat." He raised his head defiantly. "But I sure ain't gonna accept a slave of *any* age sassin' me. My job is tough enough as it is, and by you makin' me look bad or weak to the slaves—who'll surely hear about this from Lew—you're makin' things ten times harder. Just like his brother Charles did."

Catherine cocked her head and stared at him with open-mouthed contempt. "Mr. Taylor, I assure you I'm not trying to make your job harder. But I'm warning you: if I ever hear that you are refusing to follow my father's rules for this plantation when it comes to the slaves, I'll be the first to inform him. *Especially* if it involves abusing the children." She nodded curtly, then tipped her chin, spun around, and stalked back to Zino. Remounting, she tweaked the reins, prompting the horse to begin pacing down the lane.

"That's good to know, Miss Cat," Sam called after her. "Because as you'll find out before long, I happen to be a stickler for this plantation's rules myself."

She pulled on the reins to halt Zino. *What did he mean by that?* She turned back in her saddle to face him, but he was already walking back toward Charles and the other slaves.

CHAPTER 8

Emma huddled with her sister and three of their mutual girlfriends at the edge of the main house ballroom's gleaming, inlaid parquet dance floor.

Looking around the gaily decorated room, she marveled at the extent to which Papa had gone all out to impress his special guests tonight. Several expensive new colorful murals depicting Virginia countryside scenes now graced three of the walls. At points between, mirrors reflected the soft light from wall-attached candelabras, and elegantly carved wooden tables supported painted marble vases filled with cascading arrangements of several varieties of fall flowers. On a raised platform in the adjacent corner of the large room, the ten-piece orchestra that Papa had specially commissioned from Richmond played a lively popular tune, inspiring several of the early-arriving guests to clap along.

Our main house may not come close to matching the size or opulence of the Shirley Plantation's mansion across the river, Emma thought, but for the first time since Mother's death, there's no question that this ballroom is once again living up to its reputation as one of the most beautiful in the county.

Casting a quick, sidelong glance at her sister, she made a wager to herself. *I'll give Cat no more than fifteen seconds after Joe arrives to make some snide comment about Susannah York over there in the far corner.* Catherine would be of no mind to go easy on anyone who dared to threaten her self-image at tonight's harvest celebration party. Especially that part of her image involving Joe Hartwell, the handsome twenty-one-year-old planter's son, racehorse owner, and Virginia Military Institute cadet corps officer. Ever since they'd first met at a Petersburg social function last year, Catherine had been focused on one primary goal: winning Joe's exclusive affections.

"Cat," Amanda Tidwell teased, "you look unusually divine tonight. Are you expecting someone special? Mr. and Mrs. Faulkner, perhaps? Or . . . maybe someone a touch more interesting? Emma, can you shed some light on what your sister's fuss is all about this evening?"

All the girls laughed, even Catherine. Everyone knew that Catherine *always* went out of her way to look "unusually divine" at any social gathering. Tonight was no exception. Her exceptional beauty, enhanced by her low-cut, sapphire-blue, multitiered satin gown with ruffled shoulders and the expensive blue diamond necklace that adorned her neck, was on full display for all—especially Joe Hartwell—to admire.

"Well," Emma said with a giggle, "she may be thinking that our future ambassador—after observing her charms and skills tonight—will offer her a trip to France to serve as translator for his wife. If so, maybe she'll finally get a chance to meet her idol 'Sisi' at some gala diplomatic party."

Catherine groaned. "Oh, Em, stop it right now. The chances of meeting the Empress of Austria while she's just 'happening' to visit Paris during some fairy-tale diplomatic trip of my own are nil. Besides, why do you all keep thinking I'm so intrigued with her?"

"Honestly, Cat," Amanda said, "how much more evidence does anyone need than that stack of *Harper's Weekly* periodicals you keep in your bedroom? You know, the ones featuring articles like 'Empress

Elisabeth: The Most Beautiful Woman in Europe,' or 'Sisi: The World's Best Female Equestrian.'"

"Oh, yes," one of the other girls chimed in merrily, "and how about 'Sisi: The Twenty-Two-Year-Old Mother of Three with the Sixteen-Inch Waist'? Cat, stop trying to deny it. There's no woman in this world you admire more than Empress Elisabeth."

"And no *man* she admires more than Joe Hartwell," Amanda teased.

Emma held her breath, concerned that her little joke was now being blown out of proportion by the other girls. Even among friends, Catherine's mood could turn defensive and sour in a split second if she felt disrespected. Thankfully, the floor manager's announcement diverted everyone's attention toward the entrance of the ballroom.

"Ladies 'n' gentlemen, your attention, please! It's my honor to present the regimental commander for the VMI Cadet Corps Class of 1860. Ladies 'n' gentlemen . . . *Lieutenant Joseph Hartwell!*"

"Look, Cat . . . there he is!" Amanda beamed over the loud applause as she grabbed Catherine's arm and pointed toward the door.

Emma's eyes widened at her first sight of the slim, broad-shouldered young man in the tight-fitting, gray-blue cadet's uniform. Jet-black hair swept to the side; strong, angular jaw; wide, sensuous mouth turned upward at the corners—Joe Hartwell's facial features alone would be enough to melt the heart of any young lady of marriageable age, she thought. She could see why Catherine was so enchanted with him.

Seeing her sister's delighted smile, Emma cast a furtive glance to observe Susannah's reaction on the other side of the room nearer to the entrance. *Please, Susannah, just stay in your corner and don't make a show. Let Cat have first dibs on Joe tonight.*

It wasn't to be; Susannah waved excitedly to Joe, who walked over to greet her. She met him with a big smile and proffered hand, which he promptly bent down to kiss.

"Well, would you look at *that*," Catherine muttered, loud enough for all in the group to hear. "She didn't wait two seconds to start heaving her chest, batting her eyes, and flashing that polecat smile at him. Didn't even give him a chance to look our way."

"Cat, don't worry," Amanda said confidently. "The night's young. You'll have plenty of opportunity to catch Joe's eye. Just be yourself!"

Catherine glanced at her quizzically, as if uncertain whether she'd just been complimented or insulted. After a moment, she folded her arms defiantly and turned her back on Susannah and Joe. She seemed to Emma to be on the verge of tears.

Emma felt a sudden, overwhelming compassion for her sister. So happy and carefree as a young child, Catherine had undergone a rapid transformation around the age of eleven. Part of it, Emma knew from her own experience, was no doubt due to the natural physical changes to be expected around that age. The other part involved something unusual and far more sinister.

She could still remember the night she'd awakened to the sound of Papa's angry, drunken voice coming from the hallway just outside Catherine's bedroom. Emma had arisen from bed, cracked open her own bedroom door, and peered down the hall. She couldn't make out everything, but she did hear Papa accuse Catherine of engaging in "disgraceful, unladylike behavior" including "wrestling and rolling around on the hay in the barn" with one of their young male cousins who was visiting from Lynchburg. Mother had apparently spotted them and later told Papa about it, and he would not stand for it. He expected more proper conduct than that from his firstborn daughter, he'd said, and he would teach her to respect his wishes. When Catherine had meekly tried to protest her innocence, Papa had abruptly ended the "conversation" with a harsh slap to Catherine's face. She'd stood there stunned, either unable or unwilling to acknowledge Papa's demand that she confess and apologize. This had drawn a second and even more vicious slap that had sent her reeling to the floor in a fit of sobs.

Catherine had never spoken with Emma about the incident, and Emma had been too fearful to ever ask. Whatever the true reason behind Papa's excessive outburst—something that Emma had never actually witnessed him repeat, even though she suspected it might be occurring—Catherine's whole personality had changed. True happiness and peace were no longer anywhere to be seen in her, as she'd become more and more careful around Papa and more concerned with the only thing she now seemed able to control: maintaining her "perfect" face and figure. Her relations with Emma and David had gradually become more strained and fraught with arguments, even though Emma believed that—deep down—her sister still loved both of them. Just as she knew *she* would always love Catherine.

Emma turned to see Papa waving to her from the reception area beside the entrance. Mr. and Mrs. Faulkner had just arrived, and Papa no doubt wanted to ensure the entire Hodge family was there to give them a proper greeting.

Walking with Catherine toward their father, Emma saw David approaching from the opposite side of the room. She could already sense her sister's extreme discomfort over the upcoming exchange.

"Mr. and Mrs. Faulkner," Papa gushed proudly, "may I present my son David and my two daughters Catherine and Emma."

Charles Faulkner bowed as the women curtsied. "We're honored to finally meet your children, Lawrence. We've heard so many good things about them."

"I'm very proud," said Papa. "And you may have already heard, but our elder daughter Catherine here has developed quite a capacity for something I suspect you'll find of great interest—especially in view of your probable new diplomatic post."

Emma cast a worried glance at her sister. *Here it comes.*

Mr. Faulkner arched an eyebrow. "Oh, and what is that?"

"Her conversational French!" Papa said. "Catherine, why don't you treat Mr. and Mrs. Faulkner to a sampling?"

Catherine's face tightened. "Oh, Papa, does Mr. Faulkner really want to hear my simple utterings in a language I suspect he's already expert in himself?"

Papa's face darkened at the untimely display of modesty.

Mr. Faulkner broke the tension with a gracious smile. "Miss Catherine, we'd *love* to hear! Who knows if my appointment as French ambassador will ever come through. In the meantime, I have a great desire to attune my senses to all things *française.*"

Catherine hesitated, obviously trying to compose herself. Emma knew she was seething with resentment inside at the thought of being used. Finally, she flashed the sweet, obedient smile that Papa always expected both his girls to display. In a soft, melodious voice, she proceeded to speak several sentences in French.

When she'd finished, the Faulkners grinned with delight and clapped their hands. Not to be outdone, Mr. Faulkner responded with a few of his own choice French phrases.

"Catherine," Papa asked, "are you going to translate that for the rest of us?"

"Of course. I told Mr. and Mrs. Faulkner that it was my pleasure to meet them. That I've heard so many interesting things about France, and that I hope they will soon have the opportunity to serve there. I also told them I knew there was so much to be learned, especially about French cuisine and customs."

Mr. Faulkner took up the slack. "And I told Catherine that her French was beautifully spoken. That her accent is exquisite—far better than my own. And that she must have a superb tutor to have learned so much and so quickly. She is to be congratulated!"

"Well," Papa said with a self-satisfied grin, "I'm glad we've established a new bridge for communication between the Hodge and Faulkner families. And starting next year, our youngest daughter Emma here will no doubt be following suit as she begins her own private tutoring in French."

Emma offered an embarrassed smile. Like her sister, she had no desire or need to be put on display like this.

"And last but not least," Papa said, "this is my son, David. He's on semester break from the final year of his journalism studies at Princeton College."

"Is that so? You must be very proud, Lawrence!" Mr. Faulkner exclaimed as David stepped forward to shake his hand. "That's quite an accomplishment, young man. With all our national political turmoil, not many of our southern sons are graduating from or even attending the prestigious northern universities these days."

"Thank you, sir," David said. "Attending Princeton's been a great honor and a wonderful learning experience for me, and I have my father to thank for making it all possible from a financial standpoint . . . and for trusting me enough to succeed."

Faulkner grinned and clapped Papa on the shoulder. "Well done, Lawrence! You know, given your son's journalism emphasis, I'm sure he's had quite a bit of exposure to all the currents of political thought that an esteemed institution like Princeton has to offer.

"I'd be very interested to hear his scholastic insights on how I might go about advising President Buchanan concerning all this secession talk. The man seems hopelessly confused, constantly vacillating, trying to keep peace between the North and the South. He believes secession—as some in the South are now threatening—is illegal, but he also thinks it would be illegal for the North to go to war trying to stop it. In my view, his failure to deal firmly with this problem is absolutely killing our chances of unifying the whole country around a cohesive strategy for preserving the Union."

Mr. Faulkner paused and smiled hesitantly at Papa. "All that, you understand, Lawrence, is off the record—a chance for this aspiring foreign policy salesman to vent his feelings about certain domestic issues."

"Oh, of course, sir, of course," Papa said. "We would never take your comments here as anything more than a privately expressed opinion." He glanced nervously around the room, as if trying to find an excuse to end the political conversation before it took a potentially unwelcome turn with David's involvement.

"If I may, Papa?" David said suddenly. Papa glared at him briefly but then turned back to Mr. Faulkner, who seemed eager to take David up on his offer. Papa smiled tightly and nodded his consent.

David spoke with quiet confidence. "Mr. Faulkner, you asked for my insight. I know I'm young and have but limited knowledge of such things. But I do wonder if President Atent Buchanan is giving too much weight to the threats of the secessionists. Isn't it clear that the South would try to secede *only* if a federal law were passed abolishing slavery in those states like ours where it currently exists? And haven't we all learned from the recent Lincoln–Douglas debates that most responsible Northerners—both Democrats and Republicans—desire only to keep slavery from *expanding* to the new territories in the West? So . . . why take the secessionist threats so seriously? Why not instead support the good case that Senator Lincoln makes? Let the South preserve its current slave economy for the time being, but keep the South from selfishly spreading such an inhumane system beyond its current borders."

Emma, in a state of near shock, watched Papa's face contort. Catherine, for her part, stood with widened eyes and mouth ajar. Even Mr. Faulkner seemed taken aback. Emma couldn't believe that David had just expressed—with eloquence—such a condemnatory characterization of slavery and the South's role in spreading it.

"David," Papa said finally, "perhaps you shouldn't be suggesting such—"

"Papa, I'm only responding truthfully to Mr. Faulkner's request for advice. I know what I'm suggesting isn't popular around these parts, but I—"

"Would you please excuse us for a moment, Mr. Faulkner?" Papa pulled David aside by the arm and escorted him to a quiet corner of the room where the two began to engage in a heated discussion. Emma, attempting to relieve the embarrassing situation, asked the Faulkners about their own children as Catherine maintained an awkward silence.

Fortunately for all, the orchestra leader just then took to the platform to announce the first dance of the evening: a waltz—a mutual favorite of Emma and Catherine. Further, it was announced, this first dance would be gentlemen's choice.

Emma surveyed the room, wondering vaguely—but not really caring—if Billy Jensen, grandson of a Petersburg city official and her secret childhood crush, would finally get up the nerve and ask her to dance. Probably not, if his continuing animated conversation with his friends was any indication.

Catherine stood with her back turned to the dance floor, no doubt unable to endure the possibility of seeing Joe Hartwell escort Susannah York onto it.

Well, she needn't worry about that, Emma thought excitedly. *Here comes Joe!* Her pulse fluttered at the close-up view of the lieutenant's deep-set, sea-blue eyes and charming smile.

Responding to Joe's gentle tap on her shoulder, Catherine turned around to behold her prize: the one who, minutes ago, had seemed lost to a far less worthy rival.

The look on her sister's face made Emma beam with a mixture of relief and delight. For the first time in a long, long while, Catherine seemed genuinely happy.

⁂

Emma stood by the edge of the dance floor, entranced by the beautiful sight of Joe Hartwell swinging her sister round and round to the lively tune of the Virginia reel. It was their third dance together and the culminating event of the first half of tonight's program of waltzes and polkas with a few informal country dances interspersed for variety.

For Emma herself, it had been quite enough that Billy Jensen had finally requested a dance with her awhile earlier. Afterward, he'd been the perfect gentleman, bringing her a glass of punch before politely excusing himself to return to safer conversation with his goofy friends. Really, it didn't matter. Emma's heart, unlike Catherine's, wasn't drawn to anyone in the elegant ballroom tonight. Not that she would mind at all meeting a handsome, dashing young gentleman like the one in her increasingly romantic dreams of late, but by the looks of things so far—

A slight commotion by the side door leading to the kitchen building caught Emma's attention. Curious, she walked toward the door. She stopped short upon discovering the person trying to enter. It was Sallie Cobb, and her face was wet from crying.

Emma pushed her way past the attendant, through the door, and into the chilly night air with Sallie. Pulling her aside, Emma grasped her face between her hands.

"Sallie, what's wrong? Tell me." Emma grabbed her by the shoulders, trying to get the distraught girl to focus. Finally, she succeeded in getting her to calm down enough to spill out what had happened.

"Sam and his assistant, Johnny Wheeler, they caught up with Charles in the fields—he was huntin' for rabbit after supper. They all passed by our shack, and I heard Sam accuse Charles of slackin' on his field duties and makin' Sam a laughingstock to the other workers. Told him he was gonna teach Charles a lesson he'd never forget. My parents ain't around—they off with little Lew at Pastor Jones's revival service—so I ran after the men by myself, keepin' my distance. Th-They took Charles into the woods, came to a clearing, and tied him up by his hands on a tree limb. Sam started whippin' him over and over with a hickory switch. Emmy, I-I couldn't stand it—Charles cryin' out . . . oh, it was horrible. Then Sam tells Johnny it ain't enough, to go fetch his bullwhip he'd left at the barn. And that's when I got up and ran this way for help . . ." Sallie's voice broke as a fresh set of tears flowed down her cheeks. "Emmy, what do we do?"

CHAPTER 9

Hodge Family Plantation
November 18, 1859

Emma let out a horrified gasp. She tried not to think of Charles's sweet, handsome face, knowing it would only worsen her sense of panic. *What to do? Ask Papa for help?* A quick look back through the door to the far side of the packed dance floor—where Papa was immersed in conversation with at least twelve other merry, laughing guests—was enough to convince her otherwise.

Looking wildly around the yard, she spotted a solitary figure leaning casually against the fence behind the loom house. *"David!"* Grabbing Sallie's hand, she ran toward her brother.

David turned, took the pipe he'd been smoking out of his mouth, and stared in wide-eyed alarm.

"David, you've got to help," Emma said breathlessly, clutching him by his jacket collar. David listened to her frantic explanation with growing agitation, then grabbed her by the arm. "Let's go."

After a difficult sprint along the path through the moonlit woods—as Emma, with her long ball gown and limp, struggled to keep up—the three approached the clearing where Sallie said the men had taken Charles. A huge, fallen log a few feet from the edge offered concealment, and they crouched behind it with their heads down. The voices of Sam Taylor and his assistant were unmistakable.

"Here it is, Sam. Found it just where you said."

"Good, Johnny. Was wonderin' what was takin' you so long. Let me have it. This boy's about to get another round of good ole southern lovin' for all the trouble he's been causin' around here."

Her heart pounding, Emma peeked over the top of the log. It took a few moments for her eyes to focus through the misty air and dim moonlight. Once they did, she barely managed to stifle a scream at the sight. Charles—his back turned toward her—was hanging by his hands, his feet at least two feet off the ground. Sam stood casually behind him, slowly extending the coils of a long, snakelike bullwhip as Johnny pulled Charles's pants down around his ankles. To Emma's consternation, Charles did not appear to be uttering a sound in protest; she wondered for a moment if he was still alive.

"So, Charles . . ." Sam sneered, "think I was gonna let you off with just sixty strokes of my little hickory switch after you made me look like a weak supervisor to Mr. Hodge and a big joke to all your friends?"

A short pause was followed by a feeble, halting plea. "Please, Mr. Taylor sir, I-I swear I was doin' my job just like you told me to . . . c-can't help what them other no-good fools are sayin' about you."

David rose, climbed over the log, and strode into the clearing. "What the *hell* do you think you're doing, Sam?"

Sam immediately dropped his whip to the ground, as if he'd seen a ghost. "Why, uh . . . hello, Mr. David. Didn't mean to disturb your evening at the party. We were just takin' care of a little problem. This boy here's been neglectin' his duties and acting sassy the last couple days—setting a real bad example for the other slaves on my watch. You know I've been given strict orders by your father not to let that kind of thing happen."

Emma and Sallie stood up. Ignoring the disbelieving, hostile stares of Sam and Johnny, they entered the clearing. It was then that Emma got her first clear look at Charles, and she nearly fainted at the sight.

"Sam, you and Johnny pull his pants up and then help me untie him," David ordered. The two men gawked at each other, hesitating.

"*Now!*"

"Whatever you say, Mr. David."

The men untied Charles's hands from the tree limb and carefully laid him flat on his stomach on the ground. Emma and Sallie rushed over and knelt beside him. His eyes were closed, and his breathing labored. His back was a shredded, bloody mess. Emma gently cupped the side of his face with her palm. His breathing grew stronger and more regular after a few moments. Finally, he cracked open an eye. He seemed to recognize her immediately and smiled weakly.

"So, Sam," David said, rising to confront the man whose loyalty to Hodge family interests had never before been questioned. "*Bullwhipping* on top of sixty switch strokes? How would you like me to explain all this to my father? You know good and well he could fire you for going way overboard like this."

Sam appeared surprisingly unconcerned. "Guess you can explain it any way you'd like, Mr. David. I know the truth, and the truth is, I ain't done nothin' wrong. This boy had comin' to him everything he got, and everything I was gettin' ready to give him."

"*What?*" David's face contorted in utter disbelief. "Are you serious? How can you *possibly*—"

"Now you wait just a minute," Sam cut in. "You don't know the half o' what this boy's been up to, Mr. David."

Emma felt a sudden tremor pass through her body. Something began to click in her mind—something Catherine and Sallie had warned her about just yesterday.

"All right, Sam," David said. "Why don't you give me a clue as to what the hell you're talking about?"

Sam rubbed his jaw.

"I'm waiting."

Sam grimaced and shook his head sadly. Like he hated to be the bearer of bad news but knew he had no choice.

"Maybe you can find the clue you're lookin' for, Mr. David, by just turnin' around and watchin' that sister of yours holdin' that boy's face like she's found her long lost love."

Emma froze. David, eyes narrowed, stared at her hard. *Oh, God,* she thought, *what is he thinking?*

She withdrew her hand from Charles's face but continued to hold his hand in both of hers, looking up anxiously at her brother.

David whirled to face Sam. "What are you accusing my sister of, Sam? And what's this have to do with—"

Sam held up his palms in protest. "Whoa there, Mr. David. You got this all wrong. I never accused Miss Emma of what you're thinkin'. I'm just sayin', it's a mighty strange sight to see a pretty White girl so torn up, so . . . tender-feelin' toward a disrespectful slave who got what's comin' to him. Just kinda makes me wonder what might be behind it all."

Emma saw David's fists clench into tight balls. She knew without a doubt that he wanted to run over and smash Sam in his stupid, arrogant-looking face.

Clearly struggling to gather his composure, David looked up at the star-saturated night sky and exhaled slowly. For an extended moment, the soft chorus of a few chirping crickets was the only sound to mar the otherwise stark silence.

Finally, David leveled his gaze and spoke in a calm, measured tone. "Sam, you ever heard of something called simple *human compassion*?"

"Oh, sure I have, Mr. David. My daddy taught me to show it every day. Share a little o' my water with the fieldworkers if their buckets run dry. Dole out only nine lashes when ten are due. Things like that. But Daddy also taught me somethin' else."

"And what's that?"

"He taught me to do all in my power never to let a southern lady's honor get tarnished. And maybe it's been a little hard for you to see since you've been away for a while, but that's exactly what's been goin' on here, Mr. David."

David stared at him blankly for a couple of seconds, then shook his head and held his palms up in the air. "I don't understand. What are you saying?"

"I'm sayin' that slave there deserves some extra-hard punishment. Not just because he's a disrespectful shirker, but because he's been tryin' to *seduce* Miss Emma. And from what I can tell, she ain't been puttin' up a whole lotta resistance."

"All right, that's it . . ." David took two steps toward Sam with his fists clenched, but then he stopped and looked back at his sister, as if suddenly confused.

"Don't believe him, David!" Emma cried.

"No, Miss Emma?" Sam snarled. "You gonna deny flirtin' with Charles when you pass him on your way to get your clean clothes back from Priscilla every Friday afternoon—thinkin' none of the other slaves see you smilin' and oglin' each other like you're newlyweds? You gonna deny you like puttin' your hand on that boy's face like you were doin' just a moment ago? Heck, you know you could have the pick o' the litter of White gentlemen admirers, but it seems like White boys ain't good enough for you."

Emma glared at Sam, realizing now what was *really* behind his anger. *After two years, he still hasn't gotten over my rejection of his advances.*

"How is it, Sam," David asked, "that *you*, of all people, have become aware of all this supposed flirtatious behavior of my sister? How would you know? Aren't you busy enough supervising the fields? Why should anyone trust what you're saying?"

Sam spat on the ground, then leered at David with narrowed eyes and the haughtiest smile Emma had ever seen. "Somebody's gotta look out for the honor and purity of our southern ladies, Mr. David," he said archly. "And I consider it my duty to do so. I got my eyes and ears, trust me—other witnesses both colored and White who'll support me in what I've said if needs be. And if you'd like just a little more reason to believe me, I got one."

"It better be more than what you've told me so far."

Sam reached around to pull a starched-white, embroidered handkerchief from his back pocket. He held it by two corners and let it dangle in front of his chest. "I found this on Charles here. He had it stuffed in his shirt pocket. If you look closely at this, I think you'll see something interesting. Let me just read what somebody sewed on here real nice. It says: 'To Charles, From Miss Em.' Now I ask you, Mr. David, when a young southern lady gives a handkerchief to a man, don't that usually signify somethin' special between them?"

Sam crumpled up the handkerchief and smiled. "Oh, and one other thing while we're at it." He nodded to Johnny, who pulled a small object from his coat pocket. "Caught Sallie with this real nice framed set o' handwritten Bible verses yesterday. Let me read you just one o' these verses, Mr. David: 'Christ has liberated us to be free. Stand firm then and don't submit again to a yoke of slavery.'"

His lips curved in a smug smile, Sam looked up as he returned the frame to Johnny. "Sallie told me Miss Emma gave this to her for a birthday present. I couldn't help but wonder what ideas Miss Emma might secretly be tryin' to teach her two favorite slaves on this plantation, Sallie and her stepbrother Charles here. In fact, I even wonder if she might be violatin' Virginia law by teaching slaves to read and inciting 'em to disobey the people God put in charge of 'em."

The blood drained from Emma's face. Swallowing hard, she released Charles's hand and stood up. She clutched her arms to her stomach and glanced down at Sallie, who was shaking her head in obvious distress as she kept tending to her stepbrother. Looking hesitantly over at David, her heart sank even further as she watched him standing in shocked silence, at a loss for words.

Sam pressed on. "I sure hope the fact that I now have these little items in my possession will help you take the rest of what I've said seriously, Mr. David. You know, earlier you asked me what excuse I'd offer your father for my supposed terrible treatment of this poor colored boy. Well, let me return the favor now and ask *you* a question, sir: What would your father say if he was given *eyewitness proof* that his youngest daughter is cavortin' with a male slave, teachin' slaves to read, and encouraging 'em to get their freedom? Think he'd like to hear *that*?"

Emma knew there was nothing more that David could say or do in her defense. Her careless behavior had yielded its poisonous fruit, just as Catherine and Sallie had warned. Sam Taylor—the self-appointed defender of southern female honor and virtue despite his rumored shenanigans with Liz Wheeler—now held all the cards. And if anyone should report his sadistic action tonight to Papa, Sam would undoubtedly play his entire hand against Emma.

A sudden sound of voices approaching the clearing caused everyone to look up. "Momma, Daddy . . . that you?" Sallie called.

A brief pause, then: "Yes, it's us, girl. Where are you, and where's Charles?"

"We're over here, Tom," David yelled.

Upon entering the clearing, Tom and Mary Cobb at first searched around in confusion before Mary screamed in horror at the sight of their eldest son lying on the ground. They ran over to him and knelt, weeping heavily as they hovered over his bloodied back and joined Sallie in her ministrations.

"Well," Sam said, "I suppose he's got all the love and care he needs now. Guess we might as well be going, Johnny. Anything else you'd like to discuss before we leave, Mr. David?"

David shot him a look of helpless rage. "No, not now, Sam. We'll talk more later."

Emma knelt to help the Cobbs attend to Charles. She knew the parents' arrival signaled not only blessed relief for their son, but also the end of the secret joys and rhythm of life she had come to love so much. Sallie and Charles would no longer trust her special efforts to befriend and encourage them—and worse, Charles was now vulnerable to future abuse by Sam.

Unless, she thought suddenly, *I'm brave enough to call Sam's bluff.*

After confirming that Sam and Johnny had departed the scene, Emma arose and approached her brother hesitantly. "Can we talk?" she whispered.

He nodded. "You've got more than a little explaining to do."

The next morning, Lawrence Hodge leaned back in his parlor armchair, his hands massaging his forehead. Emma sat on the cushioned stool near her father's feet and held her breath, awaiting his judgment.

Of one thing she was sure: she had done the right thing. Late last night, she had spoken separately with both David and Catherine and explained everything to them. Despite their expressions of sympathy and offers of support, Emma had insisted that she needed to approach Papa privately and tell him not only about Sam's cruel treatment of Charles, but also his purported rationale behind it. She'd then gone to Papa, confessing fully to the parts of Sam's accusations against her that were true, and asking for Papa's understanding and forbearance in light of her basically good and charitable intentions. But she'd also begged him to discipline Sam, and to ensure that Sam would never again mistreat *any* Hodge slave with the vicious cruelty he'd displayed toward Charles.

By taking the initiative to confess all, Emma was sure she had obliterated Sam's ability to hold her hostage to his threats. Her father would express some disappointment in her behavior, but she was confident that in the end he would accept her apology and deal sternly with Sam. Her life ahead would be different—more scrutinized by Papa, certainly—but she would be on the right side of her father's grace, and Charles would be safe from Sam's further abuse.

Her father had listened quietly to her recounting of the night's events, his jaw tightening at Emma's description of Sam's sadistic behavior and her confession of her own actions. He'd told her that he would need to "think on things" before deciding what to do, and that they should talk about it in the morning.

The moment had arrived.

Papa finally moved his hands away from his forehead and gripped the arms of his chair as Emma stared straight ahead, her face a pale mask of worry and fatigue from lack of sleep.

Clearing his throat, Papa opened the discussion. "Emma, you did well to come to me and confess things. Sam did wrong, but that doesn't negate my responsibility to take steps to make sure something like this never happens again. From now on, Sallie will be working permanently in the loom house, and we'll find you another personal maid. You will end your misguided efforts to teach any of our slaves to read. Also, you are forbidden to express any further affections or public acknowledgment of Charles. If I find out you're doing so, you'll be confined to your room along with other punishments I deem appropriate. As long as you live in this house, you'll obey my rules."

Emma barely managed to suppress her gasp. These were not the reassuring words she had anticipated hearing from her father. "And Sam, Papa?"

Her father looked at her askance. "What about him?"

"Aren't you going to do something to discipline him for what he did to Charles? Doesn't Sam deserve your condemnation and correction as well as me?"

Lawrence Hodge let loose with all his pent-up irritation and frustration. "Daughter, you should not question your own father's judgment on this matter, especially when it comes to dealing with Sam. I know how to talk with Sam about this, and I'll do so when the time is right."

"I understand, Papa, but isn't *now* the right time? What if Sam—"

"Emma," Papa interjected, his tone harsh. "Do you have any concept of what I'm up against? Did you forget that I'll soon begin my official campaign for the Virginia House of Delegates? If I fail to get elected, there'll be one less reasonable, moderate, wealthy planter's voice that supports the institution of slavery but at the same time fights against the extreme views of the secessionist fanatics in this state. The last thing I need now is for any hint of illegal family behavior or disciplinary problems with our own slaves to become publicized and ruin my election chances. I've already been embarrassed enough by your brother's ridiculous political rantings to Mr. Faulkner last night."

Emma felt the blood rush to her face. "So . . . what are you suggesting, Papa? That by punishing me alone, you'll save your election chances? That by—"

Lawrence nearly leaped out of his chair, his right hand raised and trembling as if poised to strike. Thankfully, he slowly lowered his arm. "No more of this, Emma!" he growled. "I'm not suggesting anything. I'm *demanding* that you mind my rules from now on, and that you abstain from embarrassing me by speaking of this situation regarding you, Sam, and Charles to anyone outside of our family, especially at church. I will handle things appropriately with Sam as I see fit. Your responsibility right now is to obey me and support your family."

For the first time, Emma understood what Catherine must have felt that night years ago when Papa had slapped her to the floor for daring to argue with him over her supposed misbehavior with her male cousin.

She stood up, her face defiant. "I understand completely, Papa." Furious, she spun around and stalked out of the room. Her plan for turning the tables on Sam by confessing everything to Papa had failed. With Papa's mind consumed by his upcoming election campaign, it appeared that *she* would be the only target for his discipline and punishment; Sam would likely be spared. And if so, Charles could still face significant danger.

CHAPTER 10

Charles Town, Virginia
December 2, 1859
(Two weeks later)

Eleven o'clock.

Anticipation gripped the small crowd of civilian spectators gathered just outside the city on a low, sun-drenched hill overlooking the field designated for John Brown's execution. All eyes peered down the rock-strewn cart path stretching back in the opposite direction toward the center of Charles Town. Escorted by a strong column of solders, the wagon transporting the infamous prisoner from his city holding cell could now be seen. In only a few short minutes, it would be passing directly by.

David Hodge stood in the midst of the group, marveling at the tight security precautions in evidence everywhere. To ensure there would be no attempt at a last-minute rescue by Brown's abolitionist sympathizers, Governor Henry Wise had ordered fifteen hundred Richmond Gray militiamen to be stationed within the field itself and to establish a gated perimeter around it, backed by units of cavalry and field artillery. Save for a few notable exceptions, no civilians would be permitted inside the perimeter. Civilians could observe Brown's last movements on the hanging platform from a distance if they wished, but—much to David's disappointment—they would not be able to hear his final words.

Up before dawn today at the traveler's lodge, David had arrived at the field nearly two hours before anyone else. His goal had been to ascertain where he might obtain the best possible view of the macabre proceeding's final stage with the aid of a handheld nautical spyglass that the lodgekeeper had lent him. Not that he had any ghoulish urge to observe the actual hanging too closely, but he *was* genuinely eager to observe how this committed martyr for The Cause—and the primary subject of his recent college term paper—would handle his last moments alive in the presence of his enemies.

Spotting the small hill about fifty yards beyond the militia-protected perimeter, David had ascended it and marveled at the perspective it provided—not only of the hanging platform but of the entire surrounding region. Stretching away toward the mountain chains that bordered the scene to the east and west were large fields dotted with corn shocks and white clapboard farmhouses. Close by was the pleasant little city with its elegant suburban residences, while seven miles to the northeast—at the base of the Blue Ridge—the Potomac and Shenandoah Rivers poured their united streams at Harpers Ferry. It was there that, two months ago, Brown's effort to initiate an armed slave revolt throughout the South had been crushed and his fate sealed by a contingent of US Marines under the command of Colonel Robert E. Lee. Today, John Brown would pay the world's ultimate price.

Now, as he regarded the other spectators who'd eventually joined him on the hill, David tried to clear his mind of all the distracting memories that had been plaguing him since the night of the harvest party . . .

The trip from the plantation to Charles Town, soon to be followed by yet another long coach ride to his final destination at Princeton, had been anything but restful. The entire time, David had been burdened with concern over the unresolved situation between Emma and Sam Taylor.

After Emma told him of their father's hesitancy to confront Sam, David had guessed immediately what was really going on. As he'd learned from a guest at the harvest party, Sam and his father had reportedly joined a secretive new organization of county citizens dedicated to blocking the election to the state legislature of anyone professing even a hint of either anti-secession or antislavery political views. The "Virginia First Society," as they called themselves, was largely composed of an eclectic mixture of local planters, farmers, overseers, merchants, and businessmen who felt personally threatened by the economic and social implications of a federal government-imposed end to slavery in Virginia. They saw the state's secession from the Union as the only permanent solution, and they specialized in spreading damaging rumors about any aspirants for public office who failed to unequivocally support their full platform.

Given their association with the VFS, David knew there was good reason to fear what Sam Taylor and his father might do to hurt the election chances of a moderate candidate like Lawrence Hodge—a candidate who strongly supported slavery but who was just as adamant in opposing the unpatriotic and dangerous act of secession. Especially if such a candidate was causing them personal difficulties by confronting and punishing Sam for his treatment of Charles Cobb.

It was also easy to see why Emma was concerned. With Sam believing he'd gotten away with hurting Charles due to his possession of evidence of scandal within the Hodge family, what would stop him from repeating his sins in the future?

Recognizing these blackmail possibilities, but unable to think of any wiser and safer course of action other than to let things play out quietly for now, David could only hug Emma closely and wish her the best as he'd departed for Charles Town, where he had finally arrived late last night.

"Here they come!"

David put his troubled thoughts concerning his family aside as he and the other spectators jostled for position along both sides of the cart path to observe the approaching death parade. When the first soldiers of the escort passed by, a reverential hush fell upon the crowd. But as the open bed wagon pulled by two white horses drew closer, the predictable, angry mutterings began to swell in volume.

"Crazy old fool's about to get his due . . . the murdering, Black-lovin' scoundrel!" yelled a hawknosed old man in a bearskin coat and raccoon-tail hat as he shook his fist in the air.

"That'll teach 'im to take on Colonel Bobby Lee!" cried someone else in the crowd, drawing a chorus of loud cheers.

Standing next to David, a short, pudgy man with white hair and thick, muttonchop whiskers cupped his hands around his mouth. "Anybody wanna bet we'll have a last-minute try from Brown's abolitionist lackeys to save his neck?" he shouted to the wind.

He received his answer in the form of many boos and guffaws, prompting a tall, thin, professorial-appearing man standing beside him to put his hand on his shoulder and pat it consolingly. "You serious, my friend? With all those Richmond militia and VMI cadets locked and loaded for bear? Take a look over yonder." He nodded toward another small hill less than two hundred yards away on which a line of cannons were arrayed, all pointed menacingly at the field. "Would *you* invite a barrage from Tom Jackson's artillery, just to save the old buzzard?"

David gritted his teeth, fighting the urge to challenge the boyish bravado of his southern compatriots. Despite his annoyance, he had to admit they had a point. After all, shouldn't *all* Virginians be offended and horrified by Brown's actions and supremely confident in their own state's unflinching response?

The wagon passed by slowly, and David saw the man clearly for the first time. Brown sat on the top of his wooden coffin with his arms tied to his sides above the elbows, leaving his forearms free. His clothes appeared seedy and dilapidated, an impression reinforced by his bright-red slippers and low-crowned, broad-brimmed black hat, which somehow seemed inappropriate for the occasion. Strangely, his face wore a grim smirk—one that suggested a contemptuous disdain for the whole affair.

As if on cue, Brown turned his head and peered straight in David's direction. He raised his left forearm to wave, his face breaking out in a broad smile. "Good morning, son! Glorious day for a hanging, isn't it?"

David thought at first that Brown was addressing him directly, but then he realized the object of the greeting was someone standing immediately behind him. Turning, he beheld a handsome young man of medium height who appeared to be in his early twenties. The man was gazing past David's shoulder at Brown. His face radiated what could only be described as pure devotion, honor, and love—a rapturous expression of resigned peace, marred only by a single small tear that rolled down his left cheek. His own hand was lifted chest-high in apparent response to Brown's awkward wave.

After a moment, the young man dropped his hand before shifting his eyes to meet David's. He nodded slightly and smiled in polite acknowledgment. Embarrassed by his own intrusiveness, David turned back toward Brown and watched entranced as the wagon continued its slow progress down the hill and toward the field.

Gradually the spectators dispersed, each taking up their preferred position along the crest and facing the execution site below. David tried to spot the man he had just encountered, but he was now nowhere to be seen. Standing apart from the others, he pulled the borrowed spyglass from his coat pocket, extended it to its full sixteen-inch length, and held it up to his right eye. Two small twists of the adjustment ring brought the magnified image of the scene below into sharp focus, revealing hundreds of militiamen scrambling to assemble themselves into tight ranks facing the platform where the city sheriff and his assistants were making their final checks of the hanging apparatus.

A few minutes later, the wagon arrived near the foot of the platform. David's jaw dropped in amazement as he watched John Brown lift himself off the coffin, then jump down to the ground without help. Brown stood for a moment, looking around at the gray-uniformed men with gleaming bayonets who bordered the short, cleared path leading to the platform steps. Finally, he started walking toward them.

Absolutely no fear in the man's gait, David marveled as Brown reached the platform steps and began to ascend them with the alacrity of someone anticipating a long-delayed reunion with an old friend. Arriving at the top, he shook hands with several of the officials on the platform and walked steadily to the trapdoor over which the halter was hooked to a beam. He then offered his neck to be placed in the noose. The jailor drew a white muslin cap over his face, and the sheriff asked him something that David could only assume was an offer to receive Brown's last words.

What would I give to hear those? he thought.

Several long minutes passed as the escort soldiers took up their final positions around the platform. All the while, Brown appeared to remain stoically quiet and motionless. With his spyglass, David surveyed the sea of surrounding soldiers. How sad it was, he thought, that there was not a single colored face to be seen anywhere in the entire field. But why should he expect otherwise? The Virginia authorities would certainly not wish to have exaggerated legends of a martyr's death spreading among those for whom Brown had sacrificed his entire life.

At last, the sheriff stepped over to the halter rope attachment point. All in the crowd held their breath as he lifted a large hatchet and struck the rope a sharp blow.

The trapdoor collapsed. Brown fell three or four feet. There was profound stillness among all witnessing the scene as his struggles continued, growing feebler at each abortive attempt to breathe. His arms sank lower, and his legs hung more relaxed, until at last, he dangled straight and limp, swaying to and fro in the wind.

David pulled the spyglass away from his eye.

"No one has greater love than this, that a man lay down his life for his friends." Unexpected sobs suddenly welled up from deep within his chest at the thought of Christ's words, nearly choking him and begging to burst forth from his throat. Not wishing to disturb those around him, he covered his mouth and nose with his hands as tears flooded

his face. He remained frozen, staring toward the platform where John Brown's body continued to sway slightly in the breeze as the spectators gradually drifted away. It was a full five minutes or more before he was interrupted by the gentle touch of a hand on his shoulder.

"*Glory*. We just saw the sacrifice that it sometimes demands, don't you think?" the voice behind him said softly.

David turned and faced once again the good-looking young man whom Brown had cheerfully acknowledged when passing by in his death wagon. He could do nothing but nod and smile wanly in agreement.

"What's your name, sir . . . if I may be so bold as to ask?"

"Hodge. David Hodge."

The man extended his hand, which David accepted.

"Mr. Hodge, I would be most honored if you'd accompany me to my favorite tavern in Charles Town for a drink and bite of dinner. I find myself in great need of both after this whole taxing affair. And it appears, sir, that you may be as well."

David regarded him warily. "Did you know him?"

The man hesitated, eyeing David carefully. "Mr. Brown and I had some business dealings in the past."

Instantly, David was hooked. He wanted to learn everything he could about John Brown, what motivated him and his followers, and what it all portended for the future—not only for the country, but for himself as well. Wasn't *that* his reason for coming to view this execution in the first place?

"Thank you for the kind offer, and I'd be very pleased to accept your invitation, Mister . . . ?"

"Bowman. Abel Bowman's the name. A pleasure to meet you."

The mood in Old Henry's Tavern was dark and somber. Only four or five patrons sat at the bar, huddling close together in quiet conversation with the owner, who seemed intent on frequently and liberally refreshing each man's shot glass. The few customers who sat in pairs or trios at the small tables and booths lining the tavern walls spoke quietly or simply partook of their food and drink without conversing. The general spirit here seemed quite the opposite of what David would have expected. After all, wasn't this a southern town that had just witnessed the carrying out of almighty justice against a northern White abolitionist—one who had betrayed his own race by inspiring and even leading acts of extreme violence against it, first in Kansas and now in Virginia?

Up to this point, the conversation with Abel Bowman had been friendly and polite, mostly devoted to inquiring about each other's background and reasons for attending the execution. Bowman had briefly described his Kansas upbringing and current job as crop manager for an Ohio farm just outside Cleveland. He'd also candidly admitted to his association with the local branch of a northern abolitionist society that had once invited John Brown to speak at its annual members' meeting. After personally speaking with Brown afterward, Bowman had come away with a greatly reenergized passion and purpose for the antislavery cause. It had all made perfect sense and explained his presence here today. According to Bowman, his "acquaintance" with Brown and his motivations extended no further than this single encounter. Somehow, David sensed there was more to the story but decided not to press.

His thoughts already starting to drift toward the next leg of his trip to Princeton, David settled back in his chair as the tavern owner walked up and set a refilled snifter of apple brandy and a steaming plate of buttered, peeled shrimp in front of each man.

Abel Bowman raised the glass to his lips, then paused before taking a sip. "So, what do you plan to do, Mr. Hodge . . . David, if I may?"

"Sir?"

Bowman set his drink down, reached into his coat pocket, and pulled out the top half of a single, folded newspaper page. Pushing aside his plate of shrimp, he spread the page out on the table. The headline and its subtext spoke volumes:

SECESSION TALK RAMPANT AS BROWN EXECUTION NEARS

Southern politicians fear federal government caving to abolitionist demands

Abel stared hard at David, his dark-brown eyes gleaming like those of a ravenous tiger surveying its prey. "What I'm asking is . . . what will you do if it ever comes down to a secession vote in your state? Would you support it? Even if it would almost certainly lead to the feds sending an army to suppress your 'rebellion'?"

David sat back in his chair. "Mr. Bowman . . . Abel, if I also may . . . isn't it a little soon to be worrying about *that* extreme case?"

"I'm not so sure, David. I'm sure you know how many southerners now refer to Senator Lincoln and his party as 'reptiles' and 'Black Republicans.' Many are vowing to disregard any new federal statute that even hints at forcing their states to free or eventually release their slaves. So, what do you think would happen if Lincoln gets elected *president* next year?"

Abel's words struck David like a thunderbolt. Before Harpers Ferry, the possibility of the tall, awkward rail-splitter from Illinois occupying the highest office in the land had seemed so remote as to be laughable. But after watching Brown's body dangle in the wind today—and knowing that embellished stories of his brave demeanor and last words would soon be published in all the major northern newspapers—who could pretend any longer that Lincoln and his antislavery platform stood no chance of winning the election come November? And if *that* happened . . .

David shifted uncomfortably. "I suppose that conscientious, thinking people with divided loyalties like me would have to make a huge and terrifying decision, wouldn't we?"

"And what decision is that, David?"

"Whether to *join* the North's fight against slavery and secession—both of which I now consider to be morally dead wrong—or instead to *resist* those northern forces that could end up invading my home state and harming my family in order to impose their solutions and terms on us."

Bowman sat back and took a long sip of brandy as he watched David pick up his fork and resume eating the few remaining shrimp on his plate. "That's a choice I'm glad I'll never have to make. As you could no doubt tell from my reaction this morning, I'll have but one loyalty to drive my life from here on. But David, before we leave each other today, I want you to know something."

David put his fork down and looked up. "What's that, sir?"

Abel stared at him intently. "There's something I sensed about you the moment I saw your own reaction on that hill today. You're like me. You have a heart and eye that look beyond what many would see as the pointless personal sacrifice of a self-deluded martyr. As with Christ's suffering on the cross, because you truly believe in the ultimate goodness that will one day result from the sacrifice, you see glory—not humiliation—on display. And when you see it, you recognize the truly magnificent beauty, majesty, and grandeur of that glory's ultimate source, and it stirs you deep down inside with a longing to devote your life to that source. To shed blood for it, if needs be.

"That's why I reached out. And after hearing of your background and reasons for attending the execution, I now believe even more strongly my first impression was correct. There's something in you, David, that would *love* to know more about the source of that glory we were privileged to witness on the hanging platform today."

David blinked. This all seemed a bit much, a touch sappy. "I'm honored you would perceive me in that light, sir, though I'm not quite sure what you're—"

Bowman leaned forward, his eyes glowing with intense light. "David, what I'm getting at is this: should you ever decide that the glory of 'The Cause' is worth learning more about and possibly supporting or even fighting for, please get in touch. It would be my privilege to have you visit Ohio someday soon so I can introduce you to my friends and fellow workers. Who knows? You might become so enamored that you'll decide to come join us permanently!"

David nodded politely. It was a kind and sincere offer. But to completely abandon his family and everything he'd grown up with for the sake of the "glory" of the radical abolitionist Cause? *That* was not something he was ready to commit to.

"I definitely appreciate your invitation, Abel, and I promise I'll think it over."

Abel closed his eyes and nodded solemnly. "I'm glad to hear that. I just pray you won't overthink it as I once did, David. You never know if or when you'll get a second chance in life."

Mystified, David was tempted to press for an explanation, but something in Abel's pained expression told him to hold back.

After finishing off their drinks and the remaining food, the two men exchanged addresses and parted with a warm handshake.

Later that evening, David sat down on the single bed in his private room at the travel lodge. He opened his journal and recorded the following:

> *Today's execution of John Brown: an enthralling and emotional affair, capped off by meeting and sharing a meal with Mr. Abel Bowman—a gracious and kindhearted young Ohio farmhand devoted to abolitionist principles. Was greatly impressed with his passion for "The Cause." My professors talk smartly about it, and I'm sympathetic—but Abel lives for it. He seems to have taken a liking to me. Thinks we're kindred spirits. Perhaps some-day we'll encounter each other again.*
>
> *Back on the road to Princeton starting tomorrow. Emma's situation with Charles still heavy on my heart—but don't know how to help since it's now in Papa's hands, and after the harvest party, I doubt he'll be seeking my opinions on anything anymore.*
>
> *—DH, 12/2/59*

After reading over what he'd written, the reality struck home: the nation's division over the slavery issue was starting to divide the hearts of his own family.

He closed the journal, set it on the side table, and blew out the candle before climbing between the sheets. A wave of gloom enveloped him as he lay on the bed, staring up at the darkened ceiling.

PART II

FLIGHT AND FURY
(1861–1862)

CHAPTER 11

City of Petersburg, Virginia
April 28, 1861
(Sixteen months later; two weeks after
the Confederate attack on Fort Sumter)

Settling back on the plush, cushioned rear bench of the two-horse open carriage, Catherine closed her eyes and nestled her cheek against the gray-flanneled shoulder of recently commissioned Captain Joseph Hartwell, 1st Virginia Volunteer Infantry Regiment. The Second Presbyterian Church near the Appomattox River waterfront was still a good fifteen minutes' ride from here, and she was resolved to ignore all her worries over the impending threat of national civil war and instead to savor every precious moment before the Sunday service snuggled next to her fiancé.

She clasped Joe's hand in her lap, entertaining pleasant imaginings of their wedding day, which was now less than a month away. It would be the perfect event, she thought, for capping the past year and a half of mostly good fortune enjoyed by her entire family in the aftermath of the John Brown affair . . .

Ever since the 1859 harvest party, Papa had been making every effort to ensure that his long campaign for a seat in the next session of the Virginia House of Delegates—to open this coming December—was unhindered by any more foolhardiness from Emma or David. By ending Emma's illicit slave-teaching activity and securing David's pledge to stop expressing his negative views on slavery in the presence of Papa's friends and political associates, Papa seemed to be achieving his goal of maintaining his personal reputation as a viable candidate in firm control of his own plantation and family.

Catherine, meanwhile, had been doing her best to support Papa in all the ways she knew Mother would have during such a stressful time in his life. Ways such as performing her household oversight and charity society tasks with minimal complaint, and encouraging Emma to accept her new daily routine without Sallie around and avoid saying or doing anything that might upset Papa. She'd even sat with Papa for hours one evening, trying to raise his spirits following a bitter afternoon row with his campaign advisors over his increasingly unpopular position on the secession issue.

None of this had come easily. Occasionally, Catherine would succumb to her fits of temper, depressive moods, and cutting episodes. But as Joe Hartwell had continued to call on her and increasingly express his affections over the past year, her negative behaviors had begun to taper off. Her whole world seemed to be brightening, and all those close to her had told her they'd noticed a positive change in her disposition.

The morning of last November 7 had brought an unwelcome shock with the news of Abraham Lincoln's election as the sixteenth president of the United States. Papa was certain that the outcome would heat up secessionist fanatics all over the South, probably reducing his own chances in the upcoming elections for the Virginia House of Delegates.

That very evening, though, Papa's gloom was dispelled when Joe had surprised him with a personal visit to request his daughter Catherine's hand in marriage. With tears of joy, Papa had enthusiastically granted his blessing. The next afternoon, Joe had surprised Catherine by proposing to her following an afternoon horse ride and picnic on the bluffs overlooking the James River. She'd of course accepted, ecstatic at the prospect of beginning a new life as Joe's loving wife and mistress of the small plantation fifteen miles east of the Hodges' that he'd inherited from his father.

Catherine's engagement announcement had soon been followed by more good family news.

In early January, Papa had been honored by his selection as one of two county representatives to the all-important Virginia Secession Convention. The convention had been tasked with making a recommendation to the public on whether or not—in view of Lincoln's election—Virginia should join South Carolina in breaking all ties with the Union.

Eleven days ago on April 17, following the shelling and capture a few days earlier of the Union's base at Fort Sumter in Charleston Harbor by South Carolina military units, the convention had reversed its initial position and voted *in favor* of secession. Despite being on the "wrong" side of the convention's vote, Papa's thoughtful, erudite speeches had been highly praised by representatives on both sides of the secession issue. Many local citizens had also expressed their appreciation, renewing confidence that—despite the high probability that secession would end up being ratified by the upcoming public vote in May—Papa's prospects for winning election to the open seat in the House of Delegates were still very much alive.

On top of Papa's happy development were Catherine's receipt earlier this month of an honorary award for inspiring service from the Petersburg Charity Society, Emma's latest outstanding progress report from her private tutors, and David's expressed enjoyment of his new job with a Petersburg publishing agent, which he'd begun soon after receiving his BA degree from Princeton College last spring.

Despite all the state and national turmoil, it seemed the Hodge family had much to celebrate and anticipate . . .

Jolted out of her reverie by the clomping hooves of a passing horse pulling a small carriage, Catherine glanced toward the opposite bench, where twenty-five-year-old Oscar Hamilton—Joe's best friend since boyhood—had his arm draped around his wife Rebecca.

Elected a year and half ago to the House of Delegates, and one of its youngest members, Oscar had gained a strong reputation among his colleagues for his enthusiastic speeches in favor of secession. Clearly, his normally ebullient mood had reached new heights upon return from his recent vacation with Rebecca in Charleston.

"Hartwell, you should have seen it!" Oscar said, his left hand furiously tapping the side rail of the carriage as if he were now reliving the unforgettable experience. "Those South Carolina Citadel cadets sure helped send that baboon Lincoln a message he won't forget." He pulled his wife close, planting a kiss on her cheek before flashing a mischievous grin at Catherine and Joe. "Even the gorgeous Mrs. Rebecca Hamilton here stood up and cheered when that first shot arced out over the harbor and exploded over ole Sumter like a beautiful, red Roman candle."

Catherine smiled at Rebecca's blushing—though clearly delighted— reaction. Oscar might not have Joe's Greek-godlike looks, but he certainly knew the pathway to a young woman's heart.

"Glad you were able to perfectly time your Charleston vacation so you could join all those hotel rooftop spectators enjoying the sight, Hamilton," Joe said. "But I'm afraid the only 'message' Old Abe took from it all was that he needed to call up seventy-five thousand more Union volunteers, and from what I hear, they're already starting to arrive in Washington. If he chooses to drive them fast and hard on Richmond, it won't be easy for us Confederates to match his numbers and equipment."

Catherine lifted her head and looked at him askance. "But, Joe, haven't you been bragging to me about how one Virginia soldier's worth ten Yankees?"

Joe smiled and patted her knee. "Don't always take me *too* literally, darling! Sure, we'll lick 'em good . . . but it'll probably take a few months, not just a few weeks like the papers are saying."

Catherine rested her head back on his shoulder. Suddenly Joe's rosy prediction of only three weeks ago—that a full-scale civil war between North and South could never happen—now sounded like a cruel joke. After Sumter's takeover by the Confederates, war now seemed inevitable, and who knew when Joe would be called to galivant off somewhere with his unit as soon as General Lee sounded the alarm. What that all might mean for their wedding date wasn't entirely clear, and Joe's lack of certainty about everything recently wasn't very reassuring.

Still, she couldn't be prouder of him. A little over two weeks ago, she'd stood with Oscar, Rebecca, Papa, and Emma among at least a hundred Richmond area citizens who'd been invited to a tour of the Hermitage Camp just outside the city, where new Confederate infantry recruits were being drilled by VMI cadets. The highlight of the day was a sunset dress parade featuring complex maneuvering of units and manipulation of weaponry, all of which the audience was able to observe from a raised platform at the edge of the field.

Around 6:00 P.M., Papa shouted that Joe's unit had just come into view and was about to march in front of the reviewing stand. Everyone had run up to the platform railing for a closer look. Joe, commissioned in January following his graduation with high honors from VMI, was riding tall on a gray stallion at the head of a group of cadets. Catherine and the other women had wept and waved their white handkerchiefs as the men passed by on the ground below, cheered on by the throngs of admiring Richmond citizens. At just the right moment, Joe had raised his head and spotted Catherine. He'd lifted his hat high and grinned broadly, prompting all the ladies near her to gasp and gaze with unfeigned envy at the object of Joe's salute.

Nothing in her life—even Joe's marriage proposal—had topped the pure exhilaration of that unforgettable moment for Catherine Lynn Hodge.

"Well," Oscar said, flicking away a small insect that had just alighted on the carriage's brass siderail, "it may take a while, but at least the South got off to a good start at Sumter. Only one death on each side after all that cannonading. Still, it galls me to think it could all have been avoided. Why couldn't Lincoln get it through his ugly head? The Constitution's a contract between sovereign states. How could the northern states refuse to enforce the Fugitive Slave Act—and then somehow expect us southern states to remain bound by that same contract?"

Joe laughed. "Hamilton, did I *really* cast my vote for you? You're telling me the reason South Carolina left the Union and attacked Sumter was because they were mad at some northern states for failing to return a few of their escaped slaves? I know you're a first-rate politician, but you know good and well that's not the *main* reason."

Oscar frowned. He glanced at Rebecca, who stared at Joe with a puzzled expression. Catherine shifted uncomfortably in her seat and gripped Joe's forearm; she knew his odd theory on this issue and wasn't eager for him to talk about it now.

"Well, tell me, Hartwell," Oscar pressed, "since you seem so much more enlightened than the rest of us here . . . what *was* the main reason, then?"

"Let's just admit it. Our southern states simply don't want the federal government forcing us to give up what we consider to be rightfully ours. Lincoln's not saying it yet, but from everything I've heard, if the abolitionists force his hand, he'll legislate for *all* slaves throughout the South to go free immediately. And if that ever happens, what do you think most of them would do? Why, run north for the industry jobs, of course. And then who'd we get to work our tobacco, cotton, and rice fields? Our whole southern economy and way of life would collapse. So stop pretending, Oscar, and let's just be honest. For South Carolina, us Virginians, and the rest of the South, this conflict isn't mainly about some abstract principle of honoring a state's rights under the Constitution—it's about fighting to keep slavery alive and well for our own survival's sake, pure and simple!"

"Hartwell," Oscar objected, "have you lost your mind? Whose side are you on? You make it sound like insisting that the North respect our legitimate property rights makes us a bunch of self-obsessed animals."

"*I'm* not saying that, but that's exactly what the abolitionists are shouting in Lincoln's ear. Unlike us, they don't accept the idea that enslaved humans should be considered as 'legitimate property.'"

Rebecca spoke up. "But isn't the *Bible* on our side in that regard, Joe?"

Joe cocked his head back. "How do you mean?"

Rebecca glanced at her husband. "Well, after all, wasn't slavery accepted as a normal condition even in New Testament times? Doesn't it say: 'Slaves, obey your human masters with fear and trembling, in the sincerity of your heart, as to Christ'?"

Catherine smiled to herself. Wasn't this the same point she'd tried to make to Pastor Jones, only to be deeply humiliated for her perceived naiveté? How would her fiancé—a pastor's grandson himself—handle this one?

"She's right, Joe," Oscar chimed in. "And didn't the Apostle Paul actually tell someone to return a runaway slave to his master—just like our Fugitive Slave Act calls for today?"

"Honestly, Joe," Rebecca rejoined, suddenly sounding even more confident, "doesn't attacking the institution of slavery amount to attacking our Bible—the infallible Word of God?"

Joe grimaced. "No doubt we'll all be hearing an earful along those lines in today's sermon from Reverend Pryor. But while I admit the Bible doesn't seem to specifically condemn all forms of slavery—and while I'm certainly not an abolitionist—I swear I'll never tolerate anyone who uses the Bible or anything else to justify slaves getting mistreated and abused."

My thoughts exactly. Catherine smiled tenderly at her fiancé as Oscar and Rebecca stared at them both with bemused expressions.

"Joe," she whispered in his ear as the carriage pulled up in front of the church, "I just wish you'd occasionally spend more time worrying about the preparations for our wedding than all this abolitionism non-sense. It all gets so confusing for people."

Standing up with Emma at the conclusion of the worship service, David rubbed his forehead in abject frustration. The one-hour harangue from Reverend Pryor touting "God's blessing for our righteous southern cause" had finally convinced him there was no hope for reconciliation between North and South. Nor between himself and his past.

David gazed at his sister and struggled to maintain his composure, knowing he was on the verge of a decision that could well preclude him forever from enjoying peaceful relations with his family.

"David, why are you staring at me like that?" Emma asked, glancing around to see if anyone was paying attention. They weren't. Papa was not even present today due to a bad cough. Hopefully, that was not a sign that his chronic mild heart condition might suddenly be worsening. Everyone else in the congregation—including Catherine, Joe, and their friends who had arrived separately and sat on the opposite side of the aisle from David and Emma—was already heading toward the narthex to greet the preacher on their way out.

The sight of his sister's concerned expression brought a lump to David's throat. He avoided her eyes, unable to speak.

What a change since earlier this morning on their way to church in the new two-seat carriage that David had recently purchased for himself using earnings from his job with the publishing agency. Sitting together on the driver's bench, the two had chattered away, sharing all that had transpired since David's last visit home. Emma had lightened his heart with her assurance that she was continuing to avoid any inappropriate interactions with Charles and Sallie. But she'd also aroused his concern and anger with her reports of how Sam was continuing to take advantage of Papa's lax oversight by picking on Charles in a number of subtle but hurtful ways—such as speaking vile, degrading criticisms and insults in his ear while he was bent over working the tobacco plants.

For his own part, David had shared with Emma his growing conviction that he could no longer acquiesce in the South's decision to support slavery to the point of secession from the Union. He'd stopped short, though, of confiding that he was strongly considering a recently received invitation from Abel Bowman to move north to join the abolitionist movement in Ohio. Maybe now was the time to do so.

He glanced around to make sure none of the other congregants who hadn't already exited the sanctuary were within earshot. "Em, there's something I meant to tell—"

A woman's scream from the narthex at the front of the church brought everyone to a shocked standstill. David grabbed Emma's hand and pushed toward the doors as the sounds of commotion in the street outside grew quickly in volume.

"They've got 'im now!" shouted one gentleman, dressed in his Sunday best and beckoning other exiting congregants to join him at the edge of a gathering mob of rough-looking river dockworkers and local vagrants. The men were shouting and cursing at someone or something in their midst.

Moving forward, David and Emma edged their way through to the front of the crowd and stopped in their tracks. There in front of them, a thin, shabbily dressed man was being beaten mercilessly by two heavyset dockworkers.

"Why are they doing this to him?" David asked the man standing next to him.

"Must've snuck in on that empty merchant ship from Philadelphia come to pick up cotton and tobacco. They caught 'im trying to secretly pass out Unionist propaganda on the dock and tracked him here. Poor idiot and people like him apparently didn't learn the lesson from Sumter. Anyways, they're sure educating him now!"

A vicious punch by one of the assailants caused the victim to fall on his back.

"*That's it . . . let him have it, Hank!*" someone shouted.

The pug-faced brute sat on the helpless victim's stomach and began slapping his face alternately with each hand, ignoring his pleas for mercy.

Something inside David snapped. He turned to Emma. "Wait here."

"David, no! Don't—"

David took three running steps and launched his body at Hank, knocking him off the man. Shocked silence fell over the crowd as the two disentangled themselves, stood upright, and faced off.

"What gives, Mister?" Hank growled.

"Lay off him. You've made your point. Enough's enough. It's *Sunday*, for heaven's sake!"

"And who are *you* to be actin' like master of ceremonies, tellin' the rest of us when to quit?" the other assailant bellowed. "You one of those Black-worshippin' Union sympathizers too?"

David glowered back at him. Somehow, the words just came out. "If you and your kind are the alternative, then yes, that's exactly what I am."

Awaking groggily to a dull ache in the back of his head and the taste of blood in his mouth, David tried to make sense of the voices around him. Finally, he realized he was lying on his back in the middle of the street with the concerned faces of Catherine, Emma, Joe, Oscar, and Rebecca hovering over him. He tried to lift his head, but the pain was too much. All he could do was lay back, close his eyes again, and listen.

"Here, put this on his forehead."

"Careful, don't jostle him."

"Heavens, look at him. Joe, if you hadn't stopped them, they might've killed him, especially after what he said."

"Cat! Do you *never* stop criticizing him? Even after he tried nobly to—"

"Oh, spare me, Emma. He's my brother too, you know. I was just pointing out it's clear now where his heart lies. So will you just stop—"

"Ladies, *please*! We can talk about all this later. We need to get him into the carriage and take him to the doctor."

David doubted that any of them realized he had heard every word and understood every implication. They had only confirmed what he had long suspected but had put off admitting to himself.

No longer. His decision was now final, the future course set.

North, to Ohio.

Chapter 12

Hodge Family Plantation
May 9, 1861

Emma was growing more agitated by the moment. The heavy morning rain had forced postponement of her much-anticipated solitary horse ride along the river bluffs until later this afternoon, and her conversation with Catherine over tea on the veranda was not going the way she'd hoped.

"Em," Catherine said impatiently, "I can't believe you're going to trouble Papa yet again over this. Don't you realize how you'll upset him at a time when he most needs our support? Especially now, with the election season heating up and considering all the public criticism he's facing after that traitorous ingrate we used to call a 'brother' left us all for Ohio last week."

The tragic scene was indelibly etched in Emma's mind. Papa and David—both still seething after their huge argument the night before—had refused to embrace or even shake hands when David had walked out the door the next morning. Unlike Emma, Catherine had made no effort to run after her brother and say goodbye. When he'd lifted his arm to wave to her, disgust over his decision and its effect on Papa had overwhelmed her and she'd deliberately turned her back on him.

Emma glared at her. "I *know* what David's departure meant to Papa, Cat. But how can you sit there and tell me I should therefore just ignore what's happening to Charles? It's much worse than you think. Sallie approached me yesterday as she was leaving the loom house. She told me Sam and Johnny have been picking him out for extra-hard tasks, then mocking him constantly in front of the other fieldworkers for being 'slow' and 'stupid'—exactly the opposite of what he is. He's depressed to the point of despair, can hardly pick himself up in the mornings. He's even stopped coming to our Sunday evening prayer sessions, which he's never missed once in the past. And . . ."

"And . . . what?"

Emma could barely choke out the words. "Sallie said that two days ago, Sam pulled Charles away from the other slaves to help him unload some supplies that'd just arrived at the barn. When Charles accidentally dropped one of the sacks of seed he was carrying, Sam started cursing him, ripped his shirt off, and started to whip him with his hickory switch. Charles got riled up and started fighting back, so Sam called for Johnny to help. They got Charles pinned down, and Johnny held him while Sam doled out twenty lashes, opening up some of the cuts on his back that were scarred over from last year. When Charles finally got home, he just fell on his bed and moaned in pain the whole night."

Catherine stared at her in shell-shocked silence. "Have Charles's parents ever said anything to Papa about this?"

Emma shook her head. "They're terrified to bring things to his attention because they think it'll only make things worse. They know I've tried several times over the past year to alert Papa to what's been going on, but he just keeps downplaying it all, telling me in so many words he thinks I'm exaggerating things.

"But I'm telling you, Cat . . . after hearing this latest story from Sallie, I'm not taking this anymore. I'm going directly to Papa to tell him exactly what's happening, and this time I'll *insist* that he do something to stop it. And if that doesn't work, I swear I'll do whatever it takes to stop it myself."

Catherine put her teacup down firmly. She leaned forward, grasped Emma's forearms, and looked her in the eye. "Em, please hear me.

I know how much all this mistreatment of Charles is tearing at your heart. God knows how sick I felt when I encountered Sam abusing little Lew. But if you try to raise this with Papa before my wedding, it won't work. You know he's distracted and worried thinking about how he's going to explain David's action to all those important guests he's invited. And with that cough of his continuing, I'm concerned any extra stress could worsen his heart condition. Can't you wait just one more week when I return from my honeymoon? I promise I'll go with you to talk to Papa then. He'll be in a much better mood to listen, and I know if we *both* confront him, he'll respond better than if you try to do it alone."

Emma looked at her hesitantly. "I really don't know if it's a good idea to wait. Charles seems like he's about to—"

"*Em, please!*" Catherine placed a hand on her temple and shook her head in exasperation. "Will you stop thinking only of Charles? Yes, he needs our help, but so does Papa right now. If you want my help, just wait until next Wednesday when I get back, and we'll take care of this whole thing together—the right way. I know Papa will listen when he's a little more relaxed, especially if we both plead with him to do something to protect Charles from Sam."

Emma stared down at her lap. She suddenly felt drained of all energy. "I absolutely *hate* waiting that long, but if the only way I can get your help is to wait until next Wednesday when you're back, then so be it."

"Well, please don't thank me at all for offering my assistance, sister!" Catherine huffed. "Like I said, I promise."

Emma smiled weakly, knowing that she really had no other realistic option. "Thank you, Cat. You know I love you and I trust you. I just pray you're right about this."

Five days later on Tuesday, Catherine stood at the front door of the rustic hunting lodge with her arms folded and tapping her foot. It was nearing sunset, and as she surveyed the surrounding forested hills just south of the James River to the west of Richmond, she struggled to accept that her honeymoon was nearly over.

Only three days ago, she had been swept up in the whirlwind of the formal Saturday morning church wedding ceremony followed by the grand reception at the plantation. Never had there been such a gathering of prestigious Richmond–Petersburg society at a Hodge family function. Sadly, not every notable on the invitation list had been present; at least twenty had withdrawn their acceptance at the last moment without explanation or apology. There could be only one reason: the news about David had spread. For many of the local gentry, Catherine knew, the very idea of a privileged son of Virginia deserting his family and state for the northern havens of abolitionism was anathema.

Still, for all present, the reception had been a beautiful, happy occasion featuring many tender and memorable moments, such as best man Oscar Hamilton's grandiloquent toast followed by his close hug and lingering kiss planted on Catherine's cheek—a head-scratching display of admiration and affection that had provoked embarrassed chuckles among the guests, a reproving stare from Oscar's wife, and a polite but firm tap on the shoulder from Joe.

Moving to the lodge porch railing for a better view of the sunset, Catherine felt a shiver run up her spine as she allowed herself to savor the sweet memories of her wedding night: Joe carrying her across the threshold of the Petersburg hotel's bridal suite; their first private, deep kiss as a married couple; the slow and deliberate shedding of garments in the bedroom followed by soft, intimate caresses and the unforgettable, passionate embrace that seemed to transport her to the very gates of heaven. She had thought nothing could top the pure ecstasy of that night plus the two here at the lodge—until early this morning, when Joe had surprised her in bed with a kiss, a bouquet of wildflowers, and breakfast on a tray. Together, they'd eaten less than half the tasty meal before they'd impatiently set it aside in favor of an even more delicious mutual undertaking.

And now, it's almost over.

Two hands gently grasped her waist from behind. "A little weepy, darling?"

Catherine closed her eyes and leaned back against Joe's chest, throwing her arms up and around his neck as he kissed hers. "Mmmm . . . if the last three nights are any indication of what's in store for me, you might say I'm weeping only with joy, Captain."

If there were ever a moment in her life to be captured and bottled forever, Catherine knew that this was it. Strange, she thought, how ever since that first dance with Joe at the harvest party a year and a half ago, her thoughts had turned so completely from self-loathing and cutting herself to unbridled infatuation and affection for another human being. And to think that, from now on, nothing could ever separate her from the source of all her happiness and fulfillment, except . . .

She hesitated, unsure whether to even bring the dreadful subject up.

"Joe?"

"Yes, Mizz Hartwell?"

She turned to face him. "Will the Yankees ever make it this far south?"

Joe drew her in close and kissed her lightly, then laid her head against his chest. "At the rate things've been moving over the last couple of weeks, half the entire Confederate army will be positioned in northern Virginia by the end of the month. And with General Lee now taking over all the Virginia forces, they'll be more than able to block any federal move to take Richmond."

"Well, I'm certainly glad to hear *that*, since Richmond's only twenty-five miles north of here! But why are we using only half our army in Virginia? Where are the rest?"

Joe scratched his chin. "Rest are being spread out to defend the western territories and the lower Mississippi."

"So, what does that mean for your own unit?"

"That all depends on how Jefferson Davis and General Lee decide we're needed. We could be moving to reinforce the units north of Richmond before long, depending on how the public referendum to ratify the special convention's secession vote turns out next month."

Catherine drew back from him and turned with folded arms to stare out over the balcony at the brilliant streaks of red, orange, and lavender that hovered just above the rapidly darkening blue mountains in the distance.

Suddenly she turned back and ran over to hug him closely. "Joe, I'm so incredibly proud of you. Just promise me you won't get killed."

"It's all in God's good hands, darling," he reassured her. "Whatever he wills to happen is going to happen, and we need to accept that."

Catherine sighed and held him tighter. "That reminds me of last week when Reverend Pryor read us that verse in the Bible about what Jesus said in the garden of Gethsemane: 'Father . . . not My will, but Yours, be done.'"

Joe chuckled and gently pushed her back. He pointed a finger at her chest. "Speaking of the Bible, when's the last time you read *yours*, Mizz Hartwell?"

Catherine blushed. Regular Bible-reading was not one of her habits. "Why, just a week ago, I read one of the psalms. Captain Hartwell, I hope you're not insinuating I'm not being a good, faithful Christian woman. Just because your granddaddy was a preacher—"

"I'm not insinuating anything, Cat. Just sayin' . . . maybe it's time we both started paying it a little more heed, especially now that we're married."

"Oh, Joe, honestly! You know we go to church where the Bible's preached every single Sunday. Isn't that enough?"

"Maybe for most people." He shrugged. "All I know is, if I'm going off to fight, I want to use every good weapon our good Lord's provided to help me sense his presence right there inside me every single minute, looking out for me all the time."

Catherine lowered her eyes and sighed. *Why do I always feel so empty whenever he says something like that? It's so frustrating.*

Like Joe, she considered herself as truly believing in Jesus, loving him with sincerity, and striving to walk with integrity before him. She trusted completely in Christ's exclusive power to forgive her sins, to save her from hell and grant her eternal life in heaven after she died.

And yet, despite Joe's personal testimony and the teachings of the Bible and her church, the idea that God's Holy Spirit was actually present inside the heart of all true believers during their lifetimes—helping them to overcome sin and temptation and do good works, protecting and comforting and guiding them through trials, always loving and accepting them despite their faults—had never been one that she'd found easy to fully embrace beyond intellectually accepting it as truth.

She hoped that one day she might actually *feel* the presence of God inside her—strongly—as Joe apparently did and had testified to her about on several occasions. But given that she herself had never really experienced anything like that, she often found it difficult to relate to those who, like Joe, claimed that they had.

Still, she wanted to be supportive of her husband.

"Well, if you're going to put it *that* way," she said finally with mock petulance, "I suppose I'll *have* to follow suit."

Joe laughed. "'Wife, submit to your husband . . .'"

She gasped and playfully slapped his cheek. "Only if my husband truly loves me, Joe Hartwell!" She peeked up at him teasingly. "Joe, are you sure we can't spend an extra couple of days here? Three days is an impossibly short time to teach your new wife all she needs to learn about loving her man . . . and hunting duck."

Joe laughed. "Glad you got the order right on that! Because once we get back and start life together on our own little plantation, you'll have a few other things competing for your learning time."

"Ha!" Catherine cocked her head back playfully. "If you're talking about managing our house and our five domestic servants, I think I've had all the training I need watching and helping Mother all those years. And did you forget? She made me read Virginia Cary's *Letters on Female Character, Addressed to a Young Lady, on the Death of Her Mother* end to end. What more do I possibly have to learn about managing domestic life on a plantation?"

"Now I *know* you're pulling my leg!" Joe whispered in her ear, then kissed her cheek. "As far as staying here longer, *I* don't need to be back until Friday evening at six to make that special meeting Colonel Moore called for all his officers to discuss changes in the regiment's drilling routine. But didn't you promise Emma you'd be back by tomorrow afternoon so you two can talk to your father about that slave boy?"

"Oh, why did you have to bring *that* up?" Catherine moaned. She extricated herself from his embrace and strolled over to the railing. After a long silence staring out into the deepening shadows of the valley, she turned to face her husband.

"Joe, what if we just stay here until Friday morning? That'll give us two more wonderful nights together here. I told Papa just before leaving that we may spend an extra day or two here, and not to worry."

"But what about—"

"Emma will be just fine. I'm sure she'll understand once Papa explains our delay. She knows how much I've been dreaming of this time away with you. I mean, it's our honeymoon! Besides, a couple more days should help as far as the situation with Charles goes. Papa's usually in a better mood to hear about problems with the slaves on Friday evenings rather than during the workweek when he's all wound up with business."

Joe walked toward her and took her in his arms once again. "Cat, you'll get no argument from me. If you really want to stay till Friday, I promise I'll make it worth your while."

Catherine smiled. She tilted her head up and pulled his toward hers. "Well then, Captain Hartwell, why don't you make it worth my while starting right now?"

CHAPTER 13

Hodge Family Plantation
May 17, 1861

Starting out on her Friday morning walk with Sallie to visit her girlfriend Amanda Tidwell's plantation, Emma vented her frustration.

"Sallie, I am *so* sorry. I can't believe she let me down like this. I was so excited when Papa said you could accompany me today, and I was really hoping to share some good news with you about the talk that Cat and I were planning with him about Charles and Sam—but now I don't know when or even *if* that's going to happen."

It was late Wednesday afternoon when Emma became certain that Catherine had reneged on her promise to be home that day. Responding to Emma's inquiry as to Catherine's whereabouts, Papa had told her of her sister's previously indicated possibility of spending extra days at the lodge. Obviously, that was exactly what had happened.

"Guess Miss Cat's got other things on her mind right now," Sallie said quietly, the disappointment in her voice evident.

Emma looked at her closely, sensing something amiss. "How is Charles doing?"

Sallie said nothing as she gazed at the ground.

"Sallie, what's the matter?"

She shook her head from side to side. "He got up real early this morning and started walkin' round and round the shack outside for at least a half hour. Before the others woke up, I left for my work at the loom house and crossed his path. He was kind of stumblin' along and mutterin' and had this look in his eyes like he was seein' something a thousand miles away. I told him goodbye and that I hoped he had a good day comin'. He just came over and hugged me real close. When he pulled away, seemed like he wanted to cry, but he didn't say a word . . . just started walkin' away toward the fields—an hour earlier than he needed to."

Emma stopped in her tracks and stared at Sallie, her face a mask of worry. "Has anything else happened between him and Sam the last couple of days?"

"Who knows? After Sam's last whippin', Charles don't like to let on about nothin' connected with Sam no more if he can avoid it. Prob'ly makes him too sad, thinkin' nobody's gonna help him anyways."

Emma hung her head. "This is all my fault. None of this would be happening to Charles if I hadn't been so careless by arousing everyone's suspicions last year. And then I go and fail him yet again by not directly addressing things myself with Papa last week when I first thought about it. Instead, I stupidly trusted Catherine's promise that she'd show up to help when she said she would. I—"

Sallie touched her arm. "Miss Em, Charles don't blame you. You know what he said to me night 'fore last? He said, 'I sure miss my Sunday evenin' prayer sessions with Miss Em leadin' things. I hope she ain't too mad at me for not comin'. She's a real nice lady. Ain't nobody I'd rather o' saved from that stormy creek. Tell her I plan on comin' back on Sundays soon's I start feelin' a little better.'"

Emma's hand flew to her mouth, and she began to cry.

Sallie smiled. "Miss Em, don't you go gettin' all choked up now. We can't be late gettin' to Miss Amanda's."

After Emma had collected herself, the girls resumed their walk along the lane. The day was quickly growing hot. Emma extended her parasol and told Sallie to draw close so she could shield both of them from the glare. She stared straight ahead, confused, angry thoughts beginning to well inside despite her best efforts to quell them. *What was Catherine thinking? Did she forget or simply just not care enough to come back Wednesday?*

A quarter mile down the lane, a strange noise caused Emma and Sallie to stop yet again. It seemed to emanate from behind the tree line a hundred yards across the field to the left of the lane.

"What *is* that?" Sallie asked.

Emma walked over to the lane's fence railing and inclined her ear toward the woods. "Sounds like . . . a child wailing!"

"What would a child be doin' in them thick woods? Maybe they lost?"

The wailing increased in volume, coming now in longer spurts.

"I don't know, but I think we should check."

Emma dropped her parasol and climbed awkwardly over the fence rails. She ran as fast as her limp would allow toward the woods with Sallie close behind. When they arrived at the edge, the source of the wailing became clear.

"*Lew!*" Sallie cried out upon seeing her ten-year-old stepbrother sitting bent over on a fallen log, his head in his hands and sobbing uncontrollably. The two girls knelt beside him.

"Lew," Emma said quietly, "what are you doing out here? What happened?"

Lew could not stop crying. He lifted his arm and pointed toward what looked to be a small clearing several yards ahead. Emma rose and walked slowly toward the spot while Sallie continued trying to console her stepbrother.

Reaching the clearing's edge, Emma peered across to the far side. She screamed and fell to her knees, nearly fainting at the sight.

Sallie ran up beside her. "Oh, God," she muttered. "No, Lord, no, no, no."

It was nearly a minute before the two women were able to collect themselves and, holding on to each other, approach the large oak tree together. Near its base, they raised their eyes and beheld the dead body of Charles Cobb, hanging by the neck from a rope looped around one of the large tree limbs.

Charles's arms were not bound. It appeared that he had brought on his own demise by deliberately kicking away a small log on which he'd been standing.

Sallie fell on her knees and wrapped her arms around Charles's legs. "Brother, you didn't have to, you didn't have to . . ." she sobbed over and over, the side of her face buried against his limp thighs. "Why didn't you just tell me this mornin' . . . you know I woulda helped. Oh . . . Charles, Charles, why'd you have to go do this?" Suddenly she drew back and looked up toward his face. The sight caused her to scream and turn aside, beating the ground wildly with her fists before finally collapsing with her arms covering her head.

Emma, her hand over her mouth and her entire body racked with uncontrollable tremors, kept shaking her head. She could not bring herself to look at Charles's face, desperate as she was to preserve her beautiful memory of the brave, handsome boy who had rescued her from the raging creek waters, carrying her in his arms and smiling tenderly at her. "I sho glad you still 'live, Miss Emma," was the last thing he'd said after he'd handed her over to Papa before being dismissed to the kitchen with Papa's polite thanks for his services.

Thoughts of remorse over warning signs and opportunities missed zipped through her brain like thousands of tiny hailstones. *Should have seen this coming. He was under too much pressure. Shouldn't have trusted Cat. Should've gone to Papa myself. Oh, Charles, please forgive me.*

Through her tears, Emma spotted a small patch of what appeared to be white cloth sticking out of Charles's pants pocket. Gathering herself, she moved closer. She took hold of the cloth and pulled it out.

It was an embroidered handkerchief. She held it open in her shaking hands and stared at the cross-stitching in the lower right corner:

To Charles, From Miss Em

As their carriage approached the plantation entry gate, Catherine leaned over and kissed Joe on the cheek. "I never thought I'd say this, but the duck-hunting lessons turned out to be my favorite part of the trip."

Joe cocked his head. "Your *favorite* part?"

"Ha! I knew that would catch your attention." Catherine flashed a coy smile. "No, that was great, but my absolute favorite part was the one I can't mention in polite company."

Joe's face lit up as he dropped one hand from the reins to put his arm around her shoulders and draw her closer. "Who would've thought that my new bride would prove to be such a great shot with my favorite duck gun? Really, three kills in one day? That's unbelievable for a beginner. Hope I don't ever end up on the wrong end of a gun *you're* aiming at me, woman!"

Catherine nestled her head against Joe's shoulder. She was proud of her performance over the past five days, not only with the duck-hunting lessons, but also with the way she'd been able to please him in every way with both her body and her mind.

She'd been somewhat nervous about how he would react when she fully revealed herself to him for the first time, knowing she'd be unable to hide the three self-inflicted knife cuts that had left small but noticeable scars on her stomach and thigh. But when he'd asked about them, she had candidly admitted to their source. She'd assured him that, with him in her life, all such foolishness was now in the past. When she'd then half-seriously asked if he thought she should be committed to an asylum, he'd laughed and engaged with her in another round of passionate lovemaking.

Joe's extreme delight in her had been obvious. Intimacy at all levels would never be a problem in their marriage, she was now sure.

She was also pleased with the plan she had come up with last night for reengaging with Emma upon her return.

It was simple. First, she would immediately take Emma aside and beg forgiveness for her own selfish decision to postpone her return until today. Then, she would persuade Emma that in fact the time was now even better for mutually approaching Papa regarding Charles and Sam. Emma would be thankful, realizing that everything had worked out for the best.

Passing through the gate, Catherine lifted her head and stared at the main house a hundred yards ahead at the end of the tree-lined driveway.

"Joe, something's going on. It looks like a lot of horses are tied up at the railing. I hope Papa isn't holding another campaign meeting at our house tonight! I know the election is next Thursday, but . . ."

Joe stopped the carriage and surveyed the scene himself. "You're right, dear. Who would—"

The piercing scream cut like a knife through the still, humid air, followed quickly by more screams and wailing sounds.

Catherine glanced at Joe, her heart in her throat. Somehow, she knew immediately what this was all about. *Emma . . . oh, God, please, no!*

Joe spurred the horses forward at a gallop, arriving seconds later behind several weeping, distraught field slaves who had gathered around an old wooden wagon parked at the bottom of the veranda steps. On the veranda itself, the butler Ben Edgefield stood holding one of the female house servants in his arms, obviously trying his best to console her.

Catherine jumped out of the carriage and pushed her way to the front of the gathering, her pulse pounding with trepidation.

On the bed of the wagon lay what appeared to be a corpse wrapped in a sheet. Kneeling beside it, Tom and Mary Cobb clutched hands, crying, bending up and down in emotional agony as their stepdaughter Sallie stood next to them, holding on tightly to her little brother Lew. On the ground beside the wagon—gazing at the corpse like four ministering angels of death—stood Papa, Sheriff Johnson, Sam Taylor, and his father Philip, the plantation overseer.

"I'm sorry you had to come back to this, Catherine," Papa said.

"Papa, what happened? Oh, dear God. Is this . . . ?" She touched her throat as she stared in wide-eyed horror at the scene before her.

Papa walked over, put his arm around her shoulders, and spoke to her quietly. "Yes, daughter . . . it's Charles."

Catherine's stomach dropped, and her head began to spin. She gazed up at the blooming branches of her favorite magnolia tree on the far side of the front lawn, trying desperately to get her bearings. "Papa, what happened?"

"He hanged himself in the woods near the creek early this morning. His brother Lew was going fishing and found him. Emma and Sallie heard Lew crying in the distance while they were on their way to Amanda's and went to investigate. After they saw Charles, Emma came home with Lew. I'd already departed for the city, but she told Ben and then Sallie's parents the news. Ben went to find Sam and asked if he'd go with Charles's father and two of the other field hands here to cut his body down and bring him back along with Sallie. They all just pulled up here as I was arriving back from the city with Sheriff Johnson, whom I'd met with earlier and invited over for dinner and some campaign discussions this afternoon."

Papa shook his head. "Terrible, terrible thing to come home to and behold. I feel so badly for Charles's family."

Catherine stared in horror at the wrapped corpse. "B-But, Sam, wasn't Charles under your supervision this morning like always?"

Sam tipped his hat. "I sure woulda thought that myself, Miss Cat, but truth is Charles never showed up. I looked all around and asked everybody, but no one had seen hide nor hair of 'im. He'd been real sad-lookin' and actin' funny lately, so I started worryin' maybe he was trying to pull off an escape—as hard as that would be in these parts. Anyways, I kept lookin' all over while Johnny watched the other slaves, but had no luck. Finally, Ben sent for me. He told me the news and requested my help. I just can't say how sorry I felt when I first saw poor Charles here. I—"

"*You devil!*" Sallie screamed. "You're not sorry at all. You know good and well what you—"

"*Quiet, Sallie!*" Papa shouted. Seeing the horrified reaction of the other slaves, he softened his tone. "Sallie, I know you and your family are hurting badly over this, and I'm awfully sorry it turned out this way. But Charles brought this on himself."

"No, he *didn't*, Papa!"

All turned in unison to look toward the veranda.

At the top of the steps, Emma stepped forward and stood in front of Ben with her arms clenched around her waist. Her whole body appeared to be trembling.

Papa glowered at her. "What are you talking about, daughter? That's nonsense. Now get back in the house and get some rest."

Emma stood her ground. "Yes, Papa. I'll do as you command. But not before I ask two things about Sam. First, where exactly was he looking for Charles all that time this morning? Was anyone with him? And second, how did my handkerchief—the very handkerchief I made for Charles as a gift, the one that Sam stole from him out of spite—suddenly find its way back into Charles's pocket? Unless Sam decided to plant it there after he hanged him, just to send a message to whoever found it that this is what Miss Emma's compassion for a male slave will always lead to!"

Lawrence Hodge's mouth dropped. He stared at Sam, whose face was contorted with wild rage.

"Just what are you accusin' my son of, Miss Emma?" Sam's father snarled. "After all Sam and I've done for ten years now to support this plantation and your family and these slaves here . . . you accusin' my son of murder, Miss Emma?"

Sam launched into his own defense. "Let me tell you somethin', Miss Emma. I got witnesses who were with me the entire morning. You need any proof of that? Just go ask old man Wheeler who I must've spent three hours with lookin' all over for Charles, thinkin' he might be hidin' out somewhere in the woods behind his property. And as far as that handkerchief, I gave that back to Charles a month ago. Told him if you really wanted that bad for him to have it as a love offering from you, then so be it. I'd just as soon *spit* on it."

Emma ran down the steps toward Sam. Catherine was sure that if she'd had a knife in her hands, Sam would be dead in a matter of seconds. Before she could reach him, her father grabbed her by the waist. He half dragged and half carried her—kicking and screaming vile epithets at Sam—back up the stairs to where Ben and the cook Dorothy stood on the veranda, gawking at the drama playing out before them. "Ben," Papa said brusquely, "take her inside and lock her in her room. I won't tolerate this behavior."

Catherine started toward the veranda. "Wait, Ben," she called out, "let me go with her."

Emma wrestled out of Ben's grasp and whirled toward her sister.

"No! You stay away, Cat!" she screamed. "I don't need or want your *help* ever again!" She stood silently with her lips quivering for several seconds, then spoke again, her voice breaking. "Y-You broke your promise, Cat. You could have been here on time and helped me save Charles, but you chose *not* to!" She turned her head and glared at her father. "I'm going to my room alone now, Papa, just like you asked me. I still love this home, but I see exactly now why David left." She stalked into the house.

Papa shook with barely controlled rage, his face florid. After finally regaining his focus, he motioned to Sam. "Help the slaves take care of Charles's body and get them all settled back in their quarter. I want extra provisions for Tom, Mary, Sallie, and Lew this weekend, and give them the next week off from their tasks. We'll talk about funeral arrangements in the morning."

Sam exchanged angry glances with his father before responding. "I'll do that, sir, but what about your daughter's—"

"Sam," Papa interrupted, holding his palm in front of his chest in an obvious attempt to keep the peace, "I sincerely apologize to you and your father for my daughter's hysterical outburst, and I beg your forgiveness. Emma's very emotional, and obviously this has all been too much for her."

"We do appreciate that, Mr. Hodge," Sam's father said. "But I wonder if the sheriff, Sam, and I might have a word with you tonight about all this. Just to set the record completely straight."

"Certainly, Philip. The last thing I want is a misunderstanding between the four of us."

"Scuse me, Mr. Hodge," the sheriff drawled. "Before Sam and the others take the body away, I need to have the parents identify him in my presence for legal purposes."

Papa nodded. "All right, Sam, let 'em see."

Sam bent down and unfastened the metal clip that held the sheet covering the corpse together. He unwrapped the top of the sheet and pulled it down.

Catherine's knees buckled, and Mary Cobb screamed and pitched forward at the sight of Charles's face. Sallie pulled little Lew close and embraced him. She then lifted her head and glared straight at Catherine.

Even with the distance, Catherine understood perfectly the single word that Sallie mouthed to her in silent rage and bewilderment: *Why?*

⌘

Eight days later—on the Saturday following Election Thursday—Emma sat at her bedroom writing desk, still grieving over Charles and plotting ways to prove Sam Taylor's guilt despite his claimed alibi.

Confined to her room by Papa for two weeks as punishment for her outburst against Sam, she'd struggled mightily to keep her spirits up. Mercifully, Dorothy—at Papa's request—was making sure she suffered not the slightest lack of food or personal comfort during her confinement. Emma savored the smell of the delicious breakfast of boiled eggs, ham, and corn cakes that the maid had just brought in on a tray.

Also on the tray was a folded newspaper that the maid said Papa wanted her to read. Even before opening it, Emma could already guess what she would find, since the noisy celebration late last night in the parlor room downstairs could only mean one thing.

She quickly scanned the headline article on the front page.

VIRGINIANS PASS ORDINANCE OF SECESSION

In the special state-wide election conducted on May 23, 1861, Virginia's voting gentlemen ratified the Ordinance of Secession that the Virginia Convention had adopted on April 17. The final voting totals were 125,950 in favor and 20,373 opposed, with most of the latter cast by hardcore Unionists in counties west of the Blue Ridge Mountains. Virginia has now officially joined the Confederacy, which recently named the city of Richmond as its new capital. In response, there are already reports of Union army movements south of Washington, DC that could . . .

Impatiently, she jumped to an article on the bottom half of the front page, the title of which had been underlined—by Papa, no doubt—in black ink:

LOCAL SPECIAL ELECTION SURPRISE

Voting results for the open seat representing Piedmont County in the Virginia House of Delegates for the 1861–1863 term have now been tallied. In an extremely tight race, planter Lawrence Hodge, in the wake of his honorable participation in the Virginia Convention, barely edged out the former county prosecutor and incumbent seat-holder William Reynolds, who had been slightly favored to win. Hodge's narrow victory was secured mainly by some unexpectedly high support from Virginia First Society members, who in the previous election had favored Reynolds. In other local districts . . .

Emma threw the paper down and buried her face in her hands. So *that* was what Papa's groveling apology to Sam and Philip following her accusation last Friday had been all about. In return for their favorable influence on the votes of their fellow VFS members, Papa had publicly humiliated and questioned his own daughter's sanity. And in so doing, he'd shut down any possibility of further investigation into what she believed in her heart to be true—that Charles Cobb's hanging was *not* a suicide.

Hearing light laughter and voices from outside, she pushed the tray back and rose from her chair. She walked to the open window overlooking the backyard garden. Papa was strolling along the back path with Burton Riley, his campaign manager. The two men were laughing and talking animatedly. She hadn't seen Papa looking so serene and happy in months.

She happened to glance toward the loom house and saw one of the elderly domestic slaves sitting on a bench against the side wall, whittling away with a knife at some small wooden item in his hand. Every few seconds, he would pause in his task and lift his head to observe Papa and Mr. Riley, who were moving in his direction on their way back to the main house. Absorbed in each other's company, they passed by within a few feet, not acknowledging in the slightest the man's smile and lifted hand. In fact, they seemed not to have even noticed his existence.

Enraged, she fought the urge to scream something horrible out the window. How can they be so callous, ignoring that poor man like they would a mangy dog? The memory of Catherine's betrayal exploded once again in her brain. She yanked the curtain shut and walked back to her desk. Pulling a clean sheet of paper out of the drawer, she dipped her quill pen into the well.

She had put this off far too long. And with war now having broken out within the nation, as well as her own family, she wondered whether she was too late.

Emma pressed the ink pen onto the blank page and began writing the letter she hoped would change the entire course of her life.

Dear Pastor Jones . . .

CHAPTER 14

Cleveland, Ohio
February 17, 1862
(Nine months later)

D avid Hodge couldn't believe his good fortune.

Emerging from dinner at the Superior Street tavern into the bright afternoon sunlight, he paused to refill his pipe and reflect on his latest plum assignment. It was one which, only three days ago, he would never have dreamed possible this early in his journalistic career. After all, being chosen to interview two leading figures of the national abolitionist movement was no small prize, even for far more seasoned newspaper reporters.

Doesn't hurt to have Edwin Cowles—US Postmaster for Cleveland and cocreator of the Republican Party—for my new boss, David thought as he smiled and tipped his hat to a well-dressed passerby.

Narrowly avoiding a fast-moving stagecoach that seemed to appear out of nowhere, David crossed the street to the four-story limestone building on the corner of Superior and 6th Street—home of the editorial offices for the *Cleveland Leader*, the town's fastest growing newspaper. Upon entering, he was immediately greeted by loud rattling and clanging noises coming through the far wall, by-products of the

Leader's newest technological addition housed in the rented warehouse next door. The mammoth, twenty-one-ton monstrosity known as the "Lightning" was a ten-cylinder, rotary-type-revolving printing machine. Its sophistication was hailed in the *Leader*'s company profile as a testament to the business acumen and political clout of their owner and chief editor: Edwin Cowles.

It was Abel Bowman who had first introduced David to Mr. Cowles. After helping David to locate and secure a small, two-room residence on Detroit Street shortly after his arrival in the city last May, Abel had invited him to an informal gathering of local abolitionist leaders at which Cowles was present. The three men had struck up an animated conversation, during which Cowles had expressed great interest in learning of David's former life in Virginia, his education at Princeton, and his journalistic aspirations.

Cowles had asked David if he would consider applying for a position at the *Leader*, and within a week, David had joined four other young correspondents with their own desks on the second floor of the building. His initial reports on local political rallies and interviews of wounded Union soldiers had greatly impressed Cowles, who last Monday had called him into his office and informed him of his next assignment: to interview two nationally reputed abolitionists who would be speaking at a major conference at nearby Oberlin College over the coming weekend.

"If you don't already know much about the Reverend Charles Finney and Frederick Douglass, I suggest you read up on them—fast!" Cowles had urged.

Over the past three days, David had immersed himself in biographical study of the two men and was now chafing to return to his desk to complete his study and note-taking on the *Narrative of the Life of Frederick Douglass, an American Slave*, the famous orator's 1845 memoir of his years in bondage and his ambition to become a free man.

Bounding up to the second floor, David had just sat down at his desk and picked up the Douglass memoir to resume his reading when the door to the chief editor's office flew open and Mr. Cowles beckoned.

"Hodge, you've got two minutes to finish whatever you're doing, then get in here. We've got a couple of things to discuss."

Nervous that he had done something terribly wrong and was about to get fired, David picked up his notepad and walked hesitantly into the room.

Cowles was sitting back in his chair with both feet propped casually on the corner of his huge desk. He lit a cigar that he had just stuck in his mouth, then pointed to a corner on the side of the room behind David. "You know this gentleman, I believe?"

David turned. Leaning casually against the edge of a massive bookcase, 1st Lieutenant Abel Bowman, 7th Ohio Volunteer Infantry Regiment, stood with his arms folded and legs crossed.

Abel's face appeared thinner and ruddier than the last time David had seen him, and a thick black mustache now obscured his upper lip. But the tigerlike gleam in his large, burgundy-brown eyes appeared to be as bright as ever. A wide grin spread over his face.

"About time we linked up again, Mr. Hodge."

David strode over to hug and shake hands with his friend, whom he hadn't seen since last June when Abel had decided to enlist in the newly formed 7th, a Cleveland-based unit. Although they'd been apart since then, David had heard about Abel's exploits through a mutual acquaintance who'd kept in contact with the commanding officer of Abel's unit—Colonel Tyler—by occasional letter. According to Tyler, Abel had shown great leadership capabilities to his superiors early on in handling new recruits, and by August had been elected by his peers to the position of 2nd Lieutenant. In the 7th's first two major battles with Confederate forces at Kessler's Cross Lanes and Blue's Gap in western Virginia, he'd performed brilliantly with his unit, leading to his recent promotion to 1st Lieutenant.

So why is he here today? David wondered. He never got a chance to ask.

"All right," growled Cowles, "if you two would please stop romancing each other and come over here and sit down, we can get this meeting over with fast."

David and Abel quickly took their seats in the two wooden armchairs facing Cowles's desk and watched him expectantly.

"Lieutenant Bowman is on an important mission, Hodge, and I want you to help him with it."

David glanced at Abel, who nodded and smiled back at him.

Cowles blew out a long, thick cloud of cigar smoke. "The 7th is doing another major recruiting drive in the city to replace its recent losses, and Bowman here's been handed the thankless task of organizing it. Your job, Hodge, is to come up with the advertising copy describing the purpose, location, and other details for this effort that we can include in our Tuesday morning edition."

"But . . . sir," David asked meekly, "does this mean you don't want me attending the conference this weekend?"

"Good heavens, man! I know you're more than capable of getting this done on Monday when you return. Besides, just ask the lieutenant here to help you with all the specifics. I suspect he could write the article himself if he had to!"

Abel chuckled. "Yes, but not nearly as eloquently as my friend David here, Mr. Cowles. That's why Colonel Tyler suggested I come to *your* newspaper as opposed to the *Plain Dealer* to get this important advertising job done. Better writing, greater circulation—that's what Colonel Tyler loves about the *Leader*."

Cowles laughed. "Don't try to flatter me, Bowman. What Tyler really loves is the fact that he trusts us more. Hell, I would too. The *Leader*'s the only city paper that's always remained intensely loyal to the bedrock Republican Party priorities that I know Tyler reveres and which I personally helped to establish: 'Free labor, free speech, free press, free territories, free states—and preservation of the Union.'

"At any rate, on to our second subject. Bowman, I *love* your idea and I'm completely behind it. The only question is, will Hodge here agree with us?"

"Uh . . . which idea is that, sir?" David switched his gaze uncertainly between Abel and Cowles.

Cowles cleared his throat and leaned forward, folding his hands on top of the desk. "David, how would you like to become the *Cleveland Leader*'s first dedicated war correspondent—attached to the 7th Ohio?"

David's jaw dropped. "Seriously, sir? I-I'm totally honored, but don't we already—"

Cowles lifted his hand. "I've had it with relying exclusively on secondhand reports of battle results telegraphed by the *New York Associated Press*. I want *direct reports* on our home unit's situation from someone sympathetic and with an eye for nuance. Our Cleveland-area readers are clamoring for detailed stories on their troops' performance, camp conditions, morale, things like that—and I aim to give it to them. Oh, and one other thing: your pay would double. So, what do you think, Hodge?"

David sat shell-shocked, his hands gripping the chair and his mind swirling. It should have been a ridiculously easy decision, but . . .

"He's hesitating, Bowman," Cowles muttered. "Can you please tell me why he's hesitating?"

Abel reached over and grasped David's forearm. "It's the one thing about this proposition I was afraid might prick his conscience, Mr. Cowles. Am I right, David?"

David nodded. "One thing I promised myself when I left my family and state behind: I would *never* raise my own hand against them in violence, nor would I serve in any forces that attack them."

Cowles sat back in his chair, crossed one leg over the other, and took a long pull on his cigar. "Hodge, I'd half expected you to react like that, and I won't lie to you: there are at least seven other qualified people who would crave this job, so if you don't want it, we'll survive. But there's no doubt you're the best one by far for this, so I don't want you to tell me 'absolutely not' just yet. Think about it over the weekend at the conference, then come back on Monday and give me your final decision."

"That's very gracious of you, sir," David said, relieved that Cowles had not simply decided to throw him out of the room. "And I promise I *will* give further thought to the whole situation and what taking on that position would mean for me."

"Very good. All right, I believe we're done here. That dang Lightning sounds like she's overheating again, and I'm going to check on her. Good luck at the conference, gentlemen. And come Monday morning, I'll expect you both to go full force on that recruiting ad."

On their way out of Cowles's office, David glanced quizzically at Abel. "I didn't realize *you* were going to the conference too."

Abel laughed. "Colonel Tyler wouldn't dream of preventing the most committed abolitionist on his staff—myself—from taking a short siesta from recruiting duties to enjoy the spectacle at Oberlin. What d'you say we have supper together tonight at six at the Dunham Tavern? I'll fill you in, and you can tell me all you've learned so far about Finney and Douglass."

At the end of the workday after Abel and the other correspondents had departed, Mr. Cowles walked up to David's desk with a sealed envelope in his hand. "Almost forgot to give this to you, Hodge. It arrived today at the post office, originally postmarked last August in Richmond and addressed to you. Seems this somehow got separated from one of the last batches of mail the Adams Express Company was able to smuggle across Confederate lines—just before the US government shut down all private carriers. Something you were expecting?"

David took the envelope and immediately recognized the handwriting of Pastor Horace Jones. He looked up at Cowles with a huge grin. "Not exactly expecting it, sir, but definitely glad to see it!"

Cowles retreated to his office. David tore open the envelope, his pulse racing.

August 7, 1861

Dear David,

It was wonderful to have finally received your letter dated June 3 and to hear you are safe and now settled in your new home and job with the Leader *in Cleveland. I will certainly pass your address on to your family per your request.*

I will spare you our war news; I am sure that with your newspaper connection you are receiving far more comprehensive and reliable accounts than I (albeit from a radically different perspective).

In early June, I received a letter from your sister Emma, in which she reported some very sad news concerning your family. Three weeks prior, Charles Cobb was found hanged by his neck, and although it was officially ruled a suicide, your sister is convinced that Sam Taylor was behind it. Worse, she believes your father agreed to prevent any further investigation into the matter in exchange for votes, which led to his narrowly winning the recent election. Emma is still furious with your father and also with Catherine over their lack of empathy and support in the whole matter, and she's vowing to leave home and "follow in David's footsteps" as soon as she can find the means to do so. She is determined to make a new life for herself, helping those who suffer from undeserved trauma and oppression, including advocating and working to achieve abolitionist goals. At the end of her letter, she said she was hoping to obtain my advice and perhaps even help in eventually making it through the war zones to join up with you and other similar-minded people in the North.

Two weeks ago, unbeknownst to your father, she paid my wife and me a visit at the Wheelers' farm and we spoke for over an hour. I told her I would look into certain possibilities depending on how the war situation evolves, but in the meantime, I strongly advised her to be patient and pursue her goal of helping others in ways that would not further alienate her from your family. In that regard, my wife suggested she might consider volunteering as a nursing assistant at one of the army hospitals that are now springing up in the Petersburg area. The idea seemed to interest her, and my wife and I are praying that she will follow through.

Emma also reported that your father is basically in good health, though his heart condition occasionally acts up, and that Catherine seems happy but is constantly worried about her husband Joe's safety (his unit was involved in the recent, big Manassas battle from which, thankfully, he emerged unscathed). Sadly, Emma still bears much resentment toward both of them as a result of the incident with Charles.

As I am hearing that mail will soon cease to flow across the North–South border, this may well be the last letter I'll be able to send you for some time to come. Rest assured that my own health remains sound, and that I am constantly praying for your protection and welfare. I also pray for a quick end to this war, and that we will meet again soon. I am . . .

Sincerely Yours,

Horace D. Jones

David folded the letter and returned it to the envelope. Looking around the empty, silent room, a pervasive sadness began to overwhelm him as he reflected on the tragic news about Charles and its impact on Emma.

He recalled the day he'd left them: Papa's livid indignation and rage; Emma's devastation; Cat's cold fury over his deliberate decision not to sit down and explain his reasoning to her as he had with Emma. He'd simply assumed Cat would never be capable of understanding.

"Love is patient, love is kind . . ." Pastor Jones had urged him to remember, especially when it came to Catherine.

Please, God, forgive me for judging her so severely and for leaving her so . . .

In the midst of his silent prayer, a lump rose in his throat and tears filled his eyes. He crossed his arms on top of the desk, lay his head down, and wept.

"Men are more or less guilty, according to the knowledge they have or do not have of their moral duty," thundered the Reverend Charles Grandison Finney, the innovative Christian revivalist and President of Oberlin College.

In Acts 17:30, according to Finney, the Apostle Paul had claimed that in distant Old Testament biblical times—before the arrival of Christ and the Gospel—God had "winked" at the sins of imperfectly enlightened men.

He went on: "Not in the sense of considering them absolutely guiltless, but only comparatively so. However, there is far too much moral light shed on the institution of slavery today for a Christian to admit to neutrality in regard to it, or to assume that it is not to be regarded as a great sin. And so, what is today's Christian called to do with the light we've been given? I say it is this: to vote, to speak out against the institution of slavery and laws like the Fugitive Slave Act that help sustain it, until our entire reunified country shall purge itself from every last shred of national patronage of this horrible system!"

With one accord, the entire audience in the large lecture hall rose to applaud and cheer as Reverend Finney turned to embrace Frederick Douglass, this afternoon's conference co-speaker.

Abel leaned over and spoke into David's ear, trying to make himself heard above the din. "Finney's a lion when it comes to revivalist preaching and saving souls, but I think he's far too soft on the slavery issue. We are past the point of just 'voting and speaking out' in a genteel, Christian manner. Lincoln needs to announce clearly the immediate end of all slavery *everywhere* in the land, and state that we're directing our entire war effort toward enforcing that condition. So far, he's resisted doing that. Seems he wants to use the army to bring the South back into the Union's fold, and then try to work the slavery issue out peacefully by constitutional means."

David nodded. Many credible reports were circulating about President Lincoln's hesitancy to fully embrace the most radical abolitionist vision for the Union's objective in the civil war. Lincoln's "unity-first" position was creating serious rifts within his own cabinet and even among the Union army's general staff. Still, it was a position that David himself preferred.

The audience resumed their seats as Frederick Douglass—the mixed-race social reformer and leader of the abolitionist movement in Massachusetts and New York—stepped to the lectern. Just as in his personal interview of Douglass earlier today, David was greatly impressed by the dramatic quality of the man's appearance. With his tall, imposing figure, deep-set flashing eyes, well-formed nose, and mass of unruly gray hair, it was easy to see why Douglass had acquired his reputation for commanding the awestruck attention of any audience—both friend and foe alike.

For the next hour, David sat entranced as Douglass spoke in various degrees of light and shade, his rich baritone giving an emotional vitality to every sentence. He began by delivering an emotion-packed recounting of his former life as a Maryland slave, followed by a harsh indictment of what he saw as the false religion that supported slavery:

"I love the pure, peaceable, and impartial Christianity of Christ. I therefore *hate* the corrupt, slaveholding, women-whipping, cradle-plundering, partial, and hypocritical Christianity of this land."

Douglass went on a bit longer, concluding with an unfiltered challenge to those under the impression that belief in the "Black man's inherent inferiority" was merely a "southern" problem. Even some of the Union generals, Douglass complained, seemed to support the idea that "it would inflict an intolerable wound upon the pride and spirit of White soldiers of the Union, to see the negro in the United States uniform. If you make the negro a soldier (they say), you cannot depend on his courage: a crack of his old master's whip will send him scampering in terror from the battlefield.

"But how long, I ask you, will we fail to understand? The Union cause will never prosper until this war assumes an antislavery attitude, and until the negro is enlisted to fight on the loyal side."

Abel and David rose from their seats and clapped vigorously along with the others. Abel leaned over, his mouth close to David's ear. "Now *that's* the kind of logic that gives me hope for our cause! If only Lincoln and his generals would all accept it. From what Colonel Tyler tells me, they're hopelessly divided on the issue."

David nodded. He had been hearing much the same thing from Edwin Cowles.

After Douglass's final statement and before the applause had completely died down, David grasped Abel's arm. "Come on, I want to get to our supper table before someone steals our premium seats."

"Premium? What's so special about them?" Abel asked.

David grinned. "Mr. Douglass enjoyed my morning interview with him so much that he invited me to sit at his table tonight. I told him I'd do so on condition I could drag along my favorite military sidekick—you!"

Upon entering the dining hall, David saw immediately that his supper would not be shared with the expected random assemblage of hungry conference attendees. Some of the most distinguished Oberlin students and alumni—mostly White but several Blacks as well—were already seated and engaged in animated conversation with each other, awaiting the arrival of Reverend Finney and Frederick Douglass.

"An impressive gathering of academic elites," Abel whispered as soon as the two were seated at their reserved roundtable. "Do we really belong here?"

"Just pretend you're a professor of linguistics," David joked, "and pray that your army uniform doesn't give you away."

He turned and introduced himself to the young Black woman with kind, wide-set eyes and neck-length, wavy dark hair parted in the middle; she had just been seated next to him.

"Mary Jane Patterson's my name, sir. I'm pleased to meet you."

Intrigued by her confident manner, David started to inquire politely about the woman's connections with the college when he was interrupted by a gentle hand on his shoulder.

"Did you know, Mr. Hodge, that at the end of this term, Mary Jane will be the first negro woman in our country to earn a BA degree?"

David leaped up from his seat at the sound of the familiar, baritone voice. He turned to accept Frederick Douglass's extended hand.

"No, Mr. Douglass, I wasn't aware. But given everything I've learned about Oberlin College in the past few days, I suppose I shouldn't be surprised."

Douglass smiled. "Nor should any of us. Reverend Finney certainly has good reason to be proud of this institution: first to admit women; strong advocate for universal education; active supporter of the Underground Railroad. Quite an impressive list, I'd say. Wouldn't you agree, Mary?"

"Oh, yes, sir!" Mary beamed, obviously gratified by Douglass's recognition of her unique contribution.

"I can't imagine a more appropriate location for hosting this conference," David said.

Douglass glanced around awkwardly, as if hesitant to take his seat just yet. "Mr. Hodge, I wonder if I might have a brief word with you. Mary, would you please excuse us?"

"Oh, of course, sir."

Wondering what this might be all about, David allowed Douglass to lead him to a quiet corner of the dining hall where, on one wall, a brightly colored oil painting of Christ counseling his disciples was suspended.

Douglass clasped his hands behind his back and cleared his throat. "Mr. Hodge, I hope you'll forgive my forwardness, but there was something you mentioned during our interview this morning that I've been thinking about, and I'd like to present something for your consideration."

"Mr. Douglass, I hope I didn't offend you with my questions or—"

"Oh, no!" Douglass laughed. "Nothing of the sort. It's just that I was struck by your own story, and the dilemma you're facing now about supporting the Union war effort that could end up destroying the livelihood, if not the lives, of your own family and friends. Do I have that right?"

"Yes, the prospect does weigh heavily on me," David agreed.

Douglass lifted a hand to massage his scraggly beard. "And you also said, because of that, you were reluctant to accept your editor's offer for the war correspondent position?"

"That's true. The thought of being on the front lines, having our unit overrun and being forced—even as a reporter—to pick up a rifle and put a bullet through the head of one of my fellow Virginians causes me great misgivings."

Douglass closed his eyes and nodded slowly. "David, why did you come north?"

"To do what I could as a journalist to advocate for the elimination of slavery through peaceful, legislative means." As soon as the words left his mouth, David realized for the first time the utter naiveté of his position. Douglass's response confirmed it.

"If that's still your plan, Mr. Hodge, then at this point in our national struggle, I'd strongly advise you to repack your bags and return home to your family.

"Many of my northern abolitionist friends, including William Lloyd Garrison, used to think like you: that pursuing a nonviolent, gradual legislative solution to the slavery issue was the best course. But most of them, myself included, have now come to realize that peaceable diplomacy and legislation can *never* hope to bring about the end of slavery.

That's because it's clear the southern heart has become so hardened that anything less than all-out, violent commitment aimed at immediately eradicating the root of its darkness has no hope of succeeding.

"And so, David ... to return to my original point ... if the elimination of slavery is truly your ultimate goal, then it seems to me you have no choice but to *actively* join us in this violent struggle. I know firsthand, from reading your previous articles and experiencing your interviewing skills, the magnificent gifts you could bring to this country and the cause of abolition as a frontline war correspondent. Please, I *beg* you: don't let sentimental feelings for your family and state block your passion to destroy the evil system that has corrupted us all."

David stood frozen, his mind shocked by the clarity and logic of Frederick Douglass's words. He looked up at the painting of Christ and the disciples on the wall behind and just above Douglass's head. The inscription across the bottom of the frame stood out in bold, black lettering:

> *A man's enemies will be the members of his own household ...*
> *anyone who loves their father or mother more than Me and who*
> *does not take up his cross and follow Me is not worthy of Me.*
> *—Matthew 10:36–38*

"Mr. Douglass," David said, reaching out to grasp his hand in both of his, "I do believe you've helped me make my decision."

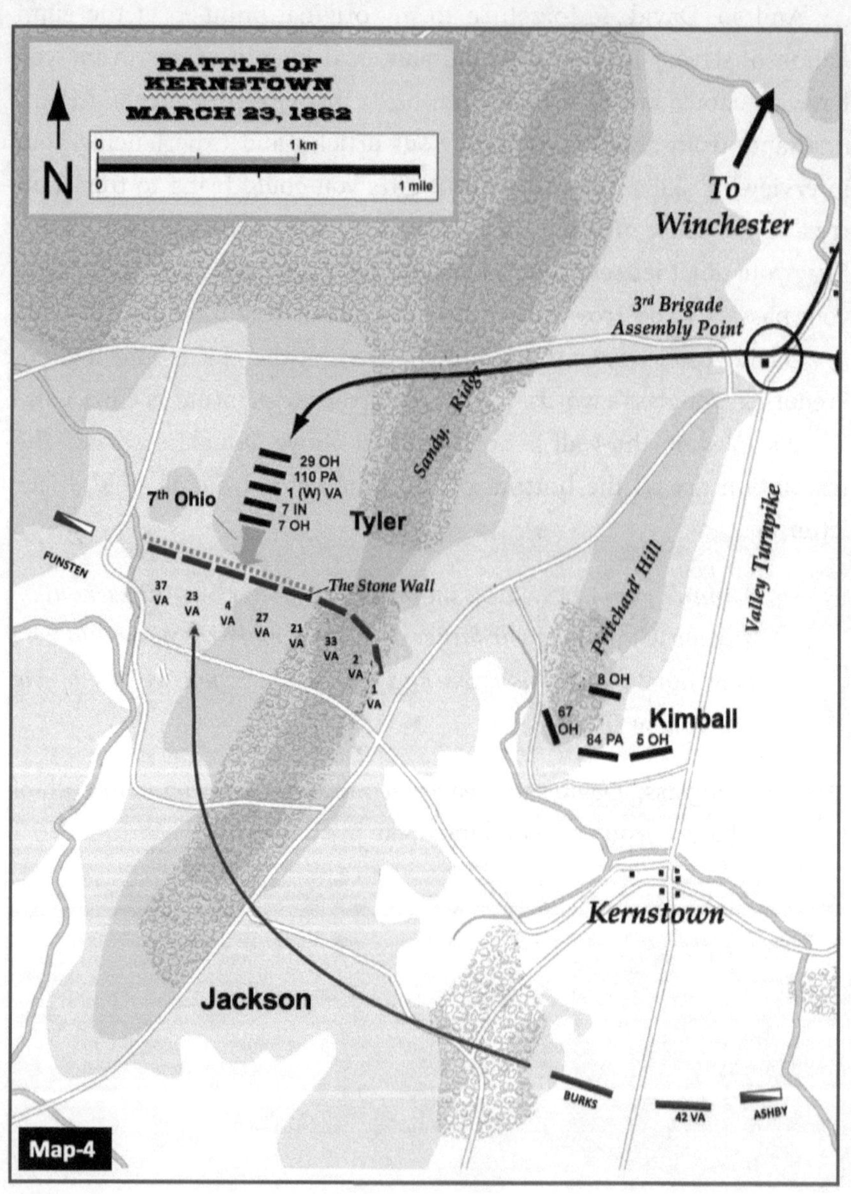

BATTLE OF KERNSTOWN
MARCH 23, 1862
N
0   1 km
0   1 mile
To Winchester
3rd Brigade Assembly Point
Sandy Ridge
29 OH
110 PA
1 (W) VA
7 IN
7 OH
7th Ohio
Tyler
The Stone Wall
FUNSTEN
37 VA
23 VA
4 VA
27 VA
21 VA
33 VA
2 VA
1 VA
Pritchard' Hill
8 OH
67 OH
84 PA
5 OH
Kimball
Valley Turnpike
Kernstown
Jackson
BURKS
42 VA
ASHBY
Map-4

CHAPTER 15

Shenandoah Valley Turnpike, South of Winchester, Virginia
March 23, 1862

The sporadic belching of cannon fire from the two Union artillery batteries on Pritchard's Hill—just north of the small village of Kernstown—had turned into a near continuous, pounding roar.

It could only mean one thing, David knew: the 7th Ohio Regiment commander's prediction was correct. Some of Stonewall Jackson's men were now making their move to flank the hill and cut off the large Union force in that area from retreating north to the safety of Winchester. If Jackson succeeded, Winchester and the entire Shenandoah Valley could soon be in Confederate hands. And if *that* happened, the Union's capital defenses around Washington, DC would face great peril.

The 7th's objective was simple and clear: help stop the rebels cold in their tracks on top of nearby Sandy Ridge. The race to get there first was now nearing the finish line.

Sitting astride his horse between Lieutenant Abel Bowman and the 7th Ohio's Company L commander, Captain White, David tried to keep his hand from shaking as he recorded in his notebook his impressions of the tense scene unfolding around him. He knew these were exactly the kind of detailed "battlefield reporting" tidbits that Edwin Cowles would be expecting from David Hodge—the *Cleveland Leader*'s first dedicated war correspondent.

Abel turned in his saddle to observe the mass of blue-uniformed 7th Ohio infantrymen pressing forward all around through the dense, leafless woods atop the ridgeline. "I'd give a thousand bucks to see the look on those reb faces when they finally see what's about to hit 'em."

"I would too, assuming they don't already know we're coming," David said worriedly.

Abel grinned. "Have no fear of *that*, David. Even if they do know, which I seriously doubt, the way Tyler's set this whole operation up, they won't be able to stop us."

Indeed, David thought, it seemed like a solid plan. Colonel Tyler, now the overall 3rd Brigade commander, had deployed his regiments in an unusual attack formation—one behind the other—intending to quickly thrust through the approaching rebel force on a narrow front and overwhelm them with wave after wave of reinforcements. Seventh Ohio Regiment, now under Lieutenant Colonel William Creighton's command, would act as the point of the spear, attacking in three successive eighty-yard-wide lines. Company L would comprise the center of the third line.

David locked his gaze on one of the company's infantrymen passing beside him. Like the others in the regiment, the man carried all the standard-issue equipment: blanket roll on top of a back-borne leather knapsack containing extra clothing and personal items; canvas haversack with shoulder strap storing four days of rations; belt-attached tin canteen, bayonet scabbard, percussion cap box, and cartridge box holding forty rounds of ammunition. Not to mention the .69 caliber Springfield Model 1816 musket with 42-inch barrel and purported effective firing range up to two hundred yards. No one could claim the Union army was failing to equip its soldiers well. By comparison, according to Abel, the rebel soldiers encountered by the 7th in earlier encounters were severely lacking in quality weaponry and equipment.

The more David considered the logic behind Colonel Tyler's attack plan and the impressively equipped troops charged with executing it, the more Abel's confidence did not seem misplaced.

"*Messenger coming!*" yelled one of the men several yards ahead. Crashing through the woods at breakneck speed and scattering all in his path, Lieutenant Johnson—Colonel Tyler's aide—headed straight for Captain White. He pulled up and saluted smartly, then spoke with White briefly before saluting again and spurring his horse on toward his next stop farther back in the column.

Captain White turned toward Abel and David, his eyes seemingly on the verge of popping out of his head. "A couple hundred yards ahead, we'll hit a large clearing that's split in the middle by a long stone wall. Seems a few advance skirmishers from the rebs' famous 'Stonewall Brigade' have already reached it. Colonel Tyler wants us to take it before the rest of Jackson's boys arrive.

"Bowman, order our men to advance on the run to the edge of the clearing and stack up close behind the first two lines of the regiment. Tell 'em to throw off their blankets and haversacks and prepare to charge the wall on Creighton's signal. I'll ride on ahead to confirm things with Creighton and Tyler and will meet you when you arrive." He wheeled his steed and dashed off toward the front.

Abel chuckled and shook his head. "How about *that*, Mr. Hodge? At last, my friend, you're about to get a taste of what my Company L 'glory-chasers' have been dealing with these past few months. And your first assignment as our battle reporter will be watching us take a stone wall away from the great Stonewall himself! We'll need to find you a nice, safe place to record your observations."

"Just show me where you want me to sit, and I'll be glad to get out of your way, Lieutenant," David said, his jocular response at odds with the wild throbbing of his heart at the prospect of what lay ahead.

Within ten minutes of Abel's communication of Captain White's orders, the men of Company L crouched in position at the clearing's edge behind the first two lines of 7th Ohio soldiers. David peered from behind a thick tree trunk at the open field stretched before them. It was a nearly perfect position to witness in relative safety the impending charge across about two hundred yards of slightly rising no-man's-land. The stone wall at the top of the rise still appeared sparsely manned, with only a few musket barrels poking over the ledge at wide intervals.

"*It's ripe for the taking, boys!*" Colonel Tyler called out to all within earshot. "Lieutenant Colonel Creighton, send out the skirmish line, then begin your advance once they're halfway across."

Creighton, now dismounted and standing at woods' edge, drew his saber.

"Seventh Ohio, fix bayonets! Skirmishers, move out now. Company commanders, prepare to advance on my signal, full charge. Keep your lines straight!"

David wiped his brow. Even as a noncombatant, the tension of the moment was so great he could hardly breathe or swallow. He peered a few yards down the line and spotted Abel, who, together with Captain White, was moving from man to man in Company L, clapping each on the shoulder and speaking a word of encouragement.

Catching Abel's eye, David placed his hand over his heart. He nodded and smiled grimly, then mouthed the words: *God be with you, my friend.* Abel grinned back, drew his pistol from his holster, and touched the barrel to the leather visor of his cap in mock salute.

The skirmish line advanced to the halfway point, drawing a few scattered shots from the rebels behind the stone wall that managed to drop only two men. The sergeant in command of the skirmishers turned and waved to the poised 7th troops. Safe to advance.

David breathed a sigh of relief. This might all be over in five minutes. But then, he thought, what would he have to write about?

Creighton raised his sword above his head. "Looks like no one's home over there, men. Let's take that wall fast!" He lowered the sword and pointed it across the clearing. "Move out . . . *now!*"

The 7th Ohio soldiers rose with a resounding cheer. One by one, the three lines emerged from the woods at twenty-yard intervals and began their full-out charge—an unstoppable tidal wave of blue.

David stood, no longer content to remain behind and miss out completely on the actual experience of rushing the lightly defended wall. No question, his own participation would make for an even more exciting and authentic newspaper story. Checking the woods behind, he saw the first troops of the next regiment in 3rd Brigade's column— the 7th Indiana—approaching rapidly. Once they all stacked up around him at the woods' edge, waiting for their own call to advance, it would be too late to join the Ohioans. If he was going to make his move, now was the time.

Pocketing his notebook and pulling his pistol from its holster, he bolted out of the woods toward Abel's unit in the center of the third line fifty yards ahead.

A sudden flash of light in a narrow gap in the stone wall straight ahead— followed almost immediately by a loud boom—caused him to freeze. Seconds later, a cannonball whizzed past his head and smashed into the trunk of a small tree behind him, snapping it in two.

Don't stop, keep running!

Seconds later, two strange-looking objects tumbled toward him, both coming to rest only a few feet away. The first was a human head, its blue soldier's forage cap still attached by the chin strap; the second a bloody, shattered arm, severed at the shoulder. David gasped and froze in place, staring incredulously as the horror of the grotesque sight began to slowly register in his brain.

The respite was short-lived. Up ahead, the stone wall along its entire length transformed suddenly into a crackling curtain of noise, flame, and smoke from the muskets of countless rebel soldiers. The vast majority must have been crouched behind the wall, awaiting the right moment to rise up in unison and blast the charging Union lines at close range.

Scores of minié balls thudded into the earth all around. David flung himself to the ground and began crawling toward the Company L soldiers, who, like all the others in the regiment, were now pinned down, absorbing the Confederates' withering fire with only isolated attempts to return it. At least a dozen men in the regiment's first two lines had been hit by the rebel musket volleys; five were motionless, and two others were writhing and screaming out in pain.

David spotted Abel just ahead, kneeling and firing his pistol at the devil knew who or what along the stone wall. He crept toward him, arriving at the same moment that Abel exhausted the revolver's chamber.

Pausing to reload, Abel did a double-take at his first sight of David lying on the ground next to him. "What in Lucifer's hell are you doing out here?"

David smiled weakly, his body still trembling from the shock of his first exposure to the human carnage of war. "Couldn't resist the thrill, I suppose."

"Well, you'll have all you want of *that* from here on. Looks like we're up against the entire Stonewall Brigade—all five regiments. Battery of artillery too. Their fire's converging on our front and both flanks. If we get stuck here, we're—"

A bullet knocked off Abel's cap and grazed the side of his head, prompting a fit of vile cursing the likes of which David suspected would have caused the devil himself to flinch.

Finally gaining control of himself, Abel reached into his pocket, pulled out a cloth bandana, and tied it around his head. He stared at David, his eyes blazing and a drop of blood trickling down his cheek. His whole face glowed with the same rapturous expression that David had observed the first time they'd met two and a half years ago— minutes before the execution of John Brown.

"It's not going to end like this, David," he said softly. "Glory won't allow it."

Abel stood, drew his saber, and began walking forward—straight into the teeth of the rebel dragon.

7th Ohio Regiment Heroism Sparks Union Victory
Kernstown, Virginia
March 24, 1862

Today at 3:00 P.M., Colonel Nathan Kimball—Acting Commander of 1st Division, V Corps, Army of the Potomac—announced to all assembled brigade and regiment commanders that further pursuit of rebel forces under the command of General Stonewall Jackson has been temporarily halted in the wake of their resounding defeat and retreat from the Winchester area in the face of bold Union army tactics and overwhelming force.

Colonel Kimball explicitly recognized the key role played by the 3rd Infantry Brigade commanded by Colonel E. Tyler in breaking the back of rebel resistance. After a fiercely contested two-hour standoff yesterday afternoon on Sandy Ridge, northwest of Kernstown, Tyler's brigade succeeded in exhausting the ammunition of the Confederate defenders entrenched behind a massive stone wall traversing the top of the ridge. The final charge, led by the Cleveland-based 7th Ohio Regiment, tore through the rebel lines at the wall's center, setting off a panicked retreat of the famous Stonewall Brigade and forcing another rebel brigade on their flank to quickly follow. By noon today, scouts reported that all of Jackson's units had fled south toward Staunton to lick their wounds and regroup. First Division, meanwhile, has been ordered by V Corps' overall commander—Major General Nathaniel Banks—to stand down from further engagement until reinforcements arrive.

The price of victory was high: 118 Union soldiers (20 from the 7th Ohio) lost their lives, with nearly four times those numbers wounded. But despite the losses, Colonel Kimball expressed immense pride at the heroic performance of 1st Division and gave special mention to the brave actions of one of the 7th Ohio's own: 1st Lieutenant Abel Bowman of Company L.

With the bulk of the regiment pinned down by intense fire from two rebel batteries protected by the wall, Lt. Bowman—armed only with his saber—personally charged one of the batteries, inspiring twenty other Ohioans to leap up and follow his lead. Fierce hand-to-hand fighting ensued, with the southern artillerymen being either killed or driven off and their brass cannon turned to fire on their comrades. This was one of several actions that helped to turn the tide and prepare the way for the final decisive charge. Bowman's action was lauded as exemplary, not only by the men who followed him, but by his superior officers who witnessed it.

Colonel Kimball said it is efforts like those yesterday of Lt. Bowman and the rest of the 7th Ohio that have given Major General Banks great confidence in V Corps' ability to maintain control of the Shenandoah Valley, thus protecting the westward approaches to our nation's capital while permitting other Union army units to press their attack on Richmond.

David S. Hodge,
Correspondent

"What do you think?" David asked the burly Company L sergeant, whom he'd just asked to review the draft article before he submitted it for review and approval by 1st Division headquarters. This being his first report as the *Leader*'s war correspondent, he wanted it to reflect well on the spirit displayed by *all* the men of the 7th Ohio—even though he'd singled out Abel for special mention. "Does it exaggerate Lieutenant Bowman's role?"

The sergeant handed the sheet of paper back to David, folded his arms, and leaned back against one of the rotting logs surrounding the company's campfire—one of dozens now dotting the nighttime landscape of hills and fields around Kernstown. He snorted and spat to the side. "It speaks well of our regiment, but if anything, I'd say it *understates* what the lieutenant did."

David nodded. "I wish I could include more about Bowman's contribution in the article, but they'll only allow me limited space in the newspaper column. But at any rate, seems the lieutenant has definitely earned his press in the eyes of his men. That's what I was trying to confirm. Thanks to you and the others I've talked to, I'm now comfortable sending this on."

As he started to walk toward Captain White's tent to inform him that the article was now ready for division headquarters review, a gruff voice called out from behind.

"He *enjoyed* it."

David stopped in his tracks and turned to see another one of the Company L men—a fortyish-looking corporal—resting against the log a short distance from the sergeant, arms behind his head. The man's forage cap was tilted so low as to nearly cover his eyes.

David approached cautiously and knelt on the other side of the soldier, out of earshot from the others around the campfire. "Excuse me, sir?" he asked quietly.

The corporal kept staring straight ahead, a smug smile on his lips. "Heard you gabbin' with the others here about your article, and just wanted to offer one more opinion. He enjoyed it. I seen men kill out of necessity and desire to save themselves or others. But I also seen the look on Bowman's face when he took out those five Johnnies tryin' to defend their precious cannon . . . slashin' and cuttin' away left and right, up and down. His eyes all lit up and whoopin' and laughin' like he was a wild hyena, slayin' the devil himself fifty times over and lovin' every second of it. Yep, he definitely enjoyed it. Maybe you'd like to mention *that* in your article?"

David shifted uncomfortably. This was not quite the clean image of 7th Ohio "heroism" that he wished to convey to the *Leader*'s readers, nor was it the picture of his friend Abel's bold, selfless action that he wanted to retain in his own mind.

He stood and tipped his cap. "Not sure I have the space in my article to include all the perspectives on Lieutenant Bowman's actions, Corporal. But I do appreciate hearing yours, and maybe I'll have a chance to interview you along with some of the others in a future article if my editor will give me the go-ahead."

"Sounds fine to me, Mr. Hodge. And regarding Lieutenant Bowman, I'm not tryin' to spoil his well-deserved publicity. I'm just sayin': there's something powerful inside that man that can drive him to excess, and I'm not sure where it's gonna take him next."

David resumed his walk toward Captain White's tent, eager to pass off the corporal's strange observation as nothing more than the delusional impressions of a battle-fatigued subordinate.

His report on the Battle of Kernstown and Abel Bowman's heroism would stand as is.

CHAPTER 16

Petersburg, Virginia
April 25, 1862

As she turned the corner and started down the street leading to the Confederate military hospital on Bollingbrook Street, Emma looked up and scowled at the lowering early morning clouds. *Again?* The previous two rain-soaked days had dampened her spirits somewhat, and she wasn't eager for the trend to continue.

Suddenly she pulled up short and grimaced in pain. Once again, as would happen occasionally, the sharp jabbing sensation in her shin just below her left knee was acting up. She reached down to massage the area, silently chiding herself for dawdling when she knew that two blocks away men were writhing in pain and agony, awaiting her comforting presence.

A well-dressed, elderly gentleman with a cane who was passing by in the opposite direction paused and lifted his hat. "May I assist you, ma'am?"

She lifted her head and blushed. "Oh, thank you . . . but no, sir. I was just walking to the hospital where I'm a nursing assistant, and I experienced a small twinge in my leg as I do occasionally. But it seems fine now."

The man smiled. "Well, then, don't let me hold you up. There's no higher calling than the caring service that you and other young ladies like yourself are providing to our gallant, wounded soldiers."

Emma beamed. "Thank you, sir. It is truly an honor, I must say."

The gentleman tipped his hat again and moved on as Emma resumed her limp-impaired walk toward the hospital. After three halting steps, a ray of sun peeked through the clouds, bringing a smile to her face—an expression more in line with the way she'd been feeling about her life lately. Indeed, it seemed as if she had, at long last, found her true calling . . .

She had first broached the idea of the nursing job to Papa soon after her clandestine visit with Pastor Jones and his wife last July. With her intense anger at her father and sister now under at least a modicum of control following her prayers with Pastor Jones, she'd approached her father calmly but firmly.

She was almost twenty years old, she had argued. She'd been allowed only a few very limited excursions beyond the plantation property following her outburst at Papa's reaction to Charles Cobb's hanging last May. She had served her sentence and now deserved a chance to experience life beyond the plantation. And although she understood that her father's natural inclination was to see her spending her time and energy attracting admiring gentlemen of means and preparing for marriage, that was simply not her priority right now. Courting and marriage could wait—especially with the war closing in and the Confederate army's recruiting efforts resulting in a decreasing availability of eligible young men. For now, she had but one driving wish: to devote herself to relieving the suffering and improving the lot in life of others less fortunate.

After days of deliberation, Papa had finally agreed that it might be a good and noble thing for Emma to take on the hospital effort, since it would keep her physically well engaged during these emotionally stressing times and would faithfully serve the cause for which all true

Virginians were fighting. Besides that—he'd suggested to Emma's silent annoyance—caring for wounded soldiers would help her to realize that *all* suffering souls were deserving of her Christian compassion and concern, not just the family's slaves.

Papa's approval had been sealed when Emma informed him that Miss Dora Lewis—a forty-five-year-old friend of Pastor Jones's wife, who was also one of the hospital's administrators—had spoken with the chief physician and received his enthusiastic consent for Emma to work there. Obviously, training would have to take place on the job in view of severe staff shortages and the constantly increasing numbers of patients. But she would learn quickly by observing and assisting the other nurses and doctors on their rounds.

In early September, Emma had begun her weekly routine: Tuesday mornings, Ben would drive her into the city to the hospital where she would work the day shift on Tuesday through Thursday until 4:00 P.M. In the evenings, she would stay with Miss Lewis, who had graciously offered her a free room and meals at the house that she shared with her elderly mother near the hospital. Early Friday mornings, Ben would arrive to escort her back to the plantation for the weekend.

During their first aftersupper conversation, Emma had learned that Dora Lewis's personal interests and passions extended far beyond hospital administration and charity work. In fact, if Papa had been fully aware of these, it was highly unlikely he would have approved the midweek boarding arrangement.

A Petersburg native, Miss Lewis revealed that in her late teens she had been sent by her parents to be educated at a Quaker boarding school for girls in Philadelphia. She'd been exposed to strong abolitionist sentiment and thinking there, for which she herself had acquired great empathy. And although she was a staunch believer in the right of the southern states to defend themselves against armed invasion by the North, she could never bring herself to accept that chattel slavery was acceptable in the eyes of God.

Miss Lewis had then listened patiently as Emma confided her own personal story, including her continuing resentment of her father's callous attitude toward protecting the family slaves from abuse and her own frustrated impulse to escape the plantation and flee north to take up the abolitionist cause like her brother.

"Emma," Miss Lewis had gently suggested, "trying to rush north on your own, with no real plan or contacts or even the skills needed to support yourself there, will only lead to destitution. You have to discipline the passion that our Lord has placed on your heart. If the abolitionist call is truly in you, as it apparently was for your brother David, you need to pray and wait for the clear circumstances and support that God will provide to begin taking you down that path. In the meantime, you should learn everything you can from those who have gone before you."

"But how do I 'learn' from them?" Emma had protested. "I can't meet them and talk with them. The famous abolitionists are all in the northern states, aren't they?"

"Why, Emma," Miss Lewis had gently chided her, "how do you go about learning *anything* from someone you admire when you can't speak with them or experience life directly with them? By reading something that they've written, of course!"

It was at that point that Miss Lewis had revealed her true inner convictions. Rising from the dining table, she'd walked into her bedroom and returned a few moments later, presenting Emma with a leather-covered document pouch. "I think you'll find this will provide some profitable bedtime reading during the evenings you stay here," she'd said.

After Emma retired to her room, her hands had trembled with excitement as she opened the pouch to discover an untitled manuscript of the now-famous *Uncle Tom's Cabin* by Harriet Beecher Stowe, along with a short biography and some printed speeches and writings of a fascinating woman named Angelina Grimké.

Born and raised on a wealthy South Carolina plantation in the early 1800s, Angelina—after witnessing the horrible whipping of a young slave by her older brother—had committed her life to the cause of abolition. But deciding that she couldn't fight slavery while living in the South among White slaveowners, she'd moved to Philadelphia at the age of twenty-one with her sister Sarah. Within ten years, in the face of great opposition and intimidation, the two had become nationally published writers and speakers for the causes of abolition and the women's suffrage movement—the only southern White women so far to do so.

The more Emma had delved into Grimké's antislavery writings—especially excerpts from her *Appeal to the Christian Women of the South*—the more she became convinced in her heart: *this* was the kind of consequential, bold, Christ-honoring woman she wanted to model her own life after. Over the following months, she'd spent her evenings at Miss Lewis's reading and journaling her own personal experiences and thoughts on slavery, abolition, and the role of women in society.

Last night after supper, she'd shared some of her writing with Miss Lewis for the first time. After reading the first ten pages, Miss Lewis had removed her spectacles and stared at Emma with arched eyebrows. Emma had held her breath, preparing herself for nothing more than some insincere, patronizing remark about the nice quality of her writing style.

"Miss Hodge, where have you been hiding?" Miss Lewis had asked sternly.

"I-I don't understand . . . where have I been . . . *hiding*?"

"Emma, this is absolutely magnificent! Not only is the content of your writing original and insightful, but your grasp and interpretation of the facts, your depth of belief, and your ability to inspire the reader to want to hear more from you on these urgent subjects are outstanding. Dear, you simply cannot hide your passion and talent for this much longer. Somehow, we have to find you a suitable outlet. The world needs to hear from you—at least that part of the world that's willing to listen."

Afterward, lying in bed but unable to sleep, Emma had tossed and turned as she mulled over Miss Lewis's reaction to her writings and the implications.

One thing, at least, was clear: God had opened up a fresh and exciting new path in her life. Volunteering to tend wounded Confederate soldiers was a major, character-building first step along that path, but it would certainly not be the last.

On her way to the hospital's recovery ward, Emma blanched at the overpowering stench of putrid wounds, festering sores, and carbolic acid disinfectant emanating from the open doorway to the first-floor operating facility.

"God Almighty, please . . . help me . . . make them stop . . . no . . . no!"

They were much the same words, the same pitiable cry for salvation from the excruciating pain of an arm or leg amputation that Emma had heard at least a hundred times since joining the hospital's staff last September.

As always, the gruesome sights and sounds of the wounded Confederate soldiers from the recent fighting on the Virginia Peninsula assaulted her senses, but she couldn't let them interfere with the peaceful, congenial demeanor she knew her assigned patients would be expecting of her.

Trying her best to ignore the hideous groanings, she struggled up the staircase to the second-floor recovery room while balancing on one arm a tray containing a bowl of water, several folded linen cloths, and a small-print pocket Bible. At the far end of the ward, she spotted the eighteen-year-old private waving to her from his bed. She waved back and began walking toward him down the narrow aisle between the rows of beds and makeshift cots lining both sides of the crowded room. She tried her best to maintain a dignified bearing, avoiding too much acknowledgment of the many appreciative smiles and occasional leers flashed her way by the recovering soldiers—most of whom had been starved for months of female affection, gratification, or both.

Reaching the private's bed, she placed the tray on a small stool and sat on the edge of his bed, taking the hand of his sole remaining arm in both of hers while pretending not to be fazed by the chorus of good-natured hoots and whistles that arose from a few nearby onlookers.

She regarded him coyly, a twinkle in her eye. "Good morning, Private Baker. My, it sounds as if some of the men on this ward have improved enough to warrant their immediate return to the battlefield. Shall we count you among their number—seeing as how much better you seem to be looking and feeling today?"

Travis Baker was undoubtedly her favorite patient of the twelve assigned to her on the ward. A roguishly handsome, blue-eyed, sandy-haired farm boy from southwestern Virginia, he was polite and kind-spoken. And yet—as Emma had quickly discovered—he was also a natural flirt and ladies' man. Not by any means the usual qualities she found herself attracted to in young gentlemen, but in this case, there was something strangely compelling in his looks and teasing way of conversing that she found nearly impossible to resist.

"Only reason I'm lookin' and feelin' so perky today, Miss Emma, is because I woke up rememberin' I had by far the nicest, prettiest nurse on this whole ward comin' to take care of me. And now here she is!"

Emma laughed, blushing at the compliment but privately thrilled to imagine that he'd meant it. "I'm sure every nurse who takes care of you here receives the exact same adulation, Private Baker. But still, I'm very grateful for your kind words." She gently returned his hand to his lap, picked up one of the linen cloths, and dabbed it into the bowl of water. "Here, let's take a look at your wound."

With one hand, she carefully unfastened the clip and unwrapped the bandage covering the end of the stump of his right arm. It had been amputated two weeks ago just above the elbow, chloroform having been administered through a cloth placed over the nose and mouth to help ease the agonizing pain. Now, everything seemed to be healing well. "Just some dried blood around the sutures, Travis. I'll wipe it off, then we'll apply a clean new cloth and wrap it with the bandage again until the surgeon comes by to examine it more closely."

Travis stared morosely at the stump. "I reckon my fightin' days are over. Not even sure how I'll be able to help Pa out on the farm, pitchin' hay and all. Least till I can get me one of those new wood and metal prosthetic arms everybody's been talkin' about. And even then . . ." His voice trailed off.

"Travis, you mustn't give up hope," Emma said tenderly as she rewrapped the wound. "You're young and strong, and I have absolutely no doubt the Lord will help you learn to work effectively in your new condition—in ways that, right now, you would never dream to be possible."

Travis gazed at her, his eyes glistening. "You really think so, ma'am?"

She smiled and placed her hand over his once again. "I *know* so, Private Baker. Now, it's my turn to be inspired. While we're waiting for your supper to arrive, I want you to finish that story about how you and your unit helped fool the Yankees at Yorktown."

Actually, Travis had regaled her with the full story at least three times already. But he never seemed to recall or care that he was repeating himself, and Emma knew it was the best way to get his mind off his own plight. Besides, his hilarious way of describing the strange battle—and his own obviously exaggerated role in it—never failed to make her laugh to the point of tears.

". . . And so, Miss Emma," he concluded after describing how General Magruder had completely hoodwinked General McClellan's Army of the Potomac by conspicuously parading Travis's unit and others back and forth behind their own defenses near Yorktown, "all our marchin' made the Yank scouts who were observin' us think they were facin' a much superior Confederate force. So, you know what those dolts did?"

Emma barely managed to suppress a giggle. "Why, no . . . but I'm expecting you're about to inform me."

"They settled in and brought up their heavy cannon, thinkin' they needed to soften us up before layin' down a big frontal assault. But General Magruder fooled 'em again, ma'am!"

"How was that, Travis?" Emma asked, her eyes wide in feigned anticipation.

"The night before the Yank attack was supposed to begin, General Magruder sent me and thirty other boys from my unit to conduct a little reconnaissance raid around their left flank. Scared 'em into thinkin' they were gettin' cut off, so they called off their whole morning attack. And they've been hunkered down to this day tryin' to decide what to do next while Magruder keeps reinforcin' our own position. That's how I lost my precious limb—took a minié ball in my forearm from a Yank sharpshooter while we were escapin' back to our lines after the raid. Yep, sacrificed my best arm so that others might live!"

Emma's hands flew to her heart as she tried to contain her mirth. "Oh, Travis, that is one of the boldest—"

A gruff laugh from the one-legged, grizzled soldier lying on the bed next to Travis expressed the obvious. "Baker, that tale gets ten feet taller every time you tell it! Just last time, you told the pretty lady here you got hit by a stray shot when you was stayin' back, bravely guardin' one of our cannons while the others went out on the raid. So . . . which is it?"

Travis's face turned beet red. "Why don't you just shut up, Anderson? You don't know nothin'. From what I heard, you were—"

"*Gentlemen, please!*" Emma broke in. "Both of you are heroes in my eyes, and there's no need to challenge each other anymore."

Travis grunted and lay his head back on his pillow. "Sorry, Miss Emma. Guess I'm just a little on edge lately. Been here too long. Wanna go home and see my family."

"You know the doctor said that'll happen in less than a week now, Travis, if you continue to improve. How about if I read you some psalms to help put you in a better frame of mind?"

"That'd be just fine, ma'am. I really love it when you read those to me."

Emma reached for her pocket Bible and was about to start reading the Twenty-third Psalm—Travis's favorite—when he suddenly sat up straight. "Scuse me, Miss Emma—supper's here! Good, I'm hungrier than a bear. Bring it over here, Jeremiah!"

The thin, thirteen-year-old Black boy edged between the beds and stood next to Travis, holding a tray with a bowl of stew and some hardtack biscuits. Travis shifted slightly and patted the side of the bed opposite Emma. "No need to stand, Jeremiah . . . just sit down here beside me, put that tray on my lap, and keep me company while Miss Emma here reads us some psalms."

Jeremiah glanced around warily, clearly not wanting to create a stir. No one seemed to be taking notice. "You sho' it's all right, sir?"

"After all you've done to tend to me these past three weeks? 'Course I'm sure. If anybody deserves to sit on this bed with me besides Miss Emma, it's you. Come on, sit right here."

Jeremiah sat down awkwardly and carefully placed the tray on Travis's lap. After waiting for Emma to say grace, Travis picked up the spoon with his left hand and began slurping away at the piping hot stew.

"Miss Emma," Travis said between swallows, "did you know Jeremiah and I have somethin' real important in common?"

Emma stared at him. "I must admit I didn't know that, Private Baker."

Travis winked at Jeremiah. "We both think catfishin' is the greatest Sunday activity God ever invented—except for church, of course. Jeremiah, tell Miss Emma about that time you and your brother were standin' on the edge of the bank and that big ole cat took hold of your line."

Jeremiah started the story haltingly, but soon his eyes widened and his whole face lit up. Emma and Travis couldn't contain their laughter as Jeremiah began swinging his arms in an animated demonstration of his unexpected tumble into the stream and its chaotic aftermath.

"I swear, Jeremiah," Travis said after finally gathering his wits, "if I ever get outta this place alive, I'm gonna come get you and we're gonna go down to Tyler's Creek just off the Appomattox. You ain't never seen catfish the size they got there. Tell you what. Since I got only one arm now, you can stand on the edge of the bank while I hold on to your belt from behind to keep you from gettin' yanked in. How's that sound?"

Jeremiah laughed. "That sound mighty fine, sir. I know I'd like that a lot."

Emma gazed admiringly at Travis. The young man had grown up on a small farm with no slaves. The results showed in the natural, affectionate, brotherly way he had just treated Jeremiah, and Emma loved what she had just seen.

"What's going on here?"

The unwelcome, strident voice of Major Theodore Steele—medical officer in charge of the recovery ward—caused Emma to freeze. Jeremiah jumped up from the bed, his thigh accidentally striking the edge of the meal tray and causing the hot stew to spill all over Travis's chest and arm stump. Travis yelped in pain.

Major Steele, who had been standing in the rear doorway with his ledger of patient recovery checklists, strode toward Travis's bed. He stared at the mess that Emma was now trying to help clean up, then leveled his gaze at Jeremiah. Emma held her breath, as she knew from personal experience of Steele's explosive temper and his intolerance of the slightest sign of carelessness on the part of his staff.

"You know how much effort went into sewing and cleaning up that wound, boy?"

Jeremiah stood with his head down, too embarrassed and afraid to look at Major Steele, who'd now moved directly in front of him.

"Y-Yes, sir, I know a lotta hard work went into that."

"Then why'd you go pour that hot stew all over it?"

"It's all right, sir," Travis interjected. "I know he didn't mean it."

"*Quiet, Private!*" Steele roared. He put his ledger down on the bed. "I'll handle this. Answer me, boy."

"I-I don't know. I sorry, sir. I sure didn't mean to hurt Private Baker."

"That so? Well, you did. You know why? Because you weren't doing your job. I saw you from the door, sitting on the edge of the private's bed, laughing and joking like some kind of circus clown. Is that how I taught you to serve meals to the patients here? Now look at me. I said, *look at me!*"

Jeremiah raised his head slowly, tears in his eyes.

"Sir," Travis pleaded, "it was all *my* fault . . . I asked him to—"

"Private, I'm not telling you again. You don't know what I have to put up with every single day, dealing with these slackers. Now stay out of this." Steele turned back to face Jeremiah. His face twitched with rage. "I've a mind to cuff you right here and now, boy. If it weren't for the lady here, I'd probably do so. As it is, I'm ordering three lashes for you tonight from the quartermaster. Hopefully that'll help teach you to pay more attention to your duties. Now take the private's tray and get out of here."

Emma felt the bile rise in her throat as she watched Jeremiah pick up the tray and walk quickly down the aisle past the recovering soldiers, many of whom had witnessed what had just happened.

She could not let this pass. "Major Steele, sir, there was no call for that," she said softly, but loud enough for those nearby to hear. "It was an accident."

Steele glared at her. "Miss Hodge, please come with me." Before she could protest, he grasped her firmly by the elbow and escorted her out to the small hallway behind the rear door.

Releasing her arm, he whirled to face her. "Who do you think you are, questioning my actions in front of my patients? Miss Hodge, you truly have shown outstanding skill and compassion as an assistant nurse. But have you suddenly become the expert on the management and discipline of my entire recovery ward support staff?"

From previous experience facing Major Steele's wrath over some perceived tiny error on her part, Emma knew she should just hang her head in abject humiliation and beg for pardon and mercy. This time, though, something inside her would not allow it. "No, sir, but I do consider myself enough of a human being to know when I see unjust punishment being directed at a young boy who clearly didn't deserve it."

Major Steele stood silently for several moments, his jaw twitching.

"Miss Hodge, I've only one thing to say to you. If you can't accept my decisions and orders without it causing significant harm to your 'humanity,' then maybe it's time for you to leave your position here and go back to life on your nice, comfortable plantation."

Hot tears of indignation, hurt, and anger welled up in Emma's eyes. "Indeed, maybe it *is* time, sir." She untied the knot of her nurses' gown, then crumpled it up and thrust it against Major Steele's chest before turning away and walking deliberately down the stairwell.

The next morning, Emma sat anxiously on the porch steps of Miss Lewis's house, waiting for Ben to appear in the carriage. She wondered how she would present the news of her "firing" to Papa. Despite Miss Lewis's strong words of encouragement and commendation for the stand that she'd taken in Jeremiah's defense, she had cried all night, agonizing over the loss of her job and the patients she had come to love, as well as the bleak prospects for anything worthwhile to replace them. And while Miss Lewis had kindly offered to speak with the hospital's chief physician about the unfortunate situation, she'd admitted that it could well take some time and there was no guarantee he would agree to override Major Steele's opposition.

Emma sighed and peered down the street, just in time to spot Ben rounding the corner in the driver's seat of the carriage.

Something did not seem right; Ben seemed to be spurring the horse forward far more urgently that usual.

Ben pulled up in front of the house and jumped off the seat.

"Hello, Ben," Emma said as she stood to greet him. "Why the hurry?"

Ben took his hat off and approached her. His face had a frightened look.

"I'm sorry, Miss Em. Dorothy saw Master sittin' in the livin' room this morning. He was real pale, and his head was droopin' to the side. Looked like he was in a daze, and when he tried to talk, didn't make no sense. We called for Dr. Haynes, and he's with him now. He said come get you and bring you back quick as I can."

Emma felt as if her mind had left her body, as if she were observing Ben speaking to someone else. In the space of less than a day, her entire world had turned upside down.

CHAPTER 17

Hodge Family Plantation
May 15, 1862

Lawrence Hodge stood in front of the parlor fireplace, elbow resting on the mantle and right hand gripping his second bourbon of the morning.

Papa looks like he's aged fifty years over the past three days, Emma thought worriedly as she watched him lift the half-full glass to his lips, raise his head, and drain the rest of its contents in one long pull. She glanced across the room at Catherine, wondering if she was thinking the same thing.

Dr. Haynes had said yesterday that although Papa seemed to have recovered fully from the mild stroke he'd suffered three weeks ago, his chronic heart condition was still an issue. Haynes had also sternly cautioned Papa to temper his longtime drinking habit, as this was something that could definitely cause the condition to worsen.

Unfortunately, that was the one treatment that Lawrence Hodge was unwilling to embrace. Ever since Mother's death three years ago—a painful, drawn-out affair that had devastated him emotionally—he had relied on heavy aftersupper drinking to pull him through the evenings.

More recently, with the increasing pressure he was facing due to the war's impact on his business concerns and legislative responsibilities, he had added on a morning drinking habit that—sooner or later—might well lead to another family tragedy.

Catherine, who along with Emma had been staying at the plantation since Papa's stroke, had been hovering over him like a mother hen, ministering to his every need or request. She'd repeatedly warned everyone—especially her sister, with whom her relationship was still quite strained—to avoid doing or even saying anything that might cause Papa undue distress. But while Papa had clearly enjoyed Catherine's loving attention, even she had failed at convincing him to scale back on his dangerous new routine.

Suddenly Catherine sat up straight in the round-backed armchair and dropped the shirt she was sewing for Papa in her lap. She leaned to the side, inclining her ear to the open window just behind her. "What are those noises? They sound like . . . guns booming?"

Papa approached the window, which faced northwest up the James River past City Point in the direction of Richmond. After listening for a few moments as the booms increased in frequency, he turned toward the women.

"I'm betting those are Union siege guns."

Catherine gasped. *"Siege guns?* But, Papa, I thought you said General Johnston had the Yankee army contained across the river and well to the northeast, near West Point. How'd they get so close to Richmond so fast?" Her eyes widened as her hands gripped both arms of the chair. "Papa, you don't think they've broken through . . . that Joe and his regiment have been overrun and—"

Papa waved his hand. "No, no, dear . . . there's no need to panic. Those wouldn't be land guns. They're *naval* guns. Those Union iron-clad ships people saw steaming up the James three days ago are no doubt trying to break down our river bluff defenses near the capital. Probably trying to prepare the way for the Yank army to surround and attack the city itself, eventually." He gazed at Catherine reassuringly.

"But I'm sure Joe and his First Virginia boys are still holding fast for General Johnston against McClellan's land forces."

Catherine collapsed back in her chair. "Oh, I just pray that's true. It's been three weeks since I've received any word from him."

"Papa," Emma asked cautiously, not wanting to stir up unnecessary fears but still feeling compelled to voice what everyone was certainly thinking, "what does all this mean for plantations like ours along the river? Are we safe here?"

Papa stared down at his empty glass and shook his head before ambling away from the window and sitting down in his favorite armchair. Refilling his bourbon glass yet again from the bottle on the side table, he took a small sip and settled back. "With the Union gunboats running up and down the river at will and McClellan's army closing in, we can't rule out anything—including the Confederate government evacuating Richmond and going into exile somewhere. We should probably be prepared for the worst just in case. Since I'm on record as a Virginia Assembly member, if the Yanks overrun this area, they'll be sure to confiscate our property and all our slaves . . . and they probably won't treat us too civilly.

"I'll stay here and take whatever comes—see if I can eventually bargain my way into regaining this plantation your mother and I worked so hard to rebuild and maintain. But you girls should be ready to flee to safety somewhere. Catherine, have you and Joe discussed this?"

"Joe has said if worse comes to worst, that I should go and stay with his mother in Roanoke. He said if he can't be at our plantation to defend me, then he's ready to sacrifice it for my safety."

Papa eyed her fondly. "You married well, daughter. And what about you, Emma? You should probably go stay with your Aunt Myrta and your grandmother in Lynchburg, or—"

"No, Papa," Emma interrupted. "If I have to leave here, I'll go to Miss Lewis's in Petersburg. I know she would love me to stay with her and her mother."

"Well," Papa said, clearly irritated at having his suggestion rebuffed so strongly. "If that's your wish, who am I to stop you anymore? In fact, sheltering in Petersburg might be a good idea. Maybe by that time Miss Lewis will have finally restored you back to the good graces of those hospital doctors."

Emma stared at him coldly, smoldering inside over her father's barely disguised attempt to remind her yet again of his extreme displeasure over her loss of her job and the reason behind it. "Major Steele was correct to demand your respectful behavior," Papa had scolded her when she'd first told him what had happened. "If you had an issue with his treatment of that boy, you should have brought it up privately and not in front of the patients. And anyway, it wasn't any of your business. The major's in charge there, Emma, not you." Left unsaid was Papa's obvious disappointment that Emma had sacrificed such a fine, noble calling for the sake of her seemingly insatiable commitment to protecting slaves from abuse.

Suppressing the urge to say something she knew she'd regret, Emma stood up from the settee and walked toward the window. The cannon blasts were still ebbing and flowing, but she noticed a thick column of smoke rising in the distance. Something big must have been hit.

"I just pray none of this comes to pass," said Catherine, glancing nervously at her father. "But Papa . . . in the meantime . . . how do you plan to handle things around here? Especially if you have to spend more days in Richmond helping plan the city defense strategy. What about all our accounting tasks that drain so much of your time and energy?"

Papa looked down at his lap, then raised his glass and took another sip of bourbon. "I'm confident your sister is capable of stepping up to help take care of some of those. Am I right, Emma?"

Emma turned away from the window to face her father. "What about the field slaves, Papa?"

Papa's eyes narrowed. "What about 'em?" he asked gruffly.

Emma hesitated. She had known for over two weeks that this moment would come, that she would have to confront her father with it. But until now, she had kept putting it off due to Papa's need to recover from his stroke and Catherine's warnings against upsetting him. No longer. She would not fail Sallie and her family yet again by remaining silent until it was too late.

"Sallie told me that ever since you joined the legislature and gave Sam and his father full authority over the fieldworkers, they've been suffering terribly."

Papa rolled his eyes and groaned. "So what is Sallie complaining about *this* time, daughter? How exactly are Sam and his father making them 'suffer'?"

Emma responded quietly but firmly. "First, they increased the slaves' daily quotas by a quarter and doubled the number of lashes for not meeting them. Then, they stopped allowing the families to socialize with each other after seven P.M., accusing them of plotting to escape to the Yankee lines. I suppose Mr. Taylor has already informed you about those things by now, and apparently you're just fine with them. But that's not all . . ."

Papa glared at her. "What do you mean?"

Emma averted her eyes. "Sallie said Sam's been making advances toward her, and she's had to fight him off several times."

Papa banged his bourbon glass down on the cushioned arm of the chair, causing half the contents to splash onto his trousers and the floor. "Emma, do you believe *everything* that girl says? After that far-fetched accusation the two of you made last year against Sam concerning Charles's suicide, I'd hoped you had learned your lesson. You can't just blindly trust every single cry of distress from a slave without any proof. Who, besides Sallie, witnessed any of this? Did Sam actually hurt her? How do you know she's not just trying to gain your sympathy again by starting another vicious rumor, maybe hoping this time it'll lead us to fire Sam and his father and ease up on the field slaves' workload? I must tell you, daughter, without any evidence, I don't believe her story one bit!"

Emma stood speechless as Papa rose unsteadily to his feet and staggered toward the parlor room door. Before exiting, he stopped in his tracks and spun around.

"And another thing. Unless you've got a way to *prove* all this, don't bring it up anymore. We have enough troubles to deal with around here with the Yankees threatening Richmond, your mother gone, and . . ." Unable to finish, Papa whirled and walked out.

Emma folded her arms and turned back toward the window, defiantly awaiting Catherine's verdict on what had just taken place. The two had rarely spoken directly to each other since Charles's death last year. At the time, Emma had sensed that her sister's attempt at an apology for her failure to support Emma's effort to protect Charles was half-hearted, and Emma had only half-heartedly accepted it. Ever since, they'd maintained an awkward, polite facade, avoiding anything controversial. That was about to change.

Catherine placed her sewing project on the side table and rose from her chair. She walked over to the fireplace and stood staring at the dying embers from this morning's small blaze. After a moment's reflection, she crossed her arms, turned, and glared across the room at her sister.

"Em, does it never end?" she said softly.

Emma kept staring out the window. "Does *what* never end, Cat? If you're talking about my concern for Sallie and her family and the rest of our field slaves suffering under Sam Taylor's 'care and oversight,' then no, that will never end."

"Even if your constant harping about that ends up killing Papa?"

Emma whirled, her face flushed with indignation. *"Killing Papa? What are you talking about?"*

Catherine cocked her head back. "Are you going to pretend you forgot about his heart condition? Can't you see what he's doing to himself, trying still to deal with Mother's death and all the other pressures he's facing? Are you now determined to drive the final stake into his heart, insisting that he add yet another major worry to his list—a worry that may not even be justified?"

"Maybe this will come as a surprise to you, Cat—seeing as, unlike you, I don't yet have a husband and plantation of my own to worry over—but I do understand how hard it is for Papa, and I am concerned about his health, especially his drinking. But that doesn't mean we should all therefore just turn a blind eye to what's going on under our noses and let evil have its merry old way. Honestly, Cat, what 'evidence' will it take for Papa and you to believe what Sallie is telling me? Must she be bruised and raped or . . . even worse, murdered like Charles?"

"Emma, let's just face the truth, shall we? Given Sam's alibi that Mr. Wheeler confirmed, we have no proof whatsoever that Charles's death was anything but a suicide, despite what you and Sallie would like to believe. Sallie obviously hates Sam and wants to see him gone—and heaven knows I can see why she would—but that isn't enough for Papa to take every threat she claims he's now making against her as the gospel truth."

"You know good and well, Cat, that the only reason we have no proof that Sam murdered Charles is because Papa refused to investigate. All so he could appease Sam and his father—get them to influence the votes of their stupid Virginia First Society and allow him to win his election."

"*Emma!*" Catherine exploded. "I can't believe you would accuse Papa of such a thing. Do you even know what you're saying? Have you joined our brother David in having no regard for your own family's reputation?"

Emma stared at her in utter frustration. When she finally spoke, it was with a sad conviction that made her heart want to break into a million pieces.

"You just don't see it, do you, Catherine? And you never will."

"See *what*? What is it that I don't see?"

Emma shook her head and walked out of the room.

Two days later, still simmering over the confrontation with her father and sister, Emma made her weekly evening trek to the slave quarters carrying the basket of extra food rations that Papa had decided to permanently allot to the Cobb family as partial compensation for their son's death.

She attributed the fact that Papa had permitted her to personally deliver this offering for almost a year now to one primary cause: his continuing sense of guilt over his self-serving actions in the aftermath of the incident. But regardless of his motivation, she was grateful for the opportunity to meet privately with Sallie and sustain their unlikely friendship.

Approaching the front steps of the Cobbs' shack, Emma noticed something different. Usually, the door and the small single window beside it would be wide open to let in the cool evening breeze. Tonight, though, the door was shut, and the window had a cloth curtain stretched across it. Had someone taken ill?

She lifted her hand to knock but hesitated at the sound of an unfamiliar male voice speaking softly but emphatically, followed by total silence. Before she could knock, Sallie cracked the door open and peered out. "Miss Em, thank God you're here. Just leave the basket by the door and go round to the back of the shack. I'll meet you there in a minute."

"Sallie, wait—is everyone all right?"

"It's all right, Emmy, we fine. I promise. Just go round back now."

Five minutes later, Emma stood behind the shack with arms folded, nervously tapping her foot, convinced that something was wrong. If Sallie didn't appear momentarily, Emma was prepared to go ask one of the adult male slaves in the neighboring cabin to help her investigate.

Finally, Sallie rounded the corner, walked up to Emma, and grabbed her hands. Her face seemed alight with a spirit that Emma had not seen since before Charles's death. "Miss Em," she said excitedly, "we gotta talk. Will you take a walk with me?"

"Well . . . of course. But—where are we going? And . . . who was that in the shack with you?"

Sallie put a finger to her lips. "I'll tell you soon enough. Just come with me. Don't want nobody spyin' on us here." She took Emma's hand and led her along the path through the woods toward the creek.

Reaching the bank, the women sat down together on a fallen log at the foot of the oak tree with the overhanging branch that Charles had once employed to rescue Emma from certain death in the swirling waters.

"Recognize this place?" Sallie asked quietly.

"How could I not?" Emma replied. "But, Sallie, stop keeping me in suspense. Why'd you bring me *here*?"

"I was hopin' the memory might help you understand what I'm about to tell you . . . and ask o' you."

Emma held her breath, expecting the worst.

Sallie looked directly into her eyes. "Emmy, we're leavin'."

"You're . . . leaving? What do you mean? Who's leaving?"

"All of us. Me, my parents, and Lew."

"You mean you're . . . ?"

Sallie nodded slowly, her eyes glistening.

Emma stared at her in dumbfounded silence. The peaceful, babbling waters of the creek now seemed completely overwhelmed by the odd, roaring sensation in her ears.

"Sallie," she said finally, "are you *crazy*? Where will you go? And you know what'll happen if you get caught, don't you?"

"Can't take it no more, Emmy. We stay here any longer, Daddy swears he'll end up killin' Sam. 'Specially after yesterday."

"What? What happened?"

"After the workday ended, Daddy went up to Sam and said he'd better stop puttin' his hands all over me every time I go to the barn on Wednesdays to strip the tobacco stalks and sort the leaves. Sam told him I was lyin', and that he was sick and tired of bein' falsely accused of doin' bad things to our family. Said if Daddy didn't shut up and apologize, that he'd sure find some ways to make things harder for us. Told Daddy there wasn't a dang thing he could do about it neither, 'cause Master Hodge had given him full authority over the field slaves and trusted him completely. Daddy wanted to choke Sam to death right then and there, but thank heaven he just walked away."

Emma stared at Sallie in open-mouthed horror, a helpless rage boiling up inside her. Rage at Sam, at her father and sister, at the entire way of life that seemed so content with professing its Christian love for slaves on Sundays but then turning around and beating, whipping, raping, or even murdering them any other day of the week based on the slightest of excuses. And after the confrontation with Papa and Catherine, she knew it would be pointless—even cruel—to try to talk Sallie and her parents out of their decision. Finally collecting herself, she focused on the only thing that mattered now that Sallie had trusted her enough to share her dangerous secret.

"So, what's your plan?"

"That's where the man you heard talkin' behind our door comes in."

"Who is he?"

"Daniel Samson. He's Daddy's cousin, about the same age. One of Master Eppes's field slaves at Appomattox Manor—that big plantation up the river at City Point. Master trusts 'im enough to travel back and forth to Petersburg with a wagon twice a week to pick up food and supplies."

"And . . . what's he going to do for you and your family?"

Sallie's eyes lit up. "Two nights from now, he gonna take all of us— my family, including him and his son and another cousin—out to one o' them Yankee gunboats anchored off the Point."

Emma gasped. "*What?* How's he going to get all of you there? And even if he did, how d'you know the Yankees would let you all on board?"

"He'll take us out around midnight in a big rowboat he says he'll be able to steal. As far as the Yanks lettin' us on board, Daniel's a smart man. Kept his ear open to some Petersburg shop owners gabbin' about what's been happenin' the last couple of days up the river."

"And what's that?"

"Yank boats got shot up real bad in that river bluff battle two days ago near Richmond. So they came back down the river to City Point to lick their wounds. Daniel overheard a Virginia army man on the dock sayin' they just waitin' there for replacement boats to arrive, and then they'll take off again down the river toward that big Yank fort on the coast to get fixed up. If we can just get out to 'em before they leave and tell 'em we'll be killed if we go back, Daniel says Yanks'll feel sorry for us and take us on board for the ride to the coast."

Emma stared at her, aghast at the seeming naiveté of the scheme. "Sallie, I don't mean to cast doubts on Daniel's ideas or abilities, but—first of all—where's he going to steal this 'big rowboat' from?"

Sallie gripped her forearm with both hands. "Emmy, it's like God himself's providin' a way. Daniel says there's a warehouse with a small pier along the river just below the Point. He says about eight reb soldiers come there every third day or so. They go across the river in four rowboats to pick up ammunition and supplies from the Port Walthall train depot, then come back and lock the supplies and boats in the warehouse. On days they ain't there, they post a single guard to walk around outside and watch over everything day and night."

"So how is Daniel going to get past the guard and into the warehouse to steal a boat?"

"Sneak up on him, tie him up, kill him if he puts up too much a fight. Daniel says ain't nobody or nothin' gonna stop him from gettin' that boat. Once he gets it, he'll drag it down to the water and then row it up the river just a little ways to meet us on the bank."

Emma frowned. "But even if he succeeds in all that, you and your family are going to have to travel with whatever belongings you're carrying to meet him there. That's over five miles, and you know about those citizen night patrols that are out looking for slaves trying to escape. But assuming even *that* all succeeds, how does Daniel know the Yankee sailors will be so kind and understanding as to let you all onboard their gunboat in the dead of night? They're under no obligation to take you on, and what if they turn you away? Goodness, it all seems so dangerous and complicated. But I suppose if there's no other way . . ."

Sallie lowered her head and took a deep breath. When she looked up again, she appeared about to say something but then bit her lip and hesitated.

"Sallie, what is it?" Emma prodded.

"Maybe there *is* another way, but we'd need someone to help . . ."

"Help? How? And from whom?"

Sallie grasped Emma's hand. "Emmy, will you come with us?"

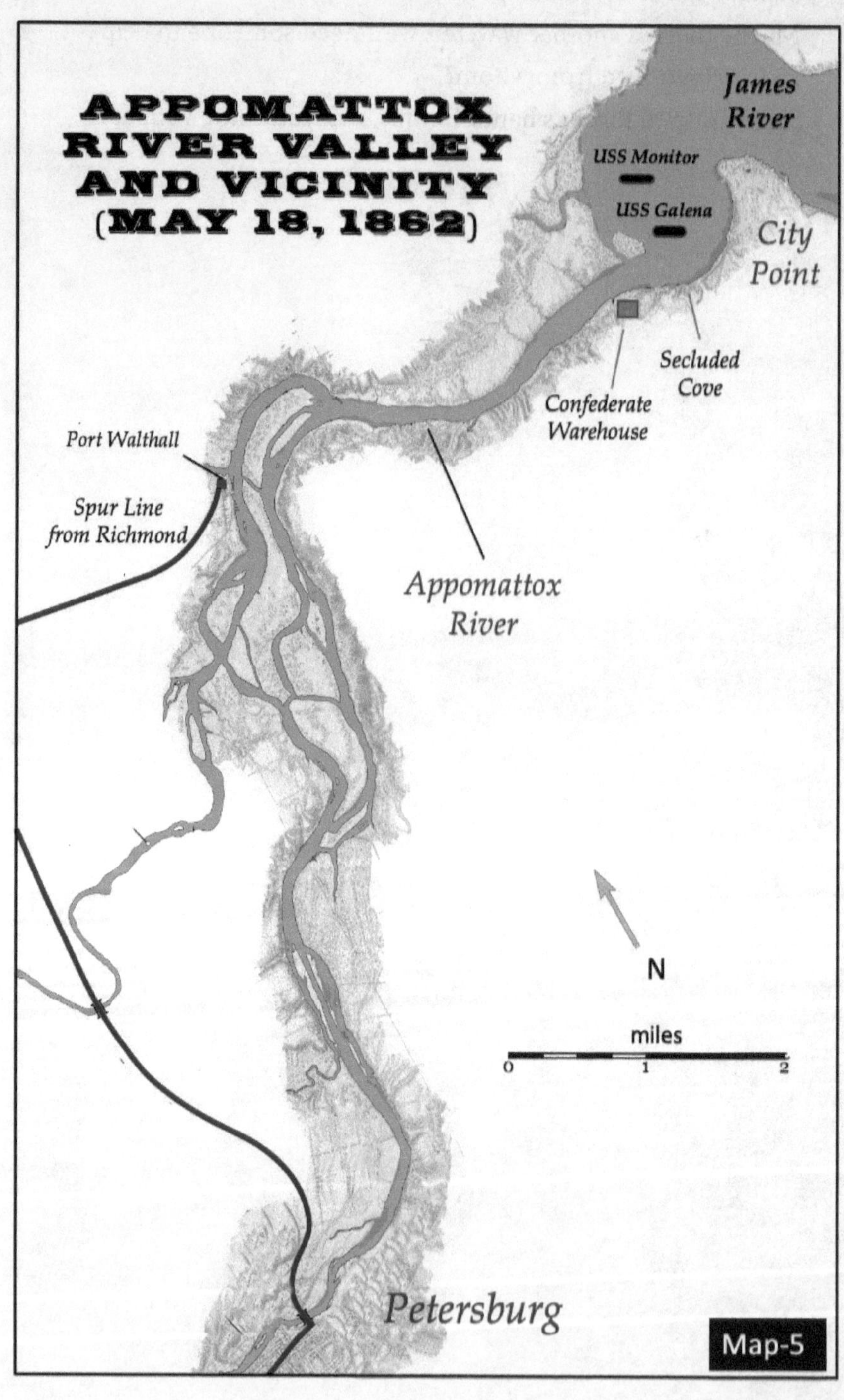

APPOMATTOX RIVER VALLEY AND VICINITY (MAY 18, 1862)
James River
USS Monitor
USS Galena
City Point
Secluded Cove
Confederate Warehouse
Port Walthall
Spur Line from Richmond
Appomattox River
N
miles
0
1
2
Petersburg
Map-5

CHAPTER 18

City of Petersburg
May 19, 1862

D aniel Samson turned around on the driver's bench of the rickety wooden supply wagon and tilted his hat back slightly. "You ready, Miss Emma?"

One look at the tall, husky Black man's weather-beaten, whiskered face flashing a confident grin made Emma suddenly ashamed of her own hesitation.

She pulled her shawl tighter around her shoulders and stood up from the narrow, makeshift sitting bench along the side of the wagon bed. She prayed silently that the ruse would work and that she would not shrink from her role in it. "Ready as I'll ever be, Daniel. Let's go."

Daniel handed the reins of the wagon horse to his cousin. "All right, Jim, take it on down to the city and unload it, just like always. Then haul your butt back to the plantation, get your things together, and you know where to meet us later tonight." Stepping off his seat to the ground, he gave the wobbly front wheel a cursory check, then went around to the back to open the rear loading gate and help Emma squeeze past the sacks of grain and step down.

At least, she thought as the two walked together toward the entrance of the rustic bait and tackle shop that also rented out small boats on the southern bank of the Appomattox River four miles north of Petersburg, her partner in crime had no lack of credentials for this perilous undertaking. In fact, according to Sallie Cobb's stepfather Tom, if there was anyone among the Virginia Peninsula slave population who was capable of organizing and pulling off a successful group escape, it was Tom's cousin—Daniel Samson.

After twenty years of plying the old dirt backroads paralleling the Appomattox between Petersburg and City Point as a food and supply hauler for Dr. Eppes, Daniel had gotten to know every single building, every sheltered nook, every hidden cove along the river's edge. He'd also developed an extensive network of contacts—"in-the-know" colored and White folk eager to share with the friendly and ever-receptive Daniel their thoughts on the war, its effects on their workloads, and the increasing pressure on city and riverbank shop owners to sell or lease their goods at inflated prices.

No doubt, Tom's confidence in Daniel's abilities had helped Sallie convince Emma that her alternative escape plan had a reasonable chance of succeeding. But it would take more than someone else's confidence for Emma to make the irreversible decision to join the effort, forever separating herself from her own family and risking a lengthy prison term and huge fine if caught. The main questions, of course, centered on what she would do if the escape succeeded. Where would she go after reaching Fort Monroe on the coast? What would she do to find sustaining work while pursuing her goal of becoming a respected writer, advocating for important social causes? Should she just go, and assume God would reveal his plan for her on the other end?

It was only after a sleepless night of prayer and a horseback ride yesterday morning to visit Pastor Jones that she finally came to have the peace in her heart that she was doing the right thing.

"Emma," Pastor Jones had said, "God knows your desire to honor your father by staying to care for him despite your differences, just as you cared for your mother. But he also knows the exceptional heart of compassion and special talent for writing that he's given you. Look at the path he's taken you on so far—your rescue by Charles; your friendship with Sallie; witnessing slaves being horribly mistreated; and getting shunned by your family and fired from your hospital job for making strong and honorable protests against that young boy's abuse. Emma, given all that, which do you see as the most likely next step that God would want you to take with the talents he's blessed you with—returning to your familiar past, or pursuing an uncertain and dangerous future with those who've captured your heart?"

Put in those terms, Emma had agreed: she had but one choice. Pastor Jones had then retreated into another room to consult privately with his wife, returning several minutes later with a small leather purse. "Judith and I have been saving for a day when we could bless someone we trust who is clearly on a God-inspired mission and would benefit from our support. We talked about it, and we've decided that the Lord has shown us today who that someone is," he'd said, handing the purse over to Emma. She'd opened it to find several stacks of ten-dollar "Old Dominion" Virginia banknotes totaling one thousand dollars in all. The offering had prompted a flood of grateful expressions and hugs.

It was that purse which Emma now clutched in her right hand as she nervously followed Daniel Samson through the door to the rest of her life.

"Hello, Master Nelson," Daniel called out to the thin, hatchet-faced boat shop owner behind the counter at the far end of the store. "Beautiful day, isn't it, sir?"

Matthew Nelson—who, according to Daniel, was the fifty-something son of a commercial fisherman with a chip on his shoulder against wealthy plantation owners and their "privileged" Black errand runners—glanced up from his accounting book and scowled. "Well, well, Daniel. It's been a while. So, what are you after today? More fish-trapping nets for the esteemed Dr. Eppes? Sorry to say, we ain't rentin' those out anymore. Gotta buy 'em if you want 'em, and I know Dr. Eppes ain't entrusted *you* with *that* kind o' money."

Daniel laughed as he approached the counter while Emma lingered several steps behind. "Oh, no, no, Mr. Nelson. Ain't after no trappin' nets today, sir."

Noticing Emma, Nelson suddenly stood up straight. "Who's the lady with you here, Daniel?" he asked suspiciously.

"Mr. Nelson, sir," Daniel said proudly, standing aside as Emma walked up to the counter, "allow me to introduce Miss Anna Parker, Master Eppes's niece. She visitin' all the way from Memphis, Tennessee!"

"Is that so?" Nelson now smiled pleasantly. "Well, Miss Parker, what brings you here with my good friend Daniel today? It's not often I get the privilege of seein' a lady walk through my door."

Emma smiled. "Why, thank you, Mr. Nelson," she said cordially before launching into her well-rehearsed rationale. She was surprised at the steadiness of her own voice. "I must admit, this is a bit unusual for me as well, but I'm rather in a bind. I received word yesterday that a shipment of wool from my father's farm—it's a gift for my uncle, Dr. Eppes—arrived by train two days ago at the Port Walthall depot across the river. We want to pick the crates up today before the depot becomes too crowded and then transport them to Appomattox Manor. And that's why we're here."

"Ma'am?" Nelson asked, head cocked and eyes narrowed.

"I'd like to rent one of your larger rowboats so we can cross the river to the depot, load it with the crates of wool, and take them upriver."

Nelson stared at her for several interminable seconds. "I'm kinda surprised Dr. Eppes would—"

"Mr. Nelson," Emma cut him off impatiently, "my uncle would have come here himself with Daniel, but these last two weeks he's had to reside at the city army hospital where he's a contract surgeon. While he's gone, his wife and daughters are completely tied up with their tasks on the plantation, and so I've taken it upon myself to make sure my father's gift reaches its destination safely."

Nelson smiled and shook his head. "Well, that sure sounds like a big, messy job for a pretty, young lady to be takin' on."

"Believe me, sir," Emma said in a lighter tone, "you don't have to worry about this 'pretty, young lady' soiling her hands a bit. I've done plenty of physical labor on my father's farm, even rolling up my sleeves to pitch hay and lift seed bags now and then. Between Daniel and me, we'll have no trouble getting the job done. So . . . may we proceed with renting a boat from you? We have an appointment across the river in one hour to complete the transaction with the railway freight agent."

Nelson scratched his jaw. "I'd love to, Miss Parker. Only problem is we ain't rentin' our rowboats anymore. Too many people these days take 'em but never return 'em. We're planning to sell all of them soon to the Confederate navy."

Emma glanced uncertainly at Daniel. Was this the end of the charade? Already?

"Mr. Nelson, how much to buy one for Dr. Eppes?" she asked on an impulse.

"*Buy?* Well, ma'am . . . it's probably a lot more than you'd want to—"

"Please just tell me, Mr. Nelson. What's your price? I'm running low on time, and I have to make a decision since yours appears to be the only boat shop around here."

"It'll cost you one hundred dollars, Miss Parker."

"*A hundred dollars!*" Emma huffed. "That's ten times your two-day rental cost, and about twice as much as I would expect."

"I'm afraid that's as low as I can go, ma'am. These are hard times for everyone."

Emma stared at him suspiciously. "Well, if that's truly the case, then I suppose I have no choice. Thankfully, my uncle advanced me an overly generous amount to cover the railway shipping cost." She opened her purse and pulled out a stack of ten-dollar bills, counting out ten and laying them on the counter. She had an uneasy awareness of Mr. Nelson watching and judging her every movement.

Nelson signed a bill of receipt and handed it to her. "You'll find boat number three tied along with the others along the small pier to the left when you exit. Best regards to you, ma'am, and I sure hope that boat will satisfy Dr. Eppes's needs for a long time to come!"

"Thank you, Mr. Nelson, I'm certain it will." She turned to walk out the door with Daniel.

"Oh, Miss Parker?"

Emma froze in her tracks. "Yes?"

"Just wanted you to know I'll be puttin' a copy of the sales record for Dr. Eppes in my next mail batch goin' to the city post office this afternoon. Always like to keep my regular customers informed of any sales takin' place on their behalf."

"Why, thank you, sir . . . I know he'll appreciate that."

Emma struggled to control the surge of panic rising in her throat. With the evidence of her foul play in the mail to Dr. Eppes, there was no longer the slightest possibility of return to the life she'd once known.

The slow current near the southern bank of the Appomattox was making for an easy downstream rowing effort. Seated on the right side of the fifteen-foot boat's aft thwart beside Daniel, Emma concentrated on duplicating his smooth, unhurried oar strokes.

"You doin' just fine, ma'am," Daniel said. "Nice and easy . . . that's right. We'll get there."

Thankfully, everything since the rowboat purchase had proceeded without incident. For appearance's sake, Daniel and Emma—still within visibility of the boat shop—had crossed the narrow channel to the Port Walthall pier and train depot. A half hour later, they'd loaded three empty wooden crates that Daniel had managed to scrounge from the depot's wasteyard into the front of the boat, then crossed back to the southern bank and set off downriver. Passing by the shop, Emma had waved to Mr. Nelson, who happened to be standing on the shop's pier talking to one of his assistants. Nelson had stared at her with mouth agape and crossed arms, as if still struggling to fathom the idea of a "pretty, young White lady" loading and rowing a boat together with a male slave. Finally, he'd offered a tentative wave of his own and turned back to his conversation.

For the next half hour, the ride had been uneventful, marked only by occasional dialogue reviewing details of tonight's activity. In ten minutes, they would be passing near the Confederate army supply warehouse that had been the original planned site for obtaining a boat by overcoming the guard and stealing it. Now, of course, the warehouse was just one more riverside structure along the route to freedom.

Emma paused in her rowing motion to marvel at the sun-speckled, mirrored surface of the middle portion of the river, broken in only a few spots by small, swirling eddies. The greenish-brown water bore the scents of algae and fish and was cool and refreshing to the touch when she dipped her hand over the side to test it.

Looking off to the side, she watched in amazement as a large crane swooped down to pluck a fish from the brackish water near the bank. "I'll never understand how they can spot their prey from so high in the air!"

Daniel chuckled. "It sure is a wonder. I don't s'pose they have to try too hard, though."

Emma observed him closely as she resumed her rowing. "Daniel, may I ask you a question?"

"O' course, ma'am."

"Has Dr. Eppes treated you poorly?"

Daniel hesitated, obviously pondering his answer carefully. "No, ma'am. Dr. Eppes, he a real nice man. At least to me. Seemed to take a likin' to me from the day he brought me and my momma home from the market 'bout twenty years ago now. Gave me more 'n more respon-sibility as I grew older to run special errands for him, buy food and supplies in the city, things like that. Even stepped in a couple times to stop his overseer from whippin' my hide over some dumb mistake I'd made. So . . . no, ma'am, I can't say Dr. Eppes ever treated me poorly."

"Why is it then that you're so intent on escaping—risking everything?"

Daniel smiled. "Miss Emma, you know that big ole white crane we just saw swoop down and fly off with the little fish wigglin' in its mouth? Way I see it, that little fish is like my eight-year-old son, just playin' around outside our shack with a couple friends, runnin' down to the creek to look for frogs, havin' a grand old time without a care in the world. Just like the little fish. Then, in a few years, he hit eleven years old, and what do you think happen? Whether he like it or don't, he gets swooped up by ole White master and his system—into the fields, servin' in the big house, whatever it take to keep ole master and his family livin' well and their bellies satisfied."

"But . . . if your son were to be treated kindly by 'old master' like you say you've been, why would that be such a bad thing?"

"First off, ma'am, ain't no sure thing he'd end up with a good master like Dr. Eppes. *I* got lucky, but what if Dr. Eppes dies? What if his son inherits the plantation, and the son turn out to be a cruel master? That's the master my own son have to live with maybe for the rest o' his life—way after I'm dead and gone. No choice in the matter. And Miss Emma, from everything Tom and Sallie tell me, you know better 'n most White folk what it mean for a slave to live under the heel of a cruel master—or overseer."

Emma nodded, her throat constricting with a sickening mixture of sadness and shame. "Daniel, why else?"

"How's that, ma'am?"

"You said fear of cruelty against your son was your 'first' reason for leaving. Is there a second?"

Daniel regarded her, his eyes moist. "I just want one chance, Miss Emma. For me and my son."

"One chance? Chance for what?"

"To build our own little farm on a river in Ohio, right next to my brother's."

Emma gaped at him. "*What?* You've got a brother in Ohio? Where?"

Daniel hesitated. "Truth is, ma'am, I don't 'xactly know. You see, my brother's a free man—his master gave him and a couple other slaves their freedom papers when he sold his plantation a few years back. After that, whenever I'd go on one o' my supply runs for Dr. Eppes, I made sure to visit my brother in Petersburg where he was workin' at the docks. He was always tellin' me stories he was hearin' 'bout some free Black families from Petersburg went north couple years 'fore the war. They started a little chain o' farms along some river somewhere in northeast Ohio. Helpin' each other out with nobody lordin' 'it over 'em—raisin' and sharin' their crops together, livin' in peace and lovin' each other like God wanted 'em to. My brother said he was gonna get there one day for sure and join 'em. I'd always laugh at 'im, tell 'im he had as much chance o' makin' it to Ohio as I had o' makin' it to the moon.

"Then one day I knock on his door, and he gone. Landlord said he up and took all his stuff. Left a note for me sayin' he'd gone to Ohio and he'd write me soon's he got there. That was right before the war started, and I ain't heard nothin' from him since. But I promise you, ma'am, if God get us outta this place, me and my son gonna go find 'im."

Emma tried not to cry as thoughts of her own brother David flooded her mind. "Daniel, I can't tell you how much I'm inspired by all you've just shared—more than you can ever imagine."

Daniel grinned. "I'm real glad you comin' with us, Miss Emma." He stopped rowing for a moment to turn around and look downriver. "Just round this bend we gonna float by the army warehouse, ma'am. Then only a half mile or so, an' we'll be at our meetin' place."

Five minutes later, Emma peered past Daniel toward the bank about fifty yards away. The reflected rays of the setting sun had turned the top of the corrugated warehouse roof into a blazing display of light. She shaded her eyes with her hand and spotted a young soldier in a light-gray tunic and blue trousers rising from his seat beside the warehouse door.

The soldier took hold of a musket leaning against the wall, slung it casually against his shoulder, and began sauntering out on the short pier toward the rowboat. Emma felt herself tensing; although they'd known this was a possibility and were ready for it, still, they were in a precarious position.

Reaching the end of the pier, the soldier raised his hand. "Whoa there, darky! What the hell you think you're doin' with that boat and them crates?"

Daniel dropped his oar deep into the water to stop the boat about twenty yards from the soldier, who Emma guessed to be about seventeen. "Afternoon, sir! We on our way to take some Tennessee wool up to Master Eppes just up the way at City Point."

"*Tennessee wool!* Now just where'd you come across *that*? And who's that beside you, boy?"

Up until then, Emma had been partially hidden from the soldier's view by one of the crates. Furrowing her brow and mustering all the authority in her voice of which she was capable, she spoke. "We got it from the train depot, soldier. It's a gift for my uncle, Dr. Eppes, and his family—from my father's farm in Tennessee." She reached for the boat purchase invoice and the forged wool shipment receipt and held them up. "If you'd like to see the papers showing all this belongs to Dr. Eppes, here they are. Otherwise, I'd appreciate it if you'd let us move on, as the sun's setting and people are waiting for us at the Point."

The soldier grinned and lifted his cap, allowing a thick tangle of blond hair to fall to his collar. The strapping, good-looking youth reminded Emma of Private Travis at the hospital.

"Oh, that's all right, ma'am," he said. "Now I see you're in charge, we're all fine. Didn't mean to hold you up, but we're always on the look for Yankee sailors from them ships anchored off the Point tryin' to pull a fast one on us—sendin' in a landing party to stir up trouble like they did just a few miles up the James a couple nights ago. Raided and set fire to one of the warehouses after stealin' a bunch o' supplies."

"I understand completely, soldier," Emma said sweetly. "I'm just glad we have brave men like you looking out for us all around here. Makes me feel a lot safer."

The soldier's face lit up. "Why, thank you, ma'am. Be even more of us tonight when my buddies come back to sleep in the warehouse. They gotta get up first thing in the morning to go pick up another big weapons haul from the depot. Y'all take care now, and tell Dr. Eppes to keep a close eye on those Yank boats and come let us know if he sees anything suspicious."

"I certainly will, and thank you again," Emma said as Daniel took a long stroke with his oar, pulling the boat away from the still water around the pier and back into the current. Breathing a huge sigh of relief, she returned her own oar to the water and resumed her stroke in rhythm with Daniel's.

They had traveled a few hundred yards downriver before conversation resumed. "There it is, Miss Emma." Daniel pointed out to the deep water where the Appomattox and James converged off City Point. In the distance, silhouetted against the setting sun, was the shot-up Union gunboat that—about six hours from now—would present itself to the escapees as either the arms of a welcoming angel or the fangs of a defensive, rabid dog.

Rowing with Daniel toward the small, wooded cove a quarter of a mile ahead, Emma said a quick prayer for Sallie, her parents and brother, Daniel's son, and his cousin Jim. *Please, God, keep them all safe from the night patrols as they make their way to our meeting place.*

CHAPTER 19

Appomattox River Shoreline, South of City Point, Virginia
May 19, 1862

Crouching behind a white oak tree with Daniel's young son Jason, Emma peered around the trunk and over the heads of Daniel and his cousin Jim. Beyond the twenty-yard stretch of river shore mud and small rocks now exposed by the low tide, out in the middle of the channel about a half mile away, two masthead lights of the *USS Galena* flickered in the midnight darkness.

"I know that's our 'scape boat, but what's that other thing off to the left about a hundred yards lyin' low in the water?" Jim asked softly, pointing toward the moonlit silhouette of what appeared to be a large round box sitting on the middle of a long, narrow flat raft.

"Dang!" Daniel marveled. "I think that's the *Monitor*—Yanks' new all-iron gunboat type. Box on top can spin around and point a big cannon any direction they want in just a second or two. Hmmm . . . I bet they gonna take over guardin' the channel so *Galena* can finally pull anchor and take off downriver to the coast."

"Now how somebody like you come to know all that?" Jim chided.

"I just listen to the Port Walthall dockworkers, cousin. They pick up all kinds o' stuff from the reb army boys haulin' supplies from the train to the piers."

After taking a minute more to survey the situation, Daniel turned toward Emma, a worried look on his face. "Can't wait much longer, Miss Em. If they ain't here in fifteen minutes, we goin' anyway."

Emma nodded, trying to control her rising sense of panic. Sallie and her family should have been here a half hour ago. Had disaster struck? She knew the consequences if they'd gotten caught: severe whipping, permanent separation from each other, possibly being sold to a new master in the Deep South where conditions were likely to be even more miserable. *Sallie, where are you?*

Only seconds later, several soft, owl-like hoots—the agreed-upon signal—emanated from the direction of some thick bushes about fifteen yards back. After Daniel responded in kind, the Cobb family emerged and crept forward to be greeted by Emma and the others with wild hugs and kisses.

Huddling next to Emma, Sallie briefly described the harrowing night-time journey from the Hodge Plantation across a five-mile patchwork of rarely used backroads, open fields, creeks, and marshes. The delay had been caused mainly by their need to detour widely around a five-man patrol that had suddenly pulled up and stopped for smokes, whiskey, and animated chatter at one of the backroad junctions along the Cobbs' planned path. "If it weren't for Daddy," she said, looking at Tom with a loving gaze, "ain't no way we'd have made it here. How he learn about all them crazy trails, and not get us lost or caught . . . I'll never know."

Daniel held up his hand and asked everyone to quiet down and sit on the damp, mossy ground in front of him. "All right, everybody," he said quietly as a slight breeze stirred the leaves in the oak tree overhead, "listen up. Here's what we doin'." He went on to give each person their instructions, starting with moving the nearby, tide-grounded boat out to the water's edge, then loading, boarding, and rowing it out to the Union ship. All with an absolute minimum of talk, noise, or unnecessary movement on the slight chance that it might attract the attention of someone who might happen to be prowling around the vicinity.

Emma's confidence grew with each passing moment. Getting past the Confederate warehouse had been the main concern . . . once past and safely hidden by the cove, there was virtually no chance of discovery. Listening to Daniel's steady voice, she was grateful for his careful, methodical approach and obvious command of the whole dangerous operation. Only one more test remained: the reaction of the Union gunboat sailors to their request to board.

Soon after Daniel concluded an emotionally wrenching prayer to Jesus on behalf of everyone for their safe journey across the water and reception by the gunboat, the moon disappeared behind some thick clouds, darkening the landscape. On Daniel's signal, he and the two other men, plus Lew, arose and crept a few yards to the tiny, tree-sheltered inlet where Daniel and Emma—six hours earlier at high tide—had steered and tied up the boat in order to hide it from view. Untying and lifting it slightly, they carried it bow first out into the open and across the shore mud before setting it down again just beyond the edge of the water.

Daniel and Jim boarded first, taking their seats on the aft thwart and working to position the oars in their locks while Tom and Lew ran back to the tree line to help Mary collect the small sacks of extra clothing articles that each would-be escapee had brought with them. Passing by them on the way, Sallie and Emma arrived at the boat next with Daniel's little son Jason in tow. They waded into the shallow water and climbed over the gunwale into the bow, making sure to leave enough room in the middle of the boat for Sallie's parents and brother, as well as the clothes sacks.

Tom Cobb emerged first from the tree line, walking quickly to the boat with three sacks in his arms, which he handed over to Emma and Sallie. At Daniel's request, he moved around to the stern of the boat and gave it a hard push off the shallow bottom so that Daniel and Jim could begin to row away with ease whenever they were ready.

As he did so, Emma happened to look over the boat's side toward the steep rise in the embankment fifty yards or so off to the right. For a split second, she thought she detected a tiny light moving among the trees on the top of the bank. Silent panic struck her heart, and she held her breath. Staring hard for a good twenty seconds, she finally discovered the light's source: a bright, twinkling star that emerged sporadically between the breeze-swayed branches. *A good omen*, she thought with relief.

Reaching into the deep side pocket of her dress, she checked to make sure the money purse was still there. It was. *So far, so good.* All that remained now was for Tom to go back and gather the remaining four clothes sacks, along with Mary and Lew, and then for all three to plod through twenty yards of muddy marsh, wade into the water, and climb into the boat.

Tom was the first to emerge from the tree line, carrying two sacks. Mary and Lew followed with the remaining two, about five yards back. As they reached the halfway point, the moon suddenly broke completely through some obscuring clouds, bathing the entire area in a ghastly, pale luminescence.

Seconds later, a flash of light on top of the embankment to the right was followed immediately by a loud bang.

Tom, Mary, and Lew froze as a small geyser of mud kicked up a second later near Tom's foot.

A second flash-bang preceded a frightening *thwack* as something struck and penetrated the side of the boat no more than a foot in front of where Emma and Sallie were seated with Jason.

"Ha, we found 'em, Lieutenant!" someone shouted from the embankment. "They thought they'd fooled me!"

Her heart in her throat, Emma recognized the voice immediately: it was that of the young soldier who'd been guarding the warehouse upriver a ways.

"We're there in a minute," a distant voice shouted back. "You and Caleb keep 'em pinned to the shore. Don't let 'em get away."

A third musket crack caused Mary to start screaming. She grabbed Lew's hand and ran back with him toward the tree line.

"Mary, wait . . . don't!" Tom yelled after her.

"Tom, hurry up! We gotta go *now*!" Daniel shouted.

Tom dropped his sacks and ran toward the boat, splashing through the water to the boat's side. Emma moved over to make room, thinking he was about to climb in. Instead, he leaned over and grabbed Sallie's outstretched arms. Crying frantically, Sallie tried to stand up, but Tom firmly pushed her back down onto the seat.

"Daughter, you know I can't leave 'em. But *you* gotta go. No life for you here no more. Remember us, Sallie. We always love you, girl. You go do good now. God be with you."

Tom waded around to the stern as a bullet zipped into the water inches from his leg. After saying a quick goodbye to the two men, he gave the boat one more hard shove out into the water before turning to run back across the mud toward Mary and Lew at the tree line. Emma held her breath, watching the scene unfold while clutching Sallie and Jason as Daniel and George began rowing with all their might out into the channel.

Tom was only a few feet from the tree line when the next shot struck him in the right side, causing him to lurch and fall onto his stomach.

Sallie let out a horrified scream. Another bullet grazed Jim's thigh just above the knee and passed through the left side of the boat right above the waterline.

"You girls, lie down *now* with Jason in the bottom of the hull . . . *and stay down!*" Daniel roared. "Don't look back no more."

They'd managed to row nearly half a mile from the bank toward the confluence of the Appomattox and James when, suddenly, a strident voice boomed out over the water.

"No closer, mister—we have orders to watch out tonight for reb sharpshooters and raiding parties sneaking around the channel in small boats just like yours. So, unless you want your heads blasted clear back to the shore, you better explain real quick. Who the *hell* are you?"

Supporting herself on her elbow, Emma lifted her head just enough to peek over the rowboat's bow. It was not at all reassuring to see at least a dozen rough-looking Union sailors crowded together on the gunboat's stern no more than fifteen yards ahead and ten feet above the water, their musket barrels all seemingly pointed directly at her.

Daniel and Jim stopped rowing and backpaddled to keep the boat from drifting into the ship. Daniel turned around on his seat and gave a friendly wave. "Hello, Master," he said, addressing the one man in the middle of the group who wasn't pointing a musket and whom Emma guessed to be the deck officer in charge. "We just a few poor slaves from the Eppes Plantation."

"Yeah? Well, what you want, mister? We heard the gunshots on the shore. Who's after you? And who you got hidin' in that bow?"

One by one, Sallie, Jason, and Emma sat up straight and faced the officer, who extended a lantern on the end of a wooden pole out over the water in order obtain a better look.

One of the sailors gasped. "That's a White woman, sir!"

The officer's voice took on an even more belligerent tone. "Thought you said you were all slaves, mister. What're you doing with that lady? They haven't hurt you, have they, ma'am?"

Prepared for this moment, Emma spoke up. "Not at all, sir. What you have here are four slaves risking their lives to escape to freedom, and a longtime friend of theirs who's bound and determined to escape her unhappy plantation life. We're asking—begging—for asylum on your boat, sir, as we understand you're getting ready to sail on downriver to Fort Monroe on the coast."

The officer hesitated, clearly uncertain how to proceed next.

Another sailor on the fringe of the group piped up. "Wouldn't do it, sir. No room for 'em belowdecks with all our wounded men. And if we gotta do any more fightin' between here and Monroe, we—"

The officer cut him off. "Enough. There's other considerations—like Congress's order just two months ago for all US military units to accept escaping slaves as contraband and stop the practice of returning 'em to their owners. What's your plan if we can't take you on, ma'am?"

Emma, uncertain, turned to Daniel.

"I s'pose we just have to try and row on down the river by ourselves, Master. But it almost a sure thing we get shot up and caught by reb patrols or slave bounty hunters on the banks along the way, 'specially once word get out in a few hours that we missin'. Escape news spread mighty far and fast round here."

After considering things for a few seconds, the officer handed the lantern pole to the sailor standing next to him. "You all wait there," he called out to Daniel. "I'm gonna have to talk to the commander."

"Sir!" Emma cried out, pulling the purse from her dress pocket and holding it up. "Please tell your commander I have nine hundred dollars in cash right here, if that's what it takes."

The officer grinned. "You can hold off on that kind offer, ma'am, but I'll be sure to let the commander know. I know he'll appreciate the gesture."

Five minutes later, the sailors on deck snapped to rigid attention as the deck officer returned alongside a tall man dressed in a buttoned-down, double-breasted blue jacket with shoulder straps and gold-laced stripes on the sleeves. The man stepped around to the stern railing, peered down for a moment, then lifted his cap and smiled.

"Commander John Rodgers, at your service, my friends. Who will speak for your party?"

"Miss Emma will, sir," Daniel called back without hesitation.

Emma, nonplussed, tentatively waved her hand.

"Well, Miss Emma," Rodgers said, "you've struck good fortune tonight. Boatswain Cox here explained your situation to me, and I've decided to take you all on—free of charge. You've put everything on the line just to get *this* far, and heaven knows after the beating my ship took up at Drewry's Bluff a few days ago, I don't mind sticking my finger in the eye of a Confederate slave owner by confiscating his property. So, if you're willing to accept the tight quarters we'll be offering you, take your boat around to the other side and we'll drop a boarding ladder for you."

"*Hallelujah!*" Jim shouted, nearly losing his oar in the water as he leaned over to hug and backslap Daniel.

Emma breathed a huge sigh of relief. She glanced down at Jason and smiled, not sure if the eight-year-old was comprehending everything that was happening. He smiled back shyly and snuggled up close by her side. She then turned toward Sallie, uncertain how she would react to the good news given her tragic separation from her entire family only twenty minutes earlier. Sallie tried to smile, but her lips immediately began quivering and she broke down in a torrent of tears. Emma knew there was nothing she could say or do at this point but hold the devastated girl in her arms as Daniel and Jim rowed the boat around the *Galena*'s stern.

Reaching the top of the boarding ladder behind Jason and Sallie, Emma was greeted by the hand of Boatswain Cox, who helped her over the railing and onto the deck. "Apologies for the appearance of our house, ma'am," Cox said as she surveyed the surroundings while waiting for Daniel and Jim to board.

It was now obvious why Commander Rodgers had lamented over his ship's beating: the deck was a shambles, with splinters of wood, pieces of iron, broken weapons, and shell fragments strewn about in one confused, horrible mass. Spots nearby, including the bottom of the steam engine's smokestack at the center of the deck, were splattered with what Emma presumed to be coagulated blood that the surviving crew had not yet had the time to clean up.

Emma hardly noticed. All her exhausted mind could comprehend was an overwhelming sense of relief and happiness as she joined Daniel, Sallie, and the others in embracing each other with tears of gratitude and thanks to God.

Daniel gripped her arms, his ecstatic grin seeming to stretch from ear to ear. "We did it, Miss Emma!"

Oblivious to the gawks of the gunboat sailors surrounding her, she threw her arms around him and hugged him closely. "It's mainly due to your great skill and courage, Daniel. Thank you."

Daniel laughed. "Ain't my place to be thanked, Miss Em. Thanks and glory be to de Lord!"

Emma smiled and nodded as tears streamed from her eyes.

"Send 'em over here, Boats," a young sailor beckoned from the top of a stairwell leading to the deck below. With Emma leading the way, the little group walked toward him, each carrying their clothing sacks.

Approaching the boyish-looking lad, Emma was struck by the dirt and grime that covered his face and clothing from top to bottom. He offered his hand to help her onto the first step. She reached out to accept it: the welcoming hand of safety, freedom, and a new life ahead for Emma and her friends.

"Thank you, sir, you are so kind to—"

A mass of blood spurted from just above the sailor's right cheekbone.

Emma watched in horror as he stared blankly at her for five seconds, then pitched forward onto the deck, flat on his face. Within seconds, all hell broke loose as whizzing bullets slammed into the lifeboats, the smokestack, and any other exposed structure on or above the deck, as well as the iron-plated landward-facing side of the ship.

"*Sharpshooters!*" Cox yelled. "*Sailors, take your stations!*" He pointed to the smokestack and motioned wildly for Emma and her party to take shelter behind it.

The fusillade continued for a full five minutes before finally tapering off to random, scattered shots. During the lull, Emma huddled next to Sallie and Jason, trying to help Sallie cover the distraught boy's ears as the agonized cries and groans of several other sailors who'd been hit resounded from various locations on the deck.

Boatswain Cox and Commander Rodgers suddenly rounded the smokestack together. They crouched beside Emma and motioned for Daniel to move closer to join the conversation.

Rodgers spoke, his voice thick with anger. "Seems you've attracted quite a following. This is the last thing my men needed on the final night of our deployment."

"Commander," Emma pleaded, "I assure you, we had no intention of—"

Rodgers touched her arm and shook his head. "I'm not blaming you, ma'am. All that matters now is to figure out exactly where all that shore firing's coming from so we can respond. Angle of the bullet strikes suggests it's a good ways off to the right from where you all were fired at, but in the darkness, it's hard to tell."

Daniel raised his hand. "Sir, if I may suggest . . . there's a reb army warehouse that Miss Em and me passed by on way to our 'scape point. It's about a half mile upriver. A few soldiers from there tracked us and started shootin' when we was leavin'. But once we got away and they saw where we was headed, they prob'ly got real mad and run back for help. That's most likely where the new firin's coming from, sir."

Rodgers nodded and pondered things for a moment. "If you and I move over to the side rail, you think you could point out about where that warehouse might be?"

"To the rail, sir?" Daniel gasped. "B-But, how we gonna keep from gettin' our heads blowed off?"

Rodgers grinned. "Simple. Just keep your head down when you crawl, like me." He turned to Cox. "Boats, once we get a bead on that warehouse with the help of our friend here, we're going to blow it sky-high."

"But, sir, with three of our guns out of commission, and—"

"Not *us*, Boats. The *Monitor*. They're within hailing distance just ahead. Go up to the bow and get their attention. Soon as I get the angle on our target, I'll relay it to you and you pass it on to them. Once they start blasting the area, we weigh anchor and take off downriver under their cover. Before you go to the bow, tell the engine crew to start heating things up. We've hung around this godforsaken place long enough."

"Sir." Cox saluted, then took off running in a low crouch toward the aft stairwell.

Rodgers removed his cap and wiped his forehead with his arm. "I'd prefer to have the rest of you down belowdecks, but getting to the stairwell's a big risk if the rebs throw another heavy volley this way. Safer to remain here behind the stack until we can get things under control. I'll have someone bring some blankets."

"Thank you, sir. We're most appreciative of everything you're doing to help us," Emma said.

Replacing his cap, the commander regarded Daniel and smiled. "Ready to crawl with me, sailor?"

Daniel grinned back. "I sure is, sir!"

Emma started to open her eyes but immediately shut them again, deciding she wasn't quite yet ready to deal with the bright early morning sunlight or the cyclical chugging noise in her right ear. Her mind and body were in a pleasantly cozy state, and she desperately wanted them to remain that way for a little while longer.

Pulling the wool blanket over her head, she folded her hands under her cheek and snuggled her back closer against the hard, warm surface behind her. As soon as she did, the memories of early this morning gradually came into focus: the ear-splitting, deck-shaking pounding of the *Monitor*'s powerful cannon; the jubilant yells of the *Galena*'s sailors as one of the cannon shots apparently hit some ammunition stores in the Confederate warehouse, igniting a huge explosion and fires; Daniel's gleeful, proud account afterward to Emma and the others of his role in helping Commander Rodgers pinpoint the target.

Daniel . . . the escape . . . that young sailor's blood exploding from his . . . oh, dear God! Now recalling vividly the entirety of last night's bittersweet drama and her own role in it, she threw off the blanket and sat bolt upright. On the deck beside her at the base of the smokestack, Sallie still lay sound asleep on her side under her blanket with Jason curled up in front of her. Daniel and Jim slept sitting up with their backs against the stack, blankets pulled up over their shoulders and heads lolling forward onto their chests. By the sound of their loud snoring, it would probably be a while before either awoke.

Looking through the gap between the top of the railing and the bottom of the suspended lifeboat on the starboard side of the deck, Emma noticed the sunbathed riverbank passing by at a rapid clip. Clearly, the steam-powered boat had been underway for some time. She stood and walked cautiously around the smokestack to assess the situation on the port side. Half-expecting to see the wounded or dead bodies of sailors from last night's battle draped over the railing, she was surprised to see the entire bullet-shredded area abandoned save for Boatswain Cox and another sailor standing casually and talking together near the forward end of the bow. The body of the young sailor who'd been shot through the back of his head in front of Emma's eyes was now gone—only a small amount of dried blood now marked the spot where he'd fallen.

Suddenly feeling nauseated, she walked up to the railing and gripped it with both hands. Even her experience nursing the recovering Confederate soldiers at the Petersburg hospital had not prepared her for the raw shock of last night's combat violence and bloodletting. Clearly, the recollection of it all was now producing a queasy stomach.

"Good morning, ma'am," Cox called cheerily. "Hope you slept well after all the fuss last night!"

Emma tried to put on a good face. "I did, Mr. Cox, all things considered. Thank you. Am I safe here—out in the open like this?" Emma asked.

"We're out of range of sharpshooters now, ma'am. And after we rounded City Point and took off down the James, not much chance of any reb shore cannons trying to block our way. We should be all right all the way to Fort Monroe, thank the good Lord! Got a lot of wounded down below who'll need tending to once we get there."

"And when will we reach the fort, sir?"

"I'd say about an hour or so, ma'am. In the meantime, you and your friends might want to talk to the commander about processing out once we get to the fort. Slaves are gonna have to apply for contraband status, but I'm not sure about your own situation."

"Thank you, Mr. Cox, I'll be sure we do that in just a little while. In the meantime, I hope it will be all right with you if I stand here a few minutes and appreciate the James River scenery—I'm not certain if or when I'll have the chance to see it again." A sudden thought struck her. "Unless, sir, you feel there might be some need for help with your wounded sailors down belowdecks, I am a trained nursing assistant, and I would be honored to offer my services."

Cox grinned and lifted his cap. "That's very kind of you, ma'am. But I'm pretty certain we have enough medical support for the men below. Better for you to stay up here and tend to your own folks. But if anything changes and we need more help, I will definitely let you know."

Emma turned again to face the shore. Thankfully, her brief wave of nausea seemed to have already passed, and she inhaled with pleasure the refreshing, salt-scented breeze that swept strongly past her face.

She realized that for the first time since accepting Sallie's invitation to join the escape effort, she was finally in a position to focus on the longer-term consequences of her decision and what she should do upon reaching Fort Monroe.

Thankfully, with the donation from Pastor Jones and his wife, she was not completely devoid of means. Unless some unforeseen huge bribe was required at the fort to secure her permanent passage into Union territory, she should have an ample amount to purchase some necessities, as well as a ticket on a steamer to Washington, DC. There, she could seek the help of her Aunt Lyla and Uncle James in finding some reasonable living quarters, and then look to obtain a job as a nurse or seamstress, for which there should be no shortage of opportunities. Once settled, she could begin to vigorously pursue her original motive for joining the escape: to fully devote her passion and writing skills in support of abolition and the uplifting of oppressed people everywhere. To do that effectively, of course, she would need to find a sponsor—someone to champion and mentor her efforts. How she would do that, she had no idea at this point. But perhaps she could start by locating and contacting her brother David using the Cleveland address supplied by Pastor Jones.

At this point, her greater concern was for Sallie. She could only imagine the depth of pain and anguish her friend must be feeling. Emma had left her own family with regret, but voluntarily. Sallie had suffered the agony of seeing her entire family ripped violently away from her, with virtually no chance for reunion—even assuming any of them were still alive. What Sallie would wish—and be permitted—to do upon reaching Fort Monroe wasn't at all clear. One possibility would be to go with Daniel to establish his dream farm in Ohio. A widower, Daniel would certainly benefit from taking on a loving, young stepmother for his child.

The other alternative, and the one that Emma was praying hard that she would choose, was for Sallie to accompany her to Washington, to live and work together with her there. Sallie's status as an escaped, contraband slave in Union territory was still uncertain, but Emma would do all in her power to see that she was granted her freedom as soon as possible. In any case, she would need to discuss the options with Sallie prior to deboarding at Fort Monroe.

As the boat rounded a bend in the river, Emma noticed what appeared to be a plantation's main house set on a hill near the northern bank up ahead. The sun had risen to the point where it was directly behind the top of the house, crowning it with a golden halo against today's sparkling blue sky. Her throat caught as she thought of Papa and Catherine, who just about now should be receiving the full news of her treachery. Would she ever see them again? Would they ever even *want* to see her?

The truth was, Emma knew she would miss Catherine far more than Papa—that was, if she could ever find it in her heart to forgive her sister for her callousness and lack of support when she most needed it. Then again, as Pastor Jones had urged in his final conversation with her just before the escape: "When it comes to the sister you were once so close to, Emma, don't let bitterness rule your heart. Remember to 'forgive one another, just as God also forgave you in Christ.' You never know what that forgiveness might accomplish—both for her and for you."

Wise words of truth, Emma thought wearily. *Someday, I know I'll have to consider them again.* For now, though, there were more urgent priorities. Fort Monroe lay just ahead. She turned away from the railing and went to rejoin Sallie and the others.

PART III

NEW VISION
(1862–1863)

CHAPTER 20

Frederick City, Maryland
September 14, 1862
(Four months later)

Entering the picturesque, border-state town on horseback along with the rest of the headquarters staff of Major General Joseph Mansfield's newly formed XII Corps, David marveled at the glorious reception.

The Union-supporting citizens were clearly ecstatic over the idea that the long column of blue-clad troops stretching forward and backward along the National Pike had come to their aid. It seemed like each civilian—regardless of age or gender—was competing with the others to be the first to welcome the march-weary soldiers and wish them well. At nearly every window, people displayed the Stars and Stripes as they bid the troops welcome and Godspeed. It was a relief knowing that once the column passed through, XII Corps would be leaving behind friends and not, as in Virginia, lurking, secret foes trying to shoot down the rear-guard pickets.

Riding along the side of the wide street, David paused his horse and reached down to take a small bouquet of flowers offered by a little girl in a yellow dress and white bonnet.

"Thank you, sir," she said shyly.

David smiled and placed the palm of his gloved hand on the girl's cheek. "I've never received a finer gift from anyone, young lady. Thank *you*!"

The girl's eyes lit up. She giggled and turned to run to her mother, who'd been observing the exchange from a few yards back. Struck by the young, brunette woman's comeliness and gracious smile, David lifted his hat, causing her to tear up and place her hand over her heart in appreciation.

The woman locked eyes with him and smiled again as the little girl clung to her waist. "Rest assured that I, Sarah Krause, and my daughter Jenny will pray every day and night for the Lord to protect you, sir," she called out.

David grinned, nodded, and replaced his hat. He coaxed his horse closer to where Sarah and Jenny were standing. "My best to the two of you and to Mr. Krause, ma'am. And tell him I said he's a mighty lucky man to have you!"

The woman lowered her eyes. "My husband passed away a year ago, sir."

David winced at his own carelessness. "Forgive me, ma'am. I am so sorry for assuming . . ."

"No need for apology, sir. We loved him and miss him, but we've adjusted. And anyway, it's you and your men whom Jenny and I wish to pray for now. God be with you."

David thanked her again, then spurred his horse to catch up with the line of staff officers. It had been two years since he'd last enjoyed close female companionship during his final year at Princeton, and the sight of the woman had awakened certain fond memories that he wished he had more time to cherish. *If I get through this next battle, I might just take a few days to come back here and thank Sarah Krause and her daughter Jenny for their prayers.*

The pleasant prospect was quickly tucked away for safekeeping as the clatter of the marching army and the sight of dense fog covering the ridgeline of South Mountain in the near distance to the west brought

David back to the present reality. He tightened his grip on the reins of his horse as the entire XII Corps column began to pick up speed.

Nearing the western outskirts of town, a low rumbling sound could be detected from the direction of the mountain. If General Mansfield's information was correct, an apocalyptic conflict was in the making. Hopefully, David thought, it was one that would reverse the frightening trend of Union army setbacks over the past six months—setbacks that, ironically, had sparked an amazing rise in David's own reputation and tasking by Union high command as a first-rate war journalist . . .

The Kernstown battle last March had clearly been a major tactical victory for the Union. Afterward, David had been highly lauded for his post-battle report, which, along with Captain White's death in subsequent fighting, had contributed strongly to Abel Bowman's recent promotion to commander of Company L.

Unfortunately, the tactical victory had soon turned into a strategic debacle for the Union army. By early June, the Confederates under Stonewall Jackson had regrouped and completely turned the tide, finally driving all Union forces out of the Shenandoah Valley following the Battle of Port Republic.

In the aftermath of that catastrophe and a subsequent major Union defeat in early August at Cedar Mountain, David had been ordered by his overall commanding officer General Banks—under heavy pressure from the US War Department—to conduct an independent, journalistic-type investigation of Banks's II Corps' troop morale and recent performance.

David's confidential, well-written final report—honest, incisive, and unsparing in its criticism of the wasteful practices and poor troop management decisions of certain II Corps mid-level commanders that had been greatly resented by many of the men serving under them— had been passed up the Union army command chain.

Within two weeks of the report's submission, David had been shocked to receive an official commendation letter from none other than US Secretary of War Edwin Stanton. At the bottom of the letter below Stanton's signature, a short note had been scrawled:

> *Mr. Hodge, please accept my sincere thanks and grati-*
> *tude. Your insightful report on troop morale, along with*
> *others I have been receiving lately, has helped greatly in*
> *informing my thinking and decisions on several matters*
> *of highest national importance. Keep up the excellent*
> *work! —Abraham Lincoln*

David's ecstatic reaction had been tempered somewhat by rumors that his report had generated significant ill will among some of the II Corps commanders—not only those mid-level officers directly implicated, but also some of their superiors, *including General Banks himself,* who felt that civilian war reporters like David had no business "pontificating" on commissioned army officer performance.

Thankfully, the rumors and negative mutterings against David had seemed to die down after a few days, and his reputation had remained untarnished.

But then came September, when the entire course of the war—and David's reporting chain of command—had turned suddenly on their heads.

It had all started when Confederate General Robert E. Lee—having previously relieved the threat to Richmond by forcing the withdrawal of all Union land and naval forces from the Virginia Peninsula—shocked the nation by quickly looping several rebel divisions totaling fifty-five thousand men around the Union's Washington, DC and northern Virginia defenses into western Maryland.

As punishment for their failure to stop Lee, General Banks was among several high-ranking Union officers who had been relieved of their commands (some insisted that David's earlier critical report had contributed heavily to Banks's demise).

The 7th Ohio Regiment, including Abel Bowman's Company L, had then been transferred to General Mansfield's newly formed XII Corps—part of Major General George McClellan's restructured Army of the

Potomac. In recognition of his exceptional reporting skills, David himself had been reassigned to report directly to the XII Corps headquarters staff, though he was still able to maintain close personal contact with Abel and his 7th Ohio unit.

"Little Mac" McClellan's orders from President Lincoln were crystal clear. He was to immediately march his massive, eighty-eight-thousand-man army northwest from Washington and intercept Lee's army near Frederick City. The objective was to engage and rout Lee's forces in a major battle, driving them out of the crucial border state of Maryland once and for all.

David knew how critically important this upcoming battle would be. If Lee was victorious, Union morale would be stretched to the breaking point—much to the delight of northern Confederate sympathizers and peace-seekers hoping to kill Lincoln's chances for reelection in November. With Lincoln gone, they knew, it was doubtful that the abolishment of slavery would ever again stand any real chance of coming about.

No doubt, the next two or three days could determine the ultimate fate of the nation. *With luck and God's help*, David thought, *I'll have a major Union victory to report on—a report that will lift the spirits of all who read it.*

At the town's edge, the unexpected order came from just ahead.

"XII Corps, halt! Officers, stand your men down and await signal to re-form!" The shouted commands from General Mansfield's adjutant were quickly passed by subordinate officers down through the ranks behind, gradually bringing the entire column of infantrymen, artillery pieces, and supply wagons grinding to a standstill with the bulk still clogging the main street of Frederick City.

David turned toward the officer next to him. "What's going on?"

"Artillery duel's heating up at South Mountain. McClellan wants XII Corps held in reserve for now," the man said, a slight note of relief in his voice. "Burnside's and Franklin's corps are about to try to shoot their way through the mountain gaps. We'll back 'em up."

"So why are we stopping?" David asked.

"Who the hell knows? Maybe trying to give Burnside and Franklin a little time and space up ahead to deploy before they make their moves."

David was about to ask another question when the clopping of hooves and a familiar, unwelcome voice calling out from behind caused him to turn suddenly in his saddle.

"Mr. Hodge! A word with you, please?"

The tone was unmistakable: this was not a request, but rather a command. Lieutenant Colonel Jonathan "Jack" Hurley—an impressive hulk of a physical specimen with barrel chest, florid face, bushy gray sideburns and beard—was not one to make polite appeals to those he considered beneath his station in life.

"Certainly, sir," David replied as Hurley pulled his horse up beside him. "How may I—"

"Best we find a private spot to converse," Hurley said brusquely. "It appears Mansfield will have us all floundering around here for at least an hour. I suggest we retreat to the little tavern I spotted just down the side street a little ways back—nice and quiet there, I'm sure. Shall we?"

David peered over his shoulder. Many of the other staff officers were already taking advantage of the stand-down order, dismounting and pulling their horses to the side of the road to swig from their canteens and engage in casual conversation with each other.

"Doesn't appear I'll be missed, sir," David said.

"Good. Follow me." Hurley turned his horse and led the way back along the side of the street as David, keenly aware of Colonel Jack's disdain for friendly small talk, trailed a few paces behind.

After tying up their horses and entering the small, well-kept tavern, the men ordered two tall glasses of cider at the bar, then seated themselves at an isolated table in the corner.

Jack Hurley leaned back and drained at least half of his drink in several huge gulps. Setting the glass down firmly, he wiped his mouth, leaned forward, and clasped his hands on top of the table. His eyes beneath the thick gray brows conveyed a clear message: he was not pleased about something.

"Mr. Hodge, let me get straight to the point."

David nodded, trying his best not to prejudge what this was all about, though he certainly had his suspicions.

"You're aware, I'm sure, that as principal assistant to McClellan's inspector general, I have a very demanding job."

"I have no doubts, sir," David said. Actually, that wasn't quite true. Hurley, an 1831 West Point graduate, had resigned his initial commission after only six months to pursue civilian notoriety as a wealthy real estate tycoon and strong supporter of radical Republican politicians. When the war broke out, he had volunteered his services— purportedly receiving his new commission as lieutenant colonel and appointment as assistant IG as a reward for his financial support of Thaddeus Stevens, the famous abolitionist congressman from Pennsylvania. Based on David's own previous interactions with Hurley, as well as some mutterings he'd picked up on from other XII Corps staff officers, Hurley's "demanding job" seemed to consist primarily of deciding the best way to ruin the military career of any lower-ranking soul who dared to cross him in the slightest fashion.

Hurley nodded and eyed him closely. "And do you know what the most difficult part of my job is, Mr. Hodge? I assure you, it is *not* the rooting out of isolated instances of waste, fraud, and abuse such as have plagued even the best performing armies in the history of the world. No, sir. The most difficult part of my job is fighting to set the record straight for good men whom I *know* have been falsely impugned for their patriotic intentions and actions."

David shifted uncomfortably under Hurley's piercing gaze. It was now clear where this conversation was headed. Collecting himself, he took a sip of cider. "That would be a difficult task for *any* honest man, sir."

"Quite true. And that's why I must express to you, Mr. Hodge, my strong disappointment in your recent report's conclusions regarding the common soldiers' views of General Banks and his officers' performance at Cedar Mountain."

"But . . . Colonel Hurley, I was only stating what I heard from—"

Hurley lifted his hand. "What you heard were the ignorant grip-ings of small men—men who've never known the pressures of having to make multiple, instantaneous decisions with minimal supporting information in the heat of a major battle."

I wonder if the noncombatant Colonel Jack would ever count him-self *among the ranks of those "small, ignorant men,"* David mused, his ire beginning to rise.

"I was especially dismayed," Hurley continued, "by that quote you included from your friend Captain Bowman, who, it seems to me, had about as much right to criticize General Banks for 'performing inade-quate reconnaissance' as *I* have to criticize Adam for failing to antic-ipate the serpent's presence in the Garden of Eden. It simply wasn't something that Bowman was in a position to judge, and in any case, it was not true. Bowman should have kept his big, arrogant mouth shut.

"And *you* should have taken care to present a more impartial report—perhaps less glowing descriptions of the performance of *your* friend Captain Bowman and his unit, and a fairer depiction of the hard decisions taken by General Banks, a magnificent officer who also happens to be a good personal friend of *mine*. Can you appreciate my position, Mr. Hodge?"

David could barely contain his fury. He struggled mightily to keep his voice calm and respectful. "Sir, I can definitely understand why my report would upset you. But I assure you, Colonel, it was not my intent to maliciously attack General Banks, but merely to follow my orders and report honestly the impact of his decisions on the morale of his men. If I had received instructions from the War Department to interview and include General Banks's counter-opinions in my report, I would gladly have done so."

Hurley stared hard at him for several seconds, then nodded and leaned back in his chair. Surprisingly, he seemed somewhat placated by David's response. *Maybe he just needed a chance to vent his frustrations,* David thought.

The colonel took another long pull from his cider glass, then set it down and reached into his coat pocket to pull out two long cigars.

He offered one to David, who politely refused, then returned it to his pocket and struck a match to light his own. After several vigorous puffs, he leaned forward once again. His eyes signaled a clear desire to strike a new tone.

"Yes, well, I suppose it's all water over the dam now, isn't it? I'm very sad that my good friend Nathaniel Banks had his reputation smeared badly by all this, but I don't doubt you reported what you did in good faith. And . . . I must admit . . . you *are* an excellent writer and journalist, Mr. Hodge. I can see why so many are impressed with you."

David blushed. Was Hurley serious? "Why, thank you, sir, it's very encouraging to hear you say that."

Hurley blustered on enthusiastically, as if his new topic was the only one he'd really wanted to discuss in the first place.

"Mr. Hodge, what is your opinion on the slave transition question?"

David stared at him blankly. "Sir?"

"The question of what should be done for the slaves as our army gradually liberates them from their plantation masters in conquered territories. I know you're a wealthy Virginia planter's son—and from what you told me before about the reasons behind your journey to the North, I would imagine this is a question you'd take great interest in."

David fondled his chin, slightly embarrassed that he hadn't already developed a cogent argument one way or another on this vitally important, emerging national issue. "Indeed, I *am* greatly interested, sir. Though with my concentration devoted to war reporting for both my newspaper and the War Department lately, I must admit to limited awareness of the latest expert views on that subject. Certainly, I'd support any view that emphasized giving all former slaves tangible help in adjusting to their freedom and preparing them for new jobs. But . . . may I inquire, sir, as to your own thoughts?"

Hurley's eyes lit up like a little child who'd just been offered a piece of candy. He took a long puff on his cigar and blew the smoke off to the side.

"Reparations, Mr. Hodge."

"Reparations, sir? In what form?"

"Land, of course. Apportion and grant them title to all plantation lands confiscated by the Union armies. God knows the poor slaves have suffered and worked hard enough to earn them."

David took another sip of cider. "On the surface, that sounds like a logical and just solution, Colonel," he ventured cautiously. "But I know personally of the resistance and outright hatred it would stir up among the southern White gentry if they were to be thrown out of their homes and stripped permanently of their property, with absolutely no chance at war's end to reclaim at least a portion of their land."

Hurley's eyes narrowed. "Seems to me that's exactly what they deserve, Mr. Hodge, whether they like it or not. What else would you suggest?"

"Well, if the main goal of this war is—as President Lincoln says—to end the rebellion and reunify the country quickly so that cooler heads from all sides can come together and pass national legislation to gradually end slavery everywhere, then it seems to me that the 'forced reparations' idea—if pushed too hard and too early—would only complicate things."

"How so?"

"By scaring the southerners and stiffening their backs—in ways that could greatly prolong the war and prevent any chance of future reconciliation."

"Hmmm." Hurley grunted. He turned to the side and crossed one leg over the other, then paused to relight his cigar. Resting his elbow casually on the table, he took another long puff before responding. "Hodge, can't you see the tragic error in that way of thinking? It is no longer privileged White southerners who will dictate how soon this war comes to an end. It is *their slaves*—enticed by an immediate national pronouncement of their freedom together with the prospect of obtaining land of their own. *They* are the oppressed, deserving souls who will rise up in droves to rupture the very foundation of the South's economy and join the invading Union armies in crushing the military forces of the Confederacy. But until our wavering, indecisive president comes to finally understand and act upon that principle, I fear we may indeed have to face the terrible prospect of a much longer war—not *because* of reparations, but rather for the lack of them. Does the argument in favor of reparations now make sense to you, Mr. Hodge?"

David scratched his jaw uneasily. "I'll admit it *does* make some sense, Colonel, though I'd have to study some more on the matter before making a final judgment."

Hurley smiled and uncrossed his legs, turning back to face David directly.

"I can respect that. And I must say, Mr. Hodge—since our time here is growing short—it encourages me to make a rather bold proposal. Could I convince you to study the matter further by reviewing a paper that I'm preparing for Congressman Stevens to illuminate President Lincoln on the subject? And if you find yourself in agreement, perhaps consider writing an article for your newspaper that would support our position? Personally, I can't imagine a better way to put your exceptional journalism skills to use in service of this nation."

David felt the blood drain from his face. The last thing he wanted was to bind himself to promoting the personal opinions of Lt. Colonel Jack Hurley, and yet when again would he ever have such an opportunity to influence the development of a historic US policy for liberating slaves? Wasn't that the primary reason he'd left home and family in the first place?

Just then, a bugle sounded outside, calling the men back to their formations. David was tempted to use the signal as an excuse to request more discussion on the subject at another time. But he could tell from Hurley's expectant stare that an answer would be required *now*.

"If you'll consent to allow me two weeks to read your paper and think about things before giving you my decision, Colonel, I'd be glad to do so."

Hurley grinned and extended his hand as the two men stood to depart. "Just as I was hoping, Mr. Hodge. I'll have a copy of the paper sent to you this evening. Given the importance of this matter to our national cause, I will definitely appreciate at the very least your honest and thorough consideration . . . quite unlike your friend

Captain Bowman's unfair and inaccurate remarks about General Banks, which I promise I will not soon forget. My best to you, sir."

David followed Colonel Jack out the door of the tavern, wondering what in the world he had got himself into.

CHAPTER 21

Antietam Creek, Maryland
September 16, 1862

The young buck private glanced back over his shoulder, observing the behavior of his company commander. Captain Abel Bowman seemed in a fury over something as he hurled a long sequence of biting observations augmented with wild gestures and vitriolic curses at the small group of junior officers gathered beside him under a nearby tree.

The private turned back to face David, who was sitting beside him just outside his undersized dog tent as the drizzle of warm, early night rain pattered against the canvas sides. A huge grin spread across his face. "I do believe I'd follow that man just about anywhere short of hell, sir."

"Is he *always* this way?" David asked.

Private John Wilcox, whom David had gotten to know during the Kernstown fighting, didn't answer immediately. He reached for his haversack and pulled out a piece of hardtack, took a bite, and then leaned back against the small log he'd placed in front of the tent's opening. "He's pretty much the same every night before a big battle. Wants to make sure none of the junior officers mess up and get their men killed for lack of understanding their orders. Have to admit, though, he does sound a bit more riled than usual tonight for some reason."

Although he hadn't yet had a chance to speak with Abel since arriving at camp earlier this afternoon for a personal visit, David could already guess the source of his friend's agitation: Lt. Colonel Jack Hurley.

Hurley had clearly decided to exact a measure of revenge for Abel's blatant criticism of Hurley's good friend, the former II Corps commander General Banks. It had come yesterday in the form of an official complaint that Hurley had filed, supposedly based on information he'd received from some "unnamed source":

> *Captain Bowman has proven derelict in his duty as Company L commander by failing to properly discipline two of his junior officers for leaving their units at night to engage in drunken and promiscuous behavior with several female citizens of Frederick City.*

... or something to that effect, according to one of the XII Corps staff officers who had overheard General Mansfield discussing the issue with Hurley.

The accused junior officers were two of Abel's best corporals—both known and respected by their men for their courage and leadership in the fiery cauldron of battle. Nonetheless, earlier this morning, Mansfield had ordered them suspended from combat duty and had called Abel into his tent for a severe dressing-down in front of Jack Hurley and some other high-ranking staff officers. Mansfield had then directed Hurley to conduct an investigation of the whole matter to see if further discipline was warranted for Abel and his two corporals.

Upon hearing the news, David had requested and been granted permission to visit Abel's camp prior to tomorrow's expected conflict in which Company L would likely play a significant role along with the rest of 7th Ohio. With two of his best men yanked away on the eve of battle and his own career now on the line, it wasn't hard to see why his friend would need some consoling and cheering up, or why his temper was now flaring.

Exactly as Colonel Jack would have it, David realized. He had no doubt that Hurley had orchestrated the whole thing. Not only to make Abel's personal life miserable and harm his reputation, but also—knowing David's concern for Abel's career—to force David's active support on the ex-slave reparations issue in return for Hurley's leniency in conducting Abel's investigation. *Two birds with one stone. Why not?* David thought bitterly.

When Abel's tirade finally died down, David sat up and prepared to go talk with him but then checked himself. *Probably best to give him a few more minutes to cool off.* He reclined against the log once again, tilted his head back, and gazed at the stars. It was nearing 9:00 P.M. Almost all the men had retired inside their tents—some to write what might be their last letter to their family or sweetheart, some simply to grab a few hours of fitful sleep before the wake-up call sounded.

Glancing over at Private Wilcox, David couldn't help but wonder what the young man was contemplating for his role in the big battle tomorrow, and what it was like for someone like him to follow an officer like Abel into battle.

"Tell me honestly, John. After Captain Bowman took over the unit following Kernstown, do you believe the other men in the company hold him in the same high esteem that you do? I promise to keep your answer in confidence."

"Oh, no worries there, sir. There's nothing to hide. Everybody respects the captain, and a whole lot of us think he's far and away the bravest company commander in the whole regiment. Loves to lead the charge from the front without the slightest hesitation, spurring the men to get off their fat arses and follow him. It's true I've heard a few say they worry the captain seems to *enjoy* fighting and killing rebs so much that maybe there's something wrong with him. But the rest of us just chalk it up as passion for his cause."

David cocked his head. "Interesting you'd say '*his* cause,' John—isn't it the same as yours and the rest of the men?"

Wilcox hesitated, seeming to bite his lip as he considered carefully his response. "Good question. To tell the truth, Mr. Hodge, I'm not so sure."

"Really? What do you see as the difference?"

"Well, sir, when I think about my own reasons for enlisting and fighting, I only had two things that drove me then—and still do now."

"And what are those?" David asked.

"Way I see it, sir, is that the founding fathers made this country, and we their children are called to save it from rebels and traitors. This war's just as holy as the Revolution that first gave us our liberties and privileges, and I'll be hanged if I'm going to just sit back and let all the good things that bind us together be destroyed. That's the first reason . . . it's my duty."

"And the second?"

"Second's kinda personal. Fact is, before enlisting, I knew I'd been living pretty much an aimless life—but fighting for my country has finally given me a way to feel like a good and useful man in this world."

"What about the slavery issue?" David asked. "Doesn't that drive you as much as your first two reasons?"

Wilcox winced slightly, thinking for a moment before offering his answer. "I *do* believe slavery's dead wrong, but I can't say in my heart that's one of the main reasons I'm fighting. I'm fighting mainly to preserve what our fathers formed for *all* our benefit: one united republic, ruled by the Constitution."

David smiled. "You sound like President Lincoln. He admits slavery's a great moral evil, but just recently I heard he told Horace Greeley, the abolitionist, that if he could only save the Union by freeing *all* the slaves, he would do that—but if he could only save it by not freeing *any* of the slaves . . . then he was just as prepared to do that as well. Saving the Union by any means is uppermost in Lincoln's mind. Freeing the slaves is important, but secondary."

Wilcox nodded. "And unless he's changed, I don't even think Lincoln holds any esteem for the slaves themselves. My pa told me when Lincoln was debating Stephen Douglas just before he got elected, Lincoln said he didn't think Blacks should vote or hold office or intermarry with Whites, and that he believed that any 'superior position' in society should be assigned to the White race. He also suggested that once the slaves were freed, they should be set up in colonies somewhere in Africa or Central America."

"Seems like, unfortunately, that's more or less the opinion of quite a few northern White folks," David said. "Can't say I agree with it, personally. I've known quite a few slaves who I'd say are far superior examples of God-fearing, society-respecting human beings than a lot of White people I've met."

"I haven't had the luxury of knowing any negroes myself, sir. But I'll take your word for it. Anyway, that is exactly what I meant when I said Captain Bowman seems driven mainly by a different cause than most of the rest of us."

"How's that?"

"Well, as I remember the captain's own words to some of us grunts recently: 'There's but one way to win this war, gentlemen, and that is through immediate and total emancipation of all slaves and their incorporation as fully equal members of society. I want to join hands with my colored brothers and sisters singing "John Brown's Body" in the streets of Charleston, and then ram red-hot abolitionism down the rebs' unwilling throats at the point of a bayonet.' He seems to equate the memory of John Brown with his own personal vision of glory. In fact, he told all the men when we assembled this afternoon that he might have some kind of surprise in store for us along those lines tomorrow, if we behave ourselves."

David chuckled. "That definitely sounds like the Abel Bowman *I* know. He met John Brown, you know, at an abolitionist meeting a few years back. In fact, Abel and I had the distinct though tragic honor of together witnessing Brown's execution at Harpers Ferry. That's where I first met your captain."

"Oh, yes, he did mention that now I recall," Wilcox said. "But," he added cautiously, "I think he knew John Brown *way* before that abolitionist meeting."

David looked at him askance. "*What?* How could that be?"

The private hesitated and shifted uncomfortably. "There's this rumor ... don't know if it has any merit ... that the captain was involved somehow with Brown and his men in those Pottawatomie murders in Kansas, and that the whole experience had a huge impact on him. I've no idea in what way, but if it's true, it might explain a lot about what's motivating him now."

"It certainly could," David muttered softly. *Why hasn't he ever told me about any of* that? Suddenly the memory of his first conversation with Abel in the Charles Town tavern following John Brown's execution flashed in his mind. Abel had mysteriously alluded to the uncertainty of receiving a "second chance in life." Was his apparent angst somehow related to his experience at Pottawatomie?

David had just begun to nod off when the sound of approaching footsteps jolted him awake. Looking up groggily, he saw he was now the only one sitting against the log—Wilcox had retired and was snoring away inside the tent.

"Well, my friend, it's only ten o'clock and it seems you've managed to bore even your good friend Private Wilcox to death," Abel Bowman said as he handed David a tin of hot coffee. "Care to take a little walk?"

David stood and allowed Abel to lead the way down the path between the rows of Company L tents bordering the east bank of Antietam Creek.

"Apologies for wasting your time making you hang around here so long." Abel's voice sounded weary, but he seemed in a slightly better humor after having ended the diatribe against his junior officers an hour ago.

"Everything in order for tomorrow?" David asked.

Abel took a sip of coffee from his own tin, then shook his head resignedly. "Who knows. The two new corporals seem smart and willing enough, but this'll be the first time either have actually led anyone in combat before, and I've had less than a day to get 'em ready. All thanks to our good 'friend' Colonel Hurley, of course."

David nodded. "I can't believe what he's trying to do to you, though I suppose it really shouldn't surprise me. After this battle, I think we should—"

Abel held his hand up. "I can't talk about that right now, David. Have to stay focused on tomorrow—may be the toughest situation we've faced yet. We had it easy during the South Mountain battle, letting the other corps win the day by punching through the gaps while our Twelfth followed merrily along in their wake. But it's our turn now. We'll be crossing the creek later tonight to get in position, and then I expect we'll be called early tomorrow to support General Hooker's I Corps' advance down the Hagerstown Turnpike to Sharpsburg. I'm told that our favorite enemy Stonewall Jackson has just arrived there with three divisions from Harpers Ferry, and make no mistake—by morning, Lee will have him reinforced to the teeth." He stared at David. "I have only one thing to say about Hurley for now."

"What's that?"

"If the good Lord wills it, after tomorrow, that jackal and everyone he's trying to deceive will swear in his heart that 'dereliction of duty' is *not* a phrase to ever mention again in connection with the name Abel Bowman."

"Why? What're you planning for tomorrow? Private Wilcox said you were hinting at something to your men today but didn't reveal it."

Abel abruptly stopped and dumped his remaining coffee on the ground. He faced David with one arm akimbo, a mile-wide grin on his face. "Guess we'll all just have to wait and see what tomorrow has in mind, won't we?"

CHAPTER 22

Approaching the outskirts of the Union's capital city, the stagecoach driver leaned to the side and called back to the vehicle's occupants. "Fifteen more minutes, sirs!"

Despite his excitement at being invited to attend the private reception at the White House celebrating Lincoln's announcement of the Emancipation Proclamation, David hardly took notice, engrossed as he was in rereading—for the fifth time—his final edited version of Private Wilcox's harrowing story.

Dear Mr. Hodge,

I hope this account of my personal experience on September 17, 1862, with Company L, 7th Ohio Regiment, XII Corps on the Antietam battlefield, will prove satisfactory to your readers. If I hadn't seen it with my own eyes, I could scarcely believe my own telling of it all.

We were ordered to fall in about 11:00 P.M. the night before and get ready to march. After crossing the northmost bridge over the creek, we arrived about 3:00 A.M. near the rebels' encampment. Our officers told us to crash on the ground and get whatever sleep we could. Dawn came quick, and with it the sounds of artillery and musketry and the order to fall in again. Barely awake and our joints stiff, we started marching southwest toward where the enemy was already engaging General Hooker's I Corps on our right. We arrived at a wooded area held by the rebels, and Major Crane deployed our regiment in line of battle to the right, with Co. L on the far-right end. At that point, we were ordered to halt and await the order to march into the woods.

Because of the severe losses Co. L had taken in our last battle, most of our men were extremely nervous—a few visibly shaking—at the prospect of advancing. That was when Captain Bowman chose to reveal the surprise he'd promised us yesterday.

Pulling a folded silk cloth out of his haversack, the captain asked Lieutenant Jones to step forward, stand beside him, and face the men. Together, they opened up the cloth and held the 5-by-4 rectangular shape up high by its top corners for all the men to see. It was a sight none of us will ever forget. In the center, two crossed silver sabers were stitched on a field of royal blue. Nestled between the blades was the most sublime, artistic rendering of an eye that I've ever seen. It seemed to be staring at us with an animal-like ferocity, challenging each man to look deep inside themselves and face the hard truth of whatever was there. Across the top, the words "Eye of Glory" were emblazoned in large, bold lettering. Across the bottom: Company L, 7th Ohio.

"What do you think, boys?" the captain asked us.

"Nice . . . but where'd ya get it, Cap'n?" one man yelled.

"Dropped right out of heaven, soldier! Hope that's good enough for you," the captain answered, making all of us laugh. I don't know exactly what it was, but right then we all felt a powerful new bond with Captain Bowman that steadied our nerves and made us eager to follow him into the woods—come what may.

"Who will carry this?" the captain shouted. Four of the boys, including myself, raised their hands immediately, and the captain picked Private Adams. The rest of us helped Adams nail the flag to a nine-foot wooden staff that one of our junior officers had obviously brought along for the occasion.

It couldn't have been more than five minutes later when the order came to form ranks and fix bayonets. I looked down the front line to the left and saw the Stars and Stripes and our regimental flag being hoisted high and waving back and forth, drawing huge roars of approval from everyone.

On our end of the line, Captain Bowman drew his saber and held it over his head. "This is it, men . . . make your 'Eye' proud. For the preservation of our Constitution, for the crushing of slavery and the evil Confederate power that controls it, for your posterity's future and God's glory . . . forward, march!" With the captain and Private Adams leading the way with our new company flag and the rousing first verse ("Mine eyes have seen the glory . . .") of the Union's new "Battle Hymn of the Republic" on our lips, onward we trekked with hearts in our mouths toward the woods just ahead. We weren't certain what we'd encounter there, but twenty yards in, we sure found out.

Three men near me dropped in rapid succession, their heads and bodies shredded by a fusillade of leaden hail spewed from somewhere up ahead. We soon discovered the source: a line of rebels masked by a fence and lying flat on the ground, their dirty, gray, ragged uniforms making it difficult at first to spot them. After sending volley after volley of our own considerable hellfire into their hiding place, we charged it, bayoneting any survivors still resisting and putting the rest to flight. At the fence, the rebel dead lay in blood-soaked piles, so sure and lethal had been our assault. We pursued the rest out of the woods and into a field of standing corn where the ground was already literally covered with dead and wounded from the rebs' engagement a little earlier that morning with Hooker's men. The carnage was terrible beyond all description. No language can describe it, nor pen even picture it.

We followed them a mile or so, but the seventy rounds of ammunition each of us had been given began to run out, and so we were all ordered to lie on the ground and wait for replenishment from the rear while shot and shell went screaming through the air above us. That's when Lieutenant Jones crawled over to where I was lying.

"Wilcox," he said, "Adams was hit. Captain wants to know if you're willing to carry the flag." I hesitated for a second, knowing as color-bearer I'd be a prime target for every reb sharpshooter on the field. But considering it a test of courage and manhood that I was too afraid to fail, I quickly assented and moved up the line with Lieutenant Jones to join Captain Bowman.

With cartridge boxes restocked, we shifted our regimental line of battle even farther to the right and marched to the top of a small hill where we saw the rebels were advancing toward us in strength. We retreated just out of sight behind the hilltop, then dropped down and lay in wait as they approached. The captain looked at me. "On my command, Wilcox, you and I will be the first to stand . . . let the 'Eye' stare them down a few seconds before the rest of our men blast 'em to hell."

Suddenly one of our advance skirmishers who'd been wounded in the arm came running back over the hilltop and dropped down beside the captain and me. "They're only fifty yards away, sir!" I tightened my grip on the flagstaff, awaiting Captain Bowman's signal.

"Now, Wilcox!" he shouted. We both jumped up and stood on the crest of the hill alone for a full ten seconds with "Eye of Glory" planted firmly on the ground between us, glaring at the mass of gray bearing down on us.

It was a moment frozen in time; the rebs in their front lines hesitated. They looked at us but seemed too shocked at the strange sight to point their weapons and shoot.

To my great relief, Captain Bowman waited no longer. "Fire, men!"

As one, our Company L soldiers rose along with the rest of the regiment down the line. We poured a deadly fire upon the rebs, mowing so many down that the rest became completely broken and confused, retiring in confusion and rout. With victorious shouts, we chased them all the way to the little white Dunkers church next to the Pike, where finally we were ordered to halt and let others take over.

As we wearily wound our way back through the cornfield and woods, the sight of the dead lying mangled and torn in horrid ghastliness of repose was truly sickening. Wounded rebel and Union soldiers lay side by side, many crying and screaming in their pain, some offering water to each other. We passed by our division commander, and he paid the entire 7th Ohio a high compliment, saying we'd shown good order, coolness, and courage in battle. Once again, Company L had taken heavy casualties, but we could not have been prouder of our unit, our captain, and our new "Eye of Glory" company flag.

Sincerely,

Private John C. Wilcox

David laid his writing pad down on his lap, closed his eyes, and wearily massaged his temple with his right hand. One of the two well-dressed businessmen seated on the opposite bench smiled sympathetically. "You look like you just finished reading an obscure Shakespeare play."

"Something like that," David muttered, too tired and preoccupied to engage in friendly conversation.

Correcting Private Wilcox's misspellings and grammar had required quite an effort over the last day and a half, but at least the substance and details of his account had been faithfully preserved. Mr. Cowles and most of his *Cleveland Leader* subscribers would be quite happy with the result, David was sure, especially since everyone on the home front had been starved for *any* inspiring report of Union battlefield fortunes over the past few months. The other beneficiary of Wilcox's account would be the US War Department under Secretary Stanton, who would no doubt read it and use it to help bolster President Lincoln's confidence that Union army morale and spirit were alive and well.

What wasn't so clear was how the story would be received by Lt. Colonel Jack Hurley and his investigatory team. Would the firsthand account of Abel's courage and leadership in battle help Abel's cause? Or would Hurley merely toss it aside as some "manufactured tale" concocted by David to help Abel escape the hook from the dereliction charges leveled against him? If there was one thing almost guaranteed to destroy the career of a young, promising infantry officer like Abel, David knew, it was being convicted of dereliction of duty in any form.

There was one other troubling aspect of Wilcox's story, David thought. It left out a disturbing incident that Wilcox had privately shared when he'd met with David yesterday morning to hand him the first draft.

"The captain and I were trailing behind the rest of the men on the way back through the cornfield," Wilcox had related. "We stopped at the sound of a wounded reb soldier off to our right begging for water. Went over to him and saw he was missing his arm and bleeding bad from his stomach as well. Obviously didn't have more than a few minutes to live. Captain Bowman offered the craggy-faced old codger a drink from his canteen. He took it, looked at the captain gratefully, and said: 'Didn't ever believe I'd have a Black-lovin' Yank givin' me a drink. Maybe you're fightin' on the wrong side?' The captain's face flushed as red as Mars, and he squeezed his eyes shut like he was trying to remember something. He finally seemed to calm down. Opened his eyes, smiled, and pulled his pistol out. 'I am most definitely fighting for the right side, soldier.' He pointed his gun and shot that poor reb bugger right between the eyes. All to put 'im out of his misery, I suppose, though it did seem harsh to me."

David had listened to Wilcox's story addendum without much comment, not wishing to reveal his growing concern over Abel's mental state. Despite Abel's inspirational leadership and heroic actions, this latest excess only confirmed the previous whispered rumors: something seemed not quite right with him. David knew that sooner or later he would need to confront his friend over it. Right now, though, it was time to clear his mind and prepare for the reception at the White House—hosted by Abraham Lincoln, President of the United States.

❦

The tall, lanky, sunken-chested leader of the Union glanced up at his audience and raised an eyebrow, as if trying to discern whether anyone besides himself had appreciated the humor in the slapstick joke he'd just told to open the festivities.

A few chuckles and nodding smiles seemed to confirm that his efforts had at least partially succeeded. He grinned hesitantly, quietly surveying the small group of cabinet officials, aides, and other invited guests standing expectantly around him near the ornate fireplace in the ovular-shaped White House Blue Room.

"No need for everyone to stand at attention the whole time," he said finally. He pointed past his audience toward the room's impressive array of furnishings in the Rococo Revival style, including pale-blue brocatelle-covered armchairs, sofas, and a large circular settee featuring a great central pouf, on top of which rested a golden ornamental vase filled with fresh flowers. "Please, make yourselves comfortable."

He looks relieved but totally exhausted . . . like he's been carrying the weight of ten thousand heavy rocks on his shoulders, David thought. Not at all surprising, given the almost unbearable pressure that President Lincoln had been under these past several months from friend and foe alike.

"Well, gentlemen," Lincoln began after the guests had taken their seats. His voice had taken on an air of grim resignation tinged with sadness. "I hope my clumsy attempt at lightening the atmosphere tonight didn't offend anyone.

"These recent times have been a rough stretch, to put it mildly. Yes, in a strategic sense, we gained a clear victory after last week's battle—finally forcing General Lee to end his Maryland campaign and withdraw all his forces across the Rappahannock, back into Virginia. But, oh, the cost, the cost! With over twenty thousand casualties combined on both sides—and still counting—there's no other way to put it: the Antietam fight was by far the worst single-day calamity in the history of our great republic. Not only that, with General McClellan's failure to follow through on our advantage to pursue and annihilate Lee's forces once and for all, they've escaped to fight another day. Once again, I fear we've needlessly prolonged this agonizing national conflict for some time to come."

Almost everyone in the room involuntarily bowed their heads, cringing at the horrible implications of what the president had just confirmed.

"And yet, gentlemen, the Antietam military outcome gave me, at long last, great reason to hope that a bright future beckons—*if* we stand firm and don't give in to the demons that threaten our courage and will to persist. As you're all aware by now, this morning I finally did what I had been putting off since July by announcing to the press the Emancipation Proclamation, which—*if* the South refuses to capitulate—will take effect on January first, 1863. Now, I don't want to stand up here and ramble on about things you undoubtedly already know about this, but before we all break for some refreshment and celebration of sorts, I'll be glad to take a couple of questions . . ."

"Mr. President!" called out Wilbur Smith, a top reporter from the *Evening Star*, "we understand the Proclamation would theoretically mean immediate freedom for all slaves in states and territories of the Confederacy. But if it can't be enforced as long as the rebels are in control there, what practical difference will it make?"

"Plenty, Mr. Smith. If we can keep strong pressure on them militarily over the next one hundred days, it'll cause the South to think seriously about the advantages of capitulating. And if they do that before the New Year, the Union will be restored, the proclamation will not go into effect, and we can negotiate a fair long-term plan—*including compensation to southern slave owners*—for the end of slavery throughout the entire nation. Otherwise, if they don't yield and the Union military eventually prevails, the southern masters will lose not only the war but also their slaves and any possible compensation."

"So, in effect, it's a bribe for the rebels to surrender early, sir?"

Lincoln smiled. "You might say that, if you wish—though the term 'bribe' sounds a bit less altruistic than what I had originally intended for my Proclamation."

After the good-natured laughter over his self-effacing remark died down, a stentorian voice boomed from the back of the room. *"Mr. President!"*

David turned toward the source and blanched at the unexpected sight of Lt. Colonel Jack Hurley standing beside the armchair in which his friend and ally, Congressman Thaddeus Stevens, was seated.

"Yes, Colonel Hurley?" Lincoln asked.

"Sir, as you know, the idea that it's the Union's moral responsibility to provide *reparations* to freed slaves is receiving strong support in many abolitionist circles lately. I was wondering how you see the Proclamation as either promoting or diminishing this possibility."

Lincoln nodded. "Ah, yes. Reparations. Definitely a thorny issue, but an important one. For now, let me just say this: we have to be very careful not to overplay our hand by claiming that the Proclamation—if and when it takes effect—will automatically require reparations from defeated southern masters to their slaves. That is *not* the intent of the Proclamation, nor should it be. At this point, we are simply striving to get the South to quit the fight. We are *not* interested in giving them another reason to keep on fighting to win in order to avoid inevitable punishment. But, that said, I'm thankful to know that you and Mr. Stevens will be meeting with me next week to further inform my thinking on the matter. I have much respect for your views on this."

Hurley beamed at the compliment. "I look forward to that, sir, and I'm pleased to say there are a growing number of people who I believe can help convince you of the value of such a policy."

Lincoln chuckled. "Oh? Someone I don't already know?"

"Some people right in this room, sir . . . such as Mr. Hodge there from the *Cleveland Leader*, who's promised to help us develop our latest position on this."

David flushed ten shades of red as Lincoln stared at him, his face lighting up in appreciation. "So *this* is the famous David Hodge who sent Secretary Stanton and me those excellent battlefield morale reports. Those reports helped my decision to hold up announcement of the Proclamation until now. Welcome, sir! I look forward to hearing what you, Colonel Hurley, and Mr. Stevens have to say in support of the reparations issue."

Struggling to hide his dismay and fury at Jack Hurley's obvious gambit to force his hand, David followed the others to the back of the room where mint juleps and glasses of champagne were being handed out in preparation for the celebratory toast to the Proclamation's release. He started to approach Hurley to vent his feelings at being unfairly boxed into a corner, but suddenly thought better of it. This was not the time or place to start a quarrel, and besides he still had to consider his behavior toward Colonel Jack in light of Hurley's investigatory power to make or break Abel Bowman's future career.

Taking a champagne glass from the server's tray, David walked toward a quiet corner to collect his thoughts. His solitude did not last; soon after the toast, he was joined by President Lincoln himself.

David had once read a southern newspaper description just before the election that described Lincoln as "the leanest, lankiest, most ungainly mass of legs, arms, and hatchet face ever strung upon a single frame." Indeed, beholding him up close now, he thought the description rather apt, and now understood Lincoln's reported decision to accept the advice of an eleven-year-old girl to grow a full beard to help distract attention from his gaunt, wrinkled, acne-scarred and asymmetrical face.

Lincoln extended his hand, his bright, dreamy gray eyes conveying an unusual combination of deep intelligence and friendliness. "A pleasure to meet you, Mr. Hodge."

David gulped. He had not expected *this*. "Thank you, Mr. President. The honor is completely mine."

After the two men had engaged briefly in small talk about the oppressive late summer heat and the president's hopes to escape it at his new cottage at the Old Soldier's Home, Lincoln took a sip of champagne and wiped his mouth with a small napkin. "Mr. Hodge, I've been thinking about something recently, and—given your background and experience growing up in Virginia—I'd like your opinion on it."

David barely suppressed a gasp. "Of course, sir."

"As I'm sure you're aware, there are many well-intended abolitionists like Jack Hurley who're absolutely convinced that once the South is defeated and humiliated, once the negroes are freed and compensated with a little plantation land and money for past mistreatment by their whipmasters, then all will be well. But I worry, Mr. Hodge. It seems to me there's another issue that must be dealt with very soon—one that will prove critical to the peace and harmony of our reunited nation in the longer run. It's the question of how to integrate the colored freedman into the normal workings of society. There are those who bluntly state that anything short of granting ex-slaves immediate, full equality in every sphere of economic and civic life would be an obscene violation of the 'all men are created equal' clause of our Declaration of Independence.

"I must admit I myself am currently torn on the matter. I'm strongly supportive of equal opportunity for any freedman to improve his economic lot in life, but I'm hesitant to immediately grant the vote and eligibility to hold civic office to people who I'm not convinced—yet at least—are ready and able to do these things responsibly. I'm curious what your own thoughts might be on that issue, Mr. Hodge. Will the freed slaves be able to handle the challenges of full citizenship, were they to be granted that status?"

Put at ease by the president's candor and friendly, disarming tone, David responded without hesitation. "Mr. President, having grown up on a large plantation with over eighty slaves—and later having the opportunity to observe and interact with many well-functioning free

Blacks, including the great Frederick Douglass in Ohio—I truly believe there's one thing that will *ensure* the 'readiness and ability' for full citizenship of the vast majority of freedmen."

"And what's that?"

"Education, sir. I'll never forget what Mr. Douglass said to me when I interviewed him: '*Some men know the value of education by having it, but I know its value by not having it.*' He said he was secretly taught basic reading by his former master's wife until the master found out, but after that, he had to learn everything on his own with little or no help. Imagine though, sir, if our reunified nation were to actively promote and support literacy, civic, and vocational education for the freedmen. Wouldn't that be one of the best and quickest ways to help them start contributing fully and equally to society and enjoying its benefits?"

Lincoln folded his arms and nodded. "Yes, yes. Many others have also stressed to me the importance of the educational aspect, and I'm inclined to agree. In fact, I've been wondering whether education should take precedence over land reparations as the immediate focus of our ex-slave transition support efforts. It seems less controversial and much easier to manage, though I admit it doesn't seem to pack quite the excitement of a 'whole new beginning' that private land ownership would provide." He bowed his head, clearly still wrestling with the options before him. "Oh, well, we won't solve all this tonight. But thank you for your insight, Mr. Hodge."

"You're most welcome, Mr. President. I'm honored that you even asked."

Lincoln looked up suddenly, a sparkle in his eye. "Mr. Hodge, this might be premature to suggest, but would you be at all interested— when the time is right—in helping the US government conduct a little experiment?"

David grinned. "It would be hard for me to say no to the President of the United States, sir."

Lincoln laughed. "You might want to hear what it is first. I don't know if you're aware, but for nearly a year, the Treasury Department's been sponsoring an effort along the Union-controlled coastal areas of

South Carolina to help us learn the best ways to help newly freed slaves move from the plantation to viable occupations in either the military or civilian life. What would you say if I asked you to lead an independent team to help my administration investigate and report on the progress of the next phase we're contemplating for that project—one that for the first time will include *both* land ownership and educational opportunities for the ex-slaves?"

David could hardly believe his ears. *Did I actually hear this right? An offer from President Lincoln himself to lead the investigation of a major governmental project?* "Why, sir, that is an astoundingly exciting request. And, yes! I would gladly accept it. My only hesitation being that I have no formal experience as a land manager or professional educator."

Lincoln nodded. "Nothing to worry about on that score. I've no doubt we can find you some well-qualified assistant investigators who would do a marvelous job of observing and analyzing all the details in each of those areas. What I'd need from you is simply to keep an eye over the whole team. Provide Treasury Secretary Chase and me with a well-balanced picture of what's really going on in terms of the overall project's progress, obstacles, morale, things like that. Inform us on whether newly freed slaves can profitably own and manage their own land, or whether it would be wiser to have them work under a supervised, wage-based system while they concentrate first on their education. Occasionally write up a few success stories for newspapers and national magazines to keep Congress and the public supportive of the project. Exactly the kinds of things you've done so well for me in your war reporting."

"*That* does sound like something I could handle, sir, and definitely something I'd be honored to accept."

"Wonderful!" Lincoln said. "Let's be patient for a while . . . see how the war situation plays out over the next several months. At that point, I'll have Secretary Chase get in contact with you. In the meantime, be prepared for a new development that the Proclamation is likely to produce: Black soldiers enlisting in the Union army. If you encounter any of them in your journalistic endeavors, I'd love to hear how they are perceiving their experience."

"I will most definitely attempt to engage them sir," David said.

Lincoln stretched out his hand, signaling the end of the conversation. "And most importantly, Mr. Hodge, whatever you do, try to stay out of harm's way in these battlefield-reporting situations. I'll soon be needing you for other purposes!"

Sitting alone that evening at a small table in the Old Ebbitt Grill on 15th Street, David pondered the momentous events of the past two weeks over a tall glass of beer and a plate of pot roast, potatoes, and coleslaw.

The Antietam experience had truly been horrific—not only in terms of the unparalleled carnage he'd witnessed afterward on the battlefield, but also in terms of the trauma experienced by David himself when his horse was shot out from under him by a whizzing rebel cannonball that had somehow managed to reach the XII Corps staff headquarters location. The poor beast had been nearly split in two, neighing in extreme agony until David was finally able to collect his wits, pick himself up, and fire a merciful bullet into its brain.

Private Wilcox's account had provided an uplifting counterpoint, but his story of Abel Bowman's post-battle behavior was alarming. If Jack Hurley were ever to get wind of it while his investigation of the Frederick prostitution incident was still ongoing, there could be no hope that Abel's military career would ever survive.

Lt. Colonel Hurley himself was turning out to be a major thorn in David's side, using his power over Abel's investigation and his influence with President Lincoln to extort David's support on the reparations issue. David had promised to respond to Hurley's "request" by next week. What his response would be, he hadn't yet decided.

Further complicating matters was Lincoln's offer for David to head up the South Carolina project investigation team. While tremendously exciting, how might Lincoln's need for his independent stance in leading such a team compete with Hurley's request for his explicit support in pushing land reparations alone as the unquestioned, penultimate national solution for the ex-slave transition issue? And if he turned Hurley down, what would that mean for Abel's military career?

"May I get you another helping of the pot roast, sir?" asked the young waitress who had been busily attending all seven of the tavern's tables by herself.

David smiled. "No, thank you, miss. But I assure you it was excellent!"

"Thank you, sir, I'll be sure to let our cook know you said so."

As she scurried off to the next table, her looks and manner reminded him of a somewhat less elegant version of his sister Catherine. *I wonder how it goes with her and her husband Joe. Was Joe involved in the Antietam fighting? Is Catherine at their new home, longing for his return while fearing the worst? Does she still hate me? And for that matter, what about Emma and Papa? How are they all faring since the Union army's withdrawal from the Virginia Peninsula? It's been over a year since I heard anything about them from the letter Pastor Jones sent. Do they ever think about me?*

The sadness in his heart over the total separation from his family eventually gave way to a more pleasant, recent memory. He had made himself a vow of sorts upon leaving Frederick City just before the battle. There was a lovely young single mother and her child there—Sarah and Jenny Krause—who had promised to pray for him. On his way back to rejoin the XII Corps headquarters staff, he would pay them both a visit.

CHAPTER 23

Hodge Family Plantation
December 12, 1862

Catherine tossed the spadeful of potatoes that she'd just extracted from the muddy ground of the Hodge Plantation's private vegetable garden into the basket beside her. Wiping the sweat off her brow with the sleeve of her work sweater, she wondered what Papa would say if he were here to advise her now.

The terrible memory of those last few moments before Papa's sudden death from heart failure in early November still burned in her soul. There hadn't even been enough time to call for a doctor or pastor. Yet despite his pain and belabored breathing as he lay on the bed, he'd still been able to clutch Catherine's arm, look her intently in the eye, and speak lucidly.

"Catherine," he'd said, his voice halting and barely audible, "I've asked the Lord's forgiveness for anything I've ever done to hurt anyone, especially David and Emma. I hope you'll forgive me too, daughter. And if you ever see them again, please tell David and Emma I hold nothing against them—and pray they'll forgive me as well for whatever I may have done or not done to drive them away."

They were his last words. It was the first time that Catherine had ever heard Papa express any hint of regret for his actions in regard to their family, and the first time he'd ever conveyed any real tenderness of feeling for her. After his eyes closed and he drifted away, she had sobbed uncontrollably, clasping and kissing his dead hand for at least half an hour, after which Ben had finally managed to gently pull her away.

Upon Papa's death, and given David and Emma's abandonment of the family, ownership and management of all aspects of the Hodge Family Plantation and its business connections had fallen immediately and entirely into her lap. After an exchange of letters with Joe, who was off fighting with his unit somewhere to the northwest, she'd gone to consult with Mr. Tidwell, her friend Amanda's father and owner of the neighboring plantation. How, she'd asked him, was she supposed to manage and care for *two* plantations—her own Hartwell Plantation and her father's Hodge Plantation—simultaneously?

The first order of business, Mr. Tidwell had suggested, was to ensure a smooth, orderly transition for the Hodges' domestic servants and field slaves—for without that, the entire plantation's operation and even survival would be imperiled. The only way he saw to accomplish that was to renew the contract with Philip Taylor and his son, Sam. She should do so immediately, he'd said, because with so many men now being called up to join the Confederate army, experienced overseers were getting extremely hard—if not impossible—to come by.

Despite her deep personal distaste for the Taylors, she'd realized she had no other real choice, and two weeks ago had signed off on a new five-year contract that even included a slight raise.

Within days of the signing, there had been indications of trouble resurfacing between Sam and some of the slaves. It was the kind of trouble that she could not avoid facing any longer, and today was the day of reckoning. *Papa, if only you were here to handle this crazy—*

"You wanted to see me, Mizz Cat?"

Catherine stood and turned to face the owner of the polite-sounding voice behind her.

"Yes, Sam . . . actually, I asked to see you a half hour ago, but I suppose you had other important priorities to attend to." *Like romancing your tramp girlfriend Liz Wheeler in your barn,* she thought angrily. What excuse would Sam Taylor offer this time for his continuing lackadaisical support of Catherine's efforts to manage the plantation following Papa's death?

Sam grinned innocently and tipped his hat. "Well, ma'am, turns out I had to give a little 'talk' to three of the fieldworkers who've been missin' their quotas lately. It's not like the old days, Mizz Cat. After that no-count sister of yours bolted with Sallie and the Eppes slaves on that Yankee gunboat, seems like proper respect and fear of masters and overseers in this whole region kinda disappeared along with 'em."

Catherine glared at him. "I'd appreciate it if you'd leave derogatory comments about my sister out of your conversations with me, Sam. Emma had her reasons for what she did—and though I definitely don't agree with them, I *know* she's a good, loving person at heart."

Sam put his hand on his hip and tilted his hat back. "Sorry I offended you, Mizz Cat. I just can't help gettin' a little miffed every time I think about what your brother's and sister's actions did to destroy your poor father's spirit and health. He—"

Catherine raised her hand. "That's enough, Sam, *please!*" Wiping a tear away from her eye, she refocused on the unpleasant task now facing her.

"Sam, I think you know the reason I called you here."

Sam observed her warily. "Ma'am?"

Catherine turned away and stooped down to resume her spading as she spoke. "When Papa willed our family's plantation and estate to me a few months after Emma left, he said he was counting on me to avoid some of the mistakes he felt he'd made. Especially in not looking out enough for the slaves' safety and welfare. He deeply regretted that in his anger over Emma and Sallie's flight he'd gone too far, taking everything out on Sallie's parents and little brother by selling Mary to that Georgia slave trader and leaving Tom—despite his badly wounded state after getting caught in the escape attempt—here alone to fend for himself and Lew."

Sam shook his head. "Hard for me to see anything but that they had it comin' to 'em, Mizz Cat. They knew what they were doin' and the consequences if caught. I'm not sure why your father felt so bad about what he did. Heck, most owners around here wouldn't have gone so easy on Tom and Lew. I know *I* wouldn't have. But anyways, what's all that got to do with me?"

Catherine threw a potato into the basket and whirled around to face him. "Sam, I know you've never gotten over Emma's and the Cobbs' accusations against you concerning Charles's death, but I am *not* going to allow you to keep pursuing a personal vendetta against Tom and Lew."

"*What?* What are you talkin' about, ma'am?"

"You know good and well what I'm talking about."

"No, I don't. Why don't you tell me?"

Catherine put her spade down and stood up once again. She folded her arms and glowered at him. "One of the other slaves told me Tom was really sick, so I went to take some food and check up on him yesterday. He looks like he's dying, Sam—that gunshot wound never really healed, and it's become seriously infected again. Lew told me he'd gone to see you at your barn the other day about getting some help, but that your 'girlfriend' Liz met him out front and said you were too busy to be bothered. That if Lew didn't shut up and skedaddle, she'd be happy to tie him up and give him a good thrashing herself. I've got Tom and Lew staying up at the main house now for the time being, with Dorothy tending to Tom and the doctor coming tomorrow.

"But what I want to know from you, Sam, is why you never told me about Tom's condition . . . and also, what is that hussy Liz Wheeler doing on *my* property, threatening *my* fieldworkers? Are you going to help me manage and care for the workers on this place properly, or do I need to look for someone else? With my husband away fighting patriotically for the South's survival, I can't possibly run *both* Hodge and Hartwell Plantations on my own without reliable help!"

Sam dropped his hand from his hip. His face was a scowling mask of hurt pride and indignation. "I am truly in awe of what your husband and many of our other brave Virginia men are doing to protect us all from the Yankees, Mizz Cat. But I *resent* your inference that those of us who haven't yet joined the fight are somehow less patriotic or honorable, or—"

"Sam, I didn't say that! I—"

"No, you let me finish. I admit I've been a little too casual with Liz lately, and I promise to make sure she stays off the property from now on. But as far as Tom, I swear I checked on him no more than four days ago, and he called out from his cabin that he was 'doing much better' and that he'd be ready to work the fields again in a few days. Maybe I shouldn't have trusted him and instead gone in to check for myself, but I didn't and I'm truly sorry for that now. Guess we all make mistakes once in a while, don't we, Mizz Cat?"

Somewhat pacified, Catherine softened her voice. "Of course, Sam. I meant no disrespect to you. I know your job isn't easy. And I'm glad you're committed to recognizing the situation with Liz for what it is and doing something about it." She sighed. "Heaven knows I've got enough to worry about just managing and caring for the eight slaves at my Hartwell Plantation, without the help of *any* overseer. I do appreciate and need your help here, Sam, as you know I can't be here all the time. I just want to make sure we do things right by our slaves."

Sam smiled genially. "I totally agree with you, ma'am. And I know what pressures and concern you must feel with Captain Hartwell away, especially with that battle at Fredericksburg going on right now."

Catherine stared at him in wide-eyed dismay. "Battle at Fredericksburg? I-I hadn't heard . . . I thought Joe's unit was still encamped up north on the Rappahannock River, not expecting to fight for a while. When did this start?"

"Just yesterday, ma'am. In fact, I heard from someone down at the City Point dock that it's a big one—Yanks are throwing everything they've got against General Lee."

After politely dismissing Sam and thanking him in advance for "tending properly to things from now on," Catherine returned home to the Hartwell Plantation and, plagued with a headache, retired early to bed without any supper.

Tossing and turning for over an hour, she finally drifted off into a long night of fitful sleep punctuated with bizarre dreams recalling past interactions with her family and a surreal replay of her husband's last visit in late October . . .

Sunset had arrived, setting the trees of the Hartwell Plantation front grounds aglow with sparkling reflections of light off the orange and yellow leaves. She drew the master bedroom window curtain open slightly and peered down the path toward the entrance gate. She gasped, and her hand flew to her chest. There he was, astride the tall, gray stallion his father had gifted him following his graduation from VMI. He reached down to grab the outstretched hands of little June, the seven-year-old daughter of Catherine's personal maid. He lifted her up onto the horse with him, clearly unconcerned about the appearance of any impropriety. As he'd once said to her, a child was a child—whether Black or White, loved equally by the Heavenly Father. He looked toward the window and raised his hat. He'd seen her!

Catherine waved back, her heart beating wildly. She turned and walked quickly to her dressing table to complete her final preparations. She could already feel the familiar, pleasant tingling of anticipation throughout her entire body. After weeks of separation, it would be all she could do to keep herself from throwing herself on him the moment she saw him up close.

A light knock on the door. She checked the tiny single bow that held her revealing chemise together at the neckline, eagerly imagining his fingers untying it. Holding her breath, she opened the door.

"Hello, darling."

She nearly fainted at the sight of him: stooped, thin, straggly long hair framing his still-handsome face; a thin, two-inch scar on the left side of his forehead; a faraway, vacant stare in his eyes as he tried to smile.

"Joe!" she cried, grabbing his limp hand and leading him to sit down on the edge of the bed. "What happened?" She removed his hat and touched his wound lightly with her forefinger.

He flinched, grasped her wrist, and pulled it away slowly. "It's all right, Catherine, it doesn't hurt. It'll be all right, please don't worry."

"But Joe, what—"

He put his finger to her lips, closed his eyes, and sighed heavily. "We're in trouble, Cat."

"Tell me, love."

He gazed at the floor, shaking his head sadly. "Disease is ravaging our camp. The men are being marched barefoot to the bone, and we have too many skulkers and cowards refusing to stand and face the Yanks' fire. Antietam just took it all out of us." He looked up at her, his eyes moist.

She placed her arms around his neck, pulling his head toward hers to where their foreheads touched. "Joe, why do you keep fighting? You've been in several hard battles and won glory enough, certainly for me. You're hurt. You've more than done your part—they'll let you off. Please, Joe, just come back to me . . ."

"Don't do that to me, Catherine. A Virginia army officer who quits on his men—before the fight for our families and our southern way of life is finished—would be held up before his countrymen in disgrace. I will not have my dear wife burdened forever by my personal dishonor."

She pulled her head away from his. Despite his present haggard condition, his face appeared just as gorgeous to her as it had on their wedding night.

"Joe, I promise . . . you will never, ever be a burden to me."

She stood and backed away from the bed. Lifting her hand shyly to the bow of her chemise, she untied it slowly and smiled at him. "Did you miss me, Captain Hartwell?"

Joe's eyes widened. "God knows how beautiful you are to me, Cat." He rose from the bed and approached her. Pressing his body against hers, he lightly stroked the curves of her waist and hips as he kissed her deeply. He lifted her and carried her to the bed, where he laid her down and covered her with a sheet before hastily removing his own clothes as she watched, giggling. He removed the sheet, and she raised her arms to welcome him.

CHAPTER 24

Hartwell Family Plantation
December 15, 1862

After three exhausting days checking on the main house's condition and conducting personal visits with some of the Hodge Plantation slaves, including Tom and Lew Cobb, Catherine finally managed to break away and return home.

The next morning, she awoke in her bed at the Hartwell Plantation, groggy and with yet another splitting headache. But there would be no opportunity to dwell on her discomfort; her maid Florence was knocking insistently on her bedroom door.

"Mizz Cat, Mizz Cat, please wake up. Miss Amanda and her friend here to see you. They been waitin' over a half hour already, and they gettin' kinda antsy."

Catherine bolted out of bed and rushed to her dressing table, calling out to Florence to bring her a bowl of fresh water and linens. With all her busyness lately, she had completely forgotten that today was the day Amanda and Charlene would be visiting for morning tea. *How can I treat them like this . . . my best friends?* They had unflaggingly supported her after Emma's flight and Papa's death and had been the main ones sustaining her during Joe's prolonged absences.

Forsaking all her usual frills, Catherine quickly washed her face and neck, brushed her hair, and threw on the most elegant morning gown in her wardrobe. Her headache having thankfully subsided, she rushed downstairs to the parlor.

"Ladies, please forgive me . . . I confess I'm losing all sense of my social schedule these days. I even forgot to tell Florence last week when we set our date so she could remind me."

Her friends laughed.

"Don't worry, Cat," Amanda said. "It's a treat for us 'common folk' to see you in your more natural appearance—which still seems a cut or two above the average princess!"

"Besides," Charlene chimed in, "who *hasn't* lost all sense of schedule lately, especially with all the news from Fredericksburg?"

Catherine felt a sudden spasm of nausea. "News? What news?" She'd been on extreme edge every day since hearing about the battle from Sam, knowing that Joe's unit was most likely involved.

Amanda and Charlene exchanged glances.

"Oh, Cat!" Amanda reached out and grabbed her hand. "My father showed me the newspaper this morning . . . our boys have won a great victory over the Yankees!"

"Yes," said Charlene, "they threw back wave after wave of bluecoats attacking the heights behind the city. I heard they killed over twelve hundred of them. General Lee was supposedly 'delirious' with joy, wanting to hug everyone after it was over. Cat, you must be so proud of Joe and everything he's—"

Charlene froze in mid-sentence at the sight of Catherine's distress and rushed over to throw her arms around her and console her. "Cat, please forgive me. I can't believe I was so insensitive."

Catherine dabbed her eyes with a handkerchief. "I'm sure he's fine. If not, I would've heard something by now, I'm sure. And after all he went through and survived at Antietam, if this victory is as grand as everyone is saying, then I'm most probably worrying over nothing."

After two hours peppered with lively speculation about the war's harsh impact on plantation life and the latest social gossip, Amanda and Charlene took their leave. In a far lighter mood and her stomach now settled completely, Catherine ate a small dinner and then lay down on the parlor couch for what she thought would be a short nap.

By the time she awoke, it was after 5:00 P.M. and the approaching mid-December evening had cast the entire room in long shadows. Catherine sat up, stretched, and leaned over to light the brass oil lamp next to the sofa. She would give herself half an hour to read the latest edition of *Harper's* magazine that had been delivered yesterday, and then it would be time to sit down with Florence and plan out the week's supply needs. With food shortages beginning to be felt everywhere in the area, this would require a lot of careful effort.

Hearing the unexpected noise of raindrops on her roof, she stood up, wrapped her cloak around her shoulders, and walked outside to the veranda. Sure enough, a cold drizzle had set in, and with it, the low layer of clouds that were causing the evening darkness to arrive sooner than usual.

She was turning to go back inside when the sight of a single-horse carriage entering the property at the far end of the pebbled driveway caused her to stop and do a double take. An odd shiver raced through her body before she recognized the vehicle as belonging to Joe's friend Oscar Hamilton, the state congressman.

Over the past year, Oscar and his wife Rebecca had made it a practice to stop by for short visits every other week or so to check on Catherine's needs, inquire for news about Joe, and generally to help lift her spirits. The last three times, however, Oscar had been coming alone, saying that Rebecca was either "busy" tending to their young children or "not feeling well today." Each time, he'd stayed longer than Catherine had thought proper, and his conversation had become just a bit too familiar and inquisitive. Given Oscar's good looks and premarital reputation for being a ladies' man, she had felt a distinct need to maintain her guard. Still, in these lonely and stressful times, she was grateful for visits from anyone friendly and familiar, and Oscar certainly met those qualifications.

What juicy tidbits will he try to pull out of me this time? she wondered. Somehow, she'd have to find a polite way to dismiss him quickly since she really needed to work on the supply list with Florence.

Oscar drove the carriage up to the bottom of the veranda steps. Without his usual wave of greeting, he stepped down from the driver's seat and handed the stable boy the reins of the horse. Head lowered, he began to walk slowly up the steps.

"Hello, Oscar," Catherine offered hesitantly. As he reached the top, he removed his hat and lifted his head. He stood only a few feet away, his eyes bearing an inexpressible sadness.

"Oscar . . . ?"

"Cat, I-I'm . . ." he stammered.

"*Oscar*, what is it?"

"I just came back from Richmond. They just published the casualty lists from the battle. It's Joe, Catherine . . . I-I'm so sorry . . . he's—"

"No." She shuffled backward and swallowed hard. "He's fine. You're wrong."

"Catherine." Oscar's eyes pleaded with her. He ran his shaky hands through his hair. "I saw his name."

Her chin trembled, and all the color drained from her face. "That's not true. The list—it must be wrong."

Oscar took a cautious step forward and reached his hand out. "Cat, I'm so sorry. I'm so terribly sorry."

She hunched over, her mouth open wide. No sound came out at first, but then a bloodcurdling scream broke free. There was no stopping it. She fell to her knees as a sob from deep within her heart overtook her body, her soul.

Oscar ran to her and helped her up, half dragging, half carrying her to the parlor sofa. He sat next to her with one arm over her shoulders and the other lightly touching her arm as she rocked back and forth, unable to speak.

Her crying lasted for a lifetime, it seemed, but she finally was able to utter one sentence: "How did it happen, Oscar?"

Oscar squeezed her arm. Strangely, a slight smile lit up his face. "I overheard two of the men in his regiment who'd survived and were looking over the lists to find out what happened to their relatives in other units. One of them said Captain Hartwell had stood his ground bravely along with ten of his men when fifty Yankees converged on the cannon position they were defending. Unbelievably, they managed to beat them off, but at the end, Joe took a stray Yank bullet to the forehead. It was over in an instant. Your husband died a true hero of Virginia and the Confederate cause, Catherine."

Tears gushed once again down Catherine's face as she absorbed the full impact of Oscar's story and recalled the strange dream of her last, sweet time together with Joe. Oscar continued to offer gentle, soothing words of comfort, gradually bringing her to the point of rationally facing the inevitable, though with what felt like an arrow piercing her heart. Joe was gone forever, just as were Papa, Mother, David, and Emma. And now she had no one.

"Cat," Oscar said as he stood to leave and held her closely in his arms, "I want you to know that there is *nothing* I won't do to help you get through the pain of this. I'll do everything I can to help with the funeral arrangements, and if you ever need and desire my help in managing or financing your plantations or providing for your personal needs, please just let me know and I will be there for you."

Catherine choked back more tears as she touched his arm. "Oscar, thank you, and I look forward to future visits from you and Rebecca." She noticed the slight wince he displayed at her mention of his wife's name. She wondered vaguely if something was wrong but said nothing. Tonight, the only pain and sorrow she could deal with belonged to her alone.

Four hours later, after Florence and the other house servants had been informed of Joe's death and expressed their sincere devastation with much weeping and wailing, Catherine sat at her dressing table and stared at herself in the mirror.

She recalled the time three years ago when she'd sat in the exact same position in her bedroom at her parents' plantation, remorseful over the way she had just accused her sister of wrongdoing with the slave-boy Charles. She'd been in the prime of her late adolescent beauty then, so eager to win Joe Hartwell's affections at the upcoming ball and oblivious to Emma's feelings for Charles. God had tolerantly granted her selfish heart's desire then. But now, things had come full circle: her siblings gone, her parents deceased, and . . . *No!* She couldn't allow herself to think of him. It was as if God had confirmed that the treasures of life were his to give and to take away, but try as she might, she simply couldn't accept it.

She glanced over to the side of the table and spotted the small penknife—the same one she used to employ so effectively in dealing with the pains that had racked her abdomen during those earlier times of concealed self-hatred and depression. Ever since Joe had swept her away, she had completely lost her need to trade one form of pain for another. But now, Joe was gone. So was her family. Forever. She was on her own.

Just a couple of cuts in the right places, and everything will feel better.

She picked up the knife and pressed the small blade's sharp tip against the inner side of her forearm. *That's it, just a little one.*

She closed her eyes, and suddenly, the sweet memory of her last time with Joe flashed through her mind. Putting the knife aside on the table, she laid her head on her arms and burst into sobs.

A week later, Catherine received a message from Joe's commanding officer, who expressed his sympathies and informed her that Joe's body had been recovered and buried by a local Christian society in a marked, single grave in the cemetery of a small church near the battlefield. At Catherine's option and expense—and at any time of her choosing—the coffin could be exhumed and transported home for final interment. This would take place at the Hodge Family Plantation cemetery, Catherine had immediately decided, since without Joe she would be unable financially to hold on to the smaller Hartwell Plantation that the two of them had founded.

Meanwhile, over the last few days, her headaches and depression had continually worsened. Responding to Florence's concerned urging, she had finally arranged for Dr. Haynes to come up from his Petersburg office for a house visit this morning—Christmas Eve.

At first, Catherine protested Haynes's suggestion to conduct an internal examination. Her mind was consumed with worries about Joe's burial arrangements and preparations for the sale of their smaller plantation. An internal exam, in her mind, wasn't going to fix her stress-induced headaches, but Dr. Haynes convinced her that it was important to be thorough.

Catherine lay back in her bed, overcome with anxiety as to the diagnosis. *What if I'm really sick, like Mother was, and have to give up the Hodge Plantation too? Where will I bury Joe?*

After finishing the exam, Haynes said nothing as he cleaned and put his instruments away in his bag.

Unable to stand the suspense, Catherine blurted out: "Doctor, what is it? Is it serious?"

Dr. Haynes looked up at her with a huge grin. "Oh, it's most definitely serious, Mrs. Hartwell. You're going to have a baby!"

CHAPTER 25

Washington, DC
February 20, 1863

Emma sat upright in one of the carved wooden chairs spaced around the perimeter of the magnificently decorated lobby of the Smithsonian Institution's auditorium.

Any minute now, the auditorium doors would be opened, releasing the small contingent of well-dressed politicians and antislavery supporters who'd been invited to critique the afternoon rehearsals for tonight's major speeches. Bringing up the rear would be the speakers themselves, with one of whom Emma had succeeded in arranging a private interview this afternoon: the famous abolitionist from South Carolina, Angelina Grimké.

Emma tapped her fingers on the arms of her chair in nervous anticipation. If someone had told her last May—when she, Sallie, and the other escapees had disembarked from the Union gunboat at Fort Monroe—that *this* is where she would be sitting nine months later, she would have thought them out of their mind.

Looking back on the events that had brought her to this point, she realized it was only by God's grace and with the help of the financial gift from Pastor Jones and his wife that a way had been found . . .

The first major hurdle had been cleared at Fort Monroe. Emma had waited patiently in a temporary shelter on the fort grounds while Sallie, Daniel, and his young son and cousin were being processed as contraband slaves under the Union army's protection. Within a week, they'd been granted their freedom papers signed by the regional army commander. It was then that Sallie had made her decision to accept Emma's invitation to accompany her north to Washington.

It had not taken much convincing. The only alternative would have been to remain with Daniel and the others, who would soon be required to transfer to the Grand Contraband Camp that had just been established in the nearby, Union-controlled city of Hampton, Virginia, to accommodate the overflow of escaped slaves arriving at Fort Monroe. But Daniel had made it clear that he and his young son would not be ready anytime soon to risk leaving the camp's protection and free services. He hadn't given up on his vision of moving north to build a farm in Ohio, he'd said, but it would have to wait until war's end. This had not sat well with Sallie, who did not like what she'd heard about the chaotic conditions in the new camp and dreaded the idea of getting "caught there forever." The greater likelihood of finding suitable permanent housing and sustained work in Washington—along with the continued availability of Emma's close friendship and emotional support—had seemed a far more attractive option.

After exchanging her Virginia state currency for US dollars at the Fort Monroe trading post despite a 20 percent loss in value, Emma had purchased some new clothing and a small space for herself and Sallie on a supply steamer headed north along the coast into the Chesapeake Bay and then northwest up the Potomac River to Washington. When they'd disembarked four days later, the Sixth Street wharf had been crowded with recently wounded soldiers awaiting transfer to local hospitals. Wading their way through the stomach-wrenching sights and sounds, the two had finally managed to extricate themselves and commission a short carriage ride to Aunt Lyla's well-appointed, three-story brick row house in the Georgetown section of the city.

Aunt Lyla and Uncle James Merton—the prosperous manager of a horsecar track line running between M Street and Pennsylvania Avenue—were initially shocked by the unexpected appearance of Emma with a former slave girl on their doorstep. But after hearing their story and lamenting over the sad Hodge family news, they had welcomed them both with open arms and offered the use of the third-floor guest rooms at a bargain rental price for as long as needed. In a stroke of luck, the Mertons' previous housemaid had just been fired for stealing silver from the kitchen pantry, and Aunt Lyla was pleased to offer Sallie her first paying job as the maid's replacement. While the work was only part-time, it took care of Sallie's room and board and permitted her the flexibility to find supplementary work elsewhere.

For Emma, the first item of business had been to write a letter to David at his Cleveland address, announcing her arrival in Washington and seeking a way to reunite if possible. The next day, she'd begun her employment search. This had proven more difficult than expected, but after a month, she finally landed steady part-time work as a seamstress for a local Georgetown tailor's shop. That left two weekdays and evenings along with weekends free to pursue her true goal of connecting with a local abolition advocacy organization to which she could volunteer her considerable writing talent and passion.

In early October, soon after the Emancipation Proclamation was announced, her quest had hit a major roadblock during her interview for an entry-level editorial writing position with the American Missionary Association's local chapter.

"Miss Hodge," the tall, imperious supervisor of AMA magazine and newsletter production had told her, "your writing samples are of outstanding quality, but we are living in rapidly changing circumstances. As you know, slavery was abolished here in the Union's capital last April, and with the Proclamation soon to take effect, we're well on our way toward achieving that same goal throughout the land. The main energy and focus of our organization is shifting . . . away from pressing politicians to support antislavery legislation and toward ministering to the many economic, medical, and educational needs of recently freed slaves. And right now, we're only accepting volunteers with strong, validated credentials and experience in Christian schoolteaching or in actively serving the hurting and underprivileged."

"Sir," Emma had entreated, "both of those are definitely skills that I've cultivated and have experience applying, beyond just my writings on the evils of slavery."

Peering impatiently over his spectacles, the supervisor had then asked the question that had brought the interview to a quick conclusion. "And *where* did you say you had acquired such credentialed skills and experiences, Miss Hodge? On a wealthy Virginia plantation where you and your family enjoyed unparalleled privileges over the slaves you were 'serving'?"

Emma had immediately grasped the pointed message. "I understand, sir. Thank you anyway for your time." Crushed with the sudden recognition that her upbringing and past associations could greatly inhibit her ability to pursue her life's passion, she'd stood and left the interview, uncertain what else she could do.

Thankfully, Uncle James—upon hearing her sad report—had urged her not to give up and to seek other connections. The following night, he'd shown her a leaflet announcing plans for a coming lecture series at the Smithsonian Institute featuring prominent people in the abolitionist movement.

Spotting Angelina Grimké's name on the schedule for February 20, Emma had excitedly recalled reading some of Grimké's works while staying with Miss Lewis in Petersburg. *This* was someone she would truly love the chance to listen to and speak with. Immediately, she'd dashed off a letter to Grimké's address, explaining her own background, enclosing some samples of her writing, and expressing her ardent desire to meet with Grimké, if possible, at the Smithsonian.

The intervening three months had passed slowly, with no word back from either David or Grimké. Her spirits sagged, and despite her constant prayers, she began to lose hope that life in the "North" would ever offer any opportunities beyond the mundane roles of shopworker and, perhaps someday, a housewife.

In early February, however, Emma's efforts had finally been rewarded when Grimké had replied with enthusiastic compliments on Emma's writings and suggested a private interview immediately following her speech rehearsal the afternoon of the event. Every day since, Emma had chafed at the bit, preparing her questions for Grimké and praying this would prove to be the way out of her recent sour mood . . .

"My word, it's absolutely stifling in here and unusually mild outside today," said the petite, fiftyish woman dressed in a cream-colored frock, her dark hair pulled back and tied in a classic Victorian bun. "Emma, would you be averse to a walk with me to the Botanic Garden in front of the capital? It's only about a mile or so away."

"It would be my honor, Mrs. Weld," Emma replied, glad that she had remembered to use Angelina Grimké's married name. "I'm thrilled to have this opportunity to meet with you."

The two women left the Smithsonian building and set out on the sun-drenched path bordering the National Mall. In the near distance, the US Capitol, with its partially constructed new dome, marked their destination; farther away, the new, half-completed Washington Monument could be seen rising against the clear blue sky. Within a minute or two, they had struck the bond of shared passion over a common cause and were conversing like old friends. At Emma's request, Angelina regaled her with a few brief stories of her own childhood and teenage years growing up on her family's wealthy South Carolina rice plantation, witnessing slave abuse and later rebelling against the pro-slavery stance of her parents' Anglican church to the point of becoming a Quaker and moving north to live with her sister Sarah in Philadelphia.

"Those were the days!" Angelina laughed. "I actually had physical stamina, my voice was strong, and by the 1830s, I was writing my heart out, speaking to halls filled with women and, later, many men as well. Not all of the latter were supportive of my abolition message, of course. I'll never forget that day I spoke at the new Pennsylvania Hall in Philadelphia, and a mob of angry rioters outside didn't like what I was doing, so they threw bricks and stones, breaking the hall windows. But that didn't stop me, and at the end of my speech, I left the building safely, arm in arm with a racially diverse group of women. The next day, an arsonist burned that building to the ground.

"My goodness, if I were faced with that today, I would collapse at the podium and they'd have to carry me out. That's what twenty-five years of marriage, child-rearing, and failing health have brought me to. Teaching the children of other abolitionists at the boarding school in Massachusetts that Sarah and I run is the extent of my labors these days. But, Emma, enough of me. I want to know about *you*. What led to your interest in abolition and your excellent writing talent? And how can I help you in your efforts to employ it?"

Over the next few minutes, Emma recounted highlights of her past life on the plantation, her flight to Fort Monroe and then to Washington with Sallie, and the disappointment and heartache she had felt at being stonewalled last October by the AMA supervisor.

"I know I have the skills and experience they require, but because of where I come from and without any credentials, I'm stuck."

Angelina nodded, then was silent for a short while as she seemed to ponder how to respond. "Emma," she said suddenly, "there are two things that you need. The first is to understand who you are dealing with in the AMA and organizations like it. You are dealing primarily with *men*. Men with good hearts and intentions, but also with great pride in their own educational accomplishments and their own grand ideas about who is qualified to help them 'fix the world.' Given your plantation-life background, it may require the strong personal testimony of someone else they feel they can trust to convince them that you truly have what it takes. Someone credible to them who's actually observed you in action as a teacher. I'm not sure who that 'someone' might be for you, but in any case, let me offer assistance on the second thing that you'll need no matter where you choose to apply next: a reference letter from someone established and known in the abolition community. Based on what I've come to know about you, Emma, there's no one for whom I'd feel more compelled and delighted to write one."

Emma pulled up short and gaped at her with shocked delight. "Oh, Mrs. Weld, I can't thank you enough. That is just so kind."

Angelina embraced her. "Just promise me two things, dear," she said, a twinkle in her eye.

"What're those, ma'am?"

"Promise me you'll take every opportunity God gives you to express, with great boldness, that deep compassion for the less fortunate that God has placed on your heart. And also promise you'll keep in touch. An old abolitionist fighter like me needs to hear encouraging reports from the younger generation once in a while to keep her going!"

Emma laughed. "I promise, Mrs. Weld . . . on both those counts. And I can't wait to hear you speak tonight! My friend Sallie will be joining me."

Later that night, on their way home after attending the speeches, Emma and Sallie sat on the passenger bench of one of the new, covered, horse-drawn rail cars that Uncle James had commissioned to transport them between Georgetown and the Smithsonian.

Angelina Grimké, though perhaps no longer the fireball speaker of her youth, had still managed to thrill her audience with her eloquence, wit, and inspiring calls for action in the face of continued political resistance to total and immediate abolition, not just in the conquered southern areas but in the border states as well.

Sallie was still gushing over what she'd witnessed. "Emmy, I never heard nothin' like that before. Mizz Grimké sure know how to fire up a crowd."

Unsmiling, Emma simply bowed her head and nodded.

"Emmy, what's wrong? You look like you mad about somethin'. Aren't you happy Mizz Grimké gonna write that reference letter for you?"

Emma smiled sadly. "Oh, I couldn't be happier about *that*. But I'm just not sure what to do about the other thing she said I needed . . . someone who could personally 'testify' and vouch for my teaching ability with people like that AMA supervisor. I so very much would love to have that teaching position, but I just don't know how I can do anything more to convince them on my own at this point."

Sallie nodded and looked down at her own lap for a long minute. Emma thought she'd fallen asleep. Suddenly she lifted her head, a mischievous smile on her face.

"Miss Em, I got an idea . . ."

Sallie Cobb adjusted her straw capote bonnet one last time. Taking a deep breath, she clutched the sealed envelope under her arm, opened the door of the AMA's Washington, DC local chapter office, and entered.

"May I help you?"

Her first sight of the young, well-dressed Black man seated behind the large, paper-strewn wooden desk caught her by surprise. Had Emma given her the wrong address?

"G-Good mornin', sir," she stammered, "I was hopin' to see Mr. Billingham, the magazine supervisor."

The man glanced over his shoulder toward the closed door behind him. "I'm afraid Mr. Billingham's very busy this morning and isn't entertaining visitors, Miss . . . ?"

"Uh . . . Cobb, sir . . . Sallie Cobb."

Standing up and walking around the desk, the man smiled graciously and extended his hand. "My name's William Johnson—I'm Mr. Billingham's assistant. I can take your request now or schedule another appointment time for you with Mr. Billingham if you'd prefer."

Out of modesty, Sallie averted her eyes as William took her hand in his and shook it gently. He was extraordinarily good-looking—tall with medium build, square-jawed with mustache and short goatee, a full head of curly black hair parted on the side, and large, wide-set dark brown eyes set off by a pair of wire-framed gold spectacles. Overall, there was a distinctly intellectual—though not at all stuffy—air about him, something she found herself strangely attracted to.

"Well, Mr. Johnson, if it be all right with you, it ain't all that easy for me to get down this way, so I'd appreciate if I could explain things to you today. And then maybe you could tell me what else I might need to do before talkin' to Mr. Billingham."

"Certainly, Miss Cobb," William said. "Please, come take a seat." He led her to the small chair facing his desk, then resumed his own seat behind it. He quickly rearranged some of his papers, then smiled graciously and invited her to proceed.

Sallie leaned forward, holding the envelope in her lap. "I'm here on behalf of a good friend o' mine, Mr. Johnson. Her name's Miss Emma Hodge."

"Emma . . . Hodge? That name sounds familiar . . ." William mused for a short moment before his eyes lit up in recognition. "Oh, yes! *Emma Hodge.* I remember Mr. Billingham telling me about his interview with her here a few months back. He was very impressed with her writings and was sorry he couldn't offer her the teaching position because of her lack of validated credentials and relevant experience."

"That's why I'm here today, Mr. Johnson," Sallie said. "I'm here to vouch for Miss Emma. There ain't nobody in this world more qualified for that teachin' position than Miss Emma. And I can prove it."

William stared at her, a dubious smile on his face. "Excuse me?"

He listened, captivated, as Sallie proceeded to tell him the whole story of her relationship with Emma: their secret reading sessions driven by Emma's special passion and talents; their shared tragedy involving Charles; Emma's nursing experience at the Confederate army hospital; and their mutual escape on the Union gunboat at the horrible cost of separation from Sallie's family.

When she'd finished, William shook his head, leaned back in his chair, and stroked his goatee. "That is quite an inspiring tale, Miss Cobb. Especially to someone like myself who's had the luxury of being born and raised by free Black parents and graduating from a Black-run university in Ohio. And on the surface, it certainly sounds like Miss Hodge *does* have all the requisite skills and experience. But how are you going to convince Mr. Billingham that you're telling the truth?"

Sallie's eyes flashed. "You don't believe me?"

William held up his hand. "It's not me, Miss Cobb. It's Mr. Billingham. He'll want to make sure you're not just someone hired by Miss Hodge to come here and present her case, thinking we'll be more likely to believe a Black woman than a former plantation daughter. At the very least, he'd want to know if you can even read . . . if what you're saying about Miss Hodge's teaching you how to read is true, you should be able to prove it."

"Give me somethin', then," Sallie said indignantly. "I'll show you I can read right here and now."

"But, Miss Cobb, I—"

"Please, Mr. Johnson. This too important for me to let go. Just give me somethin' I can read to you."

William hesitated, then reached into one of the desk drawers and pulled out a leather-bound book. He handed it to her, and she examined the title and smiled. It was the *McGuffey Reader*, the same primer she and Emma had used during the early months of their secret reading sessions. She opened to one of the middle chapters and began to read out loud. By the middle of the third page, William reached out and grasped the top of the open book to stop her.

He laughed. "That's enough! You've convinced me, Miss Cobb. You were definitely taught to read, and read very well. But there's still the issue of Miss Hodge's lack of validated credentials, and I—"

"Right here, sir. I give you permission to open it." Sallie took the envelope from her lap, put it on the desk, and thrust it toward him.

William read through the one-page letter. When he reached the bottom and noticed the signature, his eyes widened. "*Angelina Grimké?* This is truly from *her*?"

Sallie nodded, a huge, satisfied grin on her face.

William glanced back and forth between Sallie and the letter several times. "If you'd be willing to wait here a few minutes, Miss Cobb, I think I might be able to gain a brief audience with Mr. Billingham." He rose from the desk with the reference letter in hand and walked toward the supervisor's office. Without even knocking, he opened the door and shut it behind him, leaving Sallie alone to nervously ponder what would happen next.

Ten minutes later, he returned to his desk. A bright smile lit up his face.

"Great news, Miss Cobb! I explained everything to Mr. Billingham and showed him the reference letter, and he agrees that based on that, plus your own wonderful testimony, your friend Miss Hodge does indeed meet the spirit—if not the letter—of our qualifications for the teaching position. He'd like her to come back here next week on Thursday morning at nine to formally accept our offer, and to begin some initial training. Could you convey that to her for us?"

Sallie nearly jumped out of her seat with joy. "Oh, my goodness, sir . . . I-I just don't know what to say but . . . thank you, thank you, sir!"

"Oh, and Miss Cobb, there's something else."

"Yes, sir?"

"Would *you* be interested at all in volunteering some of your time with us? We are in great need of help reading and sorting our increasing volume of subscriber mail, and based on everything you've demonstrated today, both Mr. Billingham and I think you would be ideal for the task. Perhaps you and Miss Hodge could coordinate your hours and be here together starting on Thursday? What would you say to that?"

Barely able to believe what she'd just heard, Sallie put her hand to her mouth and nodded.

William rose and came around the desk to escort her out. After he shook her hand with both of his, he held on to it and peered into her eyes. "Miss Cobb, I hope you won't think this too forward of me or that I'm taking advantage of the situation, but there's something I'd like to ask you."

Completely bewitched, Sallie could only smile and mumble. "Of course, sir, what is it?"

"There's a special exhibit starting next week at the Smithsonian that I truly believe you would enjoy. I was wondering if I might have the honor of your company in viewing it with me around noon next Thursday—after you complete your first morning of volunteer work.

After that, perhaps we could have a bite to eat in the museum café and I could then escort both you and Miss Hodge home later in the afternoon?"

Sallie stared at him, about ready to melt on the spot.

"Mr. Johnson," she managed finally, "I'd be delighted to accept your invitation."

That night, in an ecstatic mood after Sallie's report of the day's events at the AMA office, Emma decided to try again to contact David. Maybe, she thought, her first letter, sent last June, had never reached its destination. After completing a five-page reprise of all that had happened since their parting, she sealed the envelope and addressed it before offering a silent prayer: *Dear God, I can't thank you enough for all you've done for me . . . and yet, here I am again with another request. Oh, Lord, I miss David so much. My news is so good, and I'm dying to see him again. Please, God, let this one reach him.*

CHAPTER 26

Chancellorsville, Virginia
May 2, 1863

T he loud explosion in the early morning darkness jolted David awake.

Sounds like an artillery wagon just blew—hopefully the rebs' and not ours, he thought groggily, rubbing the sleep from his eyes.

Sitting up on his cot in the darkened tent, he pulled the blanket off his legs and swung them over the side, then felt around the ground underneath for his standard-issue box of Lucifer matches. He pulled one out and raked the phosphorus-laced tip across the box's striking surface, producing a tiny, sparking flame, which he then applied to the wick of the candle stub protruding from its holder on the ground beside the head of the cot. Instantly, the entire interior was illumined, revealing that David's tentmate—Lieutenant Baxter—was already up and gone, presumably conferring with his XII Corps superiors over the latest plans and orders for the coming day.

He checked his pocket watch: 3:40 A.M. Too early to get dressed— he wouldn't be expected to join the rest of the staff officers until the breakfast call was sounded around five o'clock. He yawned and rubbed his eyes once again, then sat on the ground with his back against the side of the cot.

Stretching his legs out, he pulled the small wooden lap desk from under the cot and placed it over his thighs. No doubt, this would be the last opportunity to finish writing his letter before XII Corps got swept up completely in the massive battle that had been building since yesterday in the rugged wilderness area surrounding Chancellorsville, a tiny village only twelve miles west of Fredericksburg. He picked up the first of the four pages he'd already written, rereading to make sure he'd expressed things as intended.

May 2, 1863

Dearest Emma,

Words cannot express the sheer joy that I experienced upon receiving your letter of March 1 just five days ago. (I never received your first letter; indeed, the mail services are too slow and unreliable to inspire any confidence in these challenging times.)

That was the first word I've had of you and the family since receiving Pastor Jones's letter, which was written over a year and a half ago. To hear what you and the others have been through since then leaves me simultaneously appalled yet filled with brotherly affection and pride over your bold resolve and actions. The Lord has certainly been watching over and protecting you, sister, and I'm confident that he will continue to guide and prosper your future efforts with the AMA. I can't wait for us to reunite soon so that we can share in more detail our experiences and perspectives on the exploding slavery transition issue. It's certainly a complex one, to put it mildly.

As for my own situation, where shall I begin?

Looks fine so far, David thought. After skimming over the next two and a half pages where he'd briefly recounted his experiences with Abel Bowman and the Union army after becoming the *Cleveland Leader*'s primary war correspondent, he picked up the quill pen and began writing what was closest to his heart.

Not all of my story is war and gloom. There is some great news: I am engaged to be married—to a lovely, godly young widow named Sarah Krause, whom I met in Frederick City, Maryland, last September. I fell in love with her and her young daughter Jenny the moment I first met them. I proposed to Sarah last month before I left on our present campaign, and she accepted. We've set July 10 as our wedding date and, of course, you are invited and I hope with all my heart you'll be able to attend! Following the wedding, I'll likely face some big decisions regarding my future career as a correspondent. Especially with that potential offer looming from President Lincoln to lead a government investigation team. We shall see.

Emma, I know you still bear ill feelings toward Papa and Catherine for their lack of understanding and support. Indeed, the pain of remembering Cat deliberately turning her back on me when I said my final goodbye to the family still burns terribly in my own heart. But, dear sister, Pastor Jones is right. We both must learn to forgive them. I have not given up hope that one day we can all come together and reconcile, and I pray you will not give up either. In the meantime, I pray that God will grant every blessing to both you and Sallie. If he should grant me his protection once again through this coming battle, I shall very soon be sending you both a formal invite to my wedding. I cannot wait to see you again, sister. I am . . .

Your Loving Brother,

David

There was so much more he'd wanted to express to her. But for now, it would have to do. It was 4:30—time to get moving. He folded the pages and put them in an envelope, which he then sealed, addressed, and laid on top of the cot. After folding up the lap desk and pushing it back under the cot, he rose stiffly from his sitting position and got dressed. As he did so, he wondered what the day would bring. Would this be like all the other fights so far, where he would observe the action from a relatively safe position and record his impressions that would later be turned into a "firsthand story from the battlefield" to awe and inspire the *Leader*'s subscribers? Or would this be the day that a stray bullet finally found its mark, maiming him forever or perhaps even killing him?

He strapped on his holster and pulled out the Colt .44 revolver that had been his constant companion since Kernstown. Checking to make sure each of the six chambers was fully primed and loaded, another terrible thought that he'd long struggled to suppress reared its ugly head: *Will this be the day I actually have to use this weapon against my fellow Virginians?* The idea distressed him greatly, but should unavoidable circumstances require it, he knew he would do so.

He picked up the envelope and exited the tent, his stomach rumbling in anticipation of breakfast and the tin of hot coffee that he knew awaited him at the commissary wagon just down the path. He hadn't taken two steps before he spotted Lieutenant Baxter walking hurriedly in his direction.

Baxter approached and gave an informal salute. "Mr. Hodge, headquarters just got word. That explosion we heard a while back was a rebel caisson taking a direct hit from Captain Knapp's battery of rifled guns. General Slocum's ordered 7th Ohio to move up to support Knapp and clear out any rebel skirmishers in the woods in front of the battery. The general told me to let you know you have his permission to skip staff meeting and go get another story on the 7th's actions today, if you'd like. Not sure there'll be much to report on, but you never know."

David grinned. "Somehow, I think I'll manage to dig up a few lines' worth, Lieutenant. Thank you." Freed from attending the staff meeting, he walked to the commissary wagon, dropped off the letter to Emma, and gratefully accepted the tin of coffee and the small plate of salt pork and cornmeal handed to him by the attendant. Finding a nearby fallen log, he sat down and ate his breakfast while ruminating on what lay ahead.

He couldn't believe his good fortune. Today's assignment was far more desirable than the usual one, which entailed waiting around to collect his information through stilted, post-battle interviews with officers and wounded soldiers. Now, for the first time since Kernstown, he'd have a firsthand view of the 7th Ohio—including Abel Bowman and his Company L "Eye of Glory" boys—demonstrating the bravery that had come to be expected of them.

It would also give him the chance to personally deliver to Abel some very good news. Just yesterday, David had received a short letter from Lt. Colonel Jack Hurley. In it, Hurley had confirmed his decision to drop all the dereliction charges he'd levied against Abel in connection with the Frederick, Maryland "whoring" incident seven months ago. This was done partly, Hurley had intimated, in appreciation for David's qualified public endorsement of Hurley's position paper on the ex-slave reparations issue that had recently been read and well received by President Lincoln. In the editorial David had written for the *Cleveland Leader* on the subject, he'd supported the general idea of reparations. But he had also insisted that a "wide-ranging, serious government study" be conducted on how such a policy should be implemented in a fair and effective manner. Hurley had been satisfied for the most part with David's effort on his behalf and said he hoped his own gesture toward David's good friend Abel would help secure David's cooperation on future ventures of mutual interest.

Abel seems like he could use some good news, David thought worriedly. Something was clearly bothering his friend, some internal struggle that almost certainly went beyond Hurley's wild, heretofore unresolved accusations against him. He'd seen it in Abel's eyes, ever since the Antietam battle. Was it guilt over his unwarranted execution of that wounded rebel soldier in the Antietam cornfield? Or was it yet another sign of distress over his rumored connection with those Pottawatomie murders years ago?

At least twice since Antietam, David had tried to gently coax Abel into revealing the source of his distress. Each time, Abel had evaded the issue, assuring David that he was imagining things and worrying over nothing—that Abel had but one driving concern: that he and his

men would always live up to the bold, avenging spirit of John Brown!
embodied in Company L's "Eye of Glory" flag.

Whatever was behind Abel's apparent distress, no one could question his courage and continuing passionate dedication to the Union cause. Perhaps today, David thought, Abel would provide yet another heroic example worth writing home about.

After returning his empty plate and mug to the commissary sergeant, David checked the contents of his haversack one last time. Seeing that all was in order, he began walking toward the Orange Plank Road and the growing sounds of an early morning battle.

The dead body of Company L flagbearer Private John Wilcox lay twenty yards away, sprawled faceup on the rock-hard ground in the center of the clearing. The flag was not with him.

"What happened? And where's Captain Bowman?" David asked quietly of two young soldiers surveying the scene from behind a small boulder at the clearing's edge.

One of them turned to respond, his face a mask of consternation. "Happened about a half hour ago, sir. We were just returning from reconnoitering the woods on the other side when some reb skirmishers came up on our flank and opened up on us in the clearing. They dropped Wilcox out there, and then one of those cursed Johnnies came rushing up to yank the flag out of his dead hands and take it back into the woods. We could hear 'em whooping and hollering and screaming all kinds of vile insults at us, and Captain Bowman went berserk. He ordered us to get ready to turn around and go get the flag back, but just then the order came down the line from regimental command for everyone to stay put until reinforcements came.

"The captain, though, he wasn't having any of it. He shouted to everybody within earshot: 'The hell with it. No filthy, slavery-loving rebel will ever take the Eye of Glory flag and live . . . I can't allow it!' I swear I've never seen any man's face lit up like Captain Bowman's was at that point, sir. Then he took off by himself across the clearing into the woods. A few minutes later, we heard some shots and a lot of shouting and yelling, but then it died down and it's been quiet over there ever since."

David felt the knot in his stomach tightening with each word uttered by the soldier. He struggled to maintain a calm voice. "So, are you all just going to stay here and let Captain Bowman fend for himself in the woods over there?"

"Mr. Hodge," said the other soldier, "if it were up to the two of us, we would've both followed him right into those woods. But we were ordered by Major Crane not to—"

The sound of crunching brush interrupted his protest. Someone was approaching fast from behind. The two soldiers whirled and aimed their muskets before discovering it was none other than Lieutenant Jones, Abel's deputy commander. "The major says we gotta fall back *now*, men. Can't waste any more time here. Big attack's being made by Jackson against XI Corps on our right flank, and they need our support. Come on, let's move out."

"Lieutenant!" the first soldier protested. "We can't just leave Wilcox and Captain Bowman to rot out there, sir. It just ain't right. What if the captain's still alive in the woods somewhere, sir?"

"That's right, sir," said the other. "If nobody else is goin' back for him, at least let the two of us give it a try. You know the captain would do the same for you or me."

Jones grimaced. Clearly conflicted, he looked across the clearing. "Someone will have to tend to Wilcox's body later. As far as the captain, he brought this on himself—disobeying orders and forsaking his command, trying to win the war on his own. I had a feeling sooner or later he'd do something crazy like this. But . . . all right, I suppose if you two want to insist on disobeying orders and getting yourselves killed trying to rescue him, I won't try to stop you. I can only pray to God that the court-martial—if it comes to that—will go easy on you if you all return alive." He nodded at David. "Mr. Hodge, I know you and Captain Bowman were close friends. Do you want to go with them, or pull back with the rest of us?"

David gave him a hard stare. He wasn't prepared or trained for this. Who knew how many rebel soldiers might still be lurking in the woods beyond, just waiting for the chance to blow the heads off any intruders? Thoughts of Sarah and Jenny flashed through his mind. For their sake, why take this unnecessary risk? And yet . . .

"I'll go with them, Lieutenant," he said finally.

Jones nodded. "Somehow I knew that would be your choice. God protect you, men."

Pistol drawn, David crouched low as he followed Privates Hancock and Smithfield through the thick foliage on the other side of the clearing.

A few minutes ago, he had reeled at the close-up sight of Private Wilcox—who'd been shot in the shoulder, chest, and face—and the poignant memory it had evoked of their earlier collaboration in developing the Antietam battlefield account. In Wilcox's haversack, he'd found a small, self-autographed booklet filled with prayers and hymns. David had put it in his tunic pocket, determined to send it to Wilcox's next of kin—so long as he himself survived this dangerous search mission.

My odds seem to be improving, he now thought hopefully. So far—more than fifty yards into the woods—there was no sign of a rebel presence.

A sudden crackling noise caused him to whirl to his left. He pointed his pistol in the direction of the sound, his heart in his throat and his eyes straining to locate the source in the faint early morning light. He waited a few seconds. Nothing. Must have been a small critter rustling some fallen branches.

Breathing a sigh of relief, he turned to resume his trek. He hadn't taken three steps before a muffled shout rang out from up ahead.

"Hey, Smithfield, Mr. Hodge . . . over here . . . I found him!"

David raced through the thick underbrush in the direction of Private Hancock's voice. In seconds, he arrived at the edge of a small glade where Hancock and Smithfield stood frozen, staring in speechless horror at the nightmarish scene confronting them.

The bodies of three gray-clad rebel soldiers lay in blood-soaked repose, their ghastly, mortal wounds displaying clear evidence of the overwhelming wrath and power of whoever had inflicted them.

The soldier closest to David appeared to have been run through the stomach with a sword, then shot at point-blank range in the forehead. He'd probably been the first victim, his wide-open eyes and mouth displaying the shock and force with which death had struck. Less than ten feet away, the second man, in addition to being shot twice in the abdomen, had suffered his entire head being split in two like a melon from crown to chin—no doubt the result of a viciously delivered saber strike. It was the sight of the third soldier, though, that made David realize immediately the likely motivation behind the grisly slayings—a motivation that seemed to go far beyond the usual justifications of self-defense or obedience to command or even killing for a righteous cause.

Stabbed multiple times in the chest and throat and also through his mouth and both eyes, the man lay faceup with arms outstretched, his left hand still clutching the broken-off wooden staff of the "Eye of Glory" flag. The bloodied and dirt-stained flag itself had been ripped from the staff and laid unfurled on the ground—directly in front of Captain Abel Bowman, who now sat behind the flag with arms clasping his drawn-up knees, slowly rocking back and forth.

David approached carefully and knelt beside his friend, placing his hand on his upper back as Hancock and Smithfield gathered around. It was then that he noticed the small, blood-spattered pocket Bible that Abel had opened and was now clutching in his right hand, apparently muttering verses to himself.

"Abel?" David inquired softly.

For over half a minute, Abel continued to remain in his trance, giving no sign of having heard or even recognized the presence of David and the others. Finally, he stopped muttering, placed the Bible on the ground, and turned his head toward David. His eyes had a glazed, faraway look.

"Abel, it's me . . . David. Are you all right?"

"D–David? . . . David . . . what . . . where . . . I—" Abel stared at the savaged dead bodies on the other side of the flag, as if seeing them for the first time. Suddenly tears appeared in his eyes, and his chest began to heave. "*Oh, Jesus, please forgive me!*"

David gently removed Abel's kepi hat, then put his arms around his shoulders and held his head against his own chest to absorb his friend's violent sobs.

He looked at the others. "Can you give us some time alone?"

Hancock nodded sympathetically. "Of course, sir. We'll keep an eye out for reb skirmishers trying to sneak their way back here. Call us when you're ready."

It was several minutes before Abel was finally able to collect himself and sit up without David's support.

"I see the result . . . but what happened?" David asked softly.

Abel stared at the ground. "They were degrading it, David."

"Degrading what . . . the flag?"

"Yes. They degraded 'Glory'—*my* flag— and everything it stood for. I snuck up on them and heard and saw what they were doing—insulting it, laughing, two of 'em even pissing and crapping on it—and I just went crazy. Especially after I gave 'em a chance to surrender and they taunted me. First one grabbed for his musket, but I took him out before he could aim it. Second one came at me with his bayonet, and you see what I did to him." He nodded toward the third soldier. "That one nearly did me in . . . in more ways than one."

"How do you mean?"

"Put up a helluva fight. Shot at me, but he missed, so he threw down his musket and came at me with the jagged end of the flagstaff. I parried it with my saber and let him have it in the chest with my pistol, but he kept coming at me and knocked my saber out of my hands. We grappled on the ground, and I got on top and managed to pull my officer's knife out. I started to stab him, but he caught my wrist. I said: 'Give it up, reb, you've no chance against Glory.' Last words he said to me were: 'Curse you, Yank. You fight for your Glory—I'm jes' fightin' for my home and family. I spit on your Glory, and I spit on you.' Which is exactly what he did. And you see what terrible vengeance I took in response. God help me, especially after—" Abel choked up once again.

"After what, Abel?" David asked gently, his stomach churning as he placed his hand on Abel's back.

"After I-I finished him off by plunging my knife through the poor man's pocket Bible and into his heart."

David jerked his head back, trying to absorb the full, shocking impact of what he had just heard. "Abel," he said finally, "tell me the truth. *What* is it that has driven you to all this . . . worship of Glory?"

Abel eyed him forlornly. "You remember that day I met you . . . almost two and a half years ago now . . . at John Brown's hanging?"

"Yes, how could I forget *that*? It's what ultimately drew me to come join you in Ohio."

"We dined and talked in that Charles Town tavern afterward, but I never told you the true, full story about how I first came to know Mr. Brown."

David had an eerie sense that he was about to be yanked from the deceptively calm eye of a dangerous storm into the midst of the surrounding whirlwinds. "You want to tell me now?"

Abel closed his eyes and nodded . . .

And so I started down that moonlit path following Mr. Brown's son Owen, carrying one broadsword in each hand, just like he'd asked. Guess I thought the sight of those fearsome weapons would scare James Doyle and his sons into stopping whatever resistance Owen said they were putting up against the others.

When we approached the point beside the fence next to the pasture where Mr. Doyle had said his horses were kept, I was surprised that there seemed to be no commotion at all. James and his sons were cowering with their backs to the fence—seemingly in horror and fear. We finally arrived, and Mr. Brown—who had his pistol pointed at James—turned to greet us. "Glad you're here, boys."

"What should we do with them, Father?" Owen asked, sword in hand.

Mr. Brown looked at the Doyles, and then he turned to me. "Son, bring me the other swords." I walked over to him, thinking he'd take them both. But he only took one and handed it to one of his other sons. Then he stared me in the eye and said: "Abel, this is the night when glory shows its face, as the righteous wrath of God is exercised against those who would intentionally subject their fellow human beings to the cruelty and misery of slavery. Will you join this unpleasant but glorious task as a soldier in the Lord's Army?"

I stared back at him, quaking in my boots. I knew I should, that the cause was divinely righteous, and yet I was too cowardly to bring myself to accept Mr. Brown's challenge. Wordlessly, I handed my sword to Mr. Brown, tears streaming down my face. Just as I did so, James Doyle and his sons lunged toward us, no doubt hoping to break through and escape. I jumped aside while Mr. Brown's sons used their weapons to quick, terrible advantage, cutting them to pieces. After they were done, Mr. Brown walked up and shot James between the eyes to make sure he was dead.

I was in such a state of shock I hardly remember anything of the other two raids our group undertook that night. I only know when the last one was all over and we were walking away, Mr. Brown came over and patted me on the shoulder. He looked at me, and his face didn't seem angry . . . but rather, just a bit sad. He handed me Owen's sword—still dripping with blood—and said, "Maybe, son, you'll get another chance for glory someday."

Abel shook violently, clearly racked with indescribable thoughts and emotions over what he had experienced on that horrific night in Pottawatomie, Kansas, and the realization of what it had ultimately led to.

David struggled to find the right words. "What did you do with that sword that John Brown gave you, Abel?"

Abel stopped shaking and stared grimly at the ground. "I took it home and hid it in our barn. Every day I'd sneak out for a few minutes and just stare at the word GLORY engraved on the handle. Later, when I left my family and moved to Ohio, I hung it up in my bedroom. Wanted it to be a constant reminder of what I now believed to be my true calling: to overcome my shame and cowardice by fighting boldly for the glory of the indisputably worthy cause of abolition. That carving on the sword's handle became my inspiration for the design of Company L's flag."

"And . . . what have you learned from all this?" David asked cautiously.

Abel took a long moment to respond. When he did, his voice was quiet and strained with emotion. "That my whole concept of glory has been horribly wrong. I started to realize it after I shot that wounded reb in the Antietam cornfield, and what I did today confirmed it. My obsession with overcoming my failure and rising to the personal challenge of my hero, John Brown . . . it . . . it blinded me, David. It turned me into a wild demon, reveling in my brutal, rage-driven slayings—even executions!—of any battlefield enemy daring to insult my distorted vision of glory."

"But how was it a 'distorted vision,' Abel? Yes, you may have allowed your personal motivations and passions to overwhelm you in striving to pursue it, but how was your vision of eradicating slavery from the land any more 'distorted' than John Brown's?"

Because at some point, *my* vision of glory became far more connected with wielding a blood-dripping sword to build up my own weak self-esteem . . . about proving myself—and proving myself to others—than it had to do with fighting for the glory of the Great Cause of abolition. And God help me, you can see with your own eyes what that has produced. Abel looked up, his face a mask of shame and despair. "My army days are over, David. Even if I beat the court-martial, I'm resigning. Slavery is evil, and it needs to be crushed. But not by my own bloodthirsty hands driven by impure, selfish motives. I can't do this anymore."

David closed his eyes, allowing the full impact of all Abel had just said to sink in for several moments. "So, what will you do?"

Abel shook his head sadly. "I've sat here confessing my wretched sin of blind bloodlust to God and begging his forgiveness in the Lord

Christ. But beyond that, to tell the truth, right now I haven't the slightest idea."

David tightened his grip around his friend's shoulders. "Abel, can I pray for you?"

Abel nodded as sobs welled up in him once again. "Please do. I'd covet that."

After David had finished, Abel stared morosely at the soiled Eye of Glory flag stretched out in front of him. "No use for *that* anymore. Not after what those rebs did to it. Might as well just leave it here."

David followed his gaze. *Eye of Glory . . . an inspiring motto . . . too bad it had to die here, all besmirched with blood, dirt, and human waste.*

An idea suddenly struck him. "Actually, Captain Bowman, we can leave the flag here . . . but we may have another use for that motto."

Abel cocked his head. "Another use? What do you mean?"

"Can't say right yet. I should know more in a month or two. For now, you'll just have to trust me. Come on. Let's get back to camp."

While Abel—at his own stern insistence—said a solitary prayer over the bodies of each of the slain rebels and once again asked for God's forgiveness for the unholy motive that had led him to wreak such horrific violence, David went to collect Hancock and Smithfield. Together, the four men took one last look at the soiled company battle flag stretched out on the ground, then walked back through the woods toward the Orange Plank Road and headquarters.

Approaching the outskirts of the camp area, it was clear that something catastrophic was happening. At least twenty Union soldiers ran past David and the others, warning them that "all hell was about to break loose." That Stonewall Jackson's men had overrun XI Corps and were heading this way.

Two artillery shells exploded less than thirty yards away—one of them blowing the head and legs off a soldier who'd been tending to a wagon horse.

"Let's get off the road and into that grove of trees over there!" Private Smithfield shouted. His words were the last thing David heard before the blinding flash, followed by complete blackness.

CHAPTER 27

Countryside near Cleveland, Ohio
July 28, 1863

T he Eastern bluebird wouldn't stop chirping. For some reason, it had decided to perch itself on the farmhouse's back porch rail near David's rocking chair, serenading him with its cheery song.

Putting down the book in which he'd been absorbed for over two hours now, David rose slowly and surveyed the pastoral scene stretched out before him. It was nearly noon, and the shimmering heat seemed to be rising in waves from the tops of the cornstalks in the field beyond the barn. Walking slowly across the sunlit porch, David smiled at the sight of his new, seven-year-old stepdaughter Jenny playing with her doll at the foot of the steps.

He descended and reached down to pick her up.

Not easy trying to do this with half my arm missing, he thought rue-fully, the memory still fresh in his mind of the Chancellorsville fiasco nearly three months ago.

With some extra effort from his right arm and Jenny's arms wrapped tightly around the back of his neck, he managed to lift the small girl up and cradle her in a comfortable sitting position.

"Shall we go see what Momma's doing?" he asked.

Jenny's bright blue eyes lit up. "Yes, Papa." The sound of her affectionate, trusting voice thrilled him to the core. She lay her head contentedly against his chest, and he began walking toward the far side of the vegetable garden where Sarah was stooping down to pick some ripe tomatoes and cucumbers off their vines. The sight of his wife of less than three weeks made him pause, wanting to capture forever the feeling of happiness and gratitude to God that suddenly welled up in his chest.

He knew he was fortunate to have survived the sudden explosion and piece of white-hot shrapnel that had torn through his left forearm the morning of that horrible second day of May at Chancellorsville. The arm had been completely severed just below the elbow, exposing the main artery. If not for the quick action of a nearby infantry sergeant in applying a tourniquet, he would have bled to death. Abel Bowman had been even more fortunate, suffering nothing more than a severe concussion and badly bruised thigh, despite being literally tossed ten feet in the air and hitting the ground hard. Privates Hancock and Smithfield had taken the worst of it—the former losing his entire right leg and the latter his head.

David's recovery at the field hospital had been quick. Despite the Union army's embarrassing defeat in yet another poorly led effort by its commanding general, he and the other wounded had been greatly cheered by the news that their old nemesis—General Stonewall Jackson—had been accidentally shot and wounded by some of his own men the second night of the battle. He had died of pneumonia eight days later. Further hastening David's improvement had been the constant thought of returning to Sarah and Jenny. With his wedding scheduled for July 10 in Maryland, he knew he had little time to lose in securing the loan and deed for the small produce farm outside Cleveland that would serve as a means of family subsistence and minor income, augmenting David's commissions from his continuing journalistic endeavors with the *Leader*.

The wedding at the First Methodist Church in Frederick City eighteen days ago had come off just as planned. The guest list had been sparse: Sarah's parents, in whose home Sarah and Jenny had been residing since the death of her first husband; her younger sister and her husband; and a few of their mutual friends. Abel Bowman—who had avoided court-martial and been granted an honorable discharge from the army based mainly on the overwhelmingly positive testimony of his subordinates—had acted as David's best man. Sadly, Emma and Sallie had not been able to attend—Emma had responded to their formal invitation with the news that she'd been ill with a bad case of bronchitis and was recovering slower than hoped. She'd apologized profusely and had exhorted David and his new family to come visit her and Sallie in Washington the very next time he was there on business—which he now had reason to believe might occur in September. Despite Emma's absence, it had been by far the most joyous occasion of David's life. Two days later, the family had traveled by coach to Cleveland to begin their new life together on the farm.

Sarah lifted her head and beamed at the sight of David and Jenny approaching. She put down her shears, wiped her hands on her dress, and rose to greet them. Taking Jenny into her arms, she leaned over and gave David a prolonged kiss on the cheek.

"You certainly know how to please your women, Mr. Hodge," she said coyly. "Tell me, where did you acquire all your skills?"

David laughed. "I'm glad I seem to be passing your test." As he gazed at the slender, chestnut-haired, green-eyed beauty, whom he felt blessed beyond measure to have landed, he sensed the familiar stir-rings of passionate desire in his loins. He recalled the slight jitters he'd experienced on their wedding night as he'd undressed and caressed her with the benefit of only one arm, wondering in the back of his mind if she would find him as satisfying as her first husband. It had been a relief when she'd assured him afterward with a gratified smile that *that* would never be an issue.

Obviously detecting the ravenous look in his eyes, Sarah smiled, pressed in close with Jenny, and placed her hand on his chest. "So," she whispered, "before we both lose all our self-control, my love, why don't you pass another test and take over this vegetable harvesting for a while so I can go in and make dinner for us?"

David groaned and looked helplessly up at the sky, then bent down to the task as Sarah and Jenny started to leave.

After a couple of steps, she turned back to face him. "David, what time is Mr. Bowman arriving? Should I plan on preparing dinner for him as well before you two leave for your meeting in the city this evening?"

He thought for a moment. Abel—whose agricultural savvy and skills had been sorely missed by his former employer during his army service—had recently been rehired as the farmer's crop manager. He only needed to tend to a few matters this morning, he'd said, and would get to the Hodges' farm as soon as he could.

"Actually, Abel should be here any time now, dear. I wanted to talk with him about some things before the meeting. So . . . yes, having him join us for dinner before we leave would be great. Thank you."

"Do you think he's going to accept your offer?"

"I'm not sure . . . that's what I want to talk to him about."

"David, you do know how incredibly proud I am of you, don't you?" Sarah asked hesitantly.

David tipped his hat back on his forehead and grinned. "Now remind me again, darling, why exactly is *that*?"

"How many wives can say their brand-new husband has been personally appointed by the President of the United States to lead the independent investigation of a government project dealing with one of the most important issues our country's facing?"

The copy of Lincoln's official letter had arrived two days after the wedding. In it, he had ordered twenty thousand acres of confiscated cotton plantation lands, along the Union-conquered portions of South Carolina's coast, to be sold to ex-slaves in twenty-acre plots at $1.25 per acre. To support the transition, he had appointed General Rufus Saxton—the region's Union military governor residing in the harbor city of Port Royal—as the director of an ambitious new phase of a year-old project aimed at developing a workable model for freedmen's economic sustainment after slavery.

The new phase of the "Port Royal Experiment," as it was entitled, would feature a land reparations component—managed by a small group of general district supervisors, including, of all people, recently retired Lt. Colonel Jack Hurley—and an educational component to be staffed and funded by the American Missionary Association and other northern charitable organizations. Hurley and his fellow supervisors would oversee sales of the land plots, the construction of new housing, and the organization of local community administrative structures and work arrangements within their respective districts. The AMA's responsibilities included the establishment, operation, and provision of qualified teachers for a centrally located schoolhouse in each district that would be dedicated to basic literacy, Bible, and vocational train-ing. An independent investigation team, led by David, would have full ability to review official records, observe daily activities, and personally interview supervisors, educators, and freedmen involved in the project. In mid-September, David would be meeting in Washington with the supervisors and some of the leading educators to begin coordinating their respective efforts under the overall supervision of General Saxton, who in turn would report to Salmon Chase, the US Secretary of the Treasury.

Exciting and gratifying as it had been to receive, Lincoln's letter had completely disrupted David's hopes for a peaceful, sedate life in the Cleveland countryside with Sarah and Jenny, commuting only occasionally to the city as his continuing connections with Mr. Cowles and the *Cleveland Leader* demanded.

"I just hope you can tolerate my comings and goings to Washington and South Carolina over the next year or so," he ventured cautiously. "I know this isn't what either of us expected to happen so soon."

"We'll make do," Sarah said. "Just promise you'll take Jenny and me with you at least once to Washington. I want her to see the sights with her Momma and Papa."

David grinned. "I've already got a plan for that. We're all going to stay a few days with my sister Emma when I go to Washington in September for our first project coordination meeting with Secretary Chase and General Saxton."

Sarah's eye widened. "Oh, David, that will be wonderful. Don't you think so too, Jenny?" The little girl smiled uncertainly, nodded, and pressed her head closer against Sarah's neck, prompting a laugh from both her parents.

"Jenny, why don't we go get dinner ready for Papa and Mr. Bowman?" Sarah took their daughter back into the farmhouse, closing the back porch door just as Abel Bowman rounded the side of the house and offered a hearty wave of greeting—one that David was sure hid the lingering depression and pain in his friend's heart that he'd admitted was still plaguing him ever since his actions at Chancellorsville.

"Hello, David, are we ready for Jack Hurley's big show tonight?"

"That depends on your answer to my offer, my friend. Let's go inside and talk."

"Gentlemen!" bellowed recently retired Colonel Jack Hurley from the lecture podium at the front of the Weddell House Hotel's first-floor conference room. "I cannot tell you how honored I am in my new civilian capacity to be addressing this distinguished body of Cleveland-area Republicans, abolitionists, and other loyal supporters of the Union war effort. And in view of the spectacular Independence Day victories achieved by our forces at Gettysburg in the east and Vicksburg in the West, I must say the outlook for ultimate victory has never appeared brighter. It will not happen tomorrow, and it may not happen this year or even next. But, gentlemen, rest assured . . . it *will* happen, despite the constant whinings of those treasonous northern Copperhead politicians—the 'Peace Democrats'—who would like nothing better than to see President Lincoln end the war now and reembrace the southern slave masters with open arms."

Hurley smiled, his already massive chest seeming to swell even further as he took in the loud applause elicited by his last remark.

Edwin Cowles, the *Cleveland Leader*'s editor, leaned toward David, who was seated beside him in the third row of Hurley's enraptured audience. "Does Colonel Jack always open his speeches with this kind of grandiosity?"

David smirked. "If the previous times I've heard him address gatherings like this are any indication, you haven't heard *anything* yet."

"So far . . . he's being true to form," agreed Abel, seated on the other side of Cowles.

Hurley continued. "And so, my friends, with all that in mind, I am pleased to present to you tonight the broad outlines of an exciting new phase of the Port Royal Experiment commissioned by the president. With your help, I have great confidence it will succeed. And when it does, we will have demonstrated the power and efficacy of *reparations*, the solution that Congressman Stevens, myself, and others have long supported as the only just means for compensating ex-slaves for the abuses of their owners. By making confiscated plantation lands available to freedmen at low cost, they will finally be able to enjoy the fruits of their own labors, which had previously been denied them. They will eventually create their own economic engine, contributing to the rest of society in even better ways than their former, privileged White masters."

For the next half hour, Hurley regaled his audience—which included over fifty wealthy Ohio patrons of national Republican causes—with elaborate details of his coleadership of the land reparations portion of the overall project, while barely acknowledging the educational component or the independent investigation team that David would be leading. At the conclusion of his speech—after answering some generally supportive questions—Hurley thanked the attendees, urged their continued financial backing for Republican priorities, and said that he and David would be available to take additional questions at the back of the hall where refreshments were now being served.

"Look for Hurley's line of questioners to triple yours, David," Abel joked as the audience rose from their seats and began moving down the aisle, enthusiastically chatting over what they had just heard.

His prediction was borne out—an hour later, the last of Colonel Jack's supporters filed out of the door as David, Abel, and Mr. Cowles huddled in isolated, lonely conversation in the opposite corner.

Hurley sauntered over toward their group, a huge grin on his face. "Well, quite a successful evening, wouldn't you say, Mr. Hodge?" He vigorously shook David's and Cowles's hands in turn, then turned toward Abel, his broad smile suddenly disappearing.

"Mr. Bowman," he said without extending his hand. "I'm rather surprised to see *you* here tonight."

"Oh? And why is that, Colonel?" Abel asked coolly. Despite his projected outward calm, David could sense his friend's blood beginning to boil.

"Well, I know you're a committed abolitionist like most of us here tonight. But I would have thought that after all your recent difficulties with your military superiors and service record, you might have wished to lay low for at least a year or so after your discharge. You know, tending to your farm, refraining from political gatherings, things like that. I—"

David cut him off. "Actually, Colonel, I'm pleased to let you know that—earlier today—Abel accepted my formal offer to assist me in our independent investigation effort. He'll be in charge of observing and assessing the vocational training aspect."

Hurley folded his arms and cocked his head. "Well, well, is that so? In that case, my congratulations to you, Mr. Bowman. Perhaps under Mr. Hodge's close supervision, you'll prove to be a helpful asset."

Abel, his face florid, clenched his fists and took a step toward Hurley. "Colonel, I'm not sure who it is you think you're talking to, but I do not appreciate your insinuation that I need to be watched over like a little child!"

Hurley stood unmoved, his large frame towering over the heads of the others. His smug smile oozed contempt. "Control yourself, Mr. Bowman. Control yourself. Don't allow me to believe that all those nasty stories about you from Frederick City and Chancellorsville were actually true. Sir, that would make a mockery of my decision to stop pressing those dereliction charges against you. And it would also ruin my good opinion of your friend Mr. Hodge's decision to appoint you to such an important task."

David watched Abel closely, fearing the worst. Clearly, time had not completely healed Hurley's bitterness toward Abel for speaking out against Hurley's old friend General Banks, harming the latter's military reputation and disrupting his career.

To his surprise, an amazing, unexplainable peace seemed to take hold of Abel. He simply smiled back at Hurley, saying nothing in response.

Hurley glanced at his timepiece. "Well, gentlemen, it's high time we all get out of here and let the hotel staff clean up. Mr. Hodge, I look forward to meeting with you in Washington for our project initiation in September. In the meantime, I know we both have some important work to do in preparing our plans, recruiting staff, and all that. My best regards to all of you until then." With that, he spun on his heels and exited the room, leaving David, Abel, and Mr. Cowles in speechless dismay.

Cowles shook his head. "I see the two of you have a few challenges ahead . . . I'll definitely be awaiting David's first report on your experience with sweaty palms and bated breath. Can't say I envy you."

David grabbed Abel's arm. "You sure you're ready to once again pick up and leave your nice, comfortable job as farm crop manager . . . for *this*?"

Abel grinned. "How can I possibly refuse the challenges of a magnificent new cause inspired by the Eye of Glory?"

Somehow, David noticed, the familiar, intense gleam in Abel's eyes had managed to return—in full force. He prayed that this time it would lead to a better outcome.

CHAPTER 28

Hodge Family Plantation
August 15, 1863

Catherine stood beside her open bedroom window, breathing in the hot, suffocating air that blanketed the surrounding countryside following the early afternoon rainstorm.

It was not a comforting scene. The household supply wagon, returning from its weekly run to Petersburg, had just entered the front gate. Just as she'd feared, it appeared to be half empty, a sure sign the war had taken another turn for the worse.

As she watched it draw closer, she spread her hands across her extended belly, wondering if other young, widowed Virginia women on the verge of birthing were feeling the same crushing sense of helplessness and dread over what the future held.

Before word of Joe's death and discovery of her pregnancy, her confidence in her own ability to handle the two plantations in his temporary absence had steadily grown. But ever since, fear and doubts had attacked her with unrelenting fury. And while her sale of the much smaller Hartwell Plantation six months ago at a badly deflated price had brought in some needed cash and eased her daily physical burden to an extent, the nagging questions continued to haunt her. Would she be able to continue managing the Hodge Plantation's complex affairs in the midst of the increasing turmoil everywhere, all while nurturing and raising her new infant? Would she even be able to feed and provide for her baby properly?

Acquaintances from Petersburg were predicting that if the trend of the past months continued, even the most basic foodstuffs would be hard to come by as the effects of wartime blockades, dislocations, confiscations, and inflated food prices took greater hold in the area. Tea, coffee, sugar, salt, and seed for raising food crops were already rare commodities. It wouldn't be long, they said, before milk, corn, butter, meal, and an occasional piece of meat would likely become the staple diet. The bread riots in Richmond last April—led by a group of angry housewives—had been sparked by the tenfold increase in flour prices since the war had broken out two years prior. If this was any indication of what could soon be coming to Petersburg and the countryside, the prospect was frightful indeed. *At least,* she thought gratefully, *we have our private vegetable garden to help sustain us.*

Catherine drew the curtain aside slightly, revealing the unwelcome appearance of Philip Taylor and his son Sam striding together toward the driveway to greet the wagon and check its contents. *And skim a few choice items off the top for themselves, no doubt,* she thought bitterly, regretting that her own sagging energy of late was forcing her to rely more and more on the overseer and his son to perform routine tasks that she herself used to handle with little effort.

Even more concerning were the signs of subtle manipulation and even outright disrespect that both men had been exhibiting toward her lately. Catherine closed her eyes and clenched her teeth at the memory of this morning's conversation with Philip and Sam to discuss her rising concern over the slaves' situation . . .

⌒∽⌒

Catherine, attempting to appear confident and in-command as she sat on the rear veranda settee, had opened the conversation.

"Mr. Taylor," she'd said, her hand shielding her eyes from the bright sun hovering in the now cloudless sky, "I apologize for making you take time out from your fieldwork to talk about this. But I felt it best to bring up my concern about the slaves sooner rather than later."

"Now, don't you worry yourself a bit over any of *that*, Mizz Cat," Philip Taylor had assured her as he leaned casually with folded arms against the veranda railing. "Sam's got everything under control... even with all this 'Emancipation Proclamation' nonsense, we haven't had a single escape attempt since your father passed, unlike most of the other plantations around here. Ain't that right, son?"

Sitting with his legs stretched out on the veranda top step, Sam had chimed in with his usual innocent grin. "Sure is, Pa. In fact, just yesterday ole James came up to me in the fields. Told me how thankful he was to be workin' on a plantation where he's treated real fair and his needs are provided for. Said the last thing he'd ever do is run to the Yankees, because despite all their nice words, they'd for sure try to sell him to slave drivers in Cuba or somewhere even worse. He told me all the others feel the same way as him."

Catherine had felt sure this was all a big lie; she had minced no words. "Then why is it, Sam, that I've heard complaints from four different sources that the field slaves have been receiving far less than their full ration of food ever since you and your father started managing the distribution for me last month? Why is it that Tom Cobb—who'd finally been improving from that gunshot infection—suddenly keeled over dead from heart failure while working in the field under the 'watchful care' you promised me you'd give him? His son Lew said you were working him even harder than the others."

Sam's face had turned scarlet. "You believe every lie you're told by the slaves, Mizz Cat? Haven't we all been through this before?"

"That may be true," Catherine had shot back, "but we've reached a point where the protests I'm hearing are starting to have a consistent and alarming theme, Sam. And as owner of this plantation, I consider it my responsibility before God to make sure those under my care are not being mistreated or abused. And so, I just thought I'd bring my concerns to your attention."

"Well, Mizz Cat," Philip Taylor had interjected, "all I can say is you're losing sleep over nothing. The slaves are just tryin' to pull the wool over your eyes because they know you're in a delicate state. Why don't you just try to relax and concentrate on having that baby. Leave the slaves to Sam and me . . . I promise we'll start making a thorough report to you at the end of every day. In fact, if I were you, Mizz Cat, I'd be thinkin' about getting some help with all those business decisions I know you've had to agonize over ever since your father died. Now if you'd like some advice on those, I've had some ideas that—"

"Mr. Taylor, I'm not asking for your ideas or your help on business decisions. Mr. Tidwell—Amanda's father—has been graciously helping me out with those, and I trust what he's been telling me."

Philip's expression had suddenly turned stone-cold. "For fifteen years, your father sought my advice on just about everything to do with this plantation, Mizz Cat. I don't understand why you wouldn't wish the same."

"When I need it, I'll ask for it, Mr. Taylor. In the meantime, I'll thank you and Sam just to do the jobs for which you were hired, and which you've done very well for many years."

Catherine had stood up from the veranda swing, signaling the end of the conversation. "Oh, and one more thing, Sam. I don't know what it is you have going on in your barn every Friday night recently, but I understand there are some rather unsavory men who are drunk and roaming around the slaves' quarters afterward, looking for I dread to say what. Whatever you're doing there, I want you to put an end to it."

"Nothin' to end, ma'am," Sam had retorted, his voice thick with disdain, "because there's nothin' going on. It's just another lie you're choosin' to believe from the slaves."

Feeling a sudden wave of nausea, Catherine had turned away and walked inside.

Catherine let the curtain drop. She'd seen more than enough of Sam Taylor and his father for one day.

She started toward her bed, her eyes heavy with exhaustion from the day's exertions and craving her usual two-hour, late afternoon nap.

Removing her gown and pulling down the sheets, she climbed awkwardly into the bed and lay on her back, staring at the ceiling. Once again, she placed her hands on her baby, hoping to detect another one of the reassuring little kicks that had been so prevalent up until the past two weeks or so, when for some reason they seemed to have ceased. During his checkup visit last week, Dr. Haynes had told her not to worry, that everything appeared fine and she should make preparations for delivery any day now. Greatly relieved, she'd arranged for Matilda—the middle-aged, colored midwife from Petersburg who had helped deliver Emma over twenty years ago and whose skill Mother had sworn by—to stay at the plantation for several weeks, quartered in Emma's former bedroom just down the hall. Amanda Tidwell was only a half hour away at the neighboring plantation and had also promised to come help as soon as she received word that Catherine's labor had begun.

Thoughts swirled as she began to drift off, one toppling over another.

Chief among them was the poignant memory of Joe's funeral and burial last January in the Hodge family cemetery overlooking the James River. She had asked Pastor Jones instead of her usual Presbyterian church pastor to preside over the burial service on the plantation, and he had graciously accepted. The service had been attended only by Catherine herself, Joe's widowed mother, the Hamiltons, and a few of Catherine's girlfriends. Terrible, crippling loneliness and despair had set in afterward and persisted as her friends had become more preoccupied with their own concerns, and Oscar Hamilton had suddenly seemed to lose all interest in further "social visits" after learning of Catherine's pregnancy. With her increasing isolation, she worried that permanent depression might overtake her.

Then there were the troubling suspicions concerning Sam and his father's increasingly disrespectful behavior, and the realization that she really needed to do something for twelve-year-old Lew Cobb. Like Catherine, Lew had now experienced the loss of his entire family. He'd been informally "adopted" by one of the other field-working families, but should she now bring him out of the fields and the constant threat of Sam's abusive treatment by making him part of the domestic staff?

The one consistent source of solace and comfort over the past several months had been Pastor Jones. After speaking with him following Joe's funeral, she had accepted his invitation to begin attending his Sunday services at the Wheelers' farm. Ever since, she had grown closer to him and his wife, occasionally inviting them for supper at the plantation.

And, of course, there was the undeniable joy of knowing that she would *never* be completely alone. Joe still lived on, inside her heart and the heart of her baby. Whether it was a boy or girl didn't matter . . . *he* would be in them, and he would always be with her. Everything else— all her troubles and worries—paled in comparison with the certainty that even death had not parted her from Joe's love.

Her mouth completely dry, Catherine reached for the water glass on the stand next to the bed. Discovering it was empty, she groaned and forced herself to sit up. She was pushing herself up from the edge of the bed when she felt what seemed like warm liquid running down her legs. She lifted her nightdress and gasped at the sight of the red-tinged trickles of water.

She rose and started to walk anxiously toward the door when the first hard contraction hit, causing her to double over in pain. After what seemed an eternity, it finally subsided enough for her to stand again and open the door.

"*Matilda*, please come quick!"

Arriving in seconds, Matilda helped her back into bed, then shouted for one of the other young female servants to go fetch Amanda Tidwell.

The labor lasted over five hours. Although racked at times with pain and all-consuming effort, Catherine knew that with Matilda's able help and Amanda's reassuring presence, there would ultimately be a wonderful outcome. She just needed to push through it, just as Matilda was now constantly encouraging her.

"Come on, now, Mizz Cat, one more time . . . almost there . . . almost there . . . here we come!"

One final push. Catherine screamed with the release, then fell back exhausted on her pillow. Amanda, who had been wiping Catherine's brow, moved to help Matilda complete the afterbirth procedures.

Catherine closed her eyes and breathed deeply, feeling a peace and happiness she hadn't felt in years. She waited a minute or two for Matilda to place the baby into her arms.

"Matilda," she called weakly, "can I see my baby now? Let me guess, is it a boy or a girl?"

A few seconds later, Amanda appeared at her side and gently took her hand in both of hers. Her eyes were moist.

"Catherine, I am so sorry."

Two weeks had passed since the burial of Catherine's stillborn baby boy, whom she had named after his father, Joe. With each passing day, the agony of knowing the only real hope she had left in life was now lost forever had gradually crushed her will to survive and carry on. Relentless grief and excruciating pain in her abdomen had tortured her day and night. Though she had no doubts that God was aware of her desperate situation, her constant prayers for relief and comfort had seemed to avail nothing.

When she'd awakened this morning, the old, familiar thoughts of self-recrimination had converged with memories of her recent traumatic experiences to pound on her brain like a sledgehammer. Her failure to win Papa's love. Her cruel rejection of her brother. Her betrayal of Emma and Charles. And then . . . the loss of Emma, Joe, Papa, and then their baby. It was clear: God had seen, he had judged, and he was no longer listening to her.

She'd told her maidservant that she wasn't feeling well and would be spending the day in bed—that no one should bother her. She had unlocked the small cabinet she'd sworn to herself she'd never again open—that night when the horrible news of Joe's death came. She had pulled out three full whiskey bottles and a tumbler that she'd placed on her vanity.

She'd then downed glass after glass, staring at her reflection in the mirror and hating the person she saw. Yes, that despicable human being who, it was now clear, she'd always been.

Ten minutes ago, Catherine's will to endure had finally crumbled. Head spinning wildly from the crescendoing effects of the alcohol and her horrid thoughts, she'd picked up the penknife on her dresser and closed her eyes. From nowhere, a strange, vivid imagining of her childhood had arisen and taken hold . . .

"Cat, it's too deep! It's almost over your head!" nine-year-old Emma shouted from the top of the steep creek bank.

"She's right, Cat," David yelled. "It's too far for us to swim out there and rescue you. But you can do it. Please come on in now. We all need to get home."

Catherine, eleven, stood on her toes in the neck-deep water of the storm-swelled creek with her arms folded, enjoying immensely the sounds of her siblings' concern. "No! I'm not coming back till both of you apologize."

"Apologize for what?" David asked.

"For . . . you know . . . for getting out of the water and leaving me here all alone."

"Cat, we all heard Dorothy's bell calling us to supper. Why didn't you just come out when we did?"

"Because I like it in here and I wasn't hungry for supper like you two. Maybe I'd have come with you if you'd asked me, but you never bothered. You just got out and left me here! And now, well, I don't know if I even care anymore . . ."

David and Emma exchanged worried glances.

"Cat," David said, "we're sorry. We shouldn't have walked out on you like that. Now please, come on in, Cat. The water's rising, and we've got to get to supper."

"Oh, all right," Catherine relented, pleased to see that her hesitancy seemed to have produced the desired effect on her siblings.

She pushed her way through the water and reached the embankment. She stretched out her hands for David and Emma to grasp, and together they began to help her scramble up through the mud.

Suddenly Emma gasped and let go of her left hand. "Cat, you've got things crawling all over you!"

Catherine looked down at her wet bathing costume. Dozens of what looked like tiny red crabs were spreading over her legs and stomach and were starting to crawl up onto her left arm and chest. They began to pinch and bite, causing her to scream and pull her other hand away from David's.

She ran back into the water, trying to swipe the crabs off her body with her hands, but the more she tried, the more they seemed to dig deeper into her flesh. She turned to cry out to David and Emma to come help her, but strangely, they had disappeared.

In a desperate attempt to find relief from the pain, she swam out into the jet-black water in the middle of the creek. As she did so, she felt herself caught in a vortex, swirling downward, her breath beginning to give out.

She heard a voice, but not a single voice—more like a choir of tempting demons. "Finish it!"

It was something she knew she could not yield to.

"Please, God, forgive me. Please don't let me . . . Help!" She lifted her arms, reaching up toward the surface for whatever last gleam of hope might possibly be there to latch on to. Darkness closed in . . .

The concerned faces of Matilda and Pastor Jones slowly came into view as the fog cleared from Catherine's brain.

"They're all over her arm and leg and stomach, Pastor. But it was the big one on her wrist that would've killed her if I hadn't found her, poor thing. Looks like she used that little penknife on the floor by her dresser. Thank God she asked me to stay here an extra couple o' weeks."

"Is the doctor coming soon?"

"Yes, I asked Ben to go fetch him. Should be here within the hour."

Now it was all coming back. She was in the same bed where, two weeks ago, she had given birth. She tilted her head slightly and noticed that her left forearm and wrist were heavily bandaged. A soft linen cloth covered her abdomen, and Matilda was in the process of applying another one to her left leg. Those tiny, pinching crabs of her strange dream must have reflected the horrible reality of all the little knife cuts she'd inflicted in her semiconscious delirium before finally slicing her wrist.

Pastor Jones sat on a stool beside the bed, holding her right hand and wiping her brow occasionally.

She blinked, trying to focus her eyes on his. "I almost did it, didn't I?"

Jones closed his eyes and squeezed her hand. "Yes, Catherine, you almost did."

"Pastor, I truly despise myself. Why didn't God just let me die?"

Pastor Jones smiled tenderly at her. "Because, Catherine, besides the fact that God loves you, maybe he saw that your own greater desire was to *live*."

"But . . . I cut myself and—"

"Yes, but afterward, you struggled to your door, and then you opened it and cried out for help. Over and over. That's the only reason Matilda heard you and got to you in time."

Hearing his words, the floodgates opened. She reached her arms out for Pastor Jones, who leaned over and held her head against his chest as she shook with the sobs that had been building for years. As she rested in the warmth of his embrace, she clearly sensed—for the first time in her life—that God was actually right there inside her, and that he would never, ever leave her or forsake her.

CHAPTER 29

City Point, Virginia
September 12, 1863

The picnic dinner with Pastor Jones and his wife Judith on top of the sunny bluff overlooking the riverbank southeast of City Point had done wonders for Catherine's spirit. It was the culmination of a restful, weeklong recuperative stay with the Jones family at their Wheeler Farm residence, and she regretted that their time together was drawing to a close.

At Judith's gracious urging, Catherine and Pastor Jones set out on a short walk together while she picked up the picnic paraphernalia and readied the carriage for the ride back to the farm. Holding on to the pastor's arm as they walked along the narrow footpath near the bluff's edge, Catherine closed her eyes and tilted her head back as she breathed in the refreshing scents from the clumps of Virginia wild rye and other native grasses dotting the ground nearby. For the first time in ages, the entirety of her body, mind, and soul felt at complete peace.

She smiled at him gratefully. "Pastor, I can't thank you and Judith enough for all you've done to befriend and care for me. Honestly, if the two of you hadn't so vigorously vouched for my sanity to Dr. Haynes, I know he would have had me committed to the asylum in Richmond."

She touched her throat and shook her head. "I still can't believe—after my rudeness during that supper with my family four years ago—that you'd even consider opening your door last January when I came knocking, asking you to preside over Joe's burial service."

Pastor Jones nodded. "Tell me, Catherine, what *really* made you decide to come ask me? At the time, you inflated my vanity by telling me it was because of recalling your brother David's 'high opinion' of my abilities for handling such sad occasions. But was that really the reason?"

"That was part of it," she replied hesitantly. "But . . . there was something else that I felt too awkward admitting to you at the time. I knew I would need strong pastoral comfort at the burial service—even more so than the funeral. And when I considered who might best provide that, I thought of you. There was something about you that I truly appreciated that first time we talked at the family supper. You really seemed to listen to me . . . like you truly cared about me, even though I'm sure that much of what I was saying was highly offensive to you."

Jones chuckled. "I must admit, I saw and heard some things that greatly intrigued me about you that memorable evening."

"And . . . what did you see and hear?"

He gazed at her intently. "A young lady with great intelligence and spirit, but also one carrying a lot of inner hurt and anger at herself."

Catherine turned her face aside, wanting desperately to hide her emotions. "I thought . . . I thought I had put all those negative things aside when Joe came into my life. And then he died, and then my baby . . ."

"And then," Jones suggested gently, "in addition to the pain and devastation of losing them, the old ghosts came rushing right back, didn't they, Catherine?"

She nodded, unable to speak.

Pastor Jones stopped suddenly and placed his hand on her forearm. "Catherine, why do you hate yourself?"

It took nearly a half minute for Catherine to answer. She turned to face him, her eyes moist. "It's all rather embarrassing, Pastor, and I'm not even sure it will make any sense to you."

"You'll never know if you don't give it a try . . . if you're willing."

Catherine closed her eyes, realizing the time to expunge her inner demons had finally arrived. "Up until about the age of ten, I'd been a happy, playful child without a care in the world. But then something changed. Papa started to look at me differently, as if he was now always seeing something in me that for some reason disgusted him. Instead of the hugs and kisses he used to shower both me and Emma with, for some reason I became the main object of his angry outbursts in the evenings after he'd had several drinks. He'd remember some little thing I'd done or said that day and suddenly take me to task, jumping out of his chair and yelling profanities and often slapping my face. Sometimes, he'd even switch my legs bloody with his belt for being 'disrespectful.'"

Pastor Jones grimaced. "And your mother? And Emma and David? Did they witness this?"

Catherine sighed. "Mother would just stand there petrified, begging Papa to stop but too afraid to interfere physically. Later, she'd come up to my room and try to console me, but it did little good and I'd lie awake crying for most of the night. As for David and Emma . . . neither ever seemed to be around when Papa would light up on me, and since neither seemed to be getting the same treatment, I never wanted to talk to them about it.

"Then there was the night Papa slapped my face so hard that I fell to the floor . . . all for 'wrestling too closely with my cousin in the barn' that day, as he put it, based on what my mother told him she'd spotted us doing. He told me how disappointed he was in me, especially since I was his eldest daughter and that he expected me to behave like a 'proper young Southern lady,' setting a good example for Emma. I thought it was all over until the next morning when I passed by him on my way to breakfast and he grabbed me and pulled me into the parlor. I'll never forget what he said to me: 'Catherine, if I *ever* hear again that you are behaving like a dirty little whore, I promise by God that I'll whip you myself, as hard as I've ever had to whip a slave. Your mother and I love you, daughter, and you have great potential as a growing young woman to represent this family well . . . just as your mother has for all these years. But don't let us down.' I remember well how scared and empty and alone I felt after he said that, like the whole world was on *my* shoulders to prove myself to him by taming my wilder impulses and learning to imitate Mother. And then . . . when Mother died . . ."

She looked at him beseechingly, her face a mask of frustration. "Oh, Pastor, I tried so hard to regain the love and approval that Papa had shown me when I was a very young child. I did my best to support him like Mother did, catering to him and defending him when my brother and sister would question or argue with him. But even though his open bouts of anger toward me gradually disappeared as time passed, I *never* really felt like I won that approval that I craved from him—only his grudging tolerance. And selfish weakling that I am, instead of rising to the occasion and simply accepting that, I allowed myself to become frustrated and bitter about it all."

Pastor Jones bowed his head.

Somehow, she sensed that none of this was coming as a surprise to him.

He reached out and touched her shoulder. "And as someone in my position would now be expected to ask, Cat, what did all that do to your understanding of God?"

Catherine stared at the ground, struggling to find the right words. "I-I'm ashamed to admit that I started to see him as someone like Papa . . . some distant, judging authority whom I could never really expect to please. Oh, I still believed that Christ forgave my sins, that he would save me from hell and embrace me in heaven when I died. But as far as really trusting that God was always there to provide understanding and guidance and protection and comfort in my daily life . . . well, let's just say I began to doubt seriously whether that was really true in my case."

"And what did that lead to?" Jones asked softly.

She folded her arms across her stomach. "I turned cold inside," she said, her voice almost a whisper. "I lost that sincere concern for others which, as a Christian, I knew I was supposed to have. Like the kind of selfless compassion and affection that David and Emma used to have for me ... the kind I know they both often felt for the slaves, when *I* never felt anything but emptiness and coldness. I'd get so very jealous and angry at them for having those truly caring feelings for others less fortunate. Feelings that I wanted but could never seem to drum up."

Her chin began to tremble as tears slid down her cheek. "All these thoughts about how bad a person I was kept building up—especially after Mother died. I felt like there was some evil poison inside me that I just had to release. At some point, I discovered that cutting myself a little would make things better for a while, until the poison would build up once again and the cycle would repeat. Then Joe came along and captured my mind and heart. Even after he died, the thought of having his baby gave me great hope that I'd be able to keep pushing off my bad thoughts and need to cut myself."

Jones closed his eyes and sighed. "And after losing your baby—and without your brother or sister around to support you—you tried returning to your familiar 'cure'?"

Catherine looked up at him, a huge lump forming in her throat. "Yes, starting the day after. Only this time, it didn't work. No matter how many more little cuts I inflicted all over myself, I kept feeling worse and worse, until ... finally ... one day ... well, you know the rest."

Pastor Jones peered out over the edge of the bluff at two small dark birds flitting about, just above the surface of the water. After watching them fly off together toward the far bank, he gently grasped her by the arm and they resumed their walk.

"Catherine," he said finally, "after what you've just been through, do you still believe God to be far away, judgmental, leaving you to fend for yourself without his help?"

She shook her head firmly. "I will never believe that again. Not after the way he rescued me from death by my own hand."

"And what is the single most important thing you would like God to do for you now?"

She sighed and gazed off into the distance. "I would love for him to show me a new purpose for my life. A selfless purpose like he gave David and Emma ... and the compassion for others like they have to carry it out."

Jones said nothing for a long moment.

"Catherine, I can tell you with all certainty that God has given you far more compassion for others than you give God or yourself credit for. But even so, what if God were to give you a new purpose that didn't require compassion like David's and Emma's . . . but rather some of the other good qualities that he's already given you, or perhaps some new ones that are entirely different? Qualities he's reserved for you alone—and which he'll make sure you have when the time is right? Would you be satisfied with that?"

Catherine cocked her head. "Pastor Jones, if that's the case, then God is just going to have to show me how and where to begin. Because, to tell the truth, I see no purpose for me except surviving on a big plantation that's lost its heart and soul."

Jones peered at her, a twinkle in his eye. "I wonder if *that* is exactly where God might want you to start."

Dim light and the sound of voices emitting from the cracks around the closed doors of Sam Taylor's supply barn on the Hodge Family Plantation confirmed Catherine's suspicion. It was Friday night after nine, and Sam was obviously flouting her command to stop the partying on *her* property.

Small oil lamp in hand, she stalked toward the door, preparing to push it open and confront whoever was inside.

Caught him in the act, she thought with grim satisfaction. *Glad I came back a day earlier than expected.*

Escorted home by Pastor Jones late this afternoon, she hadn't been inside the main house for five minutes before Dorothy had rushed into the parlor room with her tidings. During the week while Catherine was away, she'd said, Sam had made himself at home.

The first two days around noon, he'd told all the house servants to vacate the entire front of the house and go eat their dinner on the back porch while Sam, Philip, and four other unknown men conducted an hour-long meeting behind the locked doors of the family dining room. They'd brought their own food and drink, but they'd done only a cursory job cleaning up after themselves, requiring Dorothy to make things spotless again after they left each time. "These are some old friends of Mizz Cat's father, Dorothy," Sam had assured her. "Don't you worry none—I'll talk to her about all this when she gets back."

Yesterday, there'd been an additional trespass. Late in the afternoon, one of the young house-servant girls had been cleaning the parlor room when she heard Sam and one of his friends approaching unexpectedly. Panicked, she'd hidden behind the large couch as the two men relaxed in the plush armchairs, drinking liberally. For over an hour, they'd discussed all manner of despicable things, including a detailed accounting of Sam's recent liaison with a Petersburg prostitute and possible new roles for Papa's old Virginia First Society, such as tracking down escaping slaves and conducting guerilla raids on Union forces if they ever managed to reach the area again. After the men had left, the girl discovered a printed announcement of an upcoming VFS meeting that one of them—obviously drunk, if the empty whiskey decanter was any indication—had carelessly left behind on a side table.

Now armed with the meeting notice in her dress pocket and prepared to flash it in front of Sam's surprised face, Catherine put her hand on the barn door. She was about to shove it open when something she heard made her pause and put her ear to the door.

"Oh, Sam . . . you always say that to me." The owner of the high-pitched, giggling voice was unmistakable.

Catherine felt the blood rush to her face. *Liz Wheeler . . . that flighty little pig . . . what's* she *doing here?* She barely managed to restrain herself from bursting through the door.

"I wouldn't say it if I didn't mean it, darlin'."

"That's right, Liz," chimed in another voice that sounded like Liz's older brother Johnny. "You can trust Sam. Whatever Sam says, we all know it's always the god-honest truth." The raucous laughter of other male voices caused Catherine to cringe. *How many are in there?* It was clear they were all drunk out of their minds.

"Yeah, didn't you know, Liz?" croaked another voice. "Sam's the walking, talking epitome of his unofficial creed for the Virginia First Society."

"And what's that, Uncle Bobby?"

"First in war, first in peace, first in line for our best friend's niece!"

"Why don't you just shut up, Bobby?" Sam snarled. "What makes you think you're my best friend? And quit makin' fun of our society. There's gonna be a lot expected of us pretty soon, mark my words."

"Guess we'll be stringin' up a lot of runaway slaves, huh, Sam?"

"Could be. If we don't, they'll end up in the Yank army, comin' back to loot our houses, rape and murder our women. Now quit yappin' and play your hand, Bobby—I know you ain't got two aces left."

"Glad at least *you've* had some practice with the hangin' process, Sam," said someone else with a snicker. "Still can't believe you got away with it. I'm impressed."

"That Cobb boy deserved it. Had it comin'."

Catherine gasped and covered her mouth upon hearing Sam's confession.

"Yeah," Bobby agreed. "But the best part? That alibi." He let out a hearty laugh. "You done snookered the sheriff."

"Not without *my* help, thank you." Liz Wheeler actually sounded proud of herself. "I'm the one who got Daddy to vouch for you."

Catherine was on the verge of erupting with fury. But she pressed her ear in closer.

Bobby cut back in. "And on top o' that, hedgin' our society votes in the election to convince the sheriff and Mr. Hodge not to investigate any further. Sam, I swear, you're a genius!"

Dead silence followed. Shocked to the core, Catherine clutched her throat, struggling to grasp everything she'd just heard.

"I didn't do it for no reason, ya know."

Someone chuckled. "Well, why *did* you do it, then, Sam?"

"Couldn't allow that slave to keep on disrespectin' me. Just wouldn't stop, despite my warnings and attempts to discipline him. Just ask Johnny here. Can't have slaves runnin' all over their supervisors."

"And tryin' to steal the heart of your old flame Miss Emma, right, Sam?" Billy suggested. Now, *that's* just too disgusting to even think about— Black-boy Charles with lily-White Miss Emma. No wonder you—"

"*Sam Taylor!*" Liz protested. "You mean you once liked that gimpy, too-good-for-everybody Emma Hodge more than *me*? Why? Just 'cause she's richer?"

Sam laughed. "No, no, darlin'. That self-righteous, slave-pityin' little race traitor could *never* hold a candle to a true-blue southern girl like—"

That's it! Catherine's head nearly exploded with revulsion and rage. She put her lamp on the ground and shoved the barn door open with both hands. Sam and the others looked up in shock from the bottle- and card-strewn circular table around which they all sat.

Liz Wheeler jumped off Sam's lap as Catherine marched toward them, pulling the VFS notice out of her pocket as she approached. She stopped two feet away from the table, glaring at Sam.

"I thought I told you to stop the barn parties."

Sam stared at her in open-mouthed astonishment from the opposite side of the table. "You're back early, Mizz Cat."

"I know that, Sam. Now answer my question."

"Well now, Mizz Cat, guess I just plain forgot you told me that. I do have to apologize and beg your forgiveness."

"And what did you think you were doing taking over my house, using my dining room for dinner meetings and my parlor for your personal saloon?"

"Your *parlor*? What are you talking about? I was going to explain to you about those meetings, but . . . your parlor? I never set foot in it."

"No?"

"That's right, ma'am."

Catherine held up the VFS notice. "Then, tell me, Sam, who happened to leave *this* on the side table? And who drank nearly an entire decanter of our best whiskey?"

Sam glanced around the table at the others, all of whom sat like statues, staring straight ahead. Letting out a huge sigh, he grinned, folded his arms, and leaned back in his chair. Liz placed her hand on his shoulder. "Guess you got me there, Mizz Cat. So, what would you like to do about it? Make me pay for expenses? I'll be happy to. Fire me? You know, if you think it's easy to find a good field supervisor these days, especially around harvest time, maybe you should—"

Before he could complete his sentence, Catherine grabbed the edge of the lightweight table with both hands and flipped it upward with all her might. Playing cards and bottles of liquor crashed onto the floor and into Sam's lap, causing him to jump up from his chair and unleash a string of vile curses.

Catherine glared at the others. "*Get out!* All of you, get out now, and get off my property!" Knocking over chairs and stumbling over themselves in their haste to exit, they left her alone with Sam. He stood glowering at her with undisguised hatred and contempt.

"*You murdering bastard!*" she shouted. "I was outside the door . . . I heard everything. I can't believe I lost the love of my sister by constantly refusing to believe what she knew you'd done to Charles."

Sam shrugged. "Water over the dam. She's gone now . . . her own choice to leave. And concerning Charles, like I said, I had my reasons. Anyway . . . there's not a blessed thing either of us can do about any of it now, is there, Mizz Cat? No way the sheriff would ever open an investigation at this point, even if he wanted to. Might as well just press on with the way things are. Like I said, I'll be happy to pay you for my use of the main house, and I promise I'll stop these barn parties."

Catherine shook her head. "We're finished, Sam. I'll be visiting your father tomorrow to give your family three days' notice to get off my property, or I'll have Sheriff Johnson escort you off."

Sam's jaw dropped. "*What?* You're firing me and my father too? Evicting our entire family?"

"That's exactly what I'm doing. I'm just sorry I waited this long to do it."

Sam bent down to pick up his hat. He dusted it off, then calmly placed it on his head. He walked around the table and passed her, stopping and turning when he reached the door.

"You're making a big mistake, Mizz Catherine. Once your slaves start actin' up, you'll wish you had me back." With that, he walked off into the night.

Catherine stood alone in the barn. She looked around, surveying the mess on the ground, the mess she had caused.

Maybe that's exactly where God wants you to start, Pastor Jones had suggested earlier today.

Utterly exhausted, she collapsed to her knees and cried.

Chapter 30

Washington, DC
September 15, 1863

Sallie Cobb and her colored assistant supervisor, William Johnson, looked up from their desks in the local AMA chapter's front office to observe the newly framed, commemorative document that Emma was holding up proudly for both to see.

"It looks wonderful, Miss Em!" Sallie gushed. "I love the wording you came up with. I'm sure Mrs. Tubman will feel honored to receive that from us. I know I would."

Emma handed the frame to William for a closer look. He scrutinized it, then broke out in a broad smile. "Couldn't have said it better myself."

Emma breathed a sigh of relief. In less than an hour, the private reception for Harriet Tubman—the now-famous "Black Moses" of the Underground Railroad for escaping slaves—would be taking place in the AMA's rented speaking hall down the street.

The workday nearly over, Sallie completed reading and sorting the last piece of magazine subscriber mail in her stack. She walked over to Emma's desk to help her assemble information packets for the one hundred or more expected reception guests.

"My, this woman has done a lot with her life," Sallie mused as she scanned Tubman's one-page biography. "Underground Railroad conductor; consultant to John Brown; leader of the surprise Union army river raid last July that freed over seven hundred plantation slaves in South Carolina. I had no idea."

"Also seems she's a devout Christian," Emma said. "Driven by dreams and timely premonitions she claims God gave her to help keep her and the slaves safe as they traveled to freedom."

"Hmmm," Sallie said. "That sounds like what our preacher was talkin' about in his sermon yesterday, Emmy. Think he said God grants some people special messages in dreams to help 'em get things done that he wants 'em to do."

Emma laughed. "I'm glad we're actually getting something more out of his sermons now. When you and I first started attending that church together last month, I was afraid we'd never hear anything beyond constant reminders to 'love our neighbors as ourselves.'"

"I suspect those constant reminders are necessary, Miss Hodge," William interjected from his desk on the far side of the room. He'd obviously been listening in on their conversation. Smiling innocently, he leaned back in his chair with hands clasped behind his neck.

"And why do you say that, Mr. Johnson?" Emma asked politely.

William cleared his throat. "Well, I'm not an overly religious man, but it seems to me that a whole lot of your fellow 'Christian' churchgoers need to take that wonderful principle of 'loving your neighbor' more seriously."

Emma stared at him. "Isn't that something we *all* need to take more seriously, Mr. Johnson?"

"Some more than others, Miss Hodge," William replied, his voice tightening. "And I'd think that with all your research on female abolitionists like the Grimké sisters, you of all people would be able to see that."

"Mr. Johnson," Emma said, trying mightily to keep her tone in check, "I'm sorry, but I'm not sure what it is you're trying to imply . . . ?"

William leaned forward in his chair, folding his hands on the top of the desk. "The problem, Miss Hodge, is that too many 'good, White, churchgoing Christians'—even those with abolitionist sentiments like yourself—don't have the slightest idea of what it truly means to love their neighbor. That is, when it comes to neighbors of a different skin color than themselves."

Emma felt the blood rushing to her face. "So, please inform me, Mr. Johnson, what in your opinion is required to truly and properly love my neighbor of a different skin color than myself? What are so many White, churchgoing Christians like myself doing wrong in that regard?"

William hesitated and glanced at Sallie, who was clearly uncomfortable with the conversation. She kept her head down, assembling the information packets on her own at a furious pace.

"May I speak honestly and freely . . . without concern that you'll complain to Mr. Billingham that I'm being disrespectful to you?" William asked.

"Of course, sir," Emma said. "You have my word."

"It's not what you do or don't do, Miss Hodge. It's who you are. Generally speaking, as a White person, because of your comparatively privileged status in society and what you've learned from it, you are naturally inclined to see the Black race as inferior to your own. Yes, some of you genuinely pity us. You hate to see us suffer. You want us to be free from the chains of slavery and are willing to do everything in your power to help us achieve that. And yes, you may even wish to teach us to read and write at a basic level so that we can embrace Christianity and learn to 'love our neighbors' and not cause White society any trouble. But, Miss Hodge, that's where it stops for the vast majority of good-hearted White folks who support abolition like you . . . and that is *not* what I call truly 'loving your neighbor.' Because basically, you *still* don't see us as your neighbor. You see us as inferior beings to be held down and kept at arm's length after we're freed . . . or better yet, as President Lincoln still seems to prefer, sent off to our own foreign colony to fend for ourselves."

Emma struggled to gather her conflicting emotions. On its surface, William's logic was hard to dispute. But on the other hand . . .

"Mr. Johnson, since you must be convinced that I'm *even more bound* than most White abolition supporters to consider you an 'inferior being' due to my privileged upbringing as a wealthy southern plantation owner's daughter, then why on earth were you willing to recommend me to Mr. Billingham?"

William's face relaxed a bit. "Oh, don't get me wrong, Miss Hodge. There are exceptions to the rule that I just described. John Brown, Congressman Stevens, the Grimké sisters—rare examples of Whites who were somehow able and willing to overcome their natural prejudices and experience true love for their colored brothers and sisters. In fact, I sensed you might well be one of them after reading the recommendation from Angelina Grimké and listening to the heartfelt testimony on your behalf from Miss Cobb here." He glanced at Sallie and smiled.

"And so, after observing my work here for six months, do you believe I'm capable of properly loving my colored neighbor, Mr. Johnson?"

William grinned. "I must admit, the signs are exceptionally promising so far."

All three laughed, relieved to have the tension finally broken.

"Mr. Johnson," Emma said, "I believe there are many more White people than you think who are fully capable of loving their colored neighbor."

"Oh, I have no doubt there are many who are capable, Miss Hodge. I'm just not sure how many who—like you—are *willing*."

After exiting the horsecar at the rail line terminus on M Street, Emma and Sallie began the five-block walk home to Aunt Lyla's house. Having already discussed every delightful angle of the highly successful reception for Harriet Tubman earlier in the evening, Emma was ready for their conversation to take a new turn.

"You like him, don't you?" she teased.

"Mr. Johnson? Well, I . . . I . . . oh, I don't know, Emmy."

Emma leaned in close and lightly bumped Sallie's arm with her elbow. "Yes, you do," she chided. "You're just afraid to tell me. You think I'll be mad at you or something. Actually, I can see why you like him."

Sallie looked at her askance. "You can? Even after that high-and-mighty way he spoke to you today?"

Emma laughed. "I have to admit, *that* was a bit hard to listen to . . . but he said some things that are true, and I do admire his honesty and courage in telling a White woman what he really thinks. At least he ended it all in a genial way. And anyway, it seems to me Mr. Johnson might have a couple of other qualities worth a woman's consideration."

"Oh, I'm not gonna deny he's real good-lookin' and he works hard and he's smarter than any man I've ever known. And he *is* fun to talk to and he treats me like a real lady when we've gone out to supper. It's just that . . ."

"What, Sallie?" Emma prompted gently.

"I'm not sure what he sees in me—him bein' raised in Philadelphia by rich, free parents, attendin' that new Wilberforce University for Blacks in Ohio. Sometimes when we talk over supper, he'll get goin' with his eyes all lit up, speakin' big, fancy words about some big national or world thing. And I just have to sit there and smile and nod, not understandin' half o' what he's talkin' about. And another thing . . ."

"What's that?"

"He says he don't know if he believes in God and Jesus—at least like you and me. He can't understand why a good God would allow people to even *have* slaves, much less beat and kill 'em. Thinks too many White people just talk 'bout God and Jesus to make themselves feel better about mistreating coloreds. And too many coloreds using 'em as an excuse to just sit back and take it." Sallie shook her head. "That may be true for a lotta folks. But Mr. Johnson ain't got no idea what it means to have God right there, helpin' you keep on goin' when you see your brother hanged, or when you lose your whole family tryin' to escape to freedom through a hail of bullets. I'm tellin' you, Emmy . . . ain't no man gonna win *my* heart completely if he don't believe in God and Jesus like I do."

Emma observed her fondly, wondering if she herself would insist on such high standards in a future male partner, if one were to ever come along. "Maybe you'll be able to move him in that direction, the more he gets to know you and liking what he sees in you."

Now it was Sallie's turn to laugh. "At the rate we're going—one supper together every month—God might decide to take me up to heaven first. And there's always the chance the AMA bosses will ask him to go down to Fort Monroe to help out at the Contraband Camp. Least that's what he's been telling me. You think they gonna ask you to go down there too sometime, Emmy?"

She shook her head. "I wish I knew. I've been here far longer than I thought, and I can't wait to get my first teaching assignment. I'm not sure what's taking so long, because there *are* places I could be serving."

"What am I gonna do if *both* you and Mr. Johnson leave? It'll sure be real lonely around here."

Emma bit her lip. She'd known there would come a time when she and Sallie would need to part, and she hated the thought. She quickly shook it off and peered down the street. Aunt Lyla's house was now in view, along with an unexpected coach parked by the curb in front of it.

"Whose coach is *that*?" Sallie asked. "Your uncle James ain't supposed to be back from his trip for two more days."

"I've no idea. I suppose we're about to find out."

Approaching the front steps, Emma noticed that a light seemed to be shining behind the drawn living room window curtains. That was unusual; Aunt Lyla would normally have retired to bed by now.

She was about to grasp the handle when the door suddenly opened to reveal Aunt Lyla, standing in the foyer dressed in her informal reception gown. A huge smile lit up her face. "Come in, come in, you two. I think I have someone here who you may know."

Mystified, Emma stepped into the foyer followed by Sallie. Grabbing Emma's hand, Aunt Lyla led them into the living room where two men, a woman, and a small girl stood in front of the fireplace, all with broad smiles on their faces.

"Hello, Em."

Emma shrieked with surprise, joy, and disbelief at her first sight of David after two and a half years of separation. Dropping her purse on the floor, she ran to embrace and kiss him over and over on the cheek, barely aware of the others standing beside him.

Finally, she drew herself back, allowing Sallie a chance to embrace David next. He was still as handsome as ever, but he seemed to have lost a lot of weight, and the empty lower left sleeve of his jacket confirmed what he'd told her in his last letter.

"Your letter said you weren't going to be here for another week," Emma protested. "I wouldn't be looking so exhausted, and we'd have been here to greet you when you first arrived."

"In that case, perhaps we should all leave and come back in a week," David joked. "Actually, we received late notice that the project planning meeting with Secretary Chase had been moved up to tomorrow, and it was all we could do to pack our bags and catch the next train to Washington. I sent another letter to let you know, but obviously it didn't get here before we did."

David turned to introduce his new wife and stepdaughter. Emma could easily see why he had become so smitten with Sarah and Jenny the first time he'd seen them. The other man she saw when she first entered stood politely off to the side, giving everyone time to embrace.

Sarah tried coaxing the little girl with bright blue eyes and light-brown, long-drop barley curls, who was clinging shyly to her skirt. "Jenny, say hello to your aunt Emma."

Emma knelt and took Jenny's hand in her own. "Hello, little angel. Do you think you and your momma and Miss Sallie and I can all become best friends, and go see some Washington sights tomorrow?"

Jenny smiled, let go of her mother's skirt, and let Emma hug her closely.

"One more to go, Emma," said David, laughing.

Emma stood and gathered herself, then turned to face the man she knew had been the first to inspire her brother to leave home, family, and everything familiar for the sake of a far greater cause.

"Abel Bowman, I'm honored to introduce you to my sister Emma."

Abel bowed slowly—a bit awkwardly, Emma thought. As if he wasn't in the habit of performing this little social grace very often with ladies.

He straightened, looked her in the eyes, and smiled. "I've heard so many good things about you, Miss Emma."

Her cheeks blushing at the compliment, she smiled and offered her hand. "It's a pleasure to finally meet you, Mr. Bowman."

Sitting on the parlor room sofa next to her brother after the others had retired for the night, Emma reached over and gently touched his empty sleeve below the amputation point. "Does it hurt?"

David grinned and moved her hand up onto his bicep. "Squeeze as hard as you can, and I'll let you know."

"Oh, you!" Laughing, she yanked her hand away and slapped his leg. Within seconds, her countenance fell, and she began dabbing at her eyes with a handkerchief.

David draped his other arm around her shoulders. "Em, what's wrong?"

She took a deep breath and let it out.

"David, that day you left our plantation for Ohio, I remember watching you walk away, over the front lawn and under that huge magnolia tree we all used to love climbing. You were so angry with Papa and Cat, and I feared I would never see you again. It broke my heart. And yet, brother, another part of me was so proud of you I wanted to burst. Jumping in to defend that Unionist being assaulted outside our church in Petersburg, standing up for your beliefs to Papa despite your love and affection for him. You showed me the way, David."

David smiled and took her hand in his. "Well, sister, I never dreamed any of that would one day spur *you* to leave the family and all your comforts, to risk your own life as you did—basically for the sake of the same cause as mine. Trust me, I'm even more proud of you." He lowered his head. "I only wish to God I'd had a better parting with Catherine. Ever since, I've often kicked myself for never bothering to take her aside as I'd done with you to explain my decision. I just assumed that, like Papa, she was locked into her old ways of thinking and would never understand. I so regret that now."

Emma withdrew her hand and folded her arms. "David, it was *Cat's choice* to turn her back on you like she did, refusing to say goodbye. *Her* choice to break her promise to help me confront Papa about the danger that Charles faced from Sam Taylor. *Her* choice—just like Papa's—to always downplay my concerns about anything involving Sam and his treatment of the slaves. I hate to say this, but I just don't feel any regrets about leaving her and Papa, and I'm having a hard time forgiving Cat for her lack of concern and even respect for me."

"Do you miss Cat at all, Emma?" David asked softly.

"I miss terribly the Cat I knew in our childhood and young teenage years. I don't miss who she eventually became."

David bowed his head and nodded, saying nothing for several moments.

"Em," he asked finally, "what's next for you?"

"Now that is a question for the ages," Emma groaned in exasperation. "I wish I knew. I'd planned on receiving my first teaching assignment months ago, but it always seems that some other supposedly well-qualified woman with a northern upbringing gets selected over me when an opportunity arises. I don't know how much longer I can will myself to keep doing odd jobs around the front office just to appear useful to Mr. Billingham."

"What would you say if I could arrange to have you assigned by the AMA Board as a teacher supporting our Port Royal Experiment in the Sea Islands?"

Emma stared at him in astonishment. "David, *really*? I've heard a lot of great things about that project. But would that even be possible? And where *are* the Sea Islands, exactly?"

"They're just off the coast of South Carolina and Georgia, about a hundred and eighty miles southwest of Charleston. The Union navy invaded them early in the war and established a base of operations in the area. I know there's a huge need down there right now for missionary-teachers to support the new phase of the project involving first-time land ownership for the freed slaves in the area. I'll be speaking tomorrow with people who I think would be quite interested in having your help there as soon as possible. Would you be willing and ready to go if I can get approval?"

"My goodness, yes! *Yes!*"

David laughed. "Good. I thought you might agree. In fact, there may even be a role down there for Sallie, if she's interested and if you'd like to have her accompany you."

Emma jumped up from the couch, her hands over her mouth to stifle her shout of joy. "Oh, David, I can't wait to tell Sallie!"

David rose and hugged her closely. "All right, but remember . . . I can't promise anything until after my meeting tomorrow. In the meantime, I think you should go get a good night's sleep while I sit here a little longer to review some papers."

About to exit the room, Emma paused and turned to face her brother.

"David . . . did you say Mr. Bowman was your assistant investigator?"

"Yes, that's right. Why do you ask?"

"Oh, I was just wondering if I would ever see him again after this."

David gave her a quizzical look. "If you come to South Carolina, you'll probably have occasion to see both of us every now and then for a few days at a time in the course of our inspection travels. Would that be a problem?"

"Oh, not a problem at all. He seems very nice. I-I was curious, that's all."

David grinned. "I'll let him know you were 'curious.'"

Emma blushed. "David Hodge, you'll do no such thing! I'll deny every bit of it."

"As you command. Good night, sister."

Emma closed the parlor door and hurried toward the stairs leading to the guest bedrooms. There was no way she could wait till morning to tell Sallie the news.

PART IV

GLORY
(1864–1865)

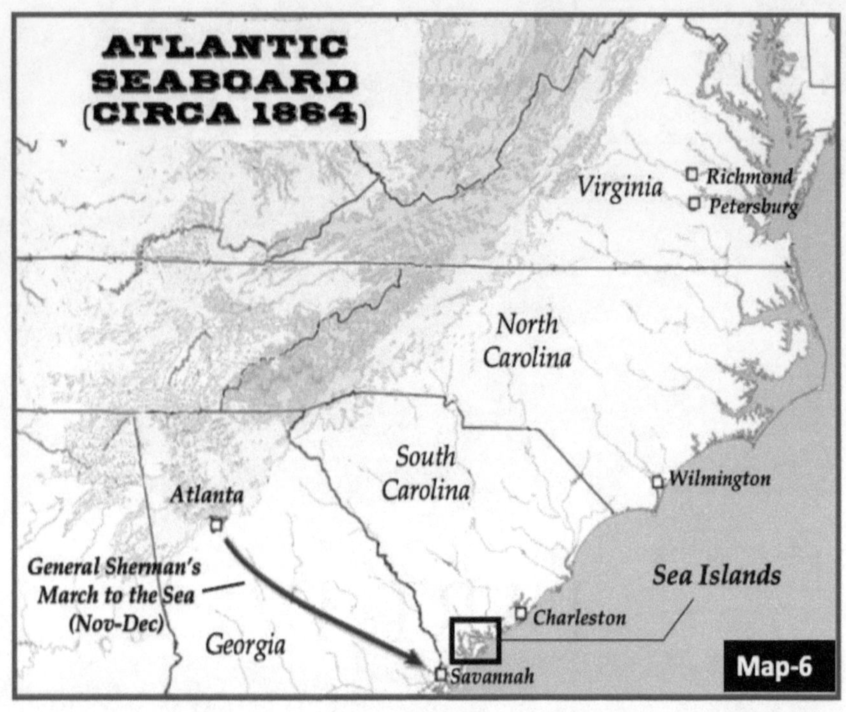

ATLANTIC
SEABOARD
(CIRCA 1864)
Virginia
Richmond
Petersburg
North
Carolina
South
Carolina
Atlanta
Wilmington
Sea Islands
General Sherman's
March to the Sea
(Nov-Dec)
Georgia
Charleston
Savannah
Map-6

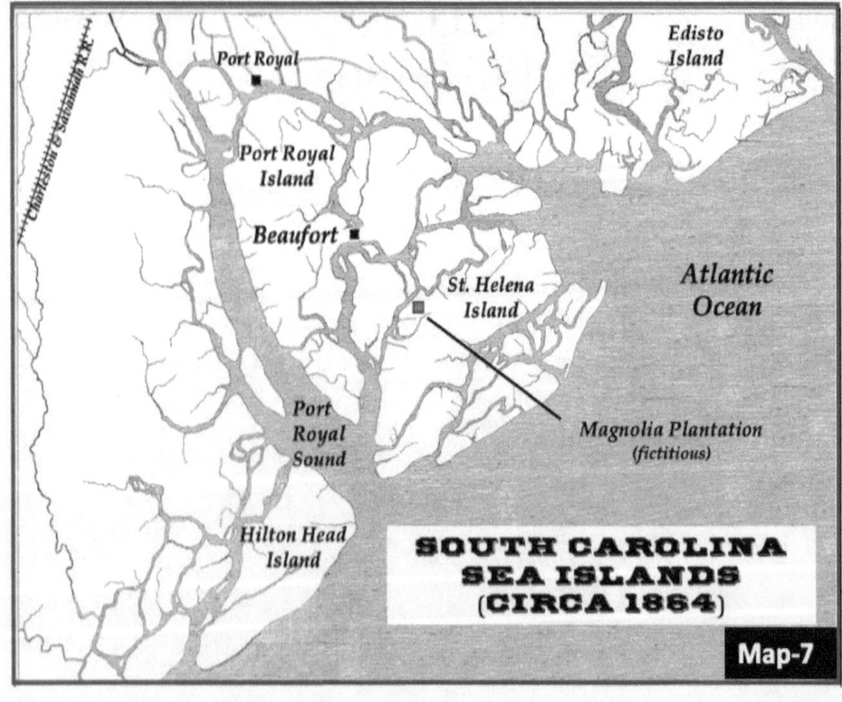

Edisto
Island
Port Royal
Charleston & Savannah R.R.
Port Royal
Island
Beaufort
St. Helena
Island
Atlantic
Ocean
Port
Royal
Sound
Magnolia Plantation
(fictitious)
Hilton Head
Island
SOUTH CAROLINA
SEA ISLANDS
(CIRCA 1864)
Map-7

CHAPTER 31

Magnolia Plantation
St. Helena Island, South Carolina Sea Islands
February 20, 1864
(Five months later)

A cold and salty Atlantic breeze swept through the palmetto and palm groves lining the ocean-facing sides of the closely interlocked Sea Islands hugging the South Carolina coast. Near the river that bordered the interior side of St. Helena Island, several large oaks with their lacy strands of Spanish moss lent somber beauty and protective shelter to the Magnolia Plantation's main house, which stood at the crest of a small, gently sloping, sandy hill facing the wind head-on.

Spring can't come soon enough, David thought, shivering slightly in his light wool coat. He'd heard many accolades from the local residents about how in spring the islands would come alive with lush greenery and the fragrance of yellow jasmine, roses, and acacia blossoms. But for the next month or so, drab and chilly days like this would be the expected norm for the region famed for producing some of the highest quality cotton in the entire world.

Seated alone on the platform that had been hastily constructed at the bottom of the hill for the special dedication ceremony, David surveyed his audience. The government-appointed plantation superintendent Milton Shaw, his wife, and over two hundred ex-slaves, along with their children, had gathered near the front of the small, makeshift stage, all waiting eagerly for the ceremony to commence as soon as the chatter quieted and Mr. Shaw gave the signal.

David closed his eyes, mentally and emotionally preparing himself to deliver the last speech on his latest round of Sea Island plantation inspection visits. This one held special significance. It would be his first time addressing the Magnolia freedmen, who, ever since the arrival of Emma, Sallie, and William Johnson on the plantation in late September, had been the beneficiaries of the AMA-commissioned teaching and administrative support mission that David had helped to arrange. David knew from Emma the special challenges they'd all faced and overcome together, and he was eager to honor and encourage them.

"I believe we're ready to begin, Mr. Hodge," called Mr. Shaw.

David nodded, stood, and walked slowly toward the podium. He glanced off to the side of the platform, wanting to make sure that his assistant investigator, Abel Bowman, along with Emma, Sallie, and William were all in their places to help with the gift presentation near the end of his speech. Seeing their reassuring smiles, he turned to look out at the crowd and the recently erected two-floor schoolhouse behind them.

"Mr. and Mrs. Shaw, together with the freed men, women, and children of the Magnolia Plantation and surrounding areas of St. Helena Island . . . on behalf of the US Treasury Department's Special Investigation Team for the Port Royal Experiment, I greet you as my dear brothers and sisters, and thank you for the opportunity to address you all today.

"My friends, when this grand experiment was begun, it had one primary goal: to prove to the nation that recently freed slaves—long oppressed by an evil system fostering degradation and dependence— would be able to sustain themselves economically and contribute to the wealth of the nation. And in that regard, there is no better way to judge the experiment's success than to recall where you started, and how far you have come.

"Who here can forget that just over two years ago, on the morning of November seventh, 1861, a fleet of Union navy gunships and troop transports entered Port Royal Sound. They began a fearsome bombardment that quickly reduced the Confederate shore defenses to rubble. Hearing the booms from the cotton fields and plantation main houses in which you were working here in St. Helena or one of the other Sea Islands, many of you ran to inquire of your masters what was happening—only to find them frantically loading their household goods and treasures onto riverboats headed toward safety in Charleston, or onto wagons headed inland to seek the protection of retreating Confederate troops.

"Some of your old masters, determined to sabotage their fields and equipment lest they fall into the hands of the invaders, sneaked back later at night to set fires and tear down their grain barns and other structures. They didn't hesitate to shoot or do even worse to many of your friends and family members who dared to resist. You were left desolate, required to fend for yourselves to avoid starvation. And yet, with only occasional, grudging help from the occupying Union soldiers, you somehow managed to survive. Some of you took up arms to help fight off rebel army raids from the mainland. *All* of you faithfully continued to work the land—not only for the next cotton crop but for your own food crops as well.

"Fortunately, humanitarian aid finally began to arrive from the North in the form of emergency provision distributors and missionary-minded preachers, teachers, and business advisors. A few of these—like Mr. Shaw here—were appointed by the government to serve as supervisors for large individual plantations like this or groups of smaller ones. And do you know what Mr. Shaw tells me was *the very first thing* these well-meaning new supervisors learned upon their arrival?"

David turned his head and cupped his hand to his ear, inviting a response. One of the freedmen spoke up immediately. "That they s'pose to be overseeing us plantin' and growin' and pickin' and balin' de cotton, but they don't have the foggiest idea how to do none of it!" A loud chorus of merry guffaws and good-natured hoots followed.

David joined in and pointed to the object of the laughter at the front of the crowd. "And what do you have to say about *that*, Mr. Shaw?"

Shaw grinned sheepishly and nodded in resigned agreement. "I have to admit, it took me only a few days to realize that as ignorant as I was of the daily operational aspects, there'd be no hope of a cotton crop for the Magnolia Plantation if I didn't seek the help of someone who knew such things from the inside out. I'm talking about one of your own, of course: George Skipwith. George, where are you?"

The crowd erupted in loud cheers as the unusually skilled and popular Black foreman—who had long served as the primary assistant to Magnolia's former White overseer—stepped forward to receive Mr. Shaw's warm handshake and pat on the shoulder.

David joined in the acclaim. After the crowd quieted, he continued. "Quite so, quite so. From what I've heard, this is the only plantation on the entire island to be blessed with a foreman of George's caliber. In fact, I was informed that under the combination of Mr. Shaw's and Mr. Skipwith's leadership, the Magnolia Plantation operation was one of the most profitable in the entire Sea Islands region last year."

More applause followed.

"Of course, it would be a great disservice if I failed to mention the second of your great achievements over the past two years. *Education!* It's the key to your future, and the evidence that you realize that is seen in the big, beautiful schoolhouse right behind you that you worked so hard to construct."

The crowd applauded with vigor once again. Many of the children jumped up and down with delight at the mention of their favorite daily activity. "We love learnin' to read and write, Mr. Hodge!" someone yelled.

David grinned, quite content to see his speech being transformed into a more casual, give-and-take dialogue with the crowd. "I'd say that's quite apparent, from everything I've been told by your teacher

Miss Emma and her assistant Miss Sallie here. Since my last inspection tour in December with Mr. Bowman, they say you've enrolled over eighty children and fifty adults in daily classes, learning their ABCs and Bible verses and a whole lot more! Which brings me to the point in our ceremony today that Mr. Bowman and I have been eagerly anticipating since our last visit. Mr. Bowman, would you and Mr. Skipwith please join me up here?"

The crowd hushed as Abel and George stepped onto the platform beside David.

He waited for the gravity of the moment to sink in before speaking once again, his voice filled with emotion.

"Friends, I know you've been through a lot these past few months. First, being told by the government that you'd be able to purchase private lots for your family on this magnificent plantation at just a dollar twenty-five an acre, something many of you could have afforded. Then, having that great hope suddenly ripped away three weeks ago, when—despite the strong objection on your behalf by the Port Royal Experiment overseer General Saxton—the federal government decided to reverse itself and sell the lands at much higher prices through a public auction in order to raise more money to support the Union war effort.

"But once again, you did not let adversity stop you. Under the leadership of Mr. Skipwith, and the financial advice of Mr. Johnson here, you worked with each other day and night. You came up with an innovative plan to pool your resources so you could put up a very strong bid at tomorrow's auction to purchase, share ownership, and cooperate together in running this entire four-hundred-seventy-acre plantation. For the first time, you will actually *own the land* that you were forced to work solely for the profit and benefit of your masters over the years. And, God willing, tomorrow night we will all be celebrating your great victory in that gorgeous schoolhouse behind you!"

A tumultuous roar of unrestrained joy and mutual pride in their accomplishment arose from the freedmen. Tears flowed freely down the faces of nearly everyone as they hugged each other, barely able to restrain their enthusiasm.

David held up his right hand. "To conclude our ceremony today, Mr. Bowman has a little gift he'd like to present in honor of everything you've already achieved, and the glorious future toward which you are certainly headed." He paused to look at Abel fondly before resuming. Choked up, he struggled to keep his voice from wavering. "Neither I nor my good friend Mr. Bowman himself can express in words the significance that I know he attaches to this gift—which he personally designed and created especially for you. Let it only be said: this gift reflects everything he now aspires to in life, and what he desires for you as well. Mr. Bowman, will you please step forward? Miss Emma, Miss Sallie, and Mr. Johnson, will you please bring me the gift?"

The crowd stared in anticipation as David and Abel bent down from the podium to pick up the ends of what appeared to be a rolled-up cloth about six feet long. Facing the crowd, they lifted the ends of the cloth shoulder-high, then allowed it to quickly unfurl on its own. Gasps and cries of astonishment arose as the crowd strained to absorb what they were seeing. David's heart pounded as he beheld once again the new flag design that Abel had first shown him last week. As before, the words Eye of Glory were emblazoned across the top in large, bold lettering. But now, instead of the two crossed silver sabers in the center, a farmer's hoe and a teacher's quill pen were crossed to frame the original image of the radiance-projecting eye. And instead of the old 7th Ohio military unit designation, the words School for Freedmen now stood out in bold relief across the bottom.

Soon, a hush once again descended on the crowd as they all continued to stare, causing David to wonder whether the gift had possibly missed its mark.

"Mr. Skipwith, please tell me what you think," he said finally, anxious for some word one way or the other.

George Skipwith stepped around Abel and stood looking at the flag for several long seconds. He turned to face the crowd, then pointed to a young negro man who was standing alone, just beyond the rear of the audience. The man was dressed in bright-red pants and a dark-blue tunic and forage cap—the uniform of a Union soldier in the new 1st South Carolina Volunteer Regiment (Colored).

"Soldier, would you please step up here?" George called out. The young man came forward and ascended the stage.

George put his arms around the man's shoulders. Once again, he gazed at the flag before facing the crowd.

"You know what I think, Mr. Hodge? I think that with this beautiful flag and the Lord's help, along with the brave, fighting men of our First South Carolina Colored, there ain't nothin' in this whole world can stop us now."

With that, the entire crowd flew into a frenzy of shouting and weeping with uninhibited joy as they mobbed the podium, straining to touch the flag that Abel and David together held over the edge.

Afterward, David carefully folded and handed the cloth to George and some of the others to take over to the flagpole in front of the schoolhouse. He and Abel stepped down from the podium and joined Emma, Sallie, and William to watch the banner being raised.

"A new and better 'Glory,'" Abel said softly, tears in his eyes.

Emma hugged David closely. "You spoke beautifully today, brother," was all she could manage.

Mr. Shaw stepped forward to offer his own congratulations and thanks as well. "Well done, David. This was a day they'll never forget."

David smiled confidently. "Tomorrow night, it gets even better."

Abel chuckled. "I wonder if we'll have the honor of our old friend Colonel Jack Hurley's attendance at the celebration? As the general district supervisor for all of St. Helena Island, it would seem impolite to remain indifferent to the happiness of the freedmen under his wing."

Mr. Shaw frowned. "Weren't you told when you arrived here yesterday? Colonel Hurley resigned from his position three weeks ago. No one knows why he resigned or what he plans to do next."

CHAPTER 32

City of Beaufort
Port Royal Island, South Carolina Sea Islands
February 21, 1864

I t seemed like ages since Jack Hurley had felt so settled about things. Heartening indeed were the strong rumors he was hearing that General Ulysses S. Grant—following his subordinate commander's November thrashing of the Confederates at Lookout Mountain in Tennessee—would soon be appointed by Lincoln to take command of *all* Union armies in both eastern and western theaters. With Grant's bulldogged tenacity and commitment to a strategy of "total war" aimed not only at killing Confederate soldiers but also at destroying the means of southern economic production, complete Union victory now seemed assured. It was just a question of when.

But besides the promising news from the warfront, there was something else. Never before had Jack enjoyed such peace when on the verge of a critical business move such as the one he was about to make. A move which, if it panned out, would place him in marvelous position to benefit personally at war's end.

Leaning back in his desk chair, Hurley puffed contentedly on his cigar and gazed around the ornately decorated office of his three-story townhome. Located on a hill near the center of the small city of Beaufort on the southern tip of Port Royal Island, the dwelling offered a commanding view of all the nearby islands, including Lady's and St. Helena.

Jack recalled his childhood connection with the Pettigrews—the townhome's wealthy former owners, who had fled along with the rest of Beaufort's citizens at the sound of Union naval guns pounding the entrance to Port Royal Sound. What would they think if they could see him now? Would they be shocked that the skinny little boy from Boston, whose family had rented the small house across the street for their annual summer vacation, had now returned after thirty years to confiscate the Pettigrews' beloved home and nearby plantation lands?

He smiled at the thought. Fitting justice for all the arrogance and disdain they had shown toward young Jack and his parents during those prewar years when the "anti-North" talk had first begun to fan the flames of secession in the hotbeds of Charleston and the Sea Islands region.

"Mr. Peterson?" Jack called out to Isaac Peterson, the bright, young negro man he'd recently hired to replace the Pettigrews' surly former house servant who had remained behind when the family fled.

Isaac appeared at the office door seconds later. "Yes, sir?"

"Will you please go downstairs and fetch that document pouch from the investors that I left on the dining table last night? The public auction starts in two hours, and it's time for me to sign off on the bid authorizations for our buying agent. Dang, Isaac. If I were married, this would be the perfect occasion to be celebrating with my wife."

Isaac grinned. "I can definitely understand *that*, sir! I'll be right back."

Good man, Jack thought approvingly. Not like that other lazy, disrespectful slug he'd finally decided to let go after several months' effort to tame him. Why that man had seemed to somehow disapprove of Jack from the moment they'd met simply had not made any sense—in large part because Jack Hurley had always thought of himself as a highly respectable, good person.

Oh, there were a few minor blemishes on Jack's conscience, to be sure. Like those two fraudulent real estate deals he couldn't resist engineering five years ago that had ended up tripling his personal wealth. And the occasional physical altercations with those attempting to thwart his plans. But these all paled in comparison with his glowing public reputation for philanthropy and dedication to the abolitionist cause.

For Colonel Jack, it all boiled down to his firm conviction that the respectable life was one where a man's personal reputation for well-intentioned patriotic or charitable undertakings was recognized and held in high esteem by those who really mattered. Where a man's publicly perceived list of "goods" was deemed to clearly outweigh their list of "bads." By Hurley's logic, the perfectly fair and just God was *obligated* to eventually reward those who sincerely strived to live by such a reasonable moral standard . . . and to eventually punish those who had ever persecuted them for trying to do so.

And if I ever doubted that, Jack mused as he looked out his third-floor window to survey the rooftops of his childhood vacation resort, *just look at where I've landed—conducting business in one of the wealthiest Sea Island districts from the former home of the family who used to treat me and mine with such contempt.*

"Mr. Peterson," Jack called out. "Are you coming?"

"Yes, sir, I'll be there in just a moment."

Jack sat at his desk, tapping his foot impatiently. With a few strokes of his pen, he would complete the last, decisive step in his arduous, months-long effort as St. Helena's general district supervisor to learn the lay of the land and determine the best course forward for all involved—a course that would balance altruistic government concerns for the welfare of St. Helena Island freedmen with his own expectation of personal reward in the form of future business profits. By resigning from his government position three weeks ago, he was finally now legally eligible to pursue that personal goal. It would be his just reward from God for having earned—in his own mind at least—his public reputation as a good and admirable citizen.

Peterson finally walked in and laid the document pouch on Hurley's desk. His face wore an agitated expression. "Colonel, your buying agent—Mr. James Robinsworth—just arrived. Says he has some important news. Shall I send him in?"

"Of course."

What now? Hurley thought. The last thing he needed at this point was any kind of unpleasant surprise.

Robinsworth entered the room. "I just found out that the freedmen who're living on one of those properties you're planning to purchase— the Magnolia Plantation—have pooled all their resources together and will offer a combined bid. It could well be higher than the maximum you've authorized for us."

Hurley shot him a look of alarm. That was the *one* part of today's bidding war that he was completely unwilling to lose. Of the three properties his agent would be bidding on, the Magnolia property had by far the best prospects of future profit-making for the Boston invest-ment firm he represented—and for himself.

"Is that so?" he asked. "Any idea what they're going to put up?"

Robinsworth winced. "Well, sir, from what I've heard, they're pre-pared to go as high as nine dollars and fifty cents an acre."

Hurley grunted and shook his head. "How in the world were they able to save up a sum like that? The government must be setting their daily work wages too high."

He sighed and pulled the bid papers from the pouch. Focusing on the Magnolia document, he stared at the bottom line and considered the potential repercussions of what he was about to do. The Magnolia freedmen would feel robbed, he knew, and Congressman Stevens and his abolitionist friends might be outraged, but they'd get over it once they saw how the plantation and all connected with it started to flour-ish under Colonel Jack Hurley's enlightened ownership. He picked up his pen and adjusted the maximum bid, then scanned it twice again to ensure its accuracy before signing and stamping his personal seal at the bottom of all three bid authorization documents.

"That should take care of it," he said, placing the papers back into the pouch and handing it to his agent. "I'll just assume my investors won't object."

The brown-suited, heavily bearded US government auctioneer stood with gavel in hand behind a large oaken table at the front of the sparsely furnished side room in the Beaufort city courthouse.

"We've received a bid of nine dollars and fifty cents an acre from the Magnolia freedmen for the Magnolia Plantation property," he announced. "Do we have another offer?"

He raised the gavel. "Going once . . . going twice . . ."

David and Abel stood with hearts pounding at the back of the room behind the Magnolia freedmen's representatives, Milton Shaw and George Skipwith. The longtime dream of the freedmen to own their own land was about to be realized.

The other fifteen or so bidders in the room—all of them White— seemed to have thrown up their hands after hearing the freedmen's generous offer, which was a full dollar above all previous bids. Everyone had heard of the collective sweat and effort that had gone into securing such a high figure, and a general sense of goodwill was clearly now prevailing. Already, concessionary nods and smiles of congratulations were being cast in Shaw's and Skipwith's direction.

The auctioneer started the downward swing of his gavel.

"Nine dollars and seventy-five cents!" someone shouted from the opposite side of the room.

The bidders' collective gasp was accompanied by all eyes turning toward the far wall where a previously unnoticed, short, well-dressed man with a moon-shaped face and thin mustache was holding up his hand.

"Please identify yourself, sir," the auctioneer demanded.

The man took a couple of steps forward and bowed slightly. "I'm James Robinsworth, the authorized buying agent for my client, retired Colonel Jack Hurley."

David exchanged glances with Abel, feeling as if his stomach was about to drop from under him.

The auctioneer frowned. "Colonel Hurley? Is he even eligible to bid on this property?"

"Sir," Robinsworth replied with a confident smile, "as you're well aware, Colonel Hurley recently resigned from his post as general district supervisor. And since he is no longer an executive agent of the US government, he is most definitely eligible to bid on this property."

So, the mystery behind Hurley's surprise resignation is now solved, David thought bitterly. *What happened to all his altruistic pretensions to Lincoln, Stevens, and Chase about "helping to elevate the freedmen" by granting them their own land?*

"Do you have papers to prove your identity?" the auctioneer asked.

"I do, sir."

"Then please bring them forward so I can examine them."

"Of course, sir." Robinsworth walked toward the table, unzipping his document pouch as he approached.

Visibly shaken, Shaw and Skipwith turned to consult with David and Abel. Skipwith appeared especially devastated, his mouth trembling and on the verge of tears. "What'll we do? It took everything we had to raise the nine fifty." Milton Shaw stared down at the ground, shaking his head sadly.

Abel grabbed David's arm and pulled him aside. "We can't let Hurley get away with this . . . not after all the freedmen did to get to this point."

David nodded. He glanced over toward the auctioneer's table where Hurley's agent was now returning his identification papers to his pouch, a satisfied smile on his face. The auctioneer picked up his gavel again, clearly preparing to announce the validity of the last bid and invite any last-gasp challengers.

In an instant, David made his decision. He walked quickly back to Shaw and Skipwith. Gripping the colored foreman's arm, he spoke quickly.

"George, if I were to personally advance you another fifty cents an acre, can you and your folks promise to pay me off in a year? I'd go higher, but it's the most I can afford right now." *In fact, it'll drain half my entire family savings,* David thought.

Skipwith's jaw dropped, and his mouth spread slowly into a wide grin. "Mr. Hodge, you serious? I know we can do that . . . we all just gotta work some extra hours for a few months, that's all!"

"The offer of nine dollars and seventy-five cents an acre from Colonel Hurley is hereby considered by the US government to be a valid bid," the auctioneer intoned. "Do we have any other bids?"

David put his hand on Shaw's shoulder and nodded. "Milton, it's in your hands."

"Going once . . . going twice . . ."

Shaw whirled and faced the table. "*Ten* dollars an acre offered by the Magnolia Plantation freedmen."

A spontaneous cheer broke out among the other bidders as Robertson's face turned pale and his shoulders slumped. He fiddled with the zipper of his document pouch, seemingly unable to get it to open.

Skipwith bounced up and down, clapping his hands. "We did it . . . we did it!"

Milton Shaw turned to hug Skipwith, David, and Abel in turn. Abel eyed David admiringly and extended his hand. "Looks like you saved the day."

David shook his head and pointed at Skipwith. "They did all the work. They deserve it."

Everyone turned toward the auctioneer. Robinsworth still stood by the side of the table. He had finally managed to open his pouch and pull out one of the documents that he now seemed to be perusing closely.

"Ten dollars an acre. Going once . . . going twice . . ."

Robinsworth looked up and raised his hand. "I am authorized by Colonel Jack Hurley to bid ten dollars and fifty cents an acre."

Silence descended over the room like a death shroud. Milton Shaw and George Skipwith turned toward David and Abel, their eyes filled with tears.

David could do nothing but stare at the ground. They were beaten, and he knew it.

"Going once . . . going twice . . . *sold!*" shouted the auctioneer.

After returning from the auction in Beaufort to the Magnolia Plantation later that evening, David cloistered with Emma, Abel, Sallie, and William at the rear of the large meeting room on the first floor of the schoolhouse. He shook his head in despair and disbelief at the appalling scene unfolding in front of them.

Instead of the blissful occasion that everyone had anticipated, tonight's "celebration" had turned into something more akin to the funeral of a murder victim—one where the surviving relatives were torn between mourning their loved one and promising revenge on the killer. Many freedmen and their families sat on the floor or in the students' chairs, weeping or shouting angry questions at Mr. Shaw and George Skipwith. Both men stood at the front of the room, attempting without much success to quell the storm that had arisen immediately following the announcement of the final auction results.

Emma suddenly grasped her brother's arm with both hands. "David, isn't there *something* we can do?"

He shook his head in dismay. "I'm afraid not, Em. Hurley's within his rights. As a private citizen, he was free to bid just like everyone else. Still, I just can't believe he would cut these people out of owning their land, forsaking the very principle of *reparations* he'd been so adamant in defending to President Lincoln and others."

"Somehow, *that* doesn't surprise me at all," Abel growled.

"So, what happens now? What about our school?" asked Sallie.

William shook his head. "It all depends on what Colonel Hurley decides. The school's no longer on government property—it's on *his* property. He could decide to shut the whole operation down and force the AMA to recall all us teachers and administrators and helpers. Especially if these people don't start behaving themselves." He waved his hand resignedly toward the front of the room where one of the freedmen was in the midst of railing at Shaw and Skipwith.

"No, I *ain't* gonna calm down, George," the man shouted. "Don't care what you sayin'. We sick and tired of all these lies—all our hopes gettin' dashed. First, they tell us each family can have our own little piece o' land for a dollar twenty-five an acre. Then the government say no to that. Next, they say if we willin' to pool all our money and equipment, we can own and work the whole plantation together. So we go to all that trouble, and now you tellin' us we still comin' up short? It don't matter what we want or what we do, boss. White man ain't *never* gonna let us Blacks own the land we slaved for 'em all these years!"

David locked eyes with Abel, suspecting immediately that they were sharing the same concern. Tomorrow morning, both would depart St. Helena to continue their inspections of other Sea Island plantations prior to returning to Washington to deliver their interim report. Once they left, the discontented Magnolia freedmen would no longer be under official government protection or observation. And given the volatile nature of the plantation's new "commander," there was no telling how they would fare.

CHAPTER 33

Magnolia Plantation
St. Helena Island, South Carolina Sea Islands
May 31, 1864
(Three months later)

Bone-weary and thankful for a few hours of rest before sunrise and another full day of classes, Emma climbed into the elegantly carved, four-post bed on the second floor of the main house. She briefly wondered how the previous occupants must have felt being suddenly forced by the invading Union soldiers into leaving such a treasured possession behind. Snuggling under the blanket, she took a deep breath and exhaled slowly, releasing some of the grating tension she'd been experiencing lately.

God, she whispered into the pillow, *things are going so well with our "Eye of Glory" School. Please don't allow the freedmen's anger to ruin everything you've been helping Sallie, William, and me accomplish here.*

Unfortunately, given developments over the past three months, Emma knew the prospects were uncertain . . .

⁂

A few days after acquiring the plantation at the auction three months ago, Jack Hurley had delivered a conciliatory speech to all the freedmen he'd asked to gather in front of the main house. Their future was bright, he'd assured them. Under the continued local supervision of Mr. Shaw and George Skipwith, they would enjoy the familiarity of their previous working arrangements. They would be provided small plots to grow their own food crops for their family and be able to either make their own clothes or buy them at one of the local government distribution centers. With their cooperation and their hard, honest work, the potential for turning a substantial profit for this year's cotton crop was great. That would lead, eventually, to higher wages, more paid time off from work to attend school, or both.

"Within five years," Hurley had gloated, "I predict you will all be enjoying a standard of living and a quality of life far greater than what you would have had if your cooperative bid for the property had won out over my own."

The speech had been generally well received. Perhaps, the freedmen speculated, their anger and suspicion of the new owner's intentions had been misplaced. Jack Hurley had sounded like a fair and decent man—a businessman committed to the original goal of the Port Royal Experiment, willing to place the freedmen's best interests on equal footing with his own profit-making motives. Perhaps they should reserve judgment. Give him the benefit of the doubt.

Two weeks ago, the illusion was shattered.

Hurley had delivered another speech on the main house lawn. He told the freedmen that he'd observed certain "inefficiencies" in the plantation's cotton production process. If allowed to continue, his required profits would fall far short of the minimum needed to sustain the operation. As a result, some big changes were needed. A new, experienced, all-White labor management team would be brought in to replace Mr. Shaw and George Skipwith—both of whom would now be assigned to "lesser duties." Wages would be reduced 20 percent, as would the allowed time for school attendance during the day. If the freedmen wished to replace their lost income, they would need to increase their daily work hours.

It was an unfortunate situation, Hurley had lamented, but his hands were effectively tied by basic business considerations. Should profits improve as hoped in the future, then the wage situation could be reevaluated. In the meantime, he'd said, "luxuries" like attending classes at the Glory School would have to be scaled back significantly. Learning to read and write were fine, but if too much charity were extended to their work habits, the freedmen would never learn to be truly self-reliant and productive, and Hurley's business would fail. Everyone would lose.

And *that's* why Hurley said the changes were necessary.

He'd concluded with an attempt to assuage: "Please know that I'm sympathetic to your situation. But I must also ask you to realize that for all of us to succeed here, the business has to succeed."

The freedmen, of course, had left Hurley's speech in a state of rage. Heated meetings were held in the schoolhouse to express their dismay and consider possible ways of resisting Hurley's new policies. They had seen through his smooth words and hollow excuses. Why was it, they asked, that they were suddenly seen by Hurley as being "inefficient" and "not producing enough"? In fact, they knew they were producing as much, if not more, than they ever had before Hurley bought the property!

There could be only one reason for Hurley's accusation: for whatever reason, he wanted to squeeze more out of them in order to further line his own pockets. Yet again, it seemed, White Master had lied to them. In this case, it all came down to Hurley's insatiable greed. Coming on top of their land ownership chance being quashed, it was beginning to feel to the freedmen like a slow and painful return to a life of slavery was being imposed upon them. And, God willing, there was no way they were going to allow *that* to happen.

Despite the pleas of William, Mr. Shaw, and George Skipwith to avoid such inflammatory public talk, many of the freedmen had not backed down. Several were still talking loudly and excitedly about the possibility of launching a general work strike. Two had actually gone so far as to walk out early on their new White foreman the other day, telling him he could just dock their pay since they had no intention of being late for their class at the Glory School.

❦

Turning over in her bed, Emma struggled to make sense of it all. The freedmen were clearly being exploited. But given David's and Abel's warnings about Hurley's vindictive nature, a more careful response seemed called for. If all the rebellious talk and actions were to get out of hand, who knew what the consequences might be?

Fortunately, she thought, there *were* some recent hopeful signs of a possible rapprochement and lessening of tensions.

Just three days ago, Hurley had summoned all the freedmen to gather once again on the lawn. In a surprising gesture, he'd thanked them for the cooperation with the new arrangements that the vast majority had demonstrated so far. He'd then said that as an expression of his goodwill, he'd decided to grant back an extra hour per week for each adult to attend Glory School classes. Education was vital to the freedmen's future, he'd explained, and he for one had no desire to thwart its progress if he could at all help it given his business pressures.

Though some of the freedmen had left the speech shaking their heads in confusion or disbelief over Hurley's latest turnabout, most seemed to have accepted his "small gift" with thanksgiving and praise to God. Perhaps, they'd said, a new spirit of mutual respect and understanding between owner and freedman had dawned over the Magnolia Plantation. A calmer atmosphere now seemed to be prevailing.

And, certainly, that wasn't the only thing to be hopeful about of late.

Especially encouraging was the reaction of young Clara Jenkins, the new AMA-appointed missionary-teacher assigned to the Magnolia Plantation who had arrived earlier this morning.

"Oh, Miss Hodge," Clara had gushed at the conclusion of the afternoon session, "I can't express how impressed I was with what I just saw in that classroom. You and Miss Sallie certainly have those students excited to recite their lessons with you. My word, to see those adults trying so hard to learn their letters so they won't be ashamed by their children's rapid progress—it's amazing to witness. And the children! So well-behaved. I think they truly do see the advantages they're going to derive from learning."

Emma knew Clara's observations were true, but she had tried to project modesty. "I'm glad you caught us on one of our good days, Miss Jenkins. If you could have seen little Hector just yesterday, acting silly and throwing a live cat into the middle of the room—and those two girls we had to lock up for fighting—you might have had a different opinion."

"That may be," Clara had conceded, "but there's no doubt the students love both of you, and they obviously respect the way you work together so smoothly with Miss Sallie—you teaching the whole class and Sallie helping the individual students. I just hope I can fit in to the system you've already perfected!"

Since Clara had shown up a few days earlier than expected, her room in the main house—which was also occupied by Emma, Sallie, William, and the Shaws—hadn't yet been vacated by the ailing, home-bound mission worker she'd come to replace. As a result, Clara had gratefully accepted temporary quarters in the small but comfortable teachers' office on the second floor of the schoolhouse.

Not wanting Clara to be alone at night, Sallie had offered to set up a cot and sleep out in the adjoining classroom. The idea had appealed not only to Clara but to ten-year-old Mandy Hostler, Sallie's favorite student, who had begged Sallie and Clara to allow her to keep them company. Her parents had given their permission, and after supper, a second cot was placed next to Sallie's.

I'll wager they're all still up, playing Mandy's favorite games and having a great time together, Emma thought drowsily. She turned onto her stomach and pulled the blanket over her head. Immediately, the delightful memory she'd been constantly rehearsing over the last two months flashed once again in her mind.

The evening before David and Abel had departed the Magnolia Plantation on the next leg of their inspection tour, Abel had invited her to take an aftersupper walk. He'd told her how inspired he'd been by her teaching and everything else that she and the others had accomplished at the Glory School. How he truly enjoyed her company and loved the way she expressed herself so eloquently and passionately on things that really mattered to him as well. He was attracted to her and—if she was not too offended by him or of the opinion that he was improperly taking advantage of his friendship with her brother—he was wondering whether she might consider allowing him to correspond with her while he was away.

Thrilled to her core and her heart beating wildly, she had struggled to maintain proper decorum as she politely accepted Abel's offer.

Since then, the two had exchanged letters twice, with Abel expressing in his last one how he could not wait to see her again and escort her on a horseback ride around the island.

I wonder where this will all lead. As sleep finally began to overtake her, Emma imagined herself at her wedding, Sallie standing beside her as her maid of honor. Then, after the vows and the bridal kiss, walking down the aisle, arm in arm with the man she'd been thinking about more and more lately: Mr. Abel Bowman . . .

Something that sounded like a muffled explosion caused Emma to bolt upright in the bed. What was *that*? Had she imagined it? What time was it? She checked her timepiece: a little after two thirty. She'd been asleep about two hours. She waited a little longer, but hearing nothing else, she lay back down and closed her eyes.

Almost immediately, she was awakened once again—this time by a faint burning smell. She lifted her head and peered around the dimly moonlit room. Everything seemed normal. She got up and walked toward the partially shuttered window, noticing that the burning odor was getting stronger. It was then that she heard the distant shout.

"*Fire!*"

Emma rushed to the window and threw the shutters open wide. Leaning out, she looked to the left—in the direction of the schoolhouse about two hundred yards away.

She recoiled and screamed out in horror at the sight. Thick smoke and flames gushed from the windows on the lower level of the front half of the building. The flames extended upward toward the second story where Sallie and the others were sleeping.

Her heart pounding, Emma threw on her robe and slippers and ran out into the hallway. Mr. Shaw and William Johnson, alerted by the burning smell, peered inquisitively out of their respective bedroom doorways.

"The schoolhouse is on fire!" Emma shouted. Within seconds, the three were racing together down the stairwell and out the front door. Emma silently cursed the limp that caused her to lag well behind the others as they cut across the lawn and down the sloping hill. She searched ahead and saw that a few people had already gathered near the front of the schoolhouse, seemingly with no other purpose than to stand there watching helplessly. Glancing to the side, she spotted George Skipwith running toward the equipment barn. "Tandey and Wilson . . . get the horses hitched up to the fire wagon! Jim, set up the bucket line!" George's booming voice was the first sign of anyone attempting to take charge of the situation.

As she drew closer to the burning building, the freedmen and their spouses began to pour from the nearby cabins. Those preassigned to the plantation's firefighting bucket brigade moved to take their positions between the schoolhouse and the equipment barn fifty yards away where the water-filled fire buckets were stored. Others ran to expand the crowd in front of the schoolhouse and gawk at the upper story, from which panicked screams and cries for help now emanated.

Emma pushed her way toward the front of the crowd, where William and Mr. Shaw were trying with all their might to restrain Jackson Hostler—Mandy's father—from making a suicidal, headlong rush into the blaze to rescue his young daughter.

"Jackson, it's no use . . . wait till the wagon gets here and we get the buckets going," Mr. Shaw pleaded. "It'll be here in just a couple of minutes."

"She'll be dead by then!" Jackson screamed, his face a contorted mask of fear and dismay.

Suddenly flames shot from one of the upper-story windows, followed closely by the chilling shriek of a child. With a violent movement of his arms and torso, Jackson wrested himself from the grips of William and Mr. Shaw and started to run toward the front door, behind which flames were no doubt lurking.

"Jackson, wait!" cried Paul Commerce, the plantation's head maintenance man who had just arrived breathlessly on the scene. "Fire's too strong . . . no way you'll make it past the front door. I got the key to the utility door—come on, follow me!"

Jackson and Paul sprinted to the small, side service door near the rear of the building where the flames had so far not yet appeared to have spread. Paul fiddled with the key for several seconds but for some reason couldn't get the door to open. Jackson shoved him aside and began back-kicking the door like a madman until it finally opened inward, releasing a thick cloud of smoke. Jackson fell back for a few seconds, then gathered himself, plunged into the abyss, and disappeared—soon to be followed by Paul.

"*Help!* Oh, please . . . somebody . . . help us . . . it's getting close!"

Emma immediately recognized the voice as Sallie's. It was all she could take.

She started to run toward the service door but was immediately arrested by a firm hand on her arm. She whirled around to face her restrainer.

"Let me go, William! I can't leave her in there." She tried to extricate herself from his grasp.

William grabbed her by both upper arms and shook her roughly. "Emma, you stay here. *I'll* go." He released her to the comforting arms of an elderly Black woman at the front of the crowd, then turned and followed Jackson's path into the building.

Moments later, the makeshift, horse-drawn fire wagon arrived. At George Skipwith's shouted request, several in the crowd jumped forward to unwind and man the hose as George and two others leaped onto the wagon to help lift the fire buckets and feed water to the manually operated pump. Soon, a steady stream was gushing from the hose nozzle and directed at the worst of the flames on the first floor.

Emma noticed the cries for help had suddenly stopped. She prayed with all her might that it was a good sign. That the stairway to the second floor—which by God's mercy was located in the rear of the building—had remained intact, and that the men had been able to find a path through the smoke and flames on the second floor to find Sallie, Mandy, and Clara unharmed. *Please, God, bring them all—*

A woman behind her screamed and pointed toward the roof. It was sagging in the middle, and flames were beginning to shoot out from under the eaves and along the entire length of its apex, as well as the remainder of the upper-story windows. A horrible cracking sound ensued as the roof sagged, then finally collapsed. The crowd let out a collective cry of horror as the entire second floor, unable to further bear the heat and stress, soon followed suit, taking large sections of the front and side walls with it.

Emma buried her head against the shoulder of the kind woman whose stout arms now encircled her. Her sobs of disbelief and grief joined with the despairing wails and cries of the others.

"They're coming out!"

In confused amazement, everyone turned toward the still-standing utility doorway.

Carrying Clara Jenkins in his arms, Paul Commerce made his way toward the crowd. Several men rushed up to help. Away from the heat, Paul laid her down on a blanket that someone had stretched out. Emma's heart and stomach dropped at the sight. Poor Clara was alive, but the entire right side of her face and body were badly burned. She moaned in agony as several of the women pushed the men aside and bent down to tend to her.

"Look, it's William and Jackson with the others!" someone cried hysterically.

Emma nearly fainted with joy at the sight of William with his arm around Sallie's waist, helping her to stagger toward the crowd. Jackson was close behind, carrying little Mandy in his arms.

Emma ran up to William and Sallie, ready to throw her arms around her friend.

"No, Emma, not yet," said William. "She's hurting. Her back's burned real bad. Just help me get her to lie down on her stomach."

Others helped them to a second blanket next to Clara's. Sallie was placed facedown with her arms cradling her head. The extent of her wounds was now evident. She trembled with pain, and Emma grabbed one of her hands with both of hers.

"Oh, God, no . . . no!" The mother of Mandy Hostler screamed over and over to the skies, but to no avail. Emma watched tearfully as Jackson and his wife bent over their daughter's still body, holding each other and rocking back and forth. She had a sudden terrible memory of Sallie's parents in the same posture, mourning the death by hanging of their beloved son Charles.

"Smoke got her," Emma heard a man say quietly behind her.

"Yeah . . . Miss Sallie tried to protect her from the flames," muttered his apparent companion. "Prob'ly how she got her back burned."

"How could a big fire like this get started?"

"Man, didn't you hear Paul say he found a Confederate flag all stretched out on the floor soon's he crashed through the door? How the hell you *think* it got started?"

CHAPTER 34

Magnolia Plantation
St. Helena Island, South Carolina Sea Islands
June 8, 1864
(One week later)

Although not in the habit of indulging temptation this early in the day, Emma sat down on the main house living room sofa and gratefully accepted the glass of bourbon that David was offering. Without *something* to calm her down quickly, she feared, her pent-up emotions over the fire's devastation—and her livid fury over Jack Hurley's arrogant, lame attempt last night to actually profit from it—would explode in a torrent of unwarranted screams and imprecations in the presence of her innocent brother. After all his effort to hasten the completion of his latest inspection task on Port Royal Island and then rush back to the plantation with Abel after receiving word of the catastrophe, her unbridled ranting and raving was the last thing he deserved.

"How is Sallie?" David asked cautiously.

Emma took a sip from her glass before staring at him sadly. "I just visited the hospital in Beaufort yesterday morning with William. She's still in a lot of pain, and the doctor said she'll have bad scarring on her back for the rest of her life. But, thank heaven, at least she's alive and will pull through. And if we ever had any doubts about her attraction to William or his to Sallie, after watching those two holding hands and staring affectionately at each other for over a half hour, I think we can put those doubts to rest. It's going to be a while before she's back on her feet, though, and she may always have difficulty performing some physical tasks."

"And what about Clara Jenkins?"

Emma shook her head. "She's in much worse shape than Sallie. They're surprised she's survived this long and still aren't convinced she'll make it. Only time will tell. And little Mandy . . . oh, David, the thought of her sweet face and wave when I said goodbye to her after our last class . . . she was so thrilled to be spending the night with Sallie and Clara. It just tears me apart. And to see Jackson and his wife so devastated at her funeral . . ." She broke down, unable to complete her sentence.

David sat down and put his arm around her shoulders, allowing her sobs to gradually run their course.

"So, what did Hurley say about it all last night?" he ventured, regretting almost immediately that he'd done so as he watched the reaction on his sister's face.

She glared at him, her eyes burning fiercely. "Before I ever have to listen to another word from that cold-blooded viper, would somebody *please* spare me the misery and bury me in my coffin thirty feet underground?" She went on to give a brief, angry recounting of Hurley's half-hour "conversation" with the main house occupants and several representatives for the freedmen.

Hurley had said he was very sorry about what had happened, especially for the injuries and loss of life. He'd said it was obviously a case of arson—sparked by the same gang of Confederate army raiders from the mainland who had torched and left a flag as their signature in at least three barns and some other large structures on St. Helena Island over the past few weeks. Unfortunately, since the schoolhouse had never been insured by the freedmen who'd built it before he purchased the property—and also since there was no way he himself could afford to pay for its replacement—they would have to do without it for the foreseeable future.

"Although," Hurley had slyly suggested, "if you're willing, there *is* a way you could recover it sooner. If you were to replace your lost schooltime with worktime—and maybe even add an hour or two to your total workday—you freedmen would increase your total income while I increase my profit due to your greater production. In a much shorter time, you'd be able to save enough to pay for the rebuilding of your school. We'd both benefit. Think about it!"

And if that self-indulgent proposal had not been insult enough, Hurley had concluded the discussion by telling Emma, William, and the Shaws in front of the others that—in view of the schoolhouse's demise—there was no longer any reason for *them* to be staying in the main house. In fact, since three of his White foremen and their families were in immediate need of housing, he would appreciate it if Emma and the others would all vacate their rooms by the first of next week. Surely, Colonel Jack had said, the AMA people could help them find temporary shelter in Beaufort, and before long, he was confident they would find "another wonderful schoolhouse" *somewhere* in the Islands or elsewhere that they could bless with their "amazing" expertise.

"His voice was dripping with contempt and complete lack of empathy for what the freedmen have suffered and lost," Emma said bitterly. "And I can't adequately describe the sarcastic, hate-filled tone of voice he directed toward William, Mr. Shaw, and me. Especially when I dared to ask whether his decision not to help rebuild the schoolhouse would be inconsistent with the goals of the Port Royal Experiment."

David closed his eyes and nodded. "That sounds like the Colonel Jack Hurley that Abel and I have had the misfortune to encounter on too many occasions."

"David, I'm telling you, there is something *wrong* with that man. Something almost . . . evil. And I'm not sure we've seen the worst of what he's capable of doing to squeeze every last ounce of labor from the freedmen. I can accept my own treatment by him, but I just pray the freedmen won't be crushed by whatever he plans to do next."

Emma stood and walked toward the large window looking out over the front lawn by the schoolhouse. She wondered when Abel would return from his trek through the burnt ruins with the maintenance man, Paul Commerce. For some reason, Abel hadn't been fully convinced by the Confederate raid explanation and wanted to see for himself if any clues might have been overlooked in the initial fruitless search that Paul, George Skipwith, and the Beaufort sheriff had conducted two days ago.

As if on cue, the sound of someone entering the front door was soon followed by the appearance at the living room entrance of a grimly smiling Abel Bowman, holding a small, brown paper sack in his hand.

"What's *that*?" David asked.

"Evidence," Abel replied.

"Evidence? Of what?"

"That fire was definitely arson . . . but it *might* not have been set by some 'gang of rebel raiders' like we all thought."

"How do you know?" asked Emma.

Abel walked over to one of the armchairs and sat down, ceremoniously placing the sack on the floor between his legs. Carefully, he put his hand in it and withdrew what appeared to be the charred bottom half of a wooden bucket. He held it up for Emma and David to see. "Found this underneath the staircase against the rear wall of the schoolhouse . . . where the fire wasn't quite as intense." He handed it to David.

"So, what does this prove?"

"Turn it over and read what's on the bottom," Abel said impatiently.

David's eyes widened as he stared at the stenciled lettering on the unburnt bottom surface. "Beaufort General Supply? But what does that have to do with—"

"David!" Abel exploded. "Can't you see? That bucket was *never* in the schoolhouse before the night of the fire. Paul Commerce swears he cleaned out under the staircase that very morning, and there was absolutely nothing there!"

"So . . . what does this tell us?" Emma asked.

"That this bucket—from the Beaufort supply store—might well have been used by the arsonist to carry whatever fuel he used to set the fire. Paul thinks it may have been gunpowder, and I'm inclined to agree."

David eyed him dubiously. "Abel, I hate to say it, but that sounds like a tall tale. Why in the world would a local arsonist leave something like this behind, take the chance that it would survive the fire and that someone would discover it? And what about that rebel flag . . . isn't that exactly what the raiders left behind in those other fires they set?"

Abel shrugged and gave David an indignant look. "How should I know? Maybe the rebs hired someone local to help 'em carry this one out. But at any rate, it's all we have at this point. Except for one other thing. In this case, something we *don't* have."

"And what's that?"

Abel leaned forward, his hands clasped with his elbows resting on his knees. "Our new Glory flag. We searched in the fire-damaged storage cabinet underneath the staircase—where Paul says they always place it folded up at night. No sign of it. Somebody must have taken it the night of the fire."

David stared at him blankly. "But who would do something like that? And why would they even bother?"

Abel leaned back in the chair and folded his arms. "I have no idea." He pointed at the charred bucket piece that David still held in his hands. "All we can do is take one step at a time to get to the bottom of all this. Tomorrow, Paul and I are going to pay the supply store owner a visit. See if we can get him to remember who he might have sold one of their buckets to recently. Want to accompany us?"

"I'd like to," David replied, "but it looks like I need to return to Washington tomorrow."

"*What?*" Emma looked at him in dismay. "I thought the two of you were here for at least another week."

"Actually, it's just me who needs to return. Abel's free to stay here longer and carry out his detective work."

Abel stared at him in confusion. "What's going on, David?"

David hesitated. "I was going to share the news with Emma privately later this evening."

Emma cocked her head. "David, it's all right. Whatever it is, you can share it with all of us."

David consented and handed the bucket piece back to Abel, then pulled an envelope from his jacket pocket and turned to face his sister.

"Em, I received a letter from Sarah yesterday."

Emma stared at the envelope. Her face went white. "Oh, David! Is she—?"

"No, no, Em . . . it's not what you think. Sarah and Jenny are fine," he reassured her. "Sarah was forwarding a letter that was in turn forwarded to her by my editor at the *Cleveland Leader*, Mr. Cowles."

"So, who was the original letter from?"

David stared at her intently. "It's from Pastor Jones, Em. He has some news about Catherine and Papa."

"*What?*" Emma gasped, her heart leaping. "How did his letter make it over the border to Ohio?"

"Cowles said there's some special new mail service that's operating undercover to transport mail across the battle lines. Pastor Jones apparently learned about it and took his chances. Would you like me to read this to you?"

"Maybe I should leave the two of you alone," Abel offered quietly.

"No, Abel, please stay," Emma pleaded. Without the slightest hesitation, she went over and clasped her hands around his arm. For some reason, she knew she wanted him to be part of this.

"Em, just . . . bear with me as I read this." David opened the folded sheets.

It had been two whole years since she'd had any word of her father and sister. She held her breath as David began reading . . .

April 30, 1864

Dear David,

I pray this letter will reach you and find you alive and well. Though I inquired several times about contacting you over the past two and a half years, until a week ago, I was told it was impossible to get mail through the lines. Praise the Lord for opening up this new private channel, and I hope it works.

Much has happened around here since I last wrote. I must first convey the sad news that your father, Lawrence Martin Hodge, passed away on November 4, 1862, after experiencing strong chest pains the prior evening . . .

Emma gasped, her hand flying to her chest. Abel put his arm around her shoulder and drew her close to his side.

"Shall I go on?" David asked gently.

She nodded. Tears flowed from her closed eyes as she listened to her brother relate the tragic details of Papa's passing, the death of Tom Cobb and his wife's exile, Catherine's loss of Joe and her baby, and her struggles to manage the plantation alone in the face of Sam Taylor's treachery.

She gripped Abel's arm even tighter as David read the last part of the letter . . .

Immediately upon returning to the plantation following her recovery with us at our residence, Catherine made some major changes. She fired and evicted Philip and Sam Taylor for seriously abusing their authority in her absence (I will spare you the sordid details), hired a free Black man from Petersburg as the new field supervisor, and sought the advice of Mr. Tidwell, who helped her find a new, more dependable overseer and someone to help her with the plantation business dealings.

Things were proceeding reasonably smoothly, all things considered, until two weeks ago when practically all the slaves—

lured by their prospects for immediate freedom due to the recent return to the area of the Union army under General Butler— deserted the plantation for Butler's lines near City Point. With no need or ability to afford the new overseer anymore, Catherine let him go the very next day. The only two who chose to remain behind with your sister were Elijah Flint—the new field supervisor—and, lo and behold, Sallie Cobb's young stepbrother Lew (whom Catherine's been showing a special concern for after Sallie and Emma's departure).

Together, the three are managing to survive reasonably well off the few remaining stores and some produce from the vegetable garden, which they all help to maintain. But the plantation's staple crops won't be harvested this year, meaning the end of business and complete loss of income for your sister. And with prices for everything now exploding out of control, the Union army threatening to overrun and confiscate all plantations in the area, and no nearby relative to turn to for help, Catherine is in a dire position and under great stress. Judith and I are doing all we can to lift her spirits with weekly visits, and she does attend our church services regularly on Sundays. But I fear it will soon not be enough.

David, do you recall that evening back in '59 when I had supper with you and your family? Afterward, you walked me out to the gate, and I predicted there could well come a future time when God may wish you to demonstrate your love for Catherine in a way that only her brother could provide.

As I'm looking at her situation now, I believe that time may have arrived. Catherine has frequently mentioned that she wishes desperately that there were some way she could find and reunite with both of you. I have no knowledge of where Emma may be, but I pray both she and Sallie are safe somewhere in God's hands after their escape. As regards yourself, assuming this letter reaches you, I can only implore you to consider if there is any possible way you might make your way back here for a visit to assess the situation and offer some much-needed love and comfort to Catherine. I believe if you do, it will be a great encouragement to her. Of course, if this proves impossible, rest assured that Judith and I will continue to provide her with every ounce of support we are capable of providing despite our own greatly diminished circumstances of late—like everyone else in the area.

May the Lord's blessings rest upon you, my dear friend. I am . . .

Sincerely Yours,

Horace D. Jones

David carefully refolded the pages of the letter and returned them to the envelope. He glanced at Emma, who appeared as if she'd been struck by a thunderbolt. Her hand covering her mouth and her body shaking, she turned her back, clearly not wishing David or Abel to observe the intense and confusing emotions she was experiencing.

Finally, she gathered herself and turned toward her brother. "I suppose this means you'll be heading back to retrieve her and bring her out here."

David gave her a puzzled look. "Well, I'll definitely be trying to get back to see her. In fact, I've decided to leave tomorrow and travel back to Washington to deliver my next report to Secretary Chase, and I'll use that opportunity to solicit a special pass through General Butler's lines to visit home. As far as bringing her back here, it's premature to assume that's what she would want. But regardless, Em, why is it that you sound as if you have some reservations about that? Don't you want to see Cat again?"

Emma folded her arms and bowed her head. "Of course I do, David, it's just that . . . well . . ."

"Well . . . *what*, Em?"

Ashamed, and realizing it would be impossible for David and Abel to understand her complicated feelings about Catherine, Emma turned and limped out of the room.

Chapter 35

Hodge Family Plantation
June 16, 1864

Alarmed by the distant blasts, Catherine paused in the middle of her weeding task. Slowly, she stood and straightened her aching back, then inclined her ear in the direction of Petersburg to the southwest.

"*Lew!*" she called to the strapping thirteen-year-old who was picking spinach leaves on the other side of the vegetable garden. "Do you hear that?"

Lew lifted his head and listened for a few seconds. "Yes, ma'am, I sure do."

Catherine unfastened her sunbonnet and wiped her brow. It had been a long, hot day, and she was grateful for any excuse to call a slightly early halt to what had become her regular afternoon litany of manual chores.

"Yankees must be starting their attack on the city, just like we expected. Go get Elijah and tell him to come on in—we need to talk. I'll go get supper started."

"Yes, ma'am. You be needin' any o' these spinach leaves for supper?"

"I'm not sure yet. Just put them all in the basket, and I'll take it inside."

"Yes, Mizz Cat."

Catherine smiled and shook her head as she watched the youngster race off toward the barn. What would she do without the boy's dependable physical help, not to mention his companionship?

On the day last month when the Hodge family slaves decided that a dash for freedom behind the nearby Union army lines was preferable to life on the plantation, the *last* person Catherine had expected to come back knocking on the main house front door that evening was Lew Cobb. Of all the slaves, Lew would certainly have had one of the most compelling arguments to forsake forever any connection with any Hodge family enablers of his own family's torment over the years. His brother's hanging, the taunting and abuse of his sister, the exile of his mother, and the death of his father—all of these had resulted directly from the hate-filled actions of Sam Taylor or indirectly from the self-concerned *lack* of action by Papa and herself.

Yes, it was true that she *had* been keeping a close and concerned eye on Lew ever since his father's death. Six months ago, she'd brought him out of the fields and made him part of the main house domestic staff. She'd quickly become quite fond of him and would often speak kindly and compliment him for his hard work. She had even gone so far as to follow Emma's example with Sallie by taking him and one of the other young male house servants aside and reading adventure stories to them on weekday evenings after supper, which both had seemed to greatly enjoy.

Still, she was surprised by his appearance that night and had asked why he wanted to stay with her when all the others—except for her new, wage-compensated field supervisor Elijah—had decided to leave. Especially after all Lew and his family had suffered under Hodge family rule.

Lew had stared down at his feet for a few seconds, then looked up. "Don't know, Mizz Cat. All I know is . . . you always been real nice to me an' you stuck up for me that time Sam was houndin' me when I was little, an' I know you gonna need some help aroun' here now."

Swept away with emotion and a thankful heart for Lew's loyalty in the midst of her now-desperate circumstances, Catherine had tossed all southern propriety aside and embraced him warmly, inviting him inside and telling him he could take up residence in the butler's vacated room.

The next day, she'd sat down at the dining table with Lew and Elijah. She'd started the conversation by telling them both that plantation life as she'd known it was dead. The tobacco fields would just have to go untended and rot. She'd then placed one hand on Lew's forearm as, with the other, she laid a single-page document with her signature on the table in front of him. He'd stared at it, looking bewildered and even scared.

"What's that, Mizz Cat?"

"It's my signed letter authorizing your freedom, Lew. As soon as I can get to Petersburg, I'm going to have a judge sign your manumission papers."

Lew peered up at her, dumbfounded. His eyes became moist as Cat gripped his arm tighter and smiled at him.

"And as far as I'm concerned, the Emancipation Proclamation is now in full, official effect on this property. From now on, Lew, you already are a freed man in my eyes—just like Elijah."

Lew had simply sat shaking in his chair as Elijah and Catherine both shed tears of joy for him. After a few moments, she'd gone on to explain that Lew would be paid weekly whatever tiny amount she could afford for his work in helping Elijah procure supplies and keep the house, barn, and smaller food-crop plots maintained. Together, the three would share cooking and gardening duties, while Catherine would be responsible for sewing and laundry tasks. The proposed arrangement had been enthusiastically embraced by Lew and Elijah, and a comfortable, amicable routine had been quickly established.

True, she'd known from the start it was an arrangement that many in the area would vehemently disapprove. When she'd visited several acquaintances in Petersburg last week, one of them had expressed her sorrow for Catherine's recent misfortune but in the next breath had questioned her decision to "live and work in such close quarters with two Black men." The woman had even gone so far as to say, "Don't you fear being molested and murdered in your bed? My, wasn't the protection of southern womanhood from that horrid possibility one of the reasons that your Joe had fought and died?"

Catherine had slammed her teacup down and angrily stalked out of the room, vowing never to speak to any of the Petersburg ladies ever again. They could think what they wanted. But none of them had faced anything close to her dilemma, and so they had no right to judge her.

Wiping the unpleasant memory from her mind, Catherine carried the basket of spinach into the house through the rear veranda door and began the process of preparing supper for herself, Lew, and Elijah. With the distant cannon fire still ebbing and flowing, it seemed they would have some unwelcome background accompaniment tonight.

Catherine ladled out bowls of thick vegetable soup for Lew and Elijah before seating herself at the head of the dining room table and serving herself.

How times have changed, she thought. Fortunately, she'd adapted quickly and without rancor to the new roles and relationships forced upon her by circumstances. In fact, it had surprised her how much more relaxed and natural she felt sharing an informal meal with her two Black workers than she often had with her own family's elegant dining experiences.

After Catherine said grace, the three ate in silence for a few minutes before Catherine raised the issue that had been troubling her for the past few days.

"Elijah, I expect the Yankee soldiers will come through here any day now. Is that your belief as well?"

"Yes, ma'am. I expect that's right. I heard yesterday they've already taken over that Eppes Plantation just up the river, and General Grant himself has set up his headquarters there."

"Whenever they come," said Catherine, "I know they'll confirm your freedom and ask both of you if you wish to leave here. And I don't want either of you to feel under any obligation to stay just for my sake. God knows you've done right by me, and I'm fortunate to have had your help and support, even if only for a brief time."

Elijah and Lew exchanged glances. Elijah spoke for both of them. "I'm not sure where else we'd wanna go right now, Mizz Cat. No relatives anywhere near, and ain't likely we gonna find a nice place like this for a good long while anyway, 'specially if the fightin' keeps up. Can't we just keep workin' for you?"

Catherine put her spoon down and folded her arms. "Of course you can, Elijah. I would *love* it if you both decided to stay with me, so long as the Yankees don't confiscate my property and turn me out, or—worse."

"You really think they'd do somethin' bad like that, ma'am?"

Catherine stared at him, trying to stop the strange trembling sensation in her upper body. She'd heard some frightening stories from the Petersburg ladies, two of whom had received letters from relatives in the Union-conquered territories to the west. "As far as confiscation goes, I hear it depends on the whims and prejudices of whoever's in command of their larger units. But it usually goes worse for plantation owners who've either fought for the Confederate army or served as a Confederate state or national government representative. In my case, I had a husband and father who are *both* on the official record as matching one or the other of those criteria."

"But you a lady, Mizz Cat. You ain't done none o' them things," Lew protested.

"I just don't know how they will look at that, Lew." *Or how those battle-weary, rebel-hating Yankee soldiers will look at* me, *a young Confederate widow ripe for the taking if they choose to force themselves on me.*

Catherine knew she could not allow herself to dwell too much on such a horrid possibility. If added to the constant anxiety she was already experiencing over just about everything else these days, it would likely drive her insane. Besides, hadn't Pastor Jones promised to visit frequently to check on her safety once the Yankees arrived? And, of course, there were always Joe's hunting rifles and pistol in her bedroom closet . . . if she could just remember how to use them.

She pushed her chair back and stood up. "Gentlemen, I hope you enjoyed your meal, because I am good and ready for some entertainment to lighten my mind."

Elijah grinned. Aftersupper music and games had become the threesome's favorite shared activity. "What you have in mind for tonight, Mizz Cat?"

"Why, what do you think, sir? Don't you have that harmonica in your pocket already warmed up, ready to accompany me as I pound the piano keys and we all sing our favorite tunes?"

Elijah laughed and reached into his pocket. "Oh, no! I must've left it at my house."

"Well, sir," said Catherine with mock severity, "you *must* go fetch it immediately. We can't have an evening's entertainment without your famous harmonica leading the way."

"Yes, *ma'am*!" Elijah was clearly delighted by the compliment. "I'll be back in five minutes." He rose from his seat and bounded into the hallway, then out the back door like an excited child. Catherine laughed, knowing it would take Elijah a few more minutes than five to reach his cabin on the far side of the plantation, find his harmonica, and return.

"Lew," she suggested, "why don't you pick up the bowls and wash them while I go upstairs and get a book for us to read while we wait for Elijah? Shall we pick up where we left off last time?"

Lew's eyes lit up. "That sound fine to me, Mizz Cat!"

Halfway back down the stairs after retrieving the book, Catherine froze in mid-step at what sounded like galloping horses approaching the front of the house.

Panic struck her—had the Yankee soldiers arrived *already*? She considered turning around and running back up the stairs for one of the hunting rifles, just in case. But as she continued to listen, the sound gradually diminished and soon disappeared entirely. Had she imagined it?

She walked to the front door, cautiously opened it, and walked out onto the veranda. She shielded her eyes from the setting sun; still about an hour of daylight left. Looking all around, nothing seemed abnormal. A slight breeze stirred the leaves in the upper parts of the red maple and black gum trees lining the entrance driveway. Other than that, with the cannon fire from Petersburg having finally tapered off during supper, silence.

Relieved, she went back into the house and sat down on the parlor room sofa. Lew took his favorite seat on the piano bench, and before long, the two were completely engrossed in Catherine's reading of the third of Hawthorne's *Tanglewood Tales for Boys and Girls*: "Dragon's Teeth." Not that she herself was especially thrilled by the retelling of the well-known Greek myth, but she'd remembered marveling at her sister Emma's wide-eyed excitement as she'd watched Mother read it to her at about the same age as Lew was now. Her hunch that Lew might enjoy it as well had proven correct.

"'But, though the gray years thrust themselves between, and made the child's figure dim in their remembrance, neither of these true-hearted three ever dreamed of giving up the search.'" As she read the sentence, Catherine's throat caught and her eyes grew moist.

"You all right, Mizz Cat?" Lew asked, his voice filled with concern.

Catherine smiled weakly and dabbed at her eyes with her handkerchief. "I'm fine, Lew, thank you. I-I just had a memory of my brother David and my sister Emma . . . and I started wondering when the three of us will see each other again."

"Yes, ma'am. I can sure understand that."

"Lew, may I ask, do you ever think much about your parents, and Charles, and . . . Sallie?"

Lew stared down at his feet, the familiar sign to Catherine that he was trying to control his emotions in front of her.

"You don't have to answer if you don't want to," she offered tenderly.

"It's all right, ma'am. Guess I try not to think too much about Momma and Daddy and Charles no more. Hurts too much, and ain't nothin' gonna bring 'em back."

"What about Sallie?"

Lew raised his head, tears now brimming in his own eyes. "Mizz Cat, you think maybe Sallie's still alive? 'Cause if she is, I'd give anything to find her."

Catherine leaned over and put her hand on his. "Lew, listen to me. There is no doubt in my mind that Sallie, David, and Emma are *all* alive somewhere. And we *are* going to find them all, sooner or later."

Lew smiled at her hesitantly. "How you know that, Mizz Cat?"

"Don't ask me how . . . I just know. Somehow God's put it on my heart, and I'm not about to—"

A loud pounding on the front door brought Catherine and Lew to their feet.

"Elijah?" Catherine called. "Is that you?"

The pounding resumed, even louder this time.

"Wait here," Catherine told Lew. She went out into the hallway to the front door.

"Who's there?"

"It's me, Mizz Cat."

Catherine breathed a sigh of relief and flung open the door. "Elijah, why in the world would you—"

She gasped in horror at the sight of Elijah standing in front of her, his face badly beaten and his hands tied behind his back. At the bottom of the veranda steps, four horse-mounted, raggedly dressed Confederate militiamen pointed their rifles in Catherine and Elijah's direction.

A fifth mounted man, armed only with a pistol, tipped his hat and displayed a wide grin.

"Good evening, Mizz Cat. Remember me? Looks like your chickens have come home to roost."

Sam Taylor dismounted. He lifted what looked to be a coiled whip off the horn of his saddle and walked slowly up the veranda steps. He approached the front door and, pistol held casually in his hand, rested his elbow on Elijah's shoulder. His eyes were glazed, and the stench of alcohol was heavy on his breath as he faced Catherine.

"Might be courteous if you'd invite us all inside for a short spell, Mizz Cat. Your Virginia First Society's been doing its level best to help fight off the Yankees, and it's time we had a little reward for all our efforts on your behalf."

CHAPTER 36

After Sam gave the order, his men began ransacking every room of the main house, snatching up any small items of value they could find and stashing them in the burlap sacks they'd obviously brought along for the task.

The discoverer of the box containing Catherine's jewelry that she'd kept in her bedroom closet appeared at the top of the stairs, whooping with delight and proudly holding up her favorite blue diamond necklace. "Hey, Sam!" the man shouted. "This family must've been worth a king's fortune. And to think you used to work for 'em!"

Sitting back with one leg crossed over the other in Lawrence Hodge's favorite parlor armchair, Sam caressed the barrel of his pistol as he glared at Catherine, Lew, and Elijah—all of whom stood facing him like condemned criminals awaiting their sentences.

"'Used to' is right, Billy," Sam called back. "My father and I *used to* be real respected around here by Mr. Hodge, appreciated for our loyalty and hard work. Then one night, all that changed. Hodge's elder daughter here, the new plantation owner, suddenly forgot all the good we'd done and threw us out like dogs. Ain't that right, Mizz Cat?"

"You know good and well the reason why I had you and your father evicted, Sam," Catherine said quietly. "And watching you and your men ravage and loot my house tonight proves how correct my decision was. But I must admit, I'm still quite surprised."

"Surprised?" Sam sneered. "By what?"

"Heaven knows I expected something like this from the Yankees," she said calmly. "But from the *Virginia First Society*? To think you would stoop to such traitorous degradation, robbing the plantations you'd sworn to defend with your lives! Is there even a *shred* of honor or dignity remaining in you or your men, Sam?"

Sam stared at her dumbfounded before breaking out in a sinister chuckle. He placed his pistol down on the side table on top of the coiled whip, pulled a small flask out of his jacket pocket, and took a long pull before capping and putting it back. He pushed himself up from the chair and sauntered toward Catherine, stopping two feet in front of her. Hands on hips, he bent slightly so that his face was only inches from hers.

"It's a fine thing for someone like *you* to be speaking of honor, Mizz Catherine. Was it *honorable* for you to evict my father and me after ten years of faithful service, all over a small mistake on my part? Was it *honorable* for you to gossip about us to all your plantation and Petersburg friends, ruining our reputation in the entire area and making it impossible to find a decent-paying job ever since?" Sam pointed at Elijah, whose nose and mouth were still oozing blood. "Was it *honorable* to replace me with this good-for-nothing darky, when there are other White men around in need of a job like that who woulda done you much better?

"You wanna know what I think?" Sam growled. "I think you and that sister of yours are exactly the same. You treat these Black boys so special because, deep down, they excite somethin' unholy inside you. In fact, with just the three of you all alone in this big place now, it's easy to guess what might be goin' on at nights between you and these two boys, Mizz Cat. And if that's the case, I can't help but wonder what that poor, brave, dead soldier-husband of yours is thinkin' as he looks down from heaven on—"

The harsh slap that Catherine delivered to the cheek of Sam Taylor was enough to make him yelp in pain. Taking a few moments to recover from the shock, he touched his cheek gingerly.

The squinty-eyed smirk that Catherine had always despised spread across Sam's face. He dropped his hand and turned his face slightly to look at his friends. "I told you this slave-lovin' whore was a feisty one!" he muttered, drawing a few chuckles and grunts.

Returning his gaze to Catherine, he took two quick steps forward and delivered his own vicious strike that sent her reeling to the floor.

Lew rushed to her side and knelt beside her, gently trying to comfort and help her up.

"Well, would you look at that!" Sam shouted triumphantly to his accomplices who were now gathering around to observe the spectacle. "Didn't I tell you, Billy? Mizz Cat just loves it when a good-size young Black boy like Lew here puts his hands all over her. Just like her sister Emma enjoyed doing with Lew's sass-mouthed big brother Charles. *Now* you see why I lost all respect for the Hodge daughters? Why I had to do to Charles what I did?

"Hey, Lew, let me ask you somethin'. Charles ever tell you everything he and Miss Emma were doin' together when they thought no one was lookin'?"

With a savage cry, Lew rushed at Sam and slammed his shoulder into the larger man's midsection, knocking him onto the floor. He started to rain down heavy blows on Sam's face before being grabbed by the arms and hauled roughly up onto his feet by Billy.

Sam stood up and wiped the blood from his lips. After taking a moment to collect himself, he grabbed his pistol off the side table, pointed it at Lew's chest, and cocked the hammer. Catherine closed her eyes, expecting the fatal blast at any moment. Mercifully, it never came.

"Billy and Nate, peel his shirt off and hold 'im over the back of the chair. I got one last thrashin' I need to get outta my system. Jonah, hand me my whip."

"No, please, Sam, don't!" Catherine rose from the floor and tried to run toward Lew before she was caught by the waist from behind by another one of Sam's men and dragged toward the other side of the room.

Sam uncocked and holstered his pistol, then uncoiled the whip that Jonah had given him. He took a practice lash against the wall near Catherine, stripping off a piece of plaster. Turning back toward Lew, he positioned himself and drew back the whip, ready to dish out the first, excruciating, skin-ripping blow.

Before he could do so, Elijah stepped in front of Lew and the two men holding him over the armchair. "No, Masta Taylor. You ain't gonna do this."

Sam paused and did a double take. "You tellin' me I ain't gonna do *what*? Get outta my way *now*, boy, before I put a big ole hole through your eye socket." He pulled out his pistol once again and pointed it at Elijah's face.

"Masta Taylor, please, sir. Lew's only thirteen. Don't have a lick o' sense . . . that's why he gone after you like he did. Please, sir, spare him. If you gotta take it out on someone, then do it on me."

Sam hesitated, dropped the whip on the floor, and, still pointing the pistol at Elijah, reached into his jacket pocket with his free hand. Pulling the cap off the flask with his bloodied teeth and spitting it on the floor, he threw his head back and took another long pull before dashing the empty container to the ground.

"I'll tell you what, Elijah. How 'bout you get down on your knees in front o' me here and *beg* me to take it out on you instead of poor little Lew? If you'll do that, then maybe . . . just maybe . . . I'll consider it."

Elijah quickly knelt down, his hands clasped in front of him. He lifted his mangled face toward Sam. "Please, Masta, I beg you in the name of Jesus, sir, take Lew's punishment out on me—not him, sir."

Sam's jaw twitched. "You admit this boy deserved some bad punishment, Elijah, for what he done to me?"

"Oh, yes, yes, sir . . . I surely do. But I'll take it *all* for 'im, Masta. I surely will."

Sam glanced around the room. Catherine could see that he was now wobbling and unsteady on his feet.

Suddenly, as if something had taken hold of him, Sam stood up straight and steadied himself. He looked down at Elijah, pressed the barrel of the gun against his swollen left temple, and pulled the trigger.

Catherine's scream mingled with the shocked shouts of Billy and Nate as blood and brains from Elijah's exit wound splattered on the back of Lew's pants. All three men jumped aside as Elijah fell backward, his head banging against the armchair's back before he rolled off to the side.

"Sam, now why the hell did you have to go do *that*?" Nate asked tentatively.

"Shut up, Nate!" Sam yelled. "He said he'd take *all* o' Lew's punishment . . . but he never asked what that punishment was gonna be!" He stared at Lew, then at Catherine. "See what you two made me do? Have a good time together cleanin' up."

He holstered his pistol and stalked out toward the front hall. "Now all of you boys, get those sacks on your horses, and let's get going before the Yanks get here."

Within seconds, Sam and his men had exited the house and the front door was slammed shut.

After checking for a heartbeat and confirming that Elijah was dead, Lew, in a mad rage, rushed toward the door and grabbed the handle.

"Lew, don't! It's no use . . . they'll kill you for sure, Lew!" Catherine shouted.

Lew spun around. His face reflected his sheer agony of soul. "He can't get away, Mizz Cat. That murdering devil has to be stopped. I can't allow it!" He turned back and started to open the door.

"Lew, wait! There's a better way than you just rushing out there alone and letting them kill you!"

Lew hesitated. He peeked out the door for several seconds, then looked back at her in panic. "Mizz Cat, think I heard Sam just say he forgot somethin' important that you still personally owed 'im." He peeked out once again. "Sam's comin' back, Mizz Cat!"

Catherine ran toward the stairs. "Lock that door and come with me!"

Three pistol blasts followed by the sound of the front door wood crack-ing indicated the obvious: Sam Taylor was attempting to reeenter the premises.

Catherine stood with her back to the shut bedroom door, trying to focus.

"Lew," she said, her face pale, but her voice strangely steady, "I just know he's going to come up here and try to have his way with me. Go over to the closet and get the duck-hunting rifle and the pistol—they're already loaded. I'll take the rifle, and I want you to take the pistol and hide under the bed."

"But, Mizz Cat, I can't let you—"

Catherine grasped his head between her hands. "Lew, please! Just do what I say, and don't make a sound or show yourself if he comes in."

Seconds later, Lew lay squeezed in the tight space between the floor and the bottom of the bedframe as Catherine stood flat up against the wall beside the hinged side of the door. She held the rifle pointed upward, having already checked that it was properly loaded and primed.

She tried to breathe as little as possible, sweat pouring from her brow as she heard the sound of bootsteps in the entry hall.

"Hey, Sam," she heard someone call from the outside, "leave her be. She ain't worth it. Forget her—we gotta get goin'!"

The bootsteps paused.

"Y'all go on, Nate. Just leave my horse tied to the porch rail. No way I'm leavin' this place before I get my full satisfaction from the beautiful Mizz Cat."

The bootsteps paced through the downstairs rooms in fruitless search, then began ascending the stairs. They continued down the hall, stopping just outside her bedroom door.

Catherine gulped and looked toward the bed. To her horror, she could clearly see Lew's face behind the barrel of his pistol, which was sticking out from under the frame and pointed at the door. But it was too late to warn him.

The knob turned, and the door creaked open, pinning Catherine back against the wall. She held her breath and gripped the rifle with both hands, her finger on the trigger. *Lord, I know you will never leave me or forsake me.*

Sam Taylor stepped cautiously into the room, not yet aware of Catherine, who stood partially concealed behind the door. He held his pistol in his right hand, ready to fire as he approached the foot of the bed peering from left to right.

"What the hell . . . ?" he muttered as he spotted Lew's pistol barrel pointing up at him.

Now! Catherine took two steps forward and jammed the barrel of the rifle in Sam's back.

"Don't move!"

Sam froze. Ever so slowly, he lowered his weapon.

Catherine took a step back. "Now drop the pistol and turn around."

Sam let the gun drop on the floor and turned to face her. His face was a mask of drunken fury.

The two stood glaring at each other for what seemed an eternity. With each passing moment, Catherine's racing heart felt on the verge of exploding from her chest as her short-lived calm began to yield to fear and uncertainty over what to do next. Her trembling arms suddenly felt like lead, and she struggled to keep the barrel of the gun pointed straight at Sam's chest.

Finally, Sam slowly spread his arms with palms up. "So, this is it . . . right, Mizz Cat? Looks like you won the day. Who woulda thought?" His mouth twisted in a resigned, snarling smile as he gazed down at the rifle muzzle six inches from his chest. "So . . . go ahead. Have your justice, Mizz Cat."

Catherine's finger tightened on the trigger. "It's not *my* justice, Sam. It's justice for Elijah and Charles . . . and Lew and Sallie and Emma and . . ."

Sam lifted his head. His eyes had a vacant, faraway expression—as if he were already contemplating his fate in eternity. "And?"

Catherine trembled but opened her mouth. "And—"

Sam's hands struck like a viper, grabbing for the rifle barrel.

The deafening blast shook the room.

Sam Taylor fell back onto the bed, his arms and legs sprawled, his feet still touching the floor. A dark-red stain spread from the hole in his left upper chest.

Catherine dropped the rifle on the floor and sunk to her knees with her arms clutching her stomach. Scrambling out from under the side of the bed, Lew took stock of the scene and raced over to her. He knelt and draped one arm around her shoulders as he kept his pistol pointed at Sam, whose labored breathing could still be heard.

Lew stood and walked over to the side of the bed. He placed the muzzle of his pistol against Sam's temple, his hand shaking violently. He looked at Catherine, whose fear was palpable.

Then Lew looked back at Sam, his hand no longer shaking.

He pulled the trigger.

Catherine stood at the foot of the bed with her arm draped around Lew's shoulders, facing the closed bedroom door. In seconds, the source of the heavy bootsteps that they'd just heard coming down the hallway outside would be revealed. Whoever it was, with the rifle and pistol both now discharged, they had no further means by which to defend themselves.

Please, God, have mercy on us.

The door flung open.

Catherine stared in amazement at the sight of a short, thin, young Black man in the crisp blue uniform of a Union soldier, his forage cap pulled low over his forehead and his rifle aimed at their faces.

"Hey, Sarge," the man yelled, "got two of 'em up here. A lady and a boy. Looks like somebody dead on the bed too."

He stepped into the room and motioned menacingly with his weapon. "All right, you two. Out into the hallway. No tricks."

Catherine and Lew quickly complied with the order. The soldier continued to glare and point his rifle at them as they passed by him. "This lady been hurtin' you, boy?"

"Oh, no, sir, she been real good to me. She made me a free man."

"She made you a *what*? No plantation mistress can do that, boy. You already a free man, just like me. Abe Lincoln himself said so. Hey, Sarge, you gotta see this!"

Soon, a burly negro officer arrived from down the hall. He took a long look at Catherine and Lew, then smiled and doffed his hat. "Apologies for frightening you, ma'am. My boys were ordered to probe the area here after our first big fight yesterday with the Confeds on the outskirts of Petersburg. They're still feeling a little jittery, especially after chasing off all those militiamen we saw fleein' like rabbits from your house for reasons I'm not entirely clear. Unfortunately, all of 'em got away. But we can talk about that later—first things first: I'm Sergeant Moses Wilson, XVIII Corps, Fifth US Colored Troops Regiment. And you are . . . ?"

After Catherine and Lew had introduced themselves, the sergeant suggested they each take whatever time they needed to change clothes and refresh themselves while he and his men took care of Sam's and Elijah's bodies and cleaned up the blood. Whenever they were ready, they could join him and his commanding officer to talk about the wild sequence that had transpired on the Hodge Plantation tonight—and what would be happening next.

"Thank you, sir. You have been most considerate, and I . . . I . . ." Catherine's words trailed off as the stress of the evening took its final toll. Head spinning and knees buckling, she collapsed into the arms of Sergeant Wilson.

⚉

On the cool, misty Tuesday morning two weeks following the deaths of Elijah Flint and Sam Taylor, Catherine stepped out on the main house's front veranda, determined to revive her sagging spirits.

After wrapping a light shawl around her shoulders and extending her umbrella, she picked up the basket of dried flower bouquets with her free hand and walked down the veranda steps. It was a fifteen-minute walk to the small hillside on the edge of the property where the gravesites of Papa, Mother, Joe, and their son were located.

Spending some time alone there—praying and meditating in the spiritual presence of her loved ones—would be the best way to clear her mind and soothe her heart in light of the depressing news she'd received last night.

Yesterday morning, Brigadier General Hinks—the White division commander for the two brigades of colored soldiers supporting XVIII Corps operations in the Petersburg area—had arrived at the main house with his staff. Hinks had fully believed and accepted Catherine's account of her actions on the evening of the shootings; "defending life, home, and property from rebel looters" was easy to justify in these dangerous times, he'd acknowledged. However, it had soon become clear that Hinks would not be as sympathetic to Catherine's situation as his subordinate, Sergeant Wilson, had been.

"With regrets, ma'am," Hinks's adjutant officer had told her after the evening meal, "I have to inform you that the Hodge Plantation property has been declared to be 'abandoned-by-owner' and confiscated by the US government. General Hinks will be establishing his headquarters in this house for the duration of the Union army's Petersburg campaign. After that, the main house, surrounding lands, and structures will become public property under federal government control, eligible for future apportionment and sale. Until that time, you will be permitted to stay here if you wish, and to retain a cordoned-off portion of the upstairs rooms for your private use—free of charge. And if you agree to help with cooking and continue tending the vegetable garden, you will also be provided with three meals per day, which you may enjoy either privately or as a regular guest at the staff officers' dining table."

The terms had sounded to Catherine like an undeserved jail sentence. But her effort to plead her case that *she*, and not her deceased father, was now the legal owner of the plantation—and that therefore it had never been abandoned—had fallen on deaf ears.

"Unless you can produce official documentation of your acquisition of the title to this property," the adjutant had insisted, "the government must rely on its prewar records. Those indicate that Lawrence M. Hodge—a member of the secessionist Virginia legislature—is the owner. And as Mr. Hodge is sadly no longer alive, we must treat this property the same as if he had abandoned it."

A frantic search of the upstairs rooms to find the notarized copy of Papa's will in which he'd granted Catherine title to the plantation had revealed yet another dimension of Sam Taylor's betrayal. Evidently, Sam's men had decided to include the small, decorative chest containing all the valuable family records as part of their loot. And without documentary proof of her right to claim title, Catherine had no hopes of reversing the government's decision.

The devastating prospect of life without family, without Joe, and now effectively forced to live as a prisoner within her own home had overwhelmed her this morning with a renewed sense of despair.

And what about the graves? she thought now as she neared the hillside cemetery. *Will I be forced to relocate my family?* The very idea sickened her heart.

She tried desperately to replace the crushing thoughts with a shred of hope. *"In everything—even the toughest of trials—Christ tells us to give thanks,"* she recalled Pastor Jones exhorting his congregation in last Sunday's sermon.

Well, I'm thankful that at least I won't be totally alone. True, her longtime neighbor and friend Amanda Tidwell and her parents had recently fled the area, but there was still Pastor Jones and his wife to visit and worship with on Sundays. And hadn't the adjutant said that Lew could continue to live in the house if he wanted, so long as he was willing to help the soldiers with their daily tasks? She would speak to Lew tonight, but she was almost certain he would be happy to accept the arrangement. If so, the familiarity of his continued presence and conversation would definitely be a source of great comfort. Ultimately, of course, there was always the hope that one day God would answer her prayer and provide a way to reunite her with David and Emma. *Thank you, God, for your comforting mercies and possibilities—both great and small.*

Reaching the gravesite near the crest of the hill, Catherine knelt in front of the pair of headstones marking the final resting places for her parents. She placed a bouquet next to each, trying as she did so to imagine Papa and Mother in their blissful resurrected state, holding hands and smiling down on her with their unconditional approval and tender affection.

As always, the effort required was much greater in Papa's case. Although she believed Papa had loved and accepted her in a resigned, dutiful sort of way, she still couldn't get over the sense that she'd never quite measured up to his high expectations for his firstborn daughter. Of course, her own view of Papa had changed drastically since his death. Especially after the night she'd overheard Sam Taylor directly confess to killing Charles, bearing out Emma's charge all along that Papa's self-interest over his election prospects had permitted the murder to happen and prompted the cover-up afterward. In some ways, realizing Papa's character flaw in this regard made it easier to forgive herself for her own shortcomings. It also made it easier to see both her parents in a more realistic and appreciative light—as two fallible human beings who had done the best they could to love, raise, and provide for their children and contribute to their society in the genteel southern tradition, the only tradition that they themselves had ever known.

After offering a prayer of thanks for the lives of her parents and for the assurance in her heart that she would one day be with them again, Catherine stood with her basket and walked the short distance to Joe's grave and the small marker immediately next to it memorializing their stillborn son. As soon as she knelt and stared at his name chiseled into the headstone, the mist suddenly turned to light rain, as if God himself were shedding tears. She broke into sobs as precious memories of her times with Joe came flooding back. He'd been the only one with whom she'd known true happiness. And though two gentlemen from Petersburg had recently expressed interest in courting her, the thought of intimacy with any other man besides Joe was repellant to her.

As she collected herself and placed the remaining bouquet in front of the stone, she wondered what it would be like to greet him again. She closed her eyes and imagined herself standing in front of a beautifully gilded heavenly door as it opened to reveal the Lord standing there, smiling and extending his hand to her . . .

She reached out to accept it, and after embracing her tenderly, he led her into a room filled with people sitting at a huge, gorgeously decorated banquet table. They all turned toward her, the newest arrival, clapping and nodding and cheering. A few she recognized from her past, but most she had never seen before. She peered across the table, and there were Papa and Mother waving to her and rising from their seats to come greet her. "I have someone else who's been especially eager to see you," she imagined Christ saying, his arm gently draped around her shoulders. She pictured a man seated immediately in front of her who was hunched over, his back turned toward her. Christ placed his hand on the man's shoulder, and he rose slowly and turned to face her. It was Joe, of course, as magnificent-looking as the first time she'd met him. In his arms, he cradled the son she had never had the chance to hold herself. He looked at her tenderly and held out his hand. "We've missed you, Cat . . ."

Catherine opened her eyes and shook her head to clear it, berating herself mildly for entertaining such presumptuous, sentimental thoughts. Her time for heavenly reward had not yet come, and she knew both Joe and Christ himself would want her to focus for now on the immense earthly dilemma facing her. How indeed, she wondered, was she going to make a new life for herself with no income, no property, no legal rights, and the city of Petersburg—her most likely hope for finding employment—now under Union army siege?

Catherine let out a long sigh and stood up, preparing herself once again to return to the main house and face the cold reality of her current situation. After kissing her palm and gently laying it one final time on Joe's headstone, she picked up her empty flower basket and turned to start down the hill.

Just as she did so, she noticed a small, one-horse carriage approaching along the rough dirt path from the house. Its canopy was drawn to protect its occupants from the rain, but she could see that two people were sitting on the driver's bench. She soon recognized it as Pastor Jones's carriage, and she guessed that he and Judith had come to pay a visit. After inquiring at the house and being told that she was out here, they had probably come to keep her company and join her in prayers for her loved ones.

Might as well wait here for them, she thought. She put the basket back down on the ground and waved. Seconds later, the carriage pulled up at the bottom of the hill. Pastor Jones peered out from the side facing her and waved back, then turned to say something to Judith. *Why are they taking so long to get out and come up here?* she wondered impatiently. Someone stepped out on the far side of the carriage and walked around the back. Catherine saw immediately she'd been mistaken. Pastor Jones's passenger was not his wife Judith.

Shocked to her core, she dropped her basket and umbrella and ran down the hill. At the bottom, she stopped.

She gazed at him, her hand on her breast and tears streaming.

"Oh, David, David, you . . . your arm . . . I . . . Emma . . . is she . . . ? And Sallie?"

He smiled and nodded. "Emma and Sallie are alive and well, Cat . . . they're waiting for me to take you to them."

Catherine covered her eyes as sobs of joy and relief began to overwhelm her. She started to run to him but once again pulled up short, her face etched with sorrow over the painful memory.

"Brother, when you left home three years ago, I turned my back on you in my self-righteous anger. Can you ever forgive me?"

David smiled, tears brimming in his own eyes. "Of course I can . . . in fact, dear sister, I gave you good reason to be angry. And I beg you to forgive me as well."

He ran to embrace her.

CHAPTER 37

City of Beaufort
Port Royal Island, South Carolina Sea Islands
July 14, 1864

Near the end of their walk to the missionary recognition supper at the plush, midtown Maxcy House—the former family mansion that now served as Union army headquarters for the Sea Island District—Emma clasped Abel's arm, trying to steady her nerves in preparation for her brief testimony tonight.

At least, she consoled herself, she wouldn't be alone. Several other AMA missionary-teachers and care workers serving at various plantations in the Sea Islands region would also be highlighting their recent progress and accomplishments in support of the Port Royal Experiment—all after Colonel Jack Hurley had delivered the evening's keynote speech. Her main challenge, she knew, would be sticking to her script and not allowing her raw emotions to derail the meeting's charitable purpose. That wouldn't be easy, given what Abel had revealed to her yesterday . . .

⁂

"You won't believe it, Emma!" Abel had said the moment Emma opened the front door of the small three-room apartment on the outskirts of town. She'd been sharing it with Sallie—who'd been released two days ago from the hospital—and one of the other female AMA missionaries who was serving in the area.

After letting him in and requesting her roommate for an hour of privacy while Sallie—still recuperating—slept soundly in her bedroom, she'd served him supper as he excitedly related the latest development in his efforts over the past month to track down the true source of the Magnolia fire.

"Last night, I finally convinced the sheriff to put aside his reservations about my idea to confront my suspected arsonist with the evidence. We went together to visit the man—a poor White river worker who lives with his sickly wife and young daughter in a ramshackle shanty near the pier—and showed him the charred half-bucket from the Beaufort supply store that I recovered from the fire. When we told him that the store owner had identified him as the purchaser of the bucket along with several large packets of gunpowder two days before the fire—and that he had the sales ledger record to prove it—the man started to tremble. And then when I said that two credible witnesses who knew him by name had spotted him snooping suspiciously around the schoolhouse the night before the fire, he broke down and confessed to the act."

"But *why*, Abel?" Emma had asked in utter dismay. "Why would anyone do such a horrible thing?"

"He told us he'd done it for money, as his wife's illness and other problems had created a mountain of personal debt. He insisted he'd had no idea that anyone was sleeping on the second floor of the schoolhouse that night, or else he would never have done what he did. Said he'd decided to leave the empty bucket, assuming it would be completely consumed by the flames."

"So, who paid him? And why?"

"We asked him that. He was extremely reluctant to reveal the answers, but the sheriff reminded him of the possible punishments he could be facing and enticed him with the idea that things would very likely go better for him if he agreed to cooperate fully with the investigation. After several minutes of hand-wringing and confiding with his wife, he told us everything."

"And . . . ?"

Abel had stared at her intently. "Are you ready? *Jack Hurley* paid him. The man has a stash of greenbacks in his bedroom to prove it— two thousand US dollars, minus the three hundred he's already spent. It's more money than he's made from his honest labors in the last four years combined."

"*Hurley?*" Emma had stared at him with her mouth agape. "But how can you prove he got that money from Hurley, and not someone else?"

"Because the idiot who personally knew and recruited the arsonist and delivered him the cash three days before the fire—Hurley's 'middleman'—made a fatal mistake. He didn't hand over the cash by itself, but instead, a leather document pouch containing it. And guess what our arsonist discovered after he pulled out the cash, stuck at the bottom between the inner folds of the pouch? Nothing less than an old business calling card for Jonathan Hurley! Now that alone doesn't prove anything, but combined with the middleman's explanation to the arsonist about Hurley's motive, the picture starts to come together."

"So, what was his motive?"

"The middleman—who turns out to be one of Hurley's three new White foremen—said Hurley was determined to make it permanently impossible for the schoolhouse and its 'AMA champions' to keep interfering with his profit-making ability. But of course, in order not to bring blame on himself, Hurley would have the arsonist plant that rebel flag so he could claim publicly it was just another malicious act by those raiders from the mainland. And if the arsonist agreed to take on the job, Hurley would not only reward him in advance with the immediate cash, but also, afterward, with a new job and a brand-new bigger boat, hauling cotton bales from Hurley's properties to the depot on the coast. That's exactly what happened a week after the fire, and ever since, the man and his family have been benefiting from his payoff despite his terrible remorse over the fire's victims."

Emma, stunned, had sat back in her chair. "Well, *I* can certainly believe all that, given everything I've heard and experienced with that serpent Hurley. And now that I think of it, that would explain all those supportive statements he made just before the fire about the Glory School and allowing a little more time for attendance—they were obviously just another ruse to throw us off his track." She'd then looked up at Abel with a perplexed frown. "But would the river worker's confession be enough to get Hurley convicted in a court of law? What needs to happen next?"

"That's where things get a bit complicated," Abel had admitted. "The arsonist said if he could be guaranteed a reduced charge or at least a lighter sentence, then he'd be willing to testify in court that Hurley's foreman recruited and paid him on Hurley's behalf. That's helpful, but the case would be much stronger if we could convince the foreman himself to confess and testify.

"Before he arrested the arsonist and escorted him off to the city jail, the sheriff pulled me aside and suggested we consult with General Saxton's people as soon as possible about the situation. As overall leader for the Port Royal Experiment, Saxton's never been happy with the hardcore, 'business-first' approach to ex-slave transition that Hurley and his investment group have been pushing to the limit. The sheriff knows Saxton personally and thinks he'd be very motivated to do whatever he legitimately can to help us get the foreman's testimony and hopefully ensure Hurley's downfall."

The full impact of everything she'd just heard finally hitting her, Emma had buried her face in her hands—overcome with emotion. At long last, justice would be served against the man ultimately responsible for crushing the honorable aspirations of the Magnolia Plantation freedmen to achieve a new, self-sustaining way of life—killing a small girl and severely burning two other young women in the process.

She'd thought of Sallie, who was still sleeping, and tried to imagine the satisfaction that all this news would bring when she awoke tomorrow morning.

"Abel, do you really think all this will bring him down?"

"I'm not sure . . . we should know soon. But I can tell you one thing. After all the trouble he's given me and you and others, *nothing* would give me more pleasure. Oh, and one other thing I forgot to mention."

"What's that?"

"The arsonist admitted to stealing our Glory flag. That was part of the foreman's instructions to him. No doubt, Hurley's got it now."

"But what on earth would he want to do with *that*?"

"Who knows? I promise, though, one day soon, I'm going to get it back."

Seated next to Abel at the elegantly decorated round table for twelve— one of four that had been set up for the occasion in the Maxcy House's second-floor conference room—Emma struggled to maintain her concentration as the aftersupper preliminary speakers droned on and on. In between mentally rehearsing yet again the key portions of her upcoming testimony, she reflected on the whirlwind of change that was poised to sweep through her life.

Next Monday, after a six-week hiatus following the Magnolia schoolhouse fire, she would finally begin commuting daily to her new AMA-sponsored teaching assignment at the nearby Smith Plantation on Port Royal Island. Though it could never replace her experience with the Glory School, nor her continuing heart-connection with the Magnolia freedmen, she was grateful for the opportunity to teach again after weeks of performing a variety of housekeeping tasks for several local Beaufort families.

Especially helpful to the transition were the generous actions of the AMA. Not only had they graciously provided for Sallie's medical treatment, but, in light of her excellent recovery progress, they had also recently approved her to remain in the Islands and work with Emma again in the same capacity as before as soon as she felt able. And after yesterday's visit from William Johnson—whom the AMA had also approved to remain working in the area—Sallie had said she should be ready to start doing light daily tasks within two weeks.

Which leads to the bigger question, Emma thought. *With Sallie now staying here and David bringing Catherine and Lew next week for an extended stay, where will we all live?*

David's letter from Virginia that she'd received just yesterday hadn't gone into a lot of detail, other than to report that Catherine and Lew had recently undergone a terrifying experience together but had emerged unscathed. Catherine was supposedly ecstatic at the prospect of seeing her, and David indicated he had noticed some "big changes in Cat—for the better!" It all sounded promising, and it would definitely be good to see her sister alive and well again. But whether she was ready and willing to take up close residence with Cat after all the animosity of their last year together was another matter completely. Maybe, she thought hopefully, David could use his Washington connections to secure the rental of a larger city townhome—one with ample rooms and space to spread out for Catherine, herself, Sallie, and Lew. In any case, it would be quite an adjustment for everyone.

And then there's Abel. She turned her face toward his and smiled coquettishly, hoping to steal his attention from the current speaker for a brief moment. She was quickly rewarded as he pretended not to notice but then quietly slipped his hand under the tablecloth to grasp hers. Things had certainly progressed rapidly between them, she thought happily. With David's abrupt departure for Virginia last month, the Washington project sponsors had requested Abel to continue temporarily conducting the Sea Island plantation inspections on his own. And despite Abel's frequent absences during the week to conduct his tours or pursue leads concerning the Hurley matter, he was a consistent companion for evening meals, long weekend walks, and horseback or carriage rides together around the island.

Whether they were apart or together, she was finding it nearly impossible to stop thinking pleasant, enticing thoughts about him, and she hoped that he was feeling the same toward her. "Watch out, Em. The man's got a passionate streak in him that would make a lion cower," David had warned her soon after they'd first met—in jest, or so she'd thought at the time. But the more she got to know and observe

Abel, the more certain she was that David had not been jesting at all. Especially after the evening walk when they'd shared their past secrets, and he'd confided to her about his involvement with John Brown, the Pottawatomie incident, and the sword that had inspired Eye of Glory.

At long last, with the preliminary speeches concluded, the fundraiser's master of ceremonies stood and approached the lectern.

"And now, ladies and gentlemen, it is my distinct honor to present to you the man who has shown us one of the best examples we've seen from the entire Port Royal Experiment of the magnificent possibilities for economics-driven slavery transition and postwar reconstruction. Ladies and gentlemen, please welcome the devoted abolitionist, the former army assistant inspector general, the successful real estate entrepreneur, and—I predict with bold confidence, the future mayor of Beaufort—tonight's keynote speaker: *Retired Lieutenant Colonel Jonathan 'Jack' Hurley!*"

With the notable exceptions of Abel and Emma, the mixed audience of local residents, Union army officers, missionaries, teachers, and clergymen clapped loudly as Colonel Jack arose from the speaker's table and strutted like a conquering emperor toward the lectern.

Emma glanced at Abel and noticed his jaw twitching, a sure sign he was thinking the same things as she.

Hurley nodded and smiled, obviously relishing the moment as he waited for the applause to die down.

"Friends, over the past ten months, my obligation to serve the primary cause of this great Port Royal Experiment—to prove the ability of newly freed slaves to become self-sufficient, effectively contributing members of society—has become far more than a mere duty. It has become the focus of my entire business enterprise and, indeed, the passion of my life . . ."

Emma's stomach knotted as applause once again filled the room. For the next twenty minutes, Hurley expounded on the "marvelous" productivity levels achieved by the freedmen on his recently purchased Sea Islands properties—especially on the Magnolia Plantation where he had instituted a number of "labor reforms" that were "already

proving beneficial—both to management and to the freedmen themselves." With his voice seeming to break, he lamented the recent tragic
Magnolia school fire that had taken the life of "a beautiful, innocent
young negro girl" and badly hurt two of the faithful missionary-teachers.
It was clear, he thundered, that the local Union army units must do
more to stop "those rebel raiders" from committing even more heinous
acts of arson in the future. But despite that awful event, he promised
in conclusion, the prospects for profitable cotton operations on Hurley
Sea Island properties—sustained by well-motivated, industrious,
wage-compensated freedmen—had never been brighter.

Livid with rage at the lies and hypocrisy she'd just heard, Emma
could barely restrain herself from standing up and walking out of the
room as the rest of the audience gave Hurley a standing ovation. She
sat through the brief, polite, uniformly positive testimonies of the three
female missionary-teachers who followed him, wondering whether
it might be better for everyone if she and Abel simply got up and left
quietly.

Finally, it was her turn.

"And lastly," announced the event moderator, "before our break prior
to dessert and the big raffle, we are fortunate to hear the testimony of
Miss Emma Hodge—who spent some time teaching on the Magnolia
Plantation prior to their tragic fire and will soon begin a new chapter
teaching on the Smith Plantation. Please, welcome Miss Hodge!"

Abel gently squeezed her knee under the table, obviously in an
attempt to calm her. She put her hand over his for a moment, then rose
from her chair. As she began limping toward the lectern, she noticed
Jack Hurley glaring at her from the speaker's table. He leaned over
and said something to the man sitting next to him, then shrugged in
apparent bewilderment. Emma wondered if Hurley had been aware
that she'd been invited to speak tonight.

Emma spoke briefly of her personal background, her passion for
abolition, her connection with Angelina Grimké, and her brief history
with the AMA and the Port Royal Experiment. Many in the audience
nodded with approval, even admiration, at the huge life transition she

had clearly undergone. She went on to describe her efforts with the Glory Schoolhouse, and the amazing educational accomplishments she had witnessed among the negro students—both children and adults. They had confirmed what she had always believed: that there was nothing at all inferior about the native intellect of the colored race. And if given the chance to learn, she said, it was clear there was *nothing* they wouldn't do to pursue that chance as joyfully and vigorously as if their very existence depended on it.

It was then that she paused, feeling a strange and sudden prompting to place her notes to the side and speak what had been on her heart since the night of the fire.

Should I do this? A memory flashed in her mind of the promise she'd made to Angelina Grimké—to use every opportunity that God gave her to boldly express her compassion for the unfortunate.

She glanced at Abel, who smiled at her encouragingly.

"In conclusion, working at the Magnolia Plantation was a wonderful experience for me, and I am eternally grateful to the AMA for supporting me in it. I have but one regret. And I realize it may cause discomfort for some who are present tonight to hear, but say it I must. There is *no truth* to the assertion that the Magnolia freedmen are perfectly content in their current situation. I have spoken recently to many of my former adult students, who tell me they and their children have been *devastated* by the loss of the schoolhouse, which they themselves built. And they cannot understand why there has been no effort from the plantation owner—Colonel Hurley—to help them rebuild it. Instead, they are told, they must completely forsake their education and work harder and longer to increase their productivity. It has left them in a demoralized state, and while I don't propose to know what should be done about it, I feel obligated that the truth of the situation be known. Thank you all for your time tonight, and for all the support you provide to the Port Royal Experiment and organizations like my own AMA that are so committed to seeing it succeed. I am most appreciative."

Walking back to her seat to smattered applause, Emma could sense the daggers of Jack Hurley's hatred directed at her from behind. She avoided looking at him as she bent down and whispered to Abel that she needed to visit the powder room before the crush that the upcoming break would certainly produce. Abel patted her hand and told her he was exceedingly proud of her. That he would be waiting for her when she returned.

Five minutes later, Emma exited the powder room having successfully avoided conversation with the others who had entered. She had planned to return to her seat, but she noticed that everyone had by now stood up and gathered in small groups to chat and digest together what they had heard this evening. She spotted Abel in one of the groups on the other side of the room, and she started to walk toward him when she suddenly felt the top of her arm grabbed from behind.

She turned to face the massive frame of Colonel Jack Hurley towering above her. His face was red, his eyes apoplectic.

"How *dare* you?" he growled. "Where did somebody like you ever get the high-minded audacity to embarrass me in public, questioning my integrity and good intentions toward the freedmen?"

Emma's heart raced. She glanced quickly behind herself toward Abel, wishing desperately that he would lift his head and notice her dilemma. But seeing he was still engrossed in his conversation, she knew she would have to face this alone.

"Colonel Hurley, I know for a fact that the freedmen don't see your policies and actions toward them as being 'well-intentioned.' To them, it was bad enough that you cut them out of the chance to buy the plantation for themselves. But then, to cut their wages and later refuse to support them in rebuilding their school after the fire? It's an entirely different picture than the pleasant one you tried to paint tonight, Colonel."

Hurley's fists clenched. He moved closer, appearing as if he might strike her. "If you know what's good for you, Miss Hodge, I strongly recommend you cease spreading such unfounded gossip and vicious characterizations of me. At some point, I could turn this into a legal process against you, you know. Believe me, I do not take slander lightly."

Emma tried to hold her tongue, but she couldn't resist. "Believe *me*, Colonel, I don't take it lightly either. But I assure you, I take *payoff for arson* even more seriously."

Hurley's eyes narrowed. "Now, what exactly is *that* supposed to mean?"

"That's for you to figure out," Emma said airily. She turned and started to walk away. Once again, he grabbed her arm and tried to pull her back.

Noticing her distress, Abel abruptly left his group and hurried over to extricate her from Hurley's grip. The two men stood glowering at each other as several people witnessing the commotion began to gather around.

"What do you think you're doing, Colonel?" Abel said. "Do you always try to manhandle young ladies like this?"

"Well, well." Hurley smirked. "If it isn't my old friend Abel Bowman. Of all people who might attempt to stand up for a lady's honor, somehow I would not have expected *you* to be that person. Tell me, did you ever manage to relieve your own guilt over that prostitution incident you and your soldiers tried to cover up during our Antietam campaign in Maryland?"

"You know good and well my men and I were completely innocent of that ridiculous dereliction charge you tried to lay on us," Abel said quietly. Emma, standing behind him, could sense his building fury.

Colonel Jack nodded slightly. "That may or may not be so. But for a raging zealot like you who is so obsessed with that harebrained Eye of Glory theme, I should think you'd have encouraged your men to avoid even the slightest hint of—"

If it hadn't been for the quick-reacting army officer who stepped in to prevent it, Abel's fist would have crashed into Jack Hurley's mouth like an iron wrecking ball. As it was, it took two additional bystanders to restrain his wild efforts to engage.

As others gathered around to observe in stunned silence, Hurley pointed his finger at Abel.

"You're threatening the wrong soldier, you lowlife son of a whore."

CHAPTER 38

City of Beaufort
Port Royal Island, South Carolina Sea Islands
July 15, 1864

The following afternoon, still mulling over events at the Maxcy House, Emma had accepted Abel's invitation to dine that evening at one of their favorite Beaufort restaurants. "Maybe you can help me get some things off my chest after last night," he'd said.

Walking home with him afterward along the narrow city sidewalk illumined dimly by widely spaced gaslit streetlamps, Emma tried to console her escort.

"Abel, you were only trying to protect me. And I *know* what the Eye of Glory means to you."

Abel shook his head. "Emma, it was wrong."

She stopped and turned to face him. "What do you mean?"

Reaching for his handkerchief, Abel wiped the hot, humid July night's perspiration from his forehead. "I wanted to kill him. And if they hadn't stopped me, I would have. I know it. I thought with my prayers to God and your brother's help that I'd left my enemy-killing impulse behind at Chancellorsville, but . . ." Unable to finish, he looked at the ground and shook his head.

Emma squeezed his forearm and looked at him intensely. "Abel, I know you. You are *not* a wanton killer. Whatever you did in your soldiering days, they're over now . . . and I know you asked God's forgiveness for your transgressions. I also know you to be a brave, good, kind, and passionate man who responded to Jack Hurley as any man of your caliber should." Lowering her eyes, she smiled shyly. "And to be perfectly honest, I couldn't have been prouder of you."

Abel's jaw trembled, and his eyes grew moist. "*You're* . . . proud of *me*? Emma, after the way you spoke the hard truth so boldly in your speech back there, it was all I could do not to jump on the table and start clapping and cheering like a wild man."

She laughed. "You would have been handcuffed and escorted out of the room immediately, I assure you."

"Honestly, Emma, how'd you get the courage to say what you did at the end—especially with all those high-powered supporters of Colonel Jack in the audience?"

Emma brushed a stray lock of hair from the side of her forehead. "I remembered that promise I made to Angelina Grimké: to speak up boldly for the oppressed whenever the Lord gave me an opportunity. And then . . ." She paused and glanced at him, a twinkle in her eye.

"And then . . . ?" Abel prompted. Emma hesitated, fearing he might consider what she was about to say to be improper.

She pressed ahead. "And then I scanned the audience and spotted a certain Mr. Bowman, whose gorgeous, encouraging smile and nod gave me all the remaining courage I needed."

Abel blushed and bowed his head, but the broad grin that spread across his face left no doubt how much he treasured her affirmation.

He offered his arm, and they resumed their walk toward her apartment. Abel was strangely quiet, responding mostly in monosyllables to her comments and not even bothering to lift his hat to acknowledge the occasional passersby. She worried that he might still be feeling burdened by his actions at the Maxcy House.

As they approached the short staircase leading up to the doorway, Emma hoped desperately that he would decide to kiss her good night. It would be their first; Abel had been the perfect gentleman on all their previous times together. True, he had frequently held her hand, and on several occasions had hugged her closely. She had craved much more, but, aware of his volatile nature, she had hesitated from pressing him beyond his self-imposed boundaries. But with the way she now felt toward him—especially after all that had happened recently—her desire for the next stage of physical intimacy could no longer be denied. She had waited long enough.

They reached the bottom step, and she turned to face him. She hesitated, wondering if she should encourage things by drawing in closer—not only offering her gloved hand for him to kiss as on previous occasions, but this time also tilting her face up toward his and looking him expectantly in the eyes.

Before she could decide, Abel reached out and grasped both of her hands. His eyes gleamed brightly as they peered directly into hers.

"Emma, tonight confirmed the feelings I've had for you from the first time I saw you . . . and . . . well . . . I want to tell you that I-I love you very much, and I was wondering . . . if it was possible . . . that you might consider marrying me?"

She blinked several times and then stared at him, her mouth slightly ajar as a wave of dizziness seemed to sweep through her entire body. *Did I hear him right?* She took a slight step back, her thoughts a jumbled mixture of elation and panic.

"Why, Mr. Bowman, I-I've always seen you as a very attractive, passionate man, and I truly adore our times together . . . but . . . do you really think we're ready for . . ." At a loss for words, her voice trailed off.

He gripped her hands tighter. "Emma, I'll tell you what I honestly think. I think you are the most beautiful, intelligent, and compassionate woman I've ever known. There is no doubt in my mind that we enjoy each other's company and share the same heart for helping others have a chance for a new and better life. Oh, Emma . . . imagine what it would be like . . . living and working together on our own farm while supporting all the good causes we value. Maybe even start our own school together someday. I can't imagine anyone else with whom I'd rather spend the rest of my days living like that. Would you be willing to consider it?"

Emma blanched, her heart pounding wildly. His proposal—and Abel himself—was everything she could ask for. And yet, now that it was upon her, tiny demons of doubt mounted their attack. *What will happen to Abel's government job and my teaching position if and when this war finally ends? Would we able to afford a farm, and how would I be able to help him tend to it if I'm also fully engaged in teaching?*

"Abel, it truly does sound wonderful, and I *am* willing to consider, but . . . oh, Abel . . . I do have very strong affections for you as well, but I'm just not sure if—"

"Emma . . . wait." He let go of one of her hands and held a finger to his pursed lips. "I knew you'd have some questions and concerns, and we won't solve them all tonight. Nor do I expect you to give me your final answer tonight. I'm just asking you to think upon the idea, and over the next few months, we should have a much better picture of where the war's headed and what it would mean for our marriage."

"So . . . we consider things and keep all this to ourselves for now?"

"I think that would be best . . . but the minute both of us are sure, we'll definitely have to inform the world in some grand way!"

Emma drew in close, wrapping her arms around his waist and laying her head against his chest. The soft caresses of his hand on her shoulders and back combined with the beating of his heart to impart the most contented, happy peace she'd ever known.

"Emma," Abel said softly, "may I kiss you?"

Her heart on the verge of exploding, she lifted her head and peered at him with half-closed eyes and a dreamy smile.

"Mr. Bowman, I was just wondering . . . why on earth has it taken you so long?"

Two days later, Emma and Sallie sat at the kitchen table of their apartment, sipping tea and discussing Emma's plans for her reading class tomorrow at the Smith Plantation.

Still basking in the glow of Abel's unofficial proposal and the memory of their passionate and prolonged first kiss, Emma found it hard to concentrate on the task at hand, as her mind kept drifting back to the incredible evening at the restaurant and afterward. *In the space of forty-eight hours,* she mused, *I was magically transformed from Colonel Hurley's despised accuser into Abel's beloved fiancée. Well, his "soon-to-be fiancée," anyway, once we finalize things.* She wondered how long she would be able to contain herself from spilling the news to Sallie.

A loud knock on the front door interrupted her pleasant thoughts.

"Coming!" She glanced at Sallie as she rose from the table, wondering who in the world would be visiting this time of the afternoon.

She opened the door.

David stood with his hat in his hand, his grin stretching ear to ear.

Beside him, clasping the arm of a young, teenaged Black boy standing shyly next to her, a woman peered beneath the wide brim of her flower-bedecked straw hat.

"Remember us?" she asked softly with a hesitant smile.

Emma stared at them with mouth agape.

Catherine was still beautiful, though her face seemed a bit thinner and the traces of crow's-feet and dark circles around her eyes gave ample evidence of the stress she must have been under the past two years. Lew appeared to have grown two feet since she'd last seen him; his face reminded her of Charles around the age that he'd saved her from the creek waters.

A plethora of confusing feelings swept through Emma as she beheld the sister she'd once loved and trusted completely without reservation.

Uncertain how to react, she turned toward the kitchen. "Sallie, come here . . . quick!"

Her back still heavily bandaged and using a cane to support herself, Sallie was at the door in a few seconds. One look at Lew, and she screamed loud enough to make the carriage horse behind them whinny and stomp its foot. She dropped her cane and threw herself into Lew's arms, nearly smothering him with her hugs and kisses.

Emma returned her gaze to Catherine, whose lips were trembling as a small tear rolled down her cheek.

Her heart melted. She held out her arms and smiled warmly. "Welcome to your new home, sister."

CHAPTER 39

City of Beaufort
Port Royal Island, South Carolina Sea Islands
October 27, 1864
(Three months later)

"There's always a chance, but right now, it doesn't look too good . . . to me at least."

David looked around the living room of the five-bedroom Beaufort townhome that he'd recently succeeded in leasing for Emma, Catherine, Sallie, and Lew. He tried to gauge whether the others present in the room this morning shared his pessimism over the probable outcome of this afternoon's civil court case decision.

There was good reason to worry, he thought. The previous effort in September to gain a criminal conviction against Jack Hurley in the Magnolia Plantation arson incident had hit a wall when Hurley's foreman had suddenly disappeared from the area with no trace. As a result, without the middleman's confession and testimony concerning Hurley's involvement, the criminal case had been dropped by the city prosecutor since he would never be able to prove Hurley's "guilt beyond a reasonable doubt." But would this second attempt—striving for a civil liability judgment, which would require less burden of proof than a criminal conviction—really stand much chance of faring any better?

Abel sat back in his armchair, massaging his jaw and nodding grimly. "I agree. Seems to me our only hope is a fair and courageous judge—one who's willing to believe we at least have enough circumstantial evidence to convince him that Hurley was more than likely behind the act, and who's also tough enough to levy a fitting penalty. But from what I've seen of our judge in the hearings so far . . . I'm not too encouraged."

Catherine entered the room, carrying a tray of rice griddle cake slices topped with blueberries that she'd prepared for this morning's informal gathering. After walking around the circle of attendees—which included David, Abel, Emma, Sallie, William Johnson, Mr. Shaw, and George Skipwith—and inviting each to partake, she set the tray down on the serving table and took her own seat next to Emma on the couch.

David couldn't help but smile at the sight of his two sisters side by side, together again. It was one that, not so long ago, he'd feared he would never see. *Thank God for Pastor Jones.* Were it not for the love and concern he'd shown toward him and his sisters with all his advice, encouragement, and determination to stay in touch over the past four years, there would likely never have been any reunion.

In fact, it was only through Pastor Jones's timely intervention after David's arrival at the Hodge Plantation that Catherine and Lew had been able to accompany him back to South Carolina. Jones had convinced General Hinks's adjutant officer to temporarily retract the "abandoned-by-owner" label for the plantation . . . allowing time for David to work with his Washington contacts to validate Catherine's claim to title and ensure that the confiscated property would revert to her full, legal control at war's end. Until then, Jones had volunteered to act as Catherine's officially designated property manager during her extended stay with her sister and friends in the Sea Islands, thus proving to the Union occupiers her continued interest and stake in the property while she was away.

It was fascinating, David thought, to watch Cat and Emma attempt to delicately navigate the treacherous waters of their past disagreements and perceived mutual offenses. Their initial reencounter had been marked by a glorious display of heartfelt joy, relief, and mutual empathy over the hardships each had faced. Catherine had gratefully accepted Emma's invitation to help her and Sallie with the teaching effort at the Smith Plantation. The new living arrangement had started out well, with both women clearly doing their best to encourage and support each other. But as the weeks of Catherine's "extended stay" had turned into months and they'd settled into their new routines while living under the same roof once again, some of the familiar patterns had begun to emerge. On occasions when he would be in town and stop by for a visit, it felt as if the old, unresolved tensions between his sisters were still simmering underneath the surface, occasionally bubbling over in the form of snippy remarks or annoyed expressions. *Oh, well,* he concluded, *this is* their *relationship to make or break together. They'll just have to learn to work things out.*

George Skipwith—the Black foreman whom Hurley had previously demoted as part of his "new labor policy" for the Magnolia freedmen— spoke up. "And what happens if the civil court judge *does* find Hurley guilty? Would he go to prison?"

"Unfortunately, no," William Johnson responded. He reached for another cake slice from the tray and handed it to Sallie, who—still experiencing occasional pain from her injuries—was reclining on the chaise longue next to him. "That's the difference between a criminal and a civil court case. The most we'll get out of these civil proceedings is a financial penalty. And how severe that will be is up to the judge."

"If you ask me," Mr. Shaw ventured, "there's no financial penalty great enough to compensate for the loss of life for poor Mandy and the injuries that Clara and Sallie suffered. The man who authorized that arson fire deserves a special place in hell."

David shook his head sadly. "All we can do at this point is hope and pray we'll see a penalty that will at least put a dent in Hurley's comfortable lifestyle for a while. Heaven knows we've given it our best shot to help bring that about." He glanced at Abel. "Those were absolutely scathing testimonies that you, Emma, and George provided to the judge last week concerning Hurley's vindictive character and his unfair policies toward the freedmen. And if you combine that with the arsonist's confession and testimony, you'd think we'd have a pretty good case. But . . . who knows? We'll find out soon." He reached for another griddle cake, but before biting into it, asked, "Cat, will you be coming with us to the court this afternoon?"

Catherine hesitated. "No, I think I'll stay behind with Sallie and Lew, if that's all right with you."

Emma's eyes flashed. "Cat, I can't believe it! After how hard the rest of us have all been working to make this day happen, don't you even care to hear the outcome?"

"Of course I care, Em. It's just that my stomach is feeling very unsettled today. And besides . . . after what I went through in Virginia with Sam Taylor, I'm not anxious to dwell on yet another evil man's horrible story. I'll learn the outcome soon enough—when you all come back and tell me."

Emma sat back with a sigh, shaking her head and rolling her eyes as Catherine stood and walked over to pick up the tray.

David glanced at his timepiece. "Well, it's time to head to court—for whoever wishes to go." He looked around the room at each person present. "And may God grant *all* of us satisfaction in this matter today."

The Beaufort city courtroom was packed with court officials, litigants, their attorneys and supporters, curious spectators, and several local newspaper reporters, all awaiting anxiously for the judge's final decision to be announced in the civil case of "Magnolia Plantation Freedmen versus Jonathan Hurley." It had been a while since this type of event had attracted such widespread interest in the region; no doubt, the involvement of the heretofore widely respected and admired Colonel Jack—the "future mayor of Beaufort"—had swelled the numbers.

David, sitting beside Emma in the first row of spectator seats, took a few moments to look around and survey the overall scene.

As the freedmen's legally appointed Caucasian representative, Abel Bowman sat with George Skipwith and Mr. Shaw, consulting with their hired attorney at the plaintiff's table in front. In the rows immediately behind David, at least twenty of the Magnolia freedmen talked animatedly among themselves—obviously hoping for a decision that would validate their cause. On the other side of the aisle, Jack Hurley stood with his team of lawyers in front of the defendant's table, laughing and joking as if the outcome of the case had already been rigged in his favor.

It was the sight of the Union officer seated in the front center row of the balcony, however, that caught David by complete surprise.

General Rufus Saxton, military governor of the Sea Islands District and overall head of the Port Royal Experiment, had obviously decided for some reason that his presence was needed at the concluding session today. Given the general's known antipathy toward Hurley and his "business-first" approach to ex-slave transition, David wondered how he would respond to today's decision—especially if it favored Hurley.

The courtroom clock struck two. Everyone took their seats, and an expectant hush settled over the audience.

From a side door, the seventy-some, frail, and tired-looking Judge William Bonnet entered the room and tottered to his seat. David closed his eyes, hung his head, and shook it. Already, he was getting a bad sense of how things were about to turn out. In the previous days' hearings, Bonnet had at times seemed to struggle staying awake despite the stirring testimonies of the plaintiffs and the heated denials and excuses of the defendant. Today, the elderly judge almost looked to be suffering from a hangover.

The clerk called the court into session and reread the charges against Hurley. All eyes fell on Judge Bonnet as he opened a black folder and launched into a rambling—at times almost incomprehensible—revisiting of the facts and his analysis of the testimonies that he'd heard. After nearly fifteen minutes, he looked up from his notes and put his spectacles down on the desk. He coughed violently, cleared his throat, and peered out at the audience . . . as if noticing them for the first time.

Emma gripped David's hand with both of hers.

Judge Bonnet spoke. "Before I announce my final decision in this matter, let me first say that—in the matter of how best to help freedmen transition from their former state into self-sufficient, contributing members of society—I do not believe there has yet been demonstrated any single, perfect solution that will work for everyone, everywhere across the nation. Accordingly, my decision today will *not* be prejudiced by my personal preference for what some abolitionists call the 'charity and reparations-first' approach over the 'business-first' approach now advocated by Colonel Hurley and others. In fact, if wisely and humanely administered, there *is* much that may be said in support of the latter— and I believe that is indeed what Colonel Hurley may have originally intended when he purchased the Magnolia Plantation..." Bonnet paused to turn to the side and engage in yet another fit of wheezing and coughing into his handkerchief.

David's heart sank. Clearly, *this* judge had neither the will nor the stamina to call out Jack Hurley's actions for what they truly were: the outworkings of a selfish, evil heart. He glanced toward the defense table and saw Hurley sitting back with his arms folded and a perfectly relaxed smile on his face. Abel turned and glanced at him with a for- lorn expression while Emma buried her face on his shoulder, preparing herself for the worst.

Judge Bonnet finally recovered from his coughing and picked up where he'd left off.

"But all that said, from the evidence and testimonies that I have heard and studied in this case over the past several sessions, it is clear to me that Colonel Hurley never followed through on his original good intentions—if indeed, he ever really had any. In fact, quite the oppo- site. Within weeks, he had implemented what can only be described as repressive labor policies that treated the freedmen as little more than serfs.

"And while that by itself is insufficient to render a criminal judgment against him for the fatal arson fire, if it is combined with the prepon- derance of evidence and testimony that have been presented to me by the arsonist and other witnesses such as Mr. Bowman, Miss Hodge, and Mr. Skipwith, then I can come to but one conclusion: Colonel Jonathan Hurley authorized and paid for the burning of the Magnolia schoolhouse, with the motive of removing it as an impediment to his own business profits. And hence, *this court deems Colonel Hurley legally liable* for the wrongful death, injury, and loss of property associated with such fire."

The collective gasp throughout the courtroom quickly transitioned to dumbfounded expressions and excited chatter. David and Abel stared at each other, mouths agape. Where was this going? Bonnet banged his gavel, and a stunned silence immediately ensued. The judge peered down once again at his notes.

"As a result of this judgment, liability in the case of 'Magnolia Plantation Freedmen versus Jonathan Hurley' is assigned as follows: Colonel Hurley is held responsible for all damages to the Magnolia Plantation schoolhouse, and for the complete payment of all reconstruction costs required.

"Furthermore, Colonel Hurley is held liable for the negligent homicide of the student Mandy Hostler, for the severe injuries suffered by the teachers Clara Jenkins and Sallie Cobb, and for the complete payment of all funeral and medical costs they and their families have so far and may continue to incur.

"Finally, in view of the malicious nature and intent of Colonel Hurley's actions, this court orders that punitive damages be awarded to the Magnolia Plantation Freedmen collectively in the amount of fifteen thousand US dollars, payable by Colonel Hurley no later than the thirty-first of December 1864."

Judge Bonnet banged his gavel to finalize the verdict, rose awkwardly, and walked out the side door. Within seconds after the clerk had repeated the verdict and handed Hurley's lawyers a printed copy, the entire plaintiff's side of the courtroom exploded with shouts and cries of joy and exhilaration. Emma leaned over the railing to hug Abel, George, and Mr. Shaw as David turned to receive the grateful embraces of Mandy Hostler's parents and the other freedmen.

After the commotion had died down a bit, David peeked cautiously in the direction of the defense table. Jack Hurley sat in his chair, angrily remonstrating with his lawyers as he wiped his florid face with a handkerchief. Catching David's glance, he stood and stalked over to the plaintiff's table where Abel, Emma, and the others were laughing and speaking in disbelief of the miracle that had just occurred. His presence brought them all to immediate attention.

"Congratulations, Mr. Bowman and Miss Hodge. Your lies and hatred of me seem to have won the day."

"It's nothing you didn't deserve, Hurley," Abel said icily.

Hurley stared at him like a cobra about to strike. Finally, he turned and walked toward the front exit.

On his own way out with the others a few minutes later, David was stopped in the lobby by General Saxton. He offered his hand. "Congratulations to your side for carrying the case today, Mr. Hodge."

David grinned. "I must admit, General, I had my doubts with Judge Bonnet there for a while."

Saxton smiled at him, a gleam in his eye. "He's an old abolitionist friend of mine. Open-minded, but tough when he has to be. We're fortunate he was the only district judge available at the time to take on this important case."

David couldn't resist. "May I be so bold as to ask . . . is it possible *you* might have had something to do with that good fortune, sir?"

Saxton laughed and clapped him on the shoulder. "Now, that one's between me and God, Mr. Hodge."

(One month later)

Ruined.

The word kept pounding over and over like a hammer inside the front lobe of Jack Hurley's brain as he sat alone at the small table in the rear of the nearly empty Beaufort waterfront tavern, hunched over his fourth glass of straight bourbon.

The mortifying realization had finally hit home earlier this afternoon—a month to the day following the courtroom debacle, and five seconds after reading the jointly written letter he'd received in the mail from his Boston investment partners:

In view of the civil judgment against you and the negative portrayal of your character and actions in the recent Boston Globe *article, we have decided that it is in our best interests to terminate our respective business agreements with you. We furthermore demand immediate repayment in full on the balance of all loans advanced to you by our respective agencies, and will pursue all legal remedies at our disposal to collect if such payments are not received by January 5, 1865.*

It was an impossible burden. The civil case judgment alone was enough to break him, forcing him to sell all three of his Sea Island properties at undesirable prices and eating up virtually all his remaining liquid assets by the end of the year. Now he would face a mountain of unpaid debt and abject poverty—forever beholden to the whims and mercies of unscrupulous partners whom he had once rescued in a big way from their own sorry plights, enriching both them and himself.

So much for ungrateful backstabbers, he thought bitterly. And so much for all those former high-level friends and supporters in the abolitionist community. Once he'd stopped supporting the idealistic "land reparations" philosophy of Congressman Stevens and purchased the Sea Islands properties for himself, Stevens and his circle had quickly cut contacts and effectively disbarred him from further interaction with them. And now, with the damaging *Globe* article, all hopes of future credibility, respect, or financial support from *any* abolitionist- or reconstruction-connected organization were forever dashed.

Yes, "ruined" was putting it mildly, he despaired.

As if an old, familiar adversary had decided they could no longer delay making their taunting presence known, another line of thought suddenly rang in his mind out of nowhere.

You know who's to blame, Jack.

Of course, he was willing to admit he himself had made a couple of stupid mistakes. Like thinking he absolutely *had* to get rid of the schoolhouse in order to ensure his profits would stay above water. In retrospect, he knew that wasn't true. Certainly, it would have been a much tighter squeeze if he'd continued to allow schooltime for the freedmen, but his finances would probably have held up. But in any case, once he'd committed to the arson idea, he had made his second error in judgment by thinking he could rely on that complete fool of a foreman he'd asked to find, recruit, and pay off a competent arsonist. At least, he tried to console himself, he'd avoided a criminal conviction and lengthy prison sentence by paying the foreman a substantial sum of money to voluntarily disappear from the area prior to the prosecutor's call to testify.

But his own mistakes aside, the real culprits behind his mostly undeserved downfall were crystal clear in Jack Hurley's eyes.

Emma Hodge, that compassionate mother hen who was constantly clucking of her never-ending concern for her "oppressed, victimized" Magnolia freedmen, had helped to stir their discontent against his policies from the day he'd purchased the property. Worse, she'd mercilessly attacked his character and reputation, publicly humiliating him at the missionary recognition supper and later in the courtroom.

However, it had been Abel Bowman—that wild-eyed, priggish moralist who loved to wrap himself in the antislavery emotionalism inspired by his Eye of Glory flag—who had done the most damage. Jumping at the offer to be interviewed by a local newspaper reporter a few days after the civil court decision, Bowman had been unsparing in resurfacing old rumors, maligning motives, and condemning certain actions that Hurley had taken in the business, political, and army spheres of his life . . . attempting to demonstrate how these had all come to shape the "evil nature" of the man who had authorized and paid for the Magnolia Plantation fire.

Obviously, Bowman had researched his subject well. His salacious comments had been reported almost verbatim, and the local article had been noticed and quickly snapped up by the *Boston Globe*. And once the *Globe* had published their story, Hurley's public reputation—not to mention his means of financial survival—had been effectively eradicated.

Hurley poured himself yet another glass of bourbon and gulped down half of it. He had tried to put off the inevitable question since receiving the letter this afternoon . . . but it was time to face it. The taunting voice inside his head was now too strong to suppress.

They beat you, Jack. But are you going to spend the rest of your life living in poverty, forever tormented with the memories of how they humiliated and disgraced you? Hell, if you're still furious over your boyhood memories of how contemptibly you and your family were treated by those rich Beaufort aristocrats, how will you ever be able to forget something like this? *And so, Jack, what's next?*

Hurley stared at the amber liquid remaining in his glass, pondering how to answer. He closed his eyes and imagined the little village in southern France that he had once visited as a child with his parents. He had loved it and had always wanted to return one day.

Like a bolt of lightning, the idea struck.

I've still got a little money . . .

He smiled and drained his glass.

CHAPTER 40

City of Beaufort
Port Royal Island, South Carolina Sea Islands
January 1, 1865
(Two months later)

Everyone agreed: it was the best New Year's Day supper they had ever had. Especially delightful for David was the company, including his wife and stepdaughter, whom he'd coaxed into accompanying him from their Ohio home to celebrate the holidays with his sisters and friends.

"Compliments to our cooks!" David said after dessert had been served, raising his champagne glass and prompting the other adults at the townhome dining table to follow suit. "To my beautiful wife Sarah and my wonderful friend Sallie Cobb . . . without doubt the two best culinary artists east of the Mississippi River!"

Sarah, sitting next to him, smiled and blushed as she slapped him playfully on the shoulder. "Oh, David . . . *really*! Isn't that just a little much?" She glanced across the table at Sallie and William. "What do you think, Sallie?"

Sallie giggled. "I think I like bein' called the best . . . um . . . *whatever* that was!"

After the laughter died down and Sarah turned to help their young daughter Jenny ladle some thick cream sauce over her bread pudding, David pushed his chair back from the table a bit, crossed one leg over the other, and rested his forearm across his abdomen.

"It seems we all had quite an eventful 1864, to put it mildly," he observed. "I think we should go around the table and have everyone share briefly the one or two things they are most looking forward to in 1865. The only thing we can't mention is the final end of this wretched war, which is coming soon, and we'll just assume it's at the top of everyone's list."

"Well, brother," Emma said, "since you suggested it, I think you should be the one to set the example for us."

David smiled fondly at Sarah and Jenny. "After my twelve extended trips by coach and steamship from Ohio to South Carolina since accepting the project inspector appointment a year and a half ago, I can safely say my family is in complete agreement. What we look forward to the most is the delivery of my final report on the Port Royal Experiment's progress to Secretary Chase in Washington on our way back home from here. After that, my loyal and 'able' assistant—does that description seem to fit, Mr. Bowman?—will take over the reins from me here as government project inspector, and after a month's vacation, I'll be starting my new position at the *Cleveland Leader* as associate editor for postwar, reconstruction-related issues."

"And *that*," Sarah explained, "means Jenny and I will finally have a captive husband and father to help tend the farm, lift our spirits, and keep us safe and sound. I know how important this project inspector job has been, but there comes a time when a wife would like to have her husband around more than one week a month."

David laughed. "No doubt, I'll have more than a few things on my dear wife's list to take care of as soon as we get back." He raised his arm with extended index finger and circled it teasingly in the air before leveling it to point at the next designated sharer of new year's hopes. "Lew! And what are *you* looking forward to the most, young man?"

The boy looked as if he'd been asked to solve the world's most complex mathematics problem. He squeezed his eyes shut and squirmed in his chair for several seconds, prompting Sallie to cuff him lightly on the back. "Come on, little brother, it ain't that hard a question."

Lew's face finally broke out in a wide grin. "I know. Thing I'm lookin' forward to the most is going deer huntin' this month with Mr. Abel."

"I think Lew just stole my answer!" Abel joked, leaning over to playfully rub the top of the boy's head. "And if he shoots as straight as he's been showing me at our weekly target practice, then between him and me, those poor deer don't stand a chance!"

David cocked his head. "'*Our* weekly target practice'? When did *that* start?"

"Right after you left for Ohio once the Hurley court case had been settled. Lew was helping me clean up my apartment one day and he saw the closet with my old hunting rifles. He expressed interest, so I asked if he'd like to learn how to shoot. Every Saturday morning since then, we've been setting up some old cans on a fence and firing away. He's a darn good shot! In fact, *so* good that I suggested we take a day in January and go after deer on Hunting Island."

Sallie, who had effectively assumed the role of unofficial guardian for Lew following his arrival in Beaufort with Catherine, offered her own perspective. "I just hope my little brother don't show up afterward on our doorstep here with a dead little doe over his shoulder—expectin' *me* to dress the poor thing. You gonna teach him how to do that too, Mr. Abel?"

Abel laughed. "No worries, Sallie. He'll be an *expert* at field-dressing by the time I've finished training him."

"So, Sallie," David suggested, "now that we've heard from Lew, why don't you share next?"

Sallie glanced hesitantly across the table at William Johnson, who smiled and nodded as if to encourage her to share whatever was on her heart.

"Well, looks like come April or May, I'll be havin' a new job."

Emma's eyes widened. Had the romantic inclinations that had been developing between Sallie and William ever since the schoolhouse fire now taken a dramatic new turn? "Sallie, are you and Mr. Johnson . . . ?"

Sallie and William gaped at her in stunned silence for a moment before breaking out in embarrassed laughter. "Oh, no, no, Emmy," Sallie finally managed. "Not *that*. I mean . . . really . . . a new *job*. Maybe I should just let William explain."

"I just received a letter from my AMA supervisor in New York," William said. "It seems some changes are afoot. After General Sherman captured Savannah just before Christmas, he had a talk with some Black Baptist and Methodist ministers there about what to do with the recently liberated Georgia slaves who've been following his army like refugees. Sherman will likely soon be marching his army up the coast toward Charleston. And when he does, it's rumored he's going to issue some kind of special new 'field order' that'll grant free plots of con-fiscated land along the way to the former slaves—and also lend them mules to help them get their new small farms started. 'Forty Acres and a Mule' for each Black family, is what my supervisor's hearing."

"Free plots of land? Mules?" David asked incredulously. "That's even better than what the government was offering to the Sea Islands freed-men when we first joined the Port Royal Experiment—that is, before they decided to yank even *that* offer away and put the lands up for auction. Let's hope General Sherman's plan doesn't also wither under the heat of Washington politics or some new 'military necessity.' But anyway . . . what's this have to do with you—and Sallie?"

"My supervisor wrote that if things turn out like they're expecting, there will soon be a huge need for AMA people—administrators and teachers—in the coastal areas south of here. They want me ready to be reassigned there at a moment's notice. And"—he looked affectionately at Sallie—"he asked me if I knew anyone else I'd recommend to help with the teaching support needs there."

Emma gasped. "Sallie, does this mean what I think it does?"

Sallie smiled at her and nodded, bittersweet tears in her eyes despite her obvious excitement at the prospects of a new life ahead with William. Emma turned to embrace her. "I am so proud and happy for you," she said softly. Still holding Sallie, she turned her face toward William. "Mr. Johnson, I only have one request."

"What's that, Miss Em?"

"That you'll never forget how lucky you are to have this amazing woman helping you, because I know I'm going to miss her terribly in so many ways!"

William smiled. "I promise, Miss Em."

David allowed a few moments for emotions to settle before calling for the next testimony. He considered asking Catherine but noticed she appeared strangely tense and out of sorts, as if for some reason she were wishing she were elsewhere.

"Mr. Bowman, would you do us the honor?"

Abel cleared his throat. "Well, besides the deer-hunting expedition with Lew, I'd say there are two things that I look forward to the most in 1865 . . . and you might say the two are, well, 'intimately connected.'"

"That certainly sounds mysterious!" David laughed. "What's the first? Something to do with your new role as lead project inspector, I suppose?"

"That's right. Overseeing the rebuilding of the Glory School—bigger and better than what it was before. Now that the Magnolia freedmen collectively *own* the plantation property that Hurley was forced to sell them at a bargain rate after the court settlement, they are bound and determined to quickly replace what he destroyed. And having just received—am I correct, William?—the funds from the extra punitive damages against Hurley that were awarded to them, they now have more than enough to get started on building the finest schoolhouse in the entire Sea Islands District."

"A worthy undertaking," David said. "Sounds like they'll be needing a new schoolhouse flag soon. Since we were never able to find out what Hurley did with the first one that his arsonist stole, will you be making them a new one?"

Abel grinned. "Only if they ask me. Of course, I'll always wish we could have gotten the original back, but with Hurley now out of the area and gone for good . . . there's no real hope for *that.*"

"So, what's that second thing you said you were looking forward to, Abel?" William asked.

"Well, I—" Abel started to respond, then turned to look at Emma. "Would *you* like to explain this one?"

Emma smiled, her face radiant as she looked around the table.

"Come on, Emma . . ." David said impatiently. "Stop keeping us in suspense."

"Abel officially proposed to me yesterday, and I accepted!"

The momentary silence in response to the shock of the announcement was immediately replaced with loud whoops and cries of joy and congratulations, followed by handshakes and hugs as everyone stood to celebrate the newly engaged couple.

After all were seated again, David picked up the conversation. "What will this mean for your teaching and AMA connections, Emma? And where will you two be living?"

"Oh, for the foreseeable future, I'll be continuing to teach at the Smith Plantation, with the AMA sponsoring me. In fact, they've asked me to consider writing up a journalistic-type account for the *Atlantic Monthly* of my experiences here in the Sea Islands teaching freedmen, which I'm very excited to do for them. As for where we'll live, in the long term, we'll just have to see how things evolve with the war, the AMA, and Abel's government position. But for the next year at least, we plan to live here on Port Royal Island somewhere. In fact, tomorrow, while Abel is working, I'll be touring a possible home-for-rent in a quiet spot just outside the city that has been recommended to us. Cat—who I confess I broke the news to about all this yesterday—said she would accompany me to give me her much appreciated 'expert opinion' on such things. Are you still up for that, Cat?"

Catherine smiled—a bit tightly, David thought. "Of course, Em."

"Well, that brings us to our last but not least testimony for the evening . . . Catherine, what are you most looking forward to in 1865?"

Catherine glanced at him oddly, her lips trembling and her eyes clearly moist. Suddenly she set her napkin down on the table, stood up, and excused herself from the room.

✑

"Cat, what's wrong? Please . . . tell me."

"Nothing's wrong, Em. Absolutely nothing. How could anything be wrong . . . especially after all the wonderful news and hopes for the future that everyone shared tonight?"

Emma hesitated. Catherine's overly breezy, slightly sarcastic tone had seemed to belie her words.

Not wishing to unduly provoke things, Emma closed her sister's bedroom door to ensure their privacy. "Well, I'm not sure, but for some reason you didn't seem very happy about any of it. I don't think I saw you smile once during the entire meal or afterward. And why didn't you want to share your hopes for next year, like the rest of us? There must be something you're looking forward to."

"Emma," said Catherine as she sat at her dresser, unpinning her hair, "do you have *any* idea what it's like to feel . . . utterly . . . *alone*?"

Emma stared at her. She'd spent hours with her sister the day she and Lew had arrived in Beaufort, welcoming the news of Sam Taylor's demise, commending Catherine for her bravery, consoling her on her hardships and personal losses—being totally supportive in every way that she could. Hadn't they been through this already?

"Certainly not in the way you have, Cat," she said softly, "having lost Joe and your baby. But I do—"

Catherine whirled on her stool to face her. "No, Em, you have *no idea* what it's like. I am very happy for you and Abel—I truly am—but when it comes to everybody expecting me to act like everything is now behind me, that I should just 'get over the past' and express a happy, joyful vision of my own for next year . . . I'm sorry, but I am not ready for that.

"There are way too many things that are still up in the air. Such as . . . will I *really* get the plantation back, and if so, when will it happen? And although I know Pastor Jones and his wife will continue to be great sources of spiritual comfort and hope, how will I restore and manage the plantation's tobacco operation completely on my own, with no husband or relatives or friends to support me and no one to work the crops? Yes, I've discovered that I have a good mind for bookkeeping and the business end of things. Out of sheer necessity, I've learned much along those lines since Papa died. But to find and hire a knowledgeable crop manager who can help me build a new, wage-based labor force and get it working profitably will be a hugely complicated and costly task—one that I'm not looking forward to taking on alone."

"Cat, I definitely understand, and please forgive me for being insensitive. But isn't there a rather obvious way to resolve your dilemma?"

Catherine grimaced and spread her arms, palms up. "What—just go advertise myself by traipsing around Petersburg when the war ends, trying to land a new husband?"

"Well, as young and attractive as you still are, that's certainly one option. But I was thinking of another one."

"Which is . . . ?"

"Cat, why don't you just sell the plantation—or perhaps lease it—and live here permanently in Beaufort near Abel and me, or . . . if you'd prefer, move to Cleveland near David and Sarah? I'm sure they'd love to have you near them, just like I would."

Catherine's face softened. She was speechless for several seconds, seeming to have been genuinely touched. "That's very kind of you to offer, Em. But . . . honestly, what would I *do* here or in Cleveland, exactly? Who would I *be*? Everything I've ever known, everything I've aspired to . . . it—it's all tied up in the life of a plantation mistress and her society connections."

Emma frowned. "But you know that glorious, old, former way of life will never return, Cat. Not with the end of slavery and the South losing the war."

"So," Catherine said, her eyes narrowed and head cocked slightly, "you're saying I should just give up our magnificent family plantation and become your typical city war widow—tending my little house with no land, watering my flowerpots, hosting a small party for other widows and spinsters once a month, attending church and occasionally the theater? Oh, it depresses me to even think about the dullness and captivity of it all."

"Cat, life in the city doesn't have to be like that. After all, there are so many great causes to serve—"

"You can stop right there, sister. I know what you're going to suggest: that I should become a freedmen-uplifting zealot like you and David. And unless I excitedly espouse some glorious personal vision for 1865 that's in line with the ones you and the others have each expressed today, then there's something wrong with me in your eyes, and you can never completely accept or respect me."

Emma threw her hands up in the air. "Cat, that's not true! Of course I accept you and I love you. It's just that . . ."

Catherine crossed her arms and sighed. "It's just . . . what, Em?"

"I'm just saying, the Confederacy is nearly finished—and good riddance as far as I'm concerned. But with it gone, there is so much that will need to be done . . . for the freedmen, I mean. And after what I personally experienced on our own plantation and learned from the writings of others, I simply can't rest. In fact, it's difficult for me to see how *anyone* who's ever been complicit with the system that enslaved them and their ancestors can rest, either. For privileged White southern women like you and me to just sit passively by and do nothing to help lift them up seems to me, well, evil."

Catherine stood up from her stool and jammed her hands onto her hips. "And so, given my 'privilege,' since I have no real concern or desire like you to devote the rest of my life and resources to uplifting the poor, Black masses, then I suppose that makes *me* evil in your sight and the sight of God as well?"

Emma shook her head impatiently. "I'm not saying *you* are evil, Cat. All I'm saying is that, in general, I believe that passivity in the face of obvious human need is profoundly immoral."

"I must say, Emma, you have become quite the expert at laying on the guilt."

"I'm not laying anything on you, Cat. Your own defensiveness speaks to the guilt that you yourself are feeling about your lack of any real interest in the future of the freedmen . . . and none of that is *my* doing. And another thing I may as well get off my chest . . . now that you've brought it up."

Catherine stared at her warily. "What?"

"You're not the only one of us who's experienced loneliness and— even worse—rejection by those they were counting on."

Catherine rolled her eyes. "If you're still thinking about my selfish choice to extend my honeymoon over returning in time to help you persuade Papa about the danger Charles was facing, I thought you'd already forgiven me—over two years ago."

"I did forgive you for that. But there were other things, Cat. Even after Charles's death, I came to you and shared my fears that more bad things were about to happen between Sam Taylor and the slaves. And if you'd been a bit more believing of the things I was warning of—and just a little less blindly supportive of Papa's constant denials—then maybe things would have turned out differently. Maybe Sallie and Lew would still have their parents. And maybe *I* wouldn't have felt so alone and rejected by my own big sister, whom I'd thought I could trust."

"Oh, so *that's* it, isn't it?" Catherine nodded angrily. "So you're saying it was all *my* fault that you came to feel that way. So much so that you decided to flee the plantation. Leaving *me* alone to watch Papa die—as much from a broken heart over both you and David deserting the family as from his physical condition."

"Don't you *dare* try to blame me for Papa's death!" Emma snapped. "You know I loved both Mother and Papa, and how I took care of Mother during her final sickness. And I would have stayed to care for Papa as well, had it not been for his stubborn refusal to acknowledge and stop the abuse he was allowing to happen on his own plantation."

Catherine folded her arms and stared at the floor. In a quiet voice, she said, "It's true Papa had his blind spots—whether intentional or not—and I was willing to look the other way for far too long, trying not to upset him."

Emma's face softened. "But you did finally look at the truth, Cat, and you acted on it—as boldly and decisively as anyone could possibly be expected to do. It's just that times have changed. You can't keep holding on to your old ways of thinking about the glory of the 'good old life' on the plantation if you expect to have any hope or vision for the future."

"Well," Catherine retorted with unexpected vehemence, "if *that's* what you believe I'm doing and you disapprove, then far be it from someone like *me* to advise someone like *you* on a house to lease. My old, traditional ways of thinking about things would obviously cloud my judgment. I'm staying here tomorrow. You and Abel can go together and make your own final decision."

Emma stared at her. "*What?* Cat, I can't believe you're doing this. You know good and well Abel can't go with me tomorrow because he'll be off doing another inspection tour. If you want to know the truth . . . *this* is what I most feared about reuniting with you—that you'd still be the same self-centered sister I left behind at the plantation." Exasperated, she threw her hands in the air. "All right then, *don't* go with me. I'll get Sallie to go with me. Or maybe I'll just go by myself. It won't be the first time you've left those as my only options."

She stalked out of the room.

CHAPTER 41

City of Beaufort
Port Royal Island, South Carolina Sea Islands
January 2, 1865

Awaking the next morning earlier than usual, Abel lay staring at the darkened ceiling of the bedroom in his rented two-story apartment overlooking the Beaufort River waterfront.

He rolled over and checked his timepiece. It was only 4:30 A.M.— five hours before Lew would be arriving to accompany him on today's scheduled inspection of two plantations located in remote areas of St. Helena's Island. The boy had certainly been a great help on these tours over the past two months: driving the carriage while Abel reviewed or wrote up his findings in the passenger seat; aiding the measurement of food-crop plots; checking farming equipment for proper functioning; running miscellaneous errands, and the like.

He wondered for a moment if he should have released Lew to accompany Emma and Sallie on their own final inspection of the house-for-rent this morning. After Emma had informed him at the conclusion of last night's supper about Catherine's petulant decision to stay home today, he'd tried once again to convince her to wait until he was free next week so that the two of them could go look things over together. Emma, though, had countered that to wait another day might well mean their ideal opportunity could be lost to another interested leaser. Besides, she'd argued, it would be broad daylight, the rental agent whom she'd met last week at his Beaufort office to arrange the tour was a kind and gentle old man, and she would have Sallie to accompany her. Things would go fine. Plus, since Abel and she had previously seen the outside of the place, having Emma check out the interior should be sufficient to make a final decision by this evening. They could put their initial deposit down tomorrow morning. Abel would then be able to give up his Beaufort apartment and take up residence alone in their newly rented house until the wedding, which was now planned for early March.

Unable to fall back asleep, Abel lit the oil lamp, got dressed, and went to his desk to complete the report for his previous inspection that was due in the mail to Washington tomorrow morning.

I now see what David meant when he said filling out these things was the most laborious, unenjoyable—

A slight noise from downstairs caused him to start. It had sounded as if someone was at the front door, playing pranks or worse. It would not be the first time that had happened in this area of the city; there had been at least three nighttime intrusions reported over the past few weeks. Two had come to nothing, but one had resulted in the owner being tied up and robbed.

The noise occurred again, a bit softer this time. Abel quietly stood and turned to open the glass door of the tall bookcase just behind his desk. Reaching for the top shelf, he placed his hand on the cold brass handle of the weapon he had thought was destined to remain there, safely encased in its leather scabbard until the day he died—nothing more than a personal "museum piece" commemorating the legacy of John Brown, the man who had once inspired him to commit egregious acts of violence against the avowed enemies of the "Great Cause" of abolition.

He took the sheathed broadsword from the shelf and returned to his desk with it, keeping his ear attuned for further noises from downstairs. There was nothing more. *Probably just imagining things.* He relaxed a bit and sat down, laying the weapon reverently on the desk in front of him. The "Glory Sword," he'd dubbed it. He gazed at the handle, admiring the engraved lettering and the artistic eye that had made him weep with emotion the first time he'd beheld it closely in the diffuse light filtering through the barn-shed window on his family's Kansas farm.

"Maybe, son, you'll get another chance for glory someday," Mr. Brown had assured him when gifting the bloody weapon to him following the massacre at Pottawatomie.

Another sound from downstairs. Someone was definitely trying to break in the front door.

Slowly, Abel pulled the sword from its sheath. Deciding against taking the oil lamp with him, he stood up and moved with stealth toward the staircase.

He descended the stairs in the dark. Halfway down, he could see that the front door was halfway open and moonlight was illuminating the entranceway. Holding the sword with his arm raised in striking position, he advanced toward the door. Whoever it was, he was poised to help them meet their maker.

He reached the door, opened it wide, and peered outside. Nothing. Just the lapping of the river water against the pier. He heard something behind him and started to turn, but it was too late.

The rainclouds that had been hovering since early this morning had finally started to release their contents, drenching the area with a steady, cold drizzle.

Emma stood with arms folded, facing the townhome's living room window and staring out at the lowering sky as Sallie entered with a tray of tea and light breakfast items for two.

"Here we go, Miss Em," Sallie said, placing the tray on the side table. "Why don't you come eat somethin'? It'll make you feel better."

Emma turned away from the window and walked over to the side table where Sallie already had a small plate of toast and a cup of tea waiting for her.

"Thank you, Sallie," she said gloomily as she took a seat in one of the plush armchairs. "Now I'm wondering if we should just call off today's visit to the rental home."

After filling her own teacup, Sallie sat down on the sofa. "What? You gonna let a few dewdrops like this stop you from keepin' that appointment? If the agent shows up there and we don't, might be the end of your chances to get that place—unless you ready to just put that deposit money down tomorrow without first seein' the insides. Besides, it ain't pourin' that hard . . . I'll just tell Lew to go put up the rain cover on the carriage and bring it around to us, and we won't even get wet."

Emma sighed. "Yes, I suppose you're right. After my conversation with Cat last night, I think I'm feeling a little depressed, looking for any excuse to just stay home today and mope."

"Oh my goodness," Sallie said with a knowing chuckle. "Mizz Cat sure know how to get you all rattled."

Emma placed her teacup on the saucer, wondering how she should express things. "Sallie," she said finally, "let me ask you something. Do you think it's the responsibility before God of every White man and woman who was a former slaveowner—or had parents who were slaveowners—to not only ask their former slaves for forgiveness, but also to make amends with them?"

Sallie frowned. "What you mean by . . . *amends*?"

"Oh, direct payments of money or land, devoting a good portion of one's time and skills to helping freedmen get their new life started, serving or donating generously to charitable causes that work exclusively for the benefit of former slaves, things like that. After what you and your family went through on our plantation, wouldn't you demand to see things like those as true evidence of a former slaveowner's remorse and repentance before you could forgive them?"

"Hmm." Sallie thought for a moment. "That'd sure be nice to see, but it'd be best if their heart and soul were really behind it. If they doin' it just because somebody like the government makin' 'em and they end up hatin' me and other coloreds even worse for it, then we still got a problem."

"But it's your *due!*" Emma asserted. "After all the sins we've committed against you, don't we owe you that?"

Sallie cocked her head back. "Was *this* what you and Mizz Cat were arguin' over last night, Emmy?"

"Well, not exactly," Emma said. "But it really all boiled down to that. She seems to think I'm being unreasonable if I encourage her to be more like David and me in doing what she can to help make amends for what happened to you and others. Not only on our own plantation, but throughout this whole, rotten Confederacy that both my parents, Catherine, and her husband were so committed to upholding and defending."

"Miss Em, you startin' to sound like Mr. Johnson. I do love that man, but he can talk my ear off sometimes, spoutin' some big idea he heard from Frederick Douglass or them other famous abolitionist people. I don't know whether somebody like you and Cat and Mr. David 'owe' me for what happened to my family, but I do know I ain't lookin' for no handout or service that you don't wanna give. All I'd be expectin' for sure from *any* White person—whether or not they a former slaveowner—is just don't do things to step on me and hold me back no more. Treat me like a fellow human being, with the same rights and respect they'd give a White citizen. And if I'm real lucky, maybe a few of 'em might even show Jesus's love to me the way you've done all these years, Emmy."

Her eyes moist, Emma rose from her chair and went over to sit beside Sallie and embrace her. "No more than you've shown to me. And now you've got me thinking. Maybe I *have* been unreasonable toward Cat."

Sallie smiled. "Lord knows she already paid her debt off in my book. Takin' Lew in and protectin' him, helpin' him kill that devil Sam . . ."

"Yes, you're right. And I also need to stop holding on to my hurt feelings from the past and *completely* forgive her for not supporting me. Not to mention forgiving her little fit last night, refusing to accompany me today."

"You need to forgive *her*? How about also askin' her to forgive *you*?"

"For what?"

"For makin' her feel like she ain't good enough for you. Like she still gotta prove somethin' more to you than she already has for you to really respect her."

Emma buried her face in her hands and nodded. "Oh," she groaned, "I heard her say that last night, but I was so caught up in lecturing her that I thought she was just whining."

"Well, now that you see it for what it was, what you gonna do? Wait for Mizz Cat to apologize first?"

Emma winced. "I know God would say I should take the initiative. I'll talk with her when we return this afternoon."

"That sounds real good. It's time for you two to bury the hatchet once and for all, Miss Em."

After requesting Lew to bring the carriage around to the front entrance for her, Emma and Sallie stood on the porch awaiting his arrival.

The door opened behind them, and Catherine stepped out, dressed for the weather. She walked up beside Emma. "Good morning, ladies. Is it too late for me?"

"Cat!" Emma smiled. "Well, I . . ." She glanced hesitantly at Sallie. The carriage seated only two people.

"You ladies go enjoy yourselves," Sallie said graciously. "I got plenty else to keep me busy today."

Standing wordlessly next to her sister as they waited for Lew to pull up with the carriage, Emma debated what she should do next. Slowly, she reached out and clasped Catherine's hand in her own, bringing a smile to her sister's face.

"There it is!" Emma pointed ahead toward the grove of bare-branched oak trees at the end of the long and winding dirt lane five miles beyond the Beaufort city limits.

Catherine strained to see through the foggy mist that now accompanied the light rain. "I can barely make the house out. You and Abel have certainly placed a high priority on privacy."

"Just for the approach," Emma said. "Wait till you see the back side. No trees, and the view is incredible. On a clear day, you can see all the way to the coastline."

She could not believe how light her heart felt. It was as if the simple act of grasping her sister's hand while waiting for the carriage had released a thousand years of built-up tensions and hostilities. For the past half hour, the two had been chatting away excitedly with each other about all manner of things, reminding Emma of the innocent days of their childhood together—before selfishness, pride, and the war had taken their terrible tolls.

Nearing the end of the lane, the one-story, white clapboard house and nearby small equipment barn came into unobstructed view. Emma drew the carriage horse to a halt. "That must be the rental agent Mr. Korvitz's carriage parked in front. That's good—means we won't have to wait out in this cold and damp for him to arrive and let us in."

After stepping down from their carriage, Emma led the horse by its bridle to the front of the house and tied its reins to the veranda railing next to the other carriage horse. As if on cue, the heavens opened up, unleashing torrents of rain as the two women quickly ascended the veranda steps and approached the entrance.

Emma's polite rap on the door brought no response. She knocked again and again, a little louder each time. Nothing. "Cat, can you see anything inside?"

Catherine cupped her hands around her eyes and peered through the open-shuttered glass window a few feet to the left of the door. "There's a fire going in the hearth and three empty chairs in front of it on the far side of the front room. But I don't see anyone."

"The door's unlocked. Do you think we should just go in?" Emma asked.

"We might as well. Your agent must be around here somewhere. Let's just go in and wait for him."

Stepping inside and closing the door behind them, Emma and Catherine spent several moments basking in the warmth of the blazing fire and surveying their surroundings.

"It's almost *too* hot in here," Catherine muttered as she shed her winter cloak and hung it on the stand beside the door. Emma did likewise, and the two began walking around the room, inspecting the built-in cabinetry and furniture pieces.

"Well," Emma said, "what do you think so far? I know this is only the front room, but—"

"Em," Catherine interrupted, "what is this black powdery stuff on the floor? There's a whole trail of it next to the wall. And look! There's another trail over there, along the bottom of the back wall. It looks like . . . I don't know what. There's way too much of it to be rat or critter droppings."

Emma went over to look. She bent down, picked up a pinch, and held it to her nose, recoiling at the odor. "What *is* this?"

"United States military-grade black gunpowder, perhaps?" boomed a voice from the far side of the room. Emma shuddered. It was a voice that she recognized all too well, even before she stood and turned to face it.

"Good morning, ladies. I'm so glad you decided to come visit today, despite the inconvenient weather."

Colonel Jack Hurley stood in the doorway leading to the back rooms, his massive frame occupying nearly the entire opening.

CHAPTER 42

City of Beaufort
Port Royal Island, South Carolina Sea Islands
January 2, 1865

"Colonel Hurley," Emma said hesitantly, her heart in her throat. "W-Where is Mr. Korvitz?"

"Ah, yes." Hurley smiled. "As it turns out, Raymond Korvitz—an old, loyal, real estate partner of mine—received a message that his only daughter in New Hampshire has taken extremely ill, so he left the area last Friday on a northbound steamer to go tend to her. Before leaving, he informed me of his appointment here today with the two of you and asked if I'd be willing to fill in for him. I told him it would please me *greatly* to do so."

Emma's entire body began to tremble. "Cat, I think we should be going." Keeping her eye on Hurley, Emma reached out for her sister's hand and cautiously led her toward the front door. Hurley appeared in no great hurry to stop the women; he simply stood watching them with an amused expression on his face.

Emma put her hand on the doorknob. Before she could twist it, the knob turned and the door was opened from the outside.

"Can I help you, ma'am?"

Emma gasped at the sight of the tall, shaggy-haired man with a top hat. His entire appearance—especially the coal-black eyes and thin, beak-nosed face—betrayed that of a ruthless, professional killer. A killer whose large revolver was pointing directly at her face. Her lips and chin trembling, she backed away slowly and reached behind herself, searching desperately for Catherine's hand.

"Why, come in, Mr. Jacobs!" Hurley said genially. "Can't have you getting cold out there in the pouring rain."

The man entered the room and closed the door behind him. Aiming his weapon alternately between Emma and Catherine, he backed them toward the blazing hearth as Hurley moved behind the three upright wooden chairs arranged in a row in front of it.

"Here, Miss Emma," he said in an oddly polite tone, "I'd like you to take this seat on my left." He watched with a twisted smile as Emma hesitantly complied, trying to avoid his gaze.

"There you go, thank you . . . and your sister can take this one here on my right." Catherine moved slowly toward the chair, keeping her eyes locked onto Hurley's the entire time.

Once she was seated, he nodded approvingly. "Excellent. We'll reserve the center seat here for our special guest, who will arrive in just a short while. But first, I need to ask Mr. Jacobs here to secure the stage just a bit before we proceed further. Mr. Jacobs?"

Jacobs handed the pistol over to Hurley. He then reached into his coat pocket and pulled out several lengths of rope with which he bound Catherine's and Emma's hands together behind the backs of their chairs and secured their ankles to the chair legs.

Emma tried mightily to suppress the panic that overtook her mind. It was no use, for the tears began to roll down her cheeks. "What are you going to do to us? I know you bear ill will toward me, but my sister here has never—"

"Spare me your protests, Miss Hodge," Hurley interrupted, his voice now with a hard, angry edge. "After all you did to help destroy *my* life, it's a bit late for those. As for our plans today, I think we should just let things unfold, one act at a time."

Emma, at a loss for words and numb with fear, looked toward her sister. To her surprise, Catherine's face displayed a strange look of peace as she maintained her gaze on Hurley. It was obviously not a look that Hurley was at all comfortable with.

"Do you find something interesting about me . . . Mizz . . . Catherine, I believe? Why do you look at me like that?"

Catherine said not a word, just kept looking at him calmly, almost curiously—as if she were trying to ascertain his full measure as a man.

"Oh, so you refuse to answer me? Mr. Jacobs!"

"Yes, sir?"

"As my fellow Bostonian, I'd like you to come stand beside me and take a good, close look at these two exquisite examples of southern womanhood.

"Pretty Miss Emma here displays tears and histrionics, all calculated to convince me that I'm unfairly treating her . . . when in reality it was *she* who brought it all on herself with her public, slanderous condemnation of my good reputation and intentions.

"And then, over here, we have the beautiful and elegant young widow, Mizz Catherine. I've never met her before, but I can already tell she possesses all those wily southern female traits I came to see and despise in the pampered older sisters of my boyhood Beaufort friends. See the way she keeps staring at me with that cool, calm expression—as if she expects me to eventually wither with self-doubt and shame under the power of her hypnotic spell. Does it seem that way to you as well, Jacobs?"

"Of course, Colonel," Jacobs said as he took the pistol back from Hurley. "Isn't that how *all* these reb temptresses are taught by their mothers to get what they want?"

Colonel Jack edged close to Catherine and bent down with hands on his knees, his face no more than a few inches from hers. "What is it that you really *want* from me now, Mizz Catherine?"

Emma held her breath. She knew Catherine had heard the story of Hurley's contentious history with David, Abel, herself, and the Magnolia Plantation freedmen from many different angles. But now, she was experiencing his intimidating presence firsthand. She had stood up to the likes of Sam Taylor. But now? *Lord, give her strength.*

Catherine's lips trembled slightly. "I want nothing from you, Colonel," she responded in a voice so low it was hardly audible. A tear rolled down her cheek.

Hurley's eyes widened, a pleased smile on his face. "Nothing? Truly nothing?" He placed a hand gently on her cheek and wiped the tear away with his thumb. "Somehow, I don't believe you, Mizz Catherine. Do you really value your life so little? Come now. You are indeed beautiful. Perhaps there's something you might offer that would inspire me to reconsider my plans for you."

Catherine jerked her head back and spit in his face. "You'll never receive such a foul offer from *me*."

Wiping the saliva from his eye, Hurley stood and grabbed the pistol from Jacobs's hand. He placed the muzzle against Catherine's forehead and cocked the trigger.

"*No, please!*" Emma screamed.

Hurley hesitated. He stared at her for a moment, then back at Catherine. Slowly, he raised his free arm and held his index finger up in front of Catherine's eye, wagging it ever so slightly. "Not yet," he muttered.

He stood and motioned to Jacobs. "Gag 'em both. I don't want to hear their bleatings during this next part."

Jacobs nodded, carrying out the order with ruthless efficiency.

"Go bring him in," Hurley ordered.

Jacobs left the room, returning moments later leading someone by the arm.

Abel! Emma cringed at the sight of her fiancé. Abel Bowman's face had been badly beaten, his right eye black and swollen to about twice its normal size. She strained desperately to rise from her seat and run to his aid, but the tightly bound cords prevented her from moving, just as the cloth scarf that Jacobs had stuffed into her mouth and tied tightly behind her head precluded any communication. Helpless, she watched with tear-filled eyes as Jacobs escorted Abel to the middle chair and forced him to sit with his arms looped around the back of the chair.

Abel's head sagged, and he seemed only dimly aware of his surroundings. Emma tried to call out to him with a guttural cry through her gag. He managed to lift his head and turn it to intently look at her for a few seconds. But the effort proved too much, and his head collapsed again onto his chest.

"So, everyone's now in position for the final act!" Hurley clapped his hands.

"Good," Jacobs groaned. "This is taking way too long."

Hurley walked over to one of the wall cabinets and opened the door. He returned with a folded cloth that Jacobs helped him to unfold and hold up by its corners in front of Abel.

"Were you wondering where this was hiding, Mr. Bowman?"

Emma's heart sank as she watched her fiancé barely lift his head to behold the Magnolia Plantation's schoolhouse flag—the one he had poured his soul into personally designing and sewing. It had been mutilated; the large, all-seeing eye in the center had been cut out, a gaping hole now in its place.

"Go ahead and bedeck our Glory Boy with all the honor he's due, Jacobs."

Jacobs took the flag and walked around behind Abel. He draped it over him, arranging it so that his battered head stuck out through the hole and the words of the flag's inscription—EYE OF GLORY—appeared upside down across his chest.

"Turn his lover's and her sister's chairs so they can have a full-on view of this, Mr. Jacobs." After Jacobs had done so, Emma turned her face away, unable to bear the horrible, degrading sight.

"And now, my friends," Hurley said, "if you'll excuse me for one moment . . ." He walked into the room where Abel had been held captive and returned seconds later with something hidden behind his back and a broad grin on his face. With a mocking, grand gesture, he revealed the concealed object—a fearsome-looking broadsword—which he then lifted high into the air with both hands.

"Hail, King of Glory!" he intoned, his voice trembling with feigned emotion.

Jacobs snickered as Hurley held the weapon in the air for several seconds before reverently lowering and laying it at Abel's feet.

Abel stared at the sword, seemingly still in a state of half-consciousness. Emma could see his lips moving, as if he might be uttering a silent prayer . . . or perhaps a vile curse.

"Proceed with the final preparations, Mr. Jacobs, while I have a brief little chat with my friend here."

Hurley pulled another chair over and placed it in front of Abel's. He settled himself into it and lit a cigar as Jacobs—after retrieving a large bucket from a side closet—worked behind him, pouring out black powder to thicken the trails along the base of the walls and on top of furniture.

Leaning forward, Hurley blew a long cloud of cigar smoke directly into Abel's face. "So, it appears that old army rumor about your participation with John Brown in that Pottawatomie raid was true, Mr. Bowman. I must admit . . . ever since I first heard the story years ago, I had not the slightest inclination to believe it—even though it was supposedly straight from the mouth of Owen Brown, John's son.

"Until this morning, that is. Thanks to the efforts of my trusted associates, Mr. Jacobs and his assistant, to subdue and bring you here to meet your well-deserved fate, I now can see with my own eyes this wonderful masterpiece of a weapon and its beautifully engraved handle. I now have no doubt, this is indeed the very weapon that was handed to you after the raid by a disgusted John Brown, who—according to Owen—told you to take it home with you. To let it serve as a lifelong reminder of *your disgraceful and cowardly refusal* when you were urgently needed and were asked to help Brown and his sons subdue the Doyle family members. Am I correct, Mr. Bowman?"

Abel barely lifted his head. Emma couldn't tell whether he was fully comprehending what was being said. Hurley blew another long stream of cigar smoke in his face, sparking a fit of coughing, as Jacobs dumped large piles of black powder under everyone's seats.

"You know, Bowman, it's one thing to try to compensate for the guilt and shame of your youthful cowardice by wrapping yourself in the flag of a grandiose, warlike vision to free and elevate slaves . . . willing to slay with unrestrained barbarity those who openly resist you. But it's quite another thing to stab in the back and then pile on and mercilessly crush someone who actually agrees with the ultimate goal behind your vision, but who merely has a different idea for how best to pursue it. And that, Mr. Bowman, is what you have done to me. Your vicious public lies and slander in civil court and in national newspapers have completely destroyed my business and forced me into massive debt and poverty from which it will be well nigh impossible to recover. And for that, I cannot rest until I know I have obtained my full and final justice today."

Abel tried mightily once again to lift his head. "Colonel . . . please . . . spare the women."

"Oh, *they* will be spared the worst of it, sir," Hurley snarled. "With a bullet in their head, they will be spared the pain of being seared by the flames which are about to consume this house. You, however, you miserable rat, are not deserving of mercy and will not receive such a courtesy. And with that Glory sword at your feet as a reminder of your cowardice and failure to support the great John Brown in that critical moment when he called for your help, may your agony be compounded."

His lit cigar now burned down to the stub, Hurley looked at his watch. He pushed his chair back and stood.

"Enough delay, Mr. Jacobs. Our ship departs from Port Royal Sound for France in less than four hours. It's time to finish up here!"

Jacobs pulled the hammer back on his revolver. "Which one first, Colonel?"

Hurley pointed at Catherine. "The arrogant, nasty one. Please proceed."

Jacobs walked over and pressed the pistol's muzzle against Catherine's temple.

Emma turned her face and squeezed her eyes shut, feeling her own soul about to be wrenched away together with her sister's.

A sudden movement beside her caused her to look again—just in time to see Abel Bowman spring like an uncaged tiger from his chair, his hands somehow, miraculously, freed from their binding cords.

Abel hurled himself at Jacobs, striking him in the right side and deflecting the gun away from Catherine. His momentum carried both men stumbling toward the side of the room with the gun pinioned against Jacobs's chest. They crashed against the wall together as Abel grappled to wrest the gun from Jacobs's hand. He succeeded in loosening his grip and knocking it away, but not before it had discharged, the bullet passing like a flaming arrow through the upper-left side of Abel's chest.

Abel stumbled backward toward the center of the room, regaining his balance for a moment before finally sinking to his knees in front of Emma. He reached out and placed his hand on the handle of the broadsword in front of his chair as Jacobs approached with the revolver back in his possession, ready to finish him off.

"No, Jacobs!" Hurley cried from the corner of the room where he'd retreated. "Use that sword . . . the one he was not enough of a man to wield himself on that night his hero John Brown needed him."

Jacobs stared blankly at Hurley for a few seconds, then nodded. He bent down and laid his pistol on the floor, then easily took the sword away from Abel's weak grasp.

Gripping the handle with both hands, he lifted the weapon with the blade pointed downward, preparing to plunge it straight into Abel's heart.

Suddenly the front door banged open behind him, causing Jacobs to stop.

He whirled. "Who the—?"

A loud rifle blast was followed a split instant later by a mass of blood exploding from the back of Jacobs's head. He crumpled to the ground at Abel's feet.

Emma, nearly passed out from shock, stared at the front door.

Lew Cobb entered the room, warily pointing his now-discharged rifle in all directions. Spotting the pistol on the floor next to Jacobs, he laid down the rifle and went over to pick it up.

"Lew, watch out!" Abel shouted, as Hurley rushed toward the boy from behind, poised to crack a large vase over his head. Lew turned, barely in time to arrest Hurley's mad onslaught by firing the pistol into his stomach. Hurley dropped the vase and staggered backward, sprawling faceup against the sofa with his hands clutching his abdomen.

Lew approached cautiously and stood over him with the pistol cocked. He glanced back over his shoulder. "What should I do with 'im, Mr. Abel?"

Abel, blood pouring from his own wound, struggled mightily to stand. He picked up the broadsword with his right hand and staggered toward Hurley.

"Step aside, son," he said softly to Lew. He positioned the edge of the sword blade across the center of Hurley's forehead, then paused.

"What are you waiting for, Bowman?" Hurley muttered. "Have your revenge . . . *finish me off.*"

Emma held her breath as Abel raised his sword high over his head.

He closed his eyes, his arms trembling as he let out an animal-like scream.

Colonel Jack squeezed his eyes shut, awaiting the fatal blow.

It didn't come.

Abel's body seemed to suddenly relax. Slowly, he lowered the sword and rested the sharp edge of the blade once again on Hurley's forehead. Breathing heavily, he let it remain there for several seconds before he lifted it slightly and took two steps backward. Kneeling, he gently laid down the weapon crosswise on the floor in front of himself. He stared at the handle with the engraved word GLORY that had inspired his entire adult life, then looked up at Hurley with a wide grin.

"You know I could, Colonel, but I won't. Vengeance belongs to God. You have finished yourself. My own conscience is clear."

Colonel Jonathan "Jack" Hurley tried to utter something, but only a trickle of blood emerged from his mouth. His eyes rolled back as he took his last breath.

Abel turned his head and smiled dazedly at Catherine and Emma before collapsing forward—on top of GLORY.

CHAPTER 43

City of Beaufort
Port Royal Island, South Carolina Sea Islands
January 4, 1865

Emma sat beside Abel's bed in a curtained-off private section of the Beaufort city hospital, clutching his hand in both of hers as she watched him drift in and out of consciousness. After a day and a half of unsuccessful attempts by the surgeons to stop his internal bleeding, she feared the end was near.

Hopefully, the messenger dispatched by Catherine had reached David and his family at the Port Royal Sound pier with news of the tragedy prior to their scheduled departure yesterday on the steamship to Washington. If so, Emma prayed that her brother would make it back to the hospital in time since Abel had requested his presence.

The curtain behind her rustled as Sallie stepped in and sat on the stool beside her. "They're here now, Emmy—Mizz Cat, William, and Lew—all waitin' their turn to come say goodbye to him, whenever you're ready. And we're all praying Mr. David will show up anytime now."

Emma nodded, trying not to cry. "All right, Sallie, please allow me just a few more minutes alone with him."

Sallie hugged her closely, then went around behind the head of the bed. She dabbed Abel's perspiring forehead with a linen cloth, then bent down and kissed it. His eyes fluttered open for a few seconds, and he managed a weak smile, bringing Sallie to tears as she took his free hand and held it to her cheek.

"Thank you, Mr. Abel, for saving my best friend and her sister."

Abel's voice was barely audible. "Thank *you*, Sallie . . . for . . . *being* Emma's best friend all these years." Sallie squeezed his hand, then left the room sobbing.

Emma sat alone once again, gazing at Abel as she recalled the harrowing trial of two days ago, marveling at the ingenuity and lifesaving heroism that he and Lew had displayed. It was amazing enough that Abel had managed to feign so well the severity of his head injuries and to employ the "old army trick" he'd once learned to slip the rope with which Jacobs had bound his wrists. But combined with Lew's bold decision—after discovering blood droppings and other signs at Abel's apartment of his possible abduction—to arm himself with one of Abel's hunting rifles and come out to the rental house to alert the women, arriving just in time to courageously burst in and save *all* their lives, it was clear to her that the hand of God himself had empowered them both.

Until now, she hadn't realized the extent to which her inner joy had become intertwined with anticipation of a future life shared with Abel. Before he'd come into her life, her passion and devotion to the "cause" of educating and uplifting those less fortunate than she had always seemed enough, inspiring her solitary efforts as an abolitionist writer and missionary-teacher and sustaining her during times of loneliness and discouragement. But the more she'd come to know and love Abel, something had switched inside her heart. No longer did the idea of pursuing a cause-driven single life—such as her heroine, the fearless southern abolitionist warrior Angelina Grimké, had done in her youth—hold as much appeal. Far more enticing had become the prospect of sharing *everything*—not just the grand, noble causes and activities that inspired her, but also the simple joys, trials, and challenges of everyday domestic and family life—with someone she knew would respect and love her for who she was. Someone willing to take seriously her concerns without patronizing or coddling her. Someone with whom she would have loved to share every intimate secret of her physical and emotional self.

It's not to be. Sadness overwhelmed her at the realization of all she was about to lose.

Sallie drew back the curtain slightly. "Emmy, David just arrived!"

"Oh, thank God!"

Seeing that Abel's breathing was fitful, but that he appeared to be sleeping peacefully for the moment, Emma released his hand and stood up. "I suppose this is as good a time as any." After tenderly kissing Abel on the lips, with Sallie's support, she stepped outside into the waiting area where the others were seated. Catherine, Lew, William, and David all rose to greet her.

David held her in his arms and spoke to her as the other three took their individual turns sitting next to Abel, silently remembering and thanking God for his bravery and his many kind and generous ways, offering their prayers for his soul.

Catherine was the last to exit. She glanced at Emma and David and shook her head sadly. "I think he's very close. It could be any minute."

David watched Emma's reaction, uncertain as to her wishes.

She smiled at him through her tears. "Go in. He needs to see you." He nodded and disappeared behind the curtains.

Catherine took Emma in her arms and held her.

"I never really knew, sister," Emma whispered, "how much I had misjudged and underestimated you, and what losing Joe and your baby must have meant to you. Nor did I really know how much I truly, truly do love you. Until now."

"Pastor Jones promised me," Catherine said softly, "that a true reconciliation with you would one day come, if I kept praying for it. I did, Em, and the Lord has answered."

Several minutes passed before the curtains rustled and David emerged. He smiled sadly and nodded.

Taking Emma once again into his arms, he spoke to her soothingly.

"He actually woke up a bit at the end, and we were able to converse."

Emma caught her breath. "What did he say?"

"He asked me to tell you that he loved you very much . . . and that he looked forward to seeing you again one day in heaven, just as he looked forward now to seeing his Savior."

Emma tried not to completely lose her composure. "Did he say anything else?"

"Well, he made one last request, which I'll tell you and Catherine about later. And also, he . . ."

"What, David? Tell me."

"The entire time I was with him, though his breathing was labored, his eyes were intense—darting to and fro as if he were searching for something in the room. Finally, near the very end, his gaze seemed transfixed toward the far corner, where the ceiling met the wall. A slight smile appeared on his lips, and he managed to raise his arm and point in that direction. I asked him if he saw something there. He didn't answer, but I had a strong sense that he had spotted and was now being drawn by some divine presence or being who was beckoning to him. I looked and looked again, but I saw nothing. When I turned back, he was looking directly at me, his eyes as clear and fierce as the first time I met him. "Who did you see, Abel? Can you tell me?" I asked him. His whole face relaxed, and he smiled at me. Then he closed his eyes and spoke his last word before his breathing stopped.

"Tell me what he said," Emma pleaded.

David stared at her, a wide grin finally breaking out over his face. "It was the first word he spoke to me the day we met: *Glory.*"

EPILOGUE

RESTORATION

CHAPTER 44

Charles Town, West Virginia
June 30, 1865
(Six months later)

Late in the afternoon of what had been an exceptionally hot day, three horse-drawn carriages set out together from the Rutherford House Inn, heading toward the gently rolling hills outside the city that also offered a view of Harpers Ferry seven miles to the northeast. David sat with Sarah and Jenny in the lead vehicle. Sallie, William, and Lew followed in the second, while Emma, Catherine, Pastor Jones, and his wife brought up the rear of the little caravan.

It had taken quite a bit of David's time and effort to coordinate schedules and travel plans, but he now felt rewarded by the sight of everyone gathered together for the purpose of carrying out Abel's dying wish.

Sarah, sitting with her arm around Jenny on the opposite bench, looked across at him and smiled. "Can you imagine his reaction, looking down on us right now . . . nearing the place where it all started for the two of you?"

David closed his eyes and recalled the moment when Abel had first spoken to him as they'd contemplated John Brown's dead body as it dangled in the breeze at the foot of the hanging platform. He wondered whether Abel—now in his own eternal abode—would consider the momentous family decisions and national developments of the past six months as a vindication of everything he had striven for in life . . .

The day after Abel's death in early January, the decision had been made—in response to Catherine's proposal—to have the former Union army captain buried in the Hodge Plantation family cemetery near Catherine's husband, the Confederate army captain, Joe Hartwell. All had agreed that the two men would have greatly admired and liked one another had they met in life, and the idea that they would both be resting in peace in proximity to the house where the two sisters whom they loved had grown up together was impossible to resist. The only concern at the time was whether the plantation would revert to Catherine's legal ownership at the end of the war. But with Pastor Jones's assurance that, in any case, he would almost certainly be able to purchase and secure the family cemetery's hillside site for his church's purposes, the funeral and burial had taken place there in mid-January.

Shortly afterward had come the eagerly anticipated news that General Sherman had launched his final push up the Atlantic Seaboard from Georgia and through the Carolinas in order to link up with Grant's forces in Virginia. In doing so, he'd issued Special Field Orders No. 15 calling for the implementation of his "Forty Acres and a Mule" policy that was intended to benefit tens of thousands of freed slaves along his march route. The order had soon resulted in the settling of over forty thousand of these refugees on large tracts of newly captured lands in the Sea Islands as well as—for the first time—the South Carolina interior, using "lessons learned" from the Port Royal Experiment to guide the process.

Early in March, a month following the passage of the Thirteenth Amendment outlawing slavery everywhere in the land, William, Sallie, and Lew had departed Beaufort for one of the Sea Islands off the Georgia coast. Having left the AMA for employment with the new, congressionally established national "Freedmen's Bureau" that was dedicated to ex-slave land ownership, education, food aid, and legal assistance, William and Sallie's responsibilities and demands on their time had increased considerably. It had been exceedingly kind and generous of William, David thought, to arrange some time off from their new jobs and to pay for himself, Sallie, and Lew to travel all the way from Georgia to join in today's special occasion.

And then there was April, which had brought in quick succession three pivotal events—the fall of Petersburg to the Union siege; the surrender of Lee's Confederate army at the Appomattox Courthouse; and President Lincoln's assassination. These had marked the ending of the war and the beginning of a profoundly uncertain transition period under the new president, Andrew Johnson. If Johnson's Tennessee background and strong, pro-southern sympathies were any indication, the plan for reconstruction of the South and transitioning of former slaves into fully equal members of society could take on an entirely different cast than the one Lincoln had envisioned.

April had also brought on a highly positive development for both Hodge sisters. At the end of the month, Catherine—still living at the leased Beaufort townhome with Emma—had received an official message from the Washington authorities. Based on the written testimony of David, Pastor Jones, and others in the Petersburg area, she had finally been granted title as the legitimate owner of the Hodge Family Plantation. She was now free to return and settle there without Union forces occupying the property.

After much mutual discussion and soul-searching, Emma had accepted Catherine's invitation to come live with her there. It had meant the end of Emma's AMA service in the Sea Islands, but the organization had expressed a willingness to support her proposal for teaching basic literacy skills to ex-slaves in the Petersburg area with the help of her old friend Miss Dora Lewis.

Catherine had rejoiced at Emma's decision, knowing that with her sister's comforting presence and support she would certainly be able to restore a reasonable portion of the plantation's business and social operations to something of their prewar grandeur. For the first time since Joe's death, she was looking forward with eager anticipation to carrying on the family tradition by fully reembracing the role of plantation mistress—this time without reliance on slave labor. Tomorrow, the two sisters would be leaving for Petersburg to begin their new adventure together.

For David, the past six months had passed by like a whirlwind. Dividing his time between tending the farm and his new job in the city as associate editor for the *Cleveland Leader* had not been easy and had been the source of several irritated exchanges between him and Sarah. But these had been diminishing lately as David's reputation with the publisher had continued to grow, and Mr. Cowles had rewarded him with more freedom to conduct his article-writing tasks at home. This could not have come at a better time, as Sarah had just last week revealed that their new child was on the way.

"Papa, are we almost there?" Jenny asked plaintively. "I'm hot and hungry."

"Yes, sweetheart," David assured her, reaching over to stroke her light-brown curls. "It's just at the crest of this hill . . . only a couple more minutes."

Reaching their destination, the separate groups dismounted from their carriages and assembled together at a grassy spot with an unobstructed view of the open field down below in the distance that had been the site of John Brown's execution nearly six years ago.

Everyone helped to spread blankets and feast on the delicious picnic supper that the women had jointly prepared. Afterward, all settled back to listen as Pastor Jones delivered a heartfelt, emotionally wrenching yet tender message that highlighted the special meaning of the execution site and the many forms of strife that had emanated from it—not only for the nation but for each individual present today.

"Who can forget," Jones had said, "the last written words that John Brown left for his followers and the nation:

I, John Brown, am now quite certain that the crimes of this guilty land will never be purged away, but with Blood. I had . . . vainly flattered myself that without very much bloodshed, it might be done.[7]

"God knows that Captain Brown's reluctant prediction eventually became the motivating vision behind the Union's war effort, starting with the Emancipation Proclamation and ending with the Union's final, great victory on the battlefield. But I do still wonder: Would God now have us believe—with the end of the war and the passage of the Thirteenth Amendment—that the bloodshed is over and the crime of slavery has now been completely erased in our nation? Or is there more to be done, and will more bloodshed be required? Assuming the former is true, we can only pray the latter will be minimal."

After Pastor Jones had concluded, he asked William Johnson to speak on what today's occasion and location signified for him.

William began by confirming his sincere gratitude for the bold actions of John Brown, President Lincoln, Frederick Douglass, Harriet Tubman, and the many other men and women—both Black and White—who had devoted and even sacrificed their lives for the related causes of abolition and emancipation. However, he then said he feared that the road ahead would be fraught with peril and frustration. While Lincoln—in his last speech—had personally come around to supporting the right to vote for colored people who were "very intelligent" and those who "had served our cause as soldiers," his endorsement was far from universal. In fact, from everything William was seeing and hearing, White anger and resistance to full rights of citizenship, including voting and private land ownership for freed Blacks, were quickly building—not only in the defeated South but in the North as well. Clearly, for many, freedom from slavery did not imply freedom from racial inequality.

But despite his fears for the national situation, William assured his friends that he had much to be thankful for at a personal level. "Not the least of which is the fact that, just before we left to come here, the love of my life—Miss Sallie Cobb—accepted my proposal of marriage. We'll be moving with Lew to Baltimore, where the ceremony will be held in December. Of course, you all are invited and expected to attend!"

A huge cheer went up as everyone rose to congratulate Sallie and William.

"Sallie," David called out in a teasing voice after the commotion had settled, "I was just curious, were there any conditions attached to your acceptance of Mr. Johnson's proposal?"

Sallie laughed. "Only two conditions—first, that my wedding day had better not be the last time Mr. Johnson attends church with me and Lew."

William grinned. "It seems the Lord is intent on finding his lost sheep."

"And what was the second?" Pastor Jones asked.

Sallie hesitated. She glanced at William, then turned to face Emma. "The second condition was that Miss Em would agree to be my maid of honor."

Emma's hand flew to her mouth. Unable to speak, she simply rushed over to Sallie and embraced her.

"I'm guessing that's a sign that Sallie's condition was accepted, and that we can now get married," William joked.

Pastor Jones called on David next, and he invited Catherine and Emma to come stand beside him as he faced the others.

After recounting some of his vivid memories of Abel and his appreciation for their close friendship and final moments together, his voice nearly broke as he asked Lew Cobb to come forward. "Without the bravery that Abel and you displayed that terrible day on Port Royal Island, young man, my two beloved sisters would not be standing here by my side today. For that, we are all eternally grateful to you."

In his customary manner, Lew kept staring down at his feet in an effort to hide his emotions.

"Say something, Lew," Sallie urged.

Lew peeked up at David, Catherine, and Emma. Tears filled his eyes. "I woulda done it all over again if I had to. I'm only sorry I didn't save Mr. Abel too."

David put his arm around his shoulders as the women gathered close to console him. "You know what, Lew? I am absolutely sure that Mr. Abel is in heaven right now, perfectly happy and looking down on this little gathering. And I'm also sure he couldn't be more honored than to see how much you cared about him."

As the others began to pick up in preparation for the return to their hotel, David went to retrieve a wrapped object from the back of his carriage. Returning, he walked a short way down the side of the hill to a narrow, shallow, three-foot-long trench that Lew had helped him dig in the soft dirt prior to the start of Pastor Jones's message. Once there, he knelt on one leg and laid the object on the ground. He carefully unwrapped the cloth, revealing the sheathed broadsword that John Brown had bequeathed to Abel at Pottawatomie. With the hand of his intact arm, he slid the sword from its sheath and laid it flat on the ground parallel to the trench.

It was Abel's last wish—the one he'd whispered to David just before that final, magnificent vision appeared to him on his deathbed:

"It's over, David. God is merciful. I know it was his strong hand that led me at Chancellorsville to recognize and abandon my corrupted vision of glory, to lay my sword down so I could learn to see clearly what it meant to seek after *his* glory and not my own. Please, bury my Glory sword on some hill with a good view of the execution site where we first met, and bury your Hodge family swords with it."

It had taken David several days, but he'd finally come to understand the second part of Abel's request.

He'd recalled it was six years ago that he and his sisters had begun to separate from each other. Just like Abel, each had pursued their own motivating visions of glory, locking on to what each saw as their "good and righteous cause," be it the commitment that he and Emma shared to abolish slavery and uplift freedmen, or Catherine's passion for defending their father's interests and preserving the southern tradition and way of life.

As the war progressed and their differences in their aspirations and priorities became magnified, they'd resorted to brandishing their self-righteousness, judgmentalism, and lack of forgiveness against each other like sharp swords, and had ended up parting on bitter, harsh terms.

Abel had observed with great dismay and sadness the resentment of her sister that all this had produced in Emma. Little wonder, then, that his last wish had included a plea for the final laying down of those selfish, prideful attitudes that had served only to divide the family he'd come to know and love.

David looked back over his shoulder at the crest of the hill. He smiled at the sight of Emma and Catherine holding hands as they now stood on the crest together, peering down at him and no doubt wondering what he was doing. *Abel would be happy to know the second part of his wish has already been fulfilled,* he thought.

He turned back to gaze at Abel's sword one last time. He considered the violent purposes for which the weapon had been employed—from supporting the Pottawatomie Massacre to inspiring the original design of the "Eye of Glory" flag and the bold battlefield exploits of Abel and Company L. Who could deny that the weapon had served these purposes with great and devastating effect, helping to ignite and prosecute the victorious national crusade to end slavery?

And yet, as David recalled from the teachings of King Solomon: *"There is a time for war, and a time for peace."* He sighed deeply, then re-sheathed the sword and laid it reverently in the trench.

Standing up, he scooped the loose dirt over it with the shovel. After tamping down the dirt with his boot, he gazed up at the sky, above and beyond the fiery red-gold sun now setting over the blue mountains to the west. A gentle breeze stirred, and he sensed a familiar voice speaking loving words of peace and encouragement to his heart.

Tears filling his eyes, he stretched his arm out with open palm.

"It's done, my friend. Enjoy God's Glory."

AUTHOR'S NOTE

Motivation and Focus for *Seeing Glory*

Of all the major themes that are typically associated today with the era of the American Civil War, the painful legacy of *slavery* is undoubtedly the most prominent.

Many outstanding literary works (fiction and nonfiction) have been produced—especially in recent years—that address this difficult theme from the primary perspective of those who obviously suffered the most under the oppressive system: the slaves themselves.

As a Christian historical novelist and Civil War enthusiast, I had long been interested in exploring the question of how slavery and the war itself were experienced from a perspective that is not as frequently discussed: *religious belief* and *personal faith*. In particular, I wanted to better understand the critical role of these spiritual factors in influencing:

1. The general attitudes toward slavery and the war itself of two major power-broking groups at opposite ends of the era's cultural and philosophical spectrum (i.e., northern abolitionists and elite White southern plantation families).

2. The attitudes and actions of individual members of both groups (and the slaves themselves) toward God, slavery, their hard circumstances, and each other.

My initial background research on this subject led to the identification of several specific questions that I felt would be especially helpful and important to focus on in the development of a relevant historical novel:

1. Leading up to the war's outbreak:

    a. How did representative leaders of each power group employ different interpretations of the (same!) Bible to motivate and justify their radically opposed views and actions on the slavery issue?

    b.   How was it possible that their personal faith and unique experiences with slaves could motivate the privileged child of a wealthy southern plantation owner to forsake their family and vigorously pursue the abolitionist cause? (Though not common, such situations did in fact occur—as evidenced, for example, in the true-life stories of the Grimké sisters, Moncure Conway, and Mattie Griffith Browne.)

2.   During the war:

    a.   How did their strong patriotic convictions combine with personal faith to inspire individual men and women on both sides to keep on fighting and surviving under horrific battlefield conditions or severe homefront deprivation and loss?

3.   In the war's latter stages:

    a.   How did personal faith and humanitarian concerns conflict with economic and profit-making motives in shaping the emerging new visions of abolitionists, former slaveowners, and newly freed plantation workers?

Indeed, it was consideration of the above questions that ultimately inspired the titling and guided development of the overarching plot and portrayals of fictional and historical characters for this novel.

Historical versus Fictional

Locales, dates, timelines, organizational structures, and names of high-ranking officers for the strategic and tactical actions of opposing Union and Confederate army units and naval vessels depicted in chapters and scenes directly dealing with these events are consistent with historical records and sources. The sole exception is "Company L" of the 7th Ohio Volunteer Infantry Regiment. Company L's existence, actions, and associated personnel are all fictitious.

For the purposes of plot, I created the fictitious Hodge Family Plantation in fictitious Piedmont County and situated the plantation five miles downriver from the historical Eppes Plantation (also known as Appomattox Manor) located on City Point in the Hopewell district of Prince George County, Virginia. Much of the exciting action sequence that unfolds in Chapters 17–18 was inspired by the real-life adventure of Richard Slaughter, an Eppes Plantation slave, who—one dark night in May 1862, along with his father and four others—successfully escaped to a Union gunboat off City Point.

The other main fictitious setting—first employed in Part IV of the novel—was the Magnolia Plantation, which I situated on St. Helena Island in the Sea Islands district of South Carolina. Inspired by the historical Marion Chaplin Plantation that was purchased cooperatively in 1864 by an enterprising group of freedmen, this setting formed ground zero for much of the novel's action that centered on the Union government's famous Port Royal Experiment of 1862–1865. All other locales, timelines, and federal government decisions that are mentioned in connection with that project are consistent with the historical record.

I should also clarify that, while the specific events and character portrayals of Part IV are entirely fictitious, they drew their inspiration from the real-life experiences in the Sea Islands of a dedicated group of missionaries known as "Gideon's Band": preachers, teachers, and philanthropic businessmen from New York and Boston who were among the first to arrive and provide continuing aid to the newly freed slaves in the region. Among these were: the Reverend Mansfield French of the American Missionary Association; the (later) famous African American antislavery activist, poet, and educator Charlotte Forten-Grimké; and the Boston-based, private investment entrepreneur Edward Philbrick.

With the exception of the paraphrased or actual quotes from recorded speeches or writings by Charles Finney and Frederick Douglass in Chapter 14 and John Brown in Chapter 44, the specific actions and dialogue of all real historical figures (see list in front matter) who appear in the novel are products of my own speculation. However, I have striven to keep all these generally consistent with the known overall character, recorded quotes, demeanor, major decisions, and actions of these figures to the extent they could be gleaned from available biographical descriptions. My main intent as a novelist was to capture the spirit, if not the letter, of the words and behaviors that one might reasonably expect these historical characters to have displayed in the various fictitious scenes in which they are placed.

Finally, a word about the self-cutting behavior exhibited by the fictitious character Catherine Hodge in several scenes of the novel. Although there is a tendency to think of this as a modern-day phenomenon, in fact this practice and other forms of self-mutilation have (quietly) been around for centuries, with documented cases recorded as far back as ancient Greece.

Historical Aftermath and Final Reflections

The epilogue of *Seeing Glory* concludes at the end of June 1865.

At that point, one might have expected that—after all they had been through and overcome—the victorious northerners and the newly freed slaves in the South would have good cause for an optimistic outlook. After all, with Congress's recent passage of the Thirteenth Amendment outlawing slavery, the promise of "Forty Acres and a Mule," and the establishment of the national Freedmen's Bureau to support the integration of former slaves into society, the government of the reunited nation seemed poised to do all in its power to correct the evils of the past and provide a true foundation of justice and equality for all. Indeed, some positive strides were made. For instance, over the next five years, the bureau succeeded in establishing over four thousand schools that provided instruction to nearly two hundred fifty thousand former slaves or their children.

Unfortunately, as William Johnson (my novel's fictitious African American missionary-worker) had feared in the epilogue scene, the positive developments on the educational front were not matched by similar progress on the broader issues of racial inequality facing the ex-slaves. Southern White resistance and gradually flagging northern commitment to Reconstruction goals proved to be the primary obstacles.

After assuming the presidency in the aftermath of Lincoln's assassination, the Democratic southern sympathizer Andrew Johnson quickly got to "work," doing everything in his power to limit the scope of Republican-led Reconstruction plans. In May 1865, Johnson issued a proclamation calling for the transfer of all confiscated southern lands under US government control—*not* to the deserving freed people, but back to the original plantation owners, so long as they swore loyalty to the restored Union! This action pulled the rug from underneath the government's recent pledge of "Forty Acres and a Mule" for thousands of freedmen in the Sea Islands and other southeast coastal areas. Instead of farming their own privately owned lands, the vast majority now had little option but to participate in the harsh "sharecropping" system of labor that ensured their continued exploitation by White landowners for decades to come.

True, significant national progress was marked by the ratification of the Fourteenth (1868) and Fifteenth (1870) Amendments, which granted full citizenship, equal protection under the law, and the right to vote for anyone born or naturalized in the US, including ex-slaves and their descendants. However, these measures incensed many Whites in the South, leading eventually to a significant expansion of Ku Klux Klan terror activities and the passage of Jim Crow laws mandating racial segregation in southern states.

It would be nearly a hundred years before the racial inequality tide began to turn through the historic legislative achievements of the 1950s to 1960s civil rights movement. Later, evidence of the slowly changing attitudes of certain segments of White-dominated religious society toward their own past racist attitudes and behavior was seen in the formal apologies issued in 1995 and 2016, respectively, by the Southern Baptist Convention (SBC) and the Presbyterian Church in America (PCA) for their earlier support of slavery and segregation.

Still, racial violence, injustice, inequitable systems and laws, demagoguery, and general animosity have persisted. They remain among the most divisive and heartbreaking issues faced by US society today. As the many proposed national, state, local community, and faith-based approaches to dealing with these contentious problems are considered and debated by individuals and their families, few would dispute the value of a clear-eyed awareness and understanding of the human greed, pride, idolatry, and spiritual blindness that originally led to the problems and—most importantly—the new, God-centered visions and attitudes that can help us to overcome them.

In that regard, it's my hope and prayer that *Seeing Glory*—in addition to being an informative, engrossing, and inspirational read—will have contributed some helpful perspectives.

SELECT BIBLIOGRAPHY

Among the numerous nonfiction books, biographies, online articles, and primary sources employed to support the development of historical context/detail, as well as real and fictional character dialogue for *Seeing Glory*, the following proved especially helpful and are listed as recommended reading for anyone interested in further exploration.

Historical Preface and Main Body

1. Reynolds, David S., *John Brown, Abolitionist* (New York: Vintage Books, 2006).
2. Puleo, Stephen, *The Caning: The Assault That Drove America to Civil War* (Yardley, PA: Westholme Publishing, 2013).
3. Burwell, Letitia M., *A Girl's Life in Virginia Before the War* (New York: Frederick A. Stokes Company Publishers, 1895).
4. Clinton, Catherine, *The Plantation Mistress* (New York: Pantheon Books, 1982).
5. Hicken, Patricia P., *Antislavery in Virginia, 1831-1861* (University of Virginia ProQuest Dissertations Publishing, 1968).
6. Jacobs, Harriet A; Child, L. Maria (Editor), *Incidents in the Life of a Slave Girl, Written by Herself* (Boston, 1861).
7. Miller, Randall M.; Stout, Harry S.; Wilson, Charles R., *Religion and the American Civil War* (New York: Oxford University Press, 1998).
8. Finney, Charles G., President of Oberlin College (August 18, 1852), "Guilt Modified By Ignorance—Anti-Slavery Duties," The Gospel Truth, www.gospeltruth.net/1852OE/520818_guilt_ignorance.html.
9. Douglass, Frederick, *Narrative of the Life of Frederick Douglass, an American Slave* (Boston: Published at the Antislavery Office, 1845).
10. Douglass, Frederick, *The Life and Times of Frederick Douglass* (Hartford, CT: Park Publishing Company, 1881), Citadel Press Facsimile Edition (1983), Kensington Publishing Company.

11. Staats, Richard J., *A Grassroots History of the American Civil War, Vol II: The Bully Seventh Ohio Volunteer Infantry* (Heritage Books, Inc., 2009).

12. Quarstein, John V, *The Monitor Boys: The Crew of the Union's First Ironclad* (History Press, 2011).

13. Slaughter, Richard, "Federal Writers' Project: Slave Narrative Project, Vol. 17, Virginia, Berry-Wilson," Library of Congress, Manuscript/Mixed Material, www.loc.gov/item/mesn170.

14. Lerner, Gerda, *The Grimké Sisters from South Carolina*, 2nd Edition (Chapel Hill, NC: The University of North Carolina Press, 2009).

15. Foner, Eric, *The Fiery Trial: Abraham Lincoln and American Slavery* (New York, London: W. W. Norton & Company, 2010).

16. Rose, Willie L., *Rehearsal for Reconstruction: The Port Royal Experiment* (New York: Oxford University Press, 1976).

17. Lincoln, Abraham, "Last Public Address (April 11, 1865)," Abraham Lincoln Online, www.abrahamlincolnonline.org/lincoln/speeches/last.htm.

Author's Note

1. d'Entremont, John, "Moncure Daniel Conway (1832–1907)," *Dictionary of Virginia Biography*, Library of Virginia (1998–), published 2006, rev. 2017, last accessed March 14, 2022, www.lva.virginia.gov/public/dvb/bio.asp?b=Conway_Moncure_Daniel.

2. Griffith-Browne, Mattie, *Autobiography of a Female Slave* (Redfield, NY: Ohio College Library Center, 1857).

3. Spiegel, Alix, *The History and Mentality of Self-Mutilation*, NPR interview with Professor Armando Favazza (University of Missouri), June 10, 2005, www.npr.org/templates/story/story.php?storyId=4697319.

4. Anderson, James D., *The Education of Blacks in the South, 1860–1935* (Chapel Hill, NC: The University of North Carolina Press, 1988).

Acknowledgments

I am very grateful to Pat Ricucci, Marshall White, Dale Abrahams, Tina Dow, Jan MacBeth, and Janet Gardner for their invaluable reviews of the draft manuscript and their extremely helpful suggestions regarding the story's character portrayals, historical accuracy, and relevance to modern times.

Thanks also to Jason North, my brother in the Lord, for his constant challenging and encouragement to stay focused in this writing effort on what matters most, and for granting me his instant grace and humorous relief when I would *occasionally* express a few frustrations in that regard.

Enough cannot be said for the many-faceted skills and stellar work of Shayla Raquel in conducting her thorough manuscript critique, copyediting, styling, proofreading, and historical fact-checking for this novel. Shayla is a true professional and an absolute joy to work with, and I cannot imagine this effort succeeding without her help.

Many thanks also to Melinda Martin (Martin Publishing Services) for her meticulous work with the interior formatting, as well as her artistic insight and production effort for the cover design.

And, of course, to Nancy—my dear wife of nearly fifty years—who in so many ways was my inspirational coauthor for this work: Thank you for your many patient and honest reviews of individual chapters, as well as your suggestions for character development that had such a positive impact on the final form of *Seeing Glory*.

ABOUT THE AUTHOR

 **D**riven by a lifelong passion for military and religious history, Bruce Gardner researches and writes creatively about the impact of major wars on the lives and faith experiences of everyday people. Retired from a thirty-year career in national aerospace and defense systems engineering, Bruce is actively involved in church and community volunteer work. He lives with his family in northern California. He is the author of the epic historical novel, *Hope of Ages Past*, which was awarded the 2016 Chanticleer Chaucer Award for Best-in-Category and was also named by Kirkus Reviews as one of the best Indie books of 2018. *Seeing Glory* is his second novel.

CONNECT WITH THE AUTHOR

Goodreads.com/AuthorBruceGardner

LEAVE A REVIEW

If you enjoyed *Seeing Glory*,
will you consider leaving a review
on your platform of choice?
Reviews help self-published authors
find more readers like you.